Winter
Flowers

Winter Flowers

Carol Coffey

POOLBEG

Published 2011
by Poolbeg Press Ltd
123 Grange Hill, Baldoyle
Dublin 13, Ireland
E-mail: poolbeg@poolbeg.com
www.poolbeg.com

© Carol Coffey 2011

Copyright for typesetting, layout, design, ebook
© Poolbeg Press Ltd

1

A catalogue record for this book is available from the British Library.

ISBN 978-1-84223-502-7

www.poolbeg.com

About the author

Carol Coffey grew up in Dublin and now lives in County Wicklow. She has a degree in Special Education and holds a Master's Degree in Education (Emotional Disturbance). Her previous novels, *The Butterfly State* and *The Penance Room*, were also published by Poolbeg.

Also by Carol Coffey

The Butterfly State

The Penance Room

Published by Poolbeg Press

Acknowledgements

Thanks to Paula Campbell of Poolbeg Press for both the opportunity to publish this book and for her on-going support and encouragement. Thanks also to all the other Poolbeg members of staff including David Prendergast, Sarah Ormston, the accounts staff and warehouse staff for getting this book from my computer to the shelves. A special thanks to Gaye Shortland for her eagle-eyed editing and her endless patience.

*I wish to dedicate this book to
my nieces and nephews*

Chapter 1

"Iris Fay, are you in there?" The man's voice boomed from outside the rundown shop as he knocked heavily on the door.

Iris switched on her bedside lamp, leapt from her small bed and threw an old dressing-gown around her thin body. She had not been asleep. She glanced at the clock. It was one o'clock. She rarely slept before three, spending the darkest hours lying there, thinking. She pulled the belt tight and tied it, staring at her thin pale face in the dusty bedroom mirror. In the dim light she looked older than her forty years. She raced to the door.

"Wait! I'm coming!" she called weakly.

Iris opened the door and saw a tall garda with a young boy standing beside him.

"Is this your nephew, Miss Fay?"

Iris looked down at the dishevelled boy. Her heart sank. She knew this meant trouble.

"Yes," she breathed heavily. "Luke . . . my sister's boy."

"Well, he didn't know your address or phone number and your sister wouldn't say. We had to get him to direct us here."

"What's happened . . . is my sister . . . where's Jack?"

The boy stayed silent, not knowing if he should speak. He was afraid his mother might be angry at him for coming here but he hadn't known what else to do. There were black marks on his face

1

and he was dressed in a T-shirt and light track-suit top despite the cold night.

"The younger child is with hospital staff," the garda answered.

"Hospital – what's happened?" Iris asked loudly. Fear gripped her and she began to sway slightly.

"There was a fire. They're fine but they inhaled fumes. They'll probably keep your sister overnight. The boy will be discharged when someone comes to collect him."

"How did it happen?"

"The fire department thinks it was probably a chip pan left on a cooker that hadn't been turned off. Too soon to tell though. Do these boys have a father I can call? This one says you're their only relative. Is that true?"

"Yes," Iris replied sadly as she stroked her nephew's curly head.

She looked down at Luke and felt an overwhelming pity for him. What was going to become of the boys with a mother like theirs? It was over two weeks since her troubled younger sister had last visited her. The visit had ended in yet another row. That's the way it was for them. When things weren't going right for Hazel, she would barge into Iris's tiny flat looking for trouble.

Luke smiled sheepishly up at her. He liked his Aunty Iris. She was good to him even though she often made his mother cry and he didn't like it when people made his mother cry. Even though he was not yet eight years old, he was the man of the house and it was his job to protect his mother. It was a hard job though because she needed a lot of protecting and sometimes he needed Aunty Iris to help, times like now.

"Can you look after the lads tonight?" the garda asked doubtfully, peering in at the rundown sewing shop she called home.

"Yes," Iris replied, knowing what he was thinking. "There's room at the back. I'll collect Jack at the hospital."

"Miss?"

"Yes?"

"The younger lad has asthma?"

"Yes."

"You might tell the boy's mother that it's probably not smart to be smoking in a house with an asthmatic child."

2

Iris reddened and lowered her head. "I'll see that he gets his medication, officer. I'm a . . . I used to be a nurse . . ."

Thanking the garda, Iris moved Luke inside and closed the door slowly. She exhaled a loud breath and stood with her back against the cold glass of the door for a moment, digesting the news, then led her shivering nephew through the small shop and into her living area.

She washed his face in her tiny cold bathroom and gave him one of her own jumpers to keep warm.

"Don't worry – it doesn't look like a girl's jumper!" she said. "You hungry, love?"

"Just a bit."

In the kitchenette she set about making some toast and slicing some cheese.

Luke could feel the anger rising in her. He watched her neck redden and her lips moving silently and knew she was about to ask questions he didn't want to answer.

"Who was smoking in the house, Luke? Did your mam have a visitor?"

Iris hated this, using the child to find out what was going on but she had no choice. Hazel was never going to tell her what had happened.

He didn't answer, and that was answer enough.

She led him into the sitting room and put his plate and a glass of milk on the coffee table.

Luke sat and began to eat. He thought about lying but knew he'd only get himself into a bigger mess. It would be a sin. He was making his Communion next May and he knew he'd have to save it up for Confession.

"Mam's friend came round," he said at last, in his flat Dublin accent. "D'you 'member Pete?"

"Oh yeah," Iris replied, trying to hide her annoyance.

Pete Doyle only came around when Hazel collected her One-Parent Family Payment. He'd usually spend the night after talking Hazel into spending more than she could afford on booze, and then disappear for another week.

3

"Were . . . were they . . . ?" Iris hated this. She watched Luke squirm as he swallowed a huge bite of toast and cheese. She stopped herself for a moment. She knew it wasn't fair on the child but decided to continue anyway. "Were they having a good night then?"

Luke looked up, unsure how to answer the question. He knew that Iris hated it when people smoked around his younger brother and that she also didn't like it when his mam had been drinking.

"Em . . . yeah," he replied nervously. "Mam was laughing for ages . . ." He stopped, wondering if that was too much information because he knew that his mam only laughed that much when she drank too much wine.

"Ah . . . that's nice," Iris said unconvincingly. "Well, finish your milk and let's go and collect your brother. He'll be worried, won't he? I've enough for a taxi so it'll be an adventure, eh?"

Luke was looking worried, already concerned that there would be another row between his mam and his aunt.

The pair huddled together as they made their way down Fairview Strand towards the taxi rank in the bitter cold. It was pitch black and there wasn't a soul to be seen.

The taxi driver didn't seem too pleased to be woken from his slumber as he sat parked on the corner and didn't say a word to either of his depressed-looking passengers, although he was slightly interested in why the woman was going to hospital with a child at this hour. He didn't look sick. Skinny maybe, but not sick.

When they pulled up in front of the old inner-city hospital he muttered the fare and found that his passengers were as dour as he was. He watched as they walked with bowed heads towards the large wooden doors of the formidable building. Maybe they've received bad news about a relative, he thought, suddenly feeling guilty, before turning the car back towards his rank. Ah well, if I'm lucky I'll get a couple of hours' kip before the day job starts.

A&E on the ground floor of the hospital had a long miserable line of old iron trolleys that should have been replaced years before. Iris could see Hazel before the nurse pointed her out. Hazel's long narrow body almost made it to the end of the trolley while her thick fair hair covered the pillow.

4

Iris approached her sister gingerly. She didn't want another row although she did intend to find out eventually what had happened.

Iris cleared her throat, anxious not to say the wrong thing and God knew it was easy to say the wrong thing to her highly strung sister. "How are you?" she asked quietly. She leaned in to kiss Hazel but pulled back quickly when her sister turned her face away. Iris sighed. "I've brought you some toilet things and a couple of nightdresses. They're mine, hope they fit you . . . might be too short though."

She knew Hazel loved to gloat about the difference in their appearances. Although both women were considered pretty when they were younger, Iris was short and dark while Hazel was very tall with long straight fair hair. They both had their mother's eyes: large round blue eyes that made them look constantly surprised, or scared.

Iris placed the bag she was carrying on the trolley and stood with her hands in her pockets. She looked at Luke who stood like a frightened rabbit, his brown eyes narrowed beneath his curly brown hair that was badly in need of a cut. Both boys looked like their father whom they never saw and didn't remember.

"Hazel," she said softly, "I'll take the boys to my place tonight. The nurse said you'll probably be out tomorrow. Jack's in the children's ward but they said to take him – that he's fine but keeps crying – and he –"

"No! You're not taking my kids anywhere!" Hazel shouted loudly, her sudden rage frightening the entire A&E including her sister and her son whose lip began to quiver slightly.

A nurse began walking towards Hazel's bed.

"Hazel, please . . ." Iris said as softly as she could. "If they don't come with me the hospital will ring Social Services." She moved closer to the trolley to avoid Luke hearing her. "You don't want that, do you?" she whispered.

Hazel jumped from the bed and, tearing off the nightdress the hospital had supplied, began putting her clothes on. She swayed and almost fell as she was pulling her jeans on but seemed unaware of her son's acute embarrassment.

"Don't you tell me what I want for my kids!" she screamed, before coughing loudly.

"Hazel!" the nurse called out. "Get back into bed, please – your breathing is still laboured."

Hazel ignored the nurse and began walking towards the door of the ward.

"I'm signing myself out. I feel perfect now," she said sharply to the nurse, raising her voice in a mocking intonation. "That okay with you?"

The nurse had met plenty like her before. They came in looking for help, worse for wear, and then up and left without as much as a thank you. Well, she didn't care either way. One less to look after through the night.

"You'll have to sign a discharge form," she replied dryly as she watched the woman sway.

At the nurses' station she quickly filled in a form and handed it to Hazel to sign.

She looked at the young child and then at Iris. "You staying with her tonight?"

Iris nodded.

"Good luck," she said as she snapped the signed discharge form from Hazel and directed the sisters to the children's ward.

Jack slept soundly in the taxi on the way home. Iris knew not to ask how bad the fire was and whether or not they could actually sleep there tonight. These questions were pointless with Hazel when she was like this. When the taxi pulled up in the small cul-de-sac outside the house, Iris couldn't see any external damage.

They got out and walked to the front door, Hazel struggling to carry Jack, unwilling to let her sister help. She opened the door and stepped inside, then pulled Luke angrily into the hallway before slamming the door loudly in Iris's face.

Iris stood, rooted to the spot. Her shoulders dropped forward. She had used the last of her cash on the taxi. She pulled her coat around her and looked up at the dark sky as she turned to walk the three-mile journey home.

Chapter 2

The narrow sitting room which sat directly behind Iris's modest clothes-repair shop was darkly decorated with cheap furniture, some of which had been her mother's. A small television sat on a low table and faced a worn two-seater sofa-bed and equally worn armchair, a coffee table in front of them. A silver-tasselled lamp stood tall on a side table which was adorned with a photo of Hazel and the boys on one side and one of Iris and Hazel as children on the other. A small wooden kitchen table was pressed up against the wall directly behind the shop as there was no room for it in the kitchenette. To the left of the sitting room was the door to Iris's tiny bedroom which consisted of a single bed with a wardrobe and side table and looked more like a convent cell than a single woman's bedroom. A door in the far wall of the sitting room led into the kitchenette which had room only for an old gas stove, small fridge and sink. Two painted cupboards stood over by the window that faced onto a small concrete yard. Iris's cat, Marmalade, sat on the window ledge, looking in at her as she prepared her modest evening meal. It made periodic meowing sounds, hoping to get inside from the cold breeze that blew around the yard. A bathroom jutted off the kitchenette with a small shower cubicle, toilet and hand basin. It obviously had been added onto the old building as an afterthought. It had no radiator and Iris dreaded showering there in the winter.

She looked about the flat and, while she knew she didn't have to live this meagrely, she liked it. It was a simple life. She did not need much and found that she preferred to give any extra cash she had to Hazel for the boys than spend it on material things for herself.

Iris pondered the day's event as she ate while watching *EastEnders* which was her favourite programme.

Hazel had come into the shop that day, almost two weeks after slamming the door in her sister's face, all smiles and cheerfulness, as if nothing had happened. But that was Hazel. Iris was used to it and, while she liked seeing her sister, she enjoyed a strange sort of peace when Hazel was fighting with her. Even though it could be lonely, life was predictable. She would get up each morning early and walk for about an hour before spending the day repairing clothes for her few regular customers or occasionally making new dresses for young brides or debutantes who knew nothing of what life was to bring, God help them. She didn't have to worry about her sister flying off the handle about some slight comment she might make.

Yet the sisters depended on each other. Their parents had not had a happy marriage and rowed constantly. Hazel was too young to remember much about either of their parents and anything she did recall was through rose-coloured glasses. When their dad failed to return after yet another row, their mother had sat the sisters down and told them that he had been killed in a car accident. Three years later their mother died, a needless death caused by alcoholism. It haunted Iris to this day and caused great bitterness. All her mistakes, she felt, were down to that one selfish act. It had led her to this place, to this life.

Iris sighed. Tomorrow was Friday and she had agreed to take the boys for the weekend while Hazel went to Galway with some friends. Where her sister got the money to go away she didn't know, but she said nothing. As usual, she kept her mouth shut when she didn't approve – and anyway she loved having the boys. Luke was a handful, though, so she was even happier when Hazel returned for them and she could return to her peaceful, predictable existence.

Iris looked up at the clock on the wall above the television.

There was nothing good on and it was only eight o'clock. She sat in silence for a few minutes and wondered what to do with herself. She could hear the rain start to fall heavily against the window. The flat was cold and she rose to get another cardigan to put around her shoulders. She hoped that Hazel had lit the fire for the boys and wondered if she'd remembered to fill the prescription for Jack's regular inhaler. She almost phoned Hazel to remind her but stopped herself in time. She stood and walked back into the shop. May as well use the time to work, she thought. She sat down at her sewing machine and hummed as she began to work.

Chapter 3

After Hazel dropped the boys off to her sister for the weekend, she raced back to her house and began dolling herself up. She hadn't wanted to lie to Iris, telling her she was going to Galway with friends, but her sister would never understand if she said Pete was coming around. The woman lived like a nun. Hazel didn't know how Iris didn't get lonely like she herself did, but they had always been so different. Iris was always the strong one while Hazel was the emotional one, crying or laughing and nothing in between.

The three-bedroom red-bricked house that Hazel lived in was the most constant thing in her life. It had been her parents' house. She had grown up there and, except for the years when she and Iris had to go into care, she had never lived anywhere else. The house was only minutes away from the Botanic Gardens, which she loved. She couldn't understand why Iris didn't want to live there with her, preferring the grotty little flat. It was a modest house that was in need of some redecoration but it was a decent size and what Hazel loved most about it was the large back garden where her father used to tend his beloved plants. It was where he was happiest, Iris had said, although Hazel didn't really remember him. Even the photos of him looked somehow foreign to her. There was one particular photo of him, standing alone by an old-fashioned motor car, taken in Sussex where he was born and where her parents had met when her mother went to work there. He was young and handsome, smiling into the camera with a confident air. When she was a teenager she used to spend hours looking into the photo, hoping for some memory to come to her, anything at all, but it never did. He was a stranger whom she was told had loved her dearly. Hazel knew that her father had walked out during a row with her mother. Although her memories were few, she remembered her mother telling them a few days later that he had died in an accident – she remembered because Iris had screamed when she heard and had cried all night in her bed and Hazel had rarely seen Iris crying. She often wondered at how different their lives could have been if he'd come back and sorted out the problem with their mother. He wouldn't have been driving that car in England and he'd be alive. She thought of her boys and wondered how anyone could walk out on their children but then she only had to look at her sister to see that it was possible. After what Iris did, Hazel wondered if it was somehow genetic, something inherited that made you just walk out without as much as an explanation. Hazel knew she wasn't the world's greatest mother – but to abandon her kids! She'd never do it, never. No matter how bad things got, and they often got really, really bad.

She wasn't brushing the boys off now because of Pete. She wouldn't do that. It was just easier if they weren't there. She needed some time alone with Pete. It would be nice. He shouted a bit much at the boys anyway so they probably preferred to be with Iris who would spoil them, she reasoned to herself. It wasn't Pete's fault – he wasn't used to kids, that's all. If it worked out between them, he'd get used to the boys. They were good kids. All in good time, she thought, as she dressed in the skimpiest dress she could find. She applied some bright red lipstick and stood back to look at herself in the mirror. "Gorgeous!" she said, laughing. She looked great and had regained her figure despite putting on almost three stone during her pregnancies. She thought fleetingly about Gerry, the boys' father, and wondered where he was now. Probably still married to his wagon of a wife who he wouldn't leave to be with her. Bastard. He hadn't actually told her he was married until she was pregnant with Luke. He promised he'd leave his wife, start a new life with their son and she believed him. She should have known better. She was twenty-nine at the time, not a kid. Gerry was older than her, a lot older, but she didn't mind – she liked it actually. It made her feel kind of safe, protected. While Gerry was filling her full of lies about buying a house in the country where she could plant a garden as good as her dad's, she fell pregnant again with Jack. She threatened him to make him leave his wife, said she'd tell. She even begged him when she became desperate but he walked away, just like her dad – only this time she would remember it. The thought of being a single mother of two children depressed her. She was no snob but she knew she could have done better and couldn't understand why she had settled for this. It puzzled her to this day. Well, it was all history now. The boys were getting big and she hadn't had any luck with any of her boyfriends since, and there had been a lot of boyfriends, lots of losers who promised her the stars and took more than they gave in return. She felt that Pete was different. For one, he had never been married so didn't come with any baggage. Even if it didn't turn into any fairytale wedding, she had fun with Pete. He took her out of her dead-end life and made her laugh. She needed him; she needed anyone who did that for her. She was suffocating in her monotonous existence and if she had to settle for short bursts of happiness, then that would have to do. Hazel peered closer into the mirror and inspected the frown lines that appeared each time she was thinking like this, thinking like Iris did – worry, worry, worry.

The doorbell rang and Hazel glanced in the mirror again, making final touches to her make-up. It rang a second time as she quickly adjusted her dress and took one last look at herself. As she raced downstairs to open the door, Pete was already ringing the bell impatiently for the third time.

"Come on. Open the bleedin' door, will ya – it's freezing!" he shouted.

Hazel stood for a moment on the last step. She hoped Pete wasn't in a bad mood. She took a deep breath before swinging the door open. She smiled nervously.

"Sorry, Pete . . . sorry."

Chapter 4

"Luke said you used to be a nurse, Aunty Iris," Jack said absentmindedly as he drew while Iris made the boys an evening meal. "Is that true?"

"Yeah, it's true, love. A long time ago," Iris replied, wearily.

Hazel had dropped the boys off only two hours before and already Iris was tired of her youngest nephew's questions. He was typical of course for a boy his age, full of questions about the world. Luke was different though. He was the one that she worried about, quiet and watchful, an anxious child. She had been the same herself, always afraid of what was about to happen, and it both saddened her and worried her that Luke might turn out like she did. Oddly, his behaviour in school was different from his usual behaviour at home. According to Hazel, he was in trouble almost daily for fighting – which didn't make any sense to Iris and she hoped to broach the subject with him this weekend if an opportunity presented itself.

"Are you old now, Aunty Iris?" Jack asked.

"No, I'm not old," she snapped but smiled to let him know she was just joking.

"So how old are you?"

"I'm forty. Do you think that's old, Jack?"

"It's older than my mam and she's really old."

Iris and Luke laughed loudly. There was an innocence about Jack that was so endearing.

"Iris?" he asked.

"Yes?"

"Why aren't you a nurse any more? You could help with my asthma instead of the cranky nurse at the doctor's."

Iris pondered her answer. She could see Luke raise his eyes from his book as if whatever information she gave might throw some light on his ongoing investigation into the family history.

"I . . . I like fixing clothes better than people," she said, more to herself than to her nephews.

She had never thought about it like that before. It had just come out of her mouth and surprised her but it was true, she did prefer inanimate objects to people. Clothes don't depend on you – they don't need you, she thought. She knew both boys were watching her now, wondering what on earth their aunt was talking about. She swung round and painted on the brightest smile.

"But – I'll help with your asthma anytime because you're so special!" She dived across the room and started tickling Jack until he squealed and coughed.

Luke jumped up and grabbed the inhaler from the plastic bag into which his mother had shoved their weekend clothes and put it into his brother's mouth. The scene saddened Iris and brought tears to her eyes. Kind acts always did that to her. She didn't know why. She patted Luke on the head and went into the tiny kitchen to dry her eyes.

"Okay, boys, I'll serve dinner now. It's your favourite – spaghetti bolognese. Wash your hands. There might even be treats for later."

"Okay, Aunty Iris. You're the bestest aunty. We love you, don't we, Luke?"

"Yeah," replied Luke who couldn't take his eyes off his aunt as she cried silently in the kitchen.

Chapter 5

"Jesus, Hazel, will ya stop? A meal? I never said I was takin' ya out for a meal. I'm not getting much work, ya know. Think I'm made of money?"

Hazel pretended to sulk in the armchair to see if it would get her anywhere. It didn't.

"I'm starving, Pete. I didn't have dinner because I thought you were taking me out for a change."

"How 'bout a Chinese? Come on, Haze, you love Chinese!" He smiled at her as he sprawled across her sofa. He could see she was going to go into one of her moods. "I'm not in the humour for going out, Hazel, so ya can like it or lump it. If ya keep up that face I'm headin' home. Jesus, me ma has a happier face than you do tonight and that's saying something!"

Hazel smiled weakly. Pete's mam had an awful sour puss alright. She was disappointed but she didn't want to ruin the night. God knew she got few nights with adult company, especially male company and no kids asking awkward questions.

"Okay," she said, "I'll phone it in. What do you want?"

"Em . . . ya'll have to shout for it, Haze, 'cos I'm skint."

Hazel stared at her "date" and almost called the whole thing off, the whole weekend.

How on earth did she get this desperate? Pete was a fine thing alright, good-looking, but he never had a penny although he worked part-time at the garage. But if she asked him to leave he might throw one of his wobblies and she didn't want a scene. Also, she'd be on her own for the entire weekend and she hated being alone, another big difference between her and her older sister who seemed to love solitude and silence.

"Okay, Pete. I'll get it. Hope you at least brought some beer in that bag because I'm definitely not buying that."

Pete laughed and grabbed at Hazel until she fell on the floor beside him. He leant towards her and kissed her roughly. She pulled back. She wanted to wait, to have a romantic evening, not like this, not like Pete had in mind. She noticed his stare and laughed nervously, tossing his hair.

"Stop, Pete, I mean it. I'm starving . . . save the best till later, eh?"

Pete let her go. She got up and walked into the hall to phone in the order. Small beads of sweat broke out on her brow and her hand shook slightly as she dialled the takeaway. She couldn't understand why she felt nervous, couldn't put her finger on what she was feeling, but she felt dirty and it didn't make any sense to her. She wanted to run upstairs and get under the covers, like she sometimes did when the boys were getting the better of her, to hide until the feeling went away. She heard Pete put the television on loudly. Her heart beat faster as it always did when there was sudden noise, another part of her personality she didn't quite understand as she wasn't exactly mouse-like. Iris was always telling her that she talked too loudly and she knew it was true. Hazel walked swiftly down the hallway and opened the fridge. There was a bottle of cheap wine that she was saving for tonight and some night it was turning out to be. She opened it and poured herself a large glass while she set the table for dinner. She sat down at her pretty kitchen table and looked out of the window. It was raining heavily and she could hear the wind picking up. She imagined that it must be cosy in Iris's little flat on a night like this and hoped the boys were having fun. Suddenly, she began to cry. Hot tears sprang out of nowhere. She placed her hand over her mouth to avoid making noise and sat there for what seemed like an eternity as if she was looking at some horrible scene that she couldn't take her eyes off. Except she wasn't looking at any scene but at her reflection in the kitchen window – all dressed up and nowhere to go, like the song says. The doorbell rang. She stood up and dried her eyes, taking her purse from her handbag. She opened the door to the delivery man, smiling.

"Oh thanks. How much? Awful night. Are you soaked, love?"

She closed the door and walked on shaky legs back to the kitchen table.

"Pete. The dinner's here," she said flatly.

She put the two romantic scented candles she was going to light back into the drawer. It wasn't going to be that kind of night.

Chapter 6

It was Saturday and Iris's busiest day in the shop. Although the shop was really rundown and old-fashioned, she was becoming well known in the area and people were beginning to come from further afield for her mending and dressmaking skills. When she moved there first the shop had been run for over forty years by a Jewish couple who were retiring and going to live with their daughter in another part of Dublin. She paid rent monthly to the old couple's son who was glad that the place was still a repair shop and he hadn't raised the rent since she took the lease. The back of the shop was just a storeroom then, with a makeshift canteen and the same draughty bathroom. Initially, Iris hoped it would be a pit stop until she built up the business and could afford a better location but after a few years she settled in and she no longer wanted to do better. This was enough for her. She was settled and her life was predictable. Sometimes she thought it would be a good idea to live away from the shop but she couldn't afford rent in Dublin and, although Hazel had asked her, she didn't want to live with her sister. Not only did she feel that they wouldn't get along but the house held so many bad memories for her that she couldn't live there. It would be like giving up on ever being normal, of ever having hope that things could be different for her. Iris felt sorry that the boys would be cooped up in the shop all day but they didn't seem to mind and were looking forward to helping out.

The front of the shop had an old-fashioned counter that ran the width of the room, with a half door on the right-hand side that led behind the counter and into Iris's flat. A bell warned of new customers so the three sat in the back, unravelling old jumpers that Iris had bought for cash and rolling them into large balls of wool.

"Jack, be careful with that wool and let me know if you feel wheezy, okay? I can get you something different to do, something more important, right?" She winked at Luke who smiled warmly up at her.

"What do you do with the wool when we've pulled it, Iris?" Luke asked.

"I sell it. People come in and buy it to make new things. Wool is expensive so they get second-hand wool cheaper."

"Aunty Iris, will you tell us stories about when you and Mam were little girls?" Jack asked breathlessly. He loved to hear these stories, most of them made up or at least embellished by Iris.

"What one do you want to hear?" she asked, hoping she could remember what she'd told the boys last time. She knew Jack wouldn't notice a different ending but Luke definitely would.

"The one about how you and Mam got your names, please, Iris."

His aunt smiled, relieved. This one she could do no problem. This one was entirely true.

"Well," she began, "my dad was a gardener. He was almost famous in Dublin and rich people used to ask him to design their gardens for them. He loved plants and flowers and our garden at home, your home now, was like a tropical paradise. He planted palm trees that no one had back then. It was lovely." Iris smiled sadly but moved on quickly.

The boys were watching her closely.

"Dad said he would call his daughters after flowers and he had already picked out names like Rose and Daisy. Well, when I was born in December, Dad said that I should be called after a flower anyway and called me Iris after the Winter Iris. He said the Winter Iris was tough and that a baby born in winter would be a tough little creature anyway so that the name would suit me." Iris was day-dreaming and had that far-off look in her eyes.

Luke brought her back to earth. "What about Mam? Tell us about Mam's name?"

Iris could tell that Luke was missing his mam and that he wouldn't rest until she got off the train from her weekend in Galway.

"Well, two days before I was four, Hazel was born, another December baby. I wasn't happy – Dad had spoiled me."

"Did your mam spoil you as well, Aunty Iris?" Jack asked innocently.

Iris looked at Jack and moved her mouth silently as she searched for the right words. "Em . . . well, you know dads. They spoil their girls, don't they?" She was sorry as soon as she said it. The boys didn't know – they would never know what a dad did. She hated being asked about her mother – it was too painful. "Well, your mam was a lovely baby," she hurried on. "She had a huge mop of fair hair even when she was born and she hardly ever cried. Dad wondered where on earth they'd got her from."

"A cabbage leaf!" offered Jack, excited about the story.

Iris smiled. "He couldn't think of a name for her for ages. But she was a long baby. The nurses even commented on it, Dad said. Eventually, he decided to call her Hazel, after the hazel tree which I know is not a flower but its long slender flowers come out in winter, when everything else is dead. That's why he chose the name, because of the time of year and because she was going to be tall."

"And, Iris, you forgot about the nuts."

"Oh, yes, the hazel tree makes tough little nuts which fall from its branches."

"That's us!" Jack cried, loving the story even though he had heard it dozens of times.

The boys sat mesmerised, one hundred questions brewing in their heads.

"Did your mam like your names?" Luke asked.

Iris thought for a moment. "I don't know," she replied flatly. "Now, let's get this work done and there might be a treat when we close. You never know, we might even close early if it's this quiet."

20

The boys sat quietly unravelling the wool as Iris saw to the occasional customer. She wondered what her mam had thought about their unusual names. Other kids on the street were named Kathleen or Maureen. Maybe she didn't care. Maybe she couldn't even muster enough enthusiasm to name her children. Iris didn't know if her mam was drinking heavily back then but she knew that by the time her brother was born, her mother was rarely sober and her dad spent most of his time in the garden after work or went to the pub just to get away from her although he wasn't much of a drinker. Her brother's birth and death all occurred on the same day. Iris remembered her mother was in hospital for weeks before the baby was born, because their mother's older sister, Eileen, came over from London to look after Hazel and her while their dad worked. They subsequently had to live with this aunt when their mother died. Iris remembered her father coming home from the hospital and sitting with his head in his hands on the sofa. He was crying and Aunt Eileen tried to bring them outside to the garden but he grabbed them and hugged them close until both girls began to cry too. Their brother had not even taken one breath. It was summertime and if he had been a girl he could have had a summer flower name, a really pretty one.

When their mother came home, she did not speak to the girls but went to her room where she remained in bed for weeks. Iris could not remember a funeral for her brother and did not even know where he was buried. Aunt Eileen had to return to London where she was a teacher and Iris remembered her dad pleading with her mother to get up and look after the girls while he went to work. After a few weeks, Iris's mam began to get up, but not until around twelve, by which time Iris would have already washed and fed Hazel and brought her to school. In the evenings, Iris's parents fought while Iris sang loudly to Hazel in the room they shared, preparing for pop stardom on *Opportunity Knocks* where she could earn lots of money to run away with Hazel. Iris noticed her father losing weight. He rarely spoke and began to send her and Hazel to bed each evening before it was even dark. She would look out of the window at him as he sat in the garden, his head bowed, shoulders bent forward. She wanted to make him happy again but she didn't know how. He stopped tending to his plants and the grass began to grow high.

One Saturday morning that September, she heard him rise early. He had been sleeping in the spare room for months and its door creaked loudly. She followed him onto the landing and watched him walk quietly down the stairs. She called him and he looked up at her. She still remembered his face, lined and tired, although he would only have been about Iris's age now. He smiled at her and put his finger to his lips.

"Shh, love, go back to bed. You'll wake Hazel."

"Where are you going, Daddy?" she asked, knowing it was Saturday.

"You look after Hazel, love, promise me?"

Iris looked at him, confused. "Yes, Daddy. I already do."

"I know, love. You're a good girl. Do you know how much I love you?"

Iris nodded and he began to descend again, his sad eyes slipping slowly from view as he took each step down the stairs. She heard him open the front door and close it gently behind him. She never saw him again.

On Monday when she and Hazel came home from school, her mother took them aside and told them that their father had gone to visit his parents in England on Saturday morning and had died in a car accident there. Iris told her mother that she had spoken to him on that morning and he hadn't said anything about going to England but her mother insisted that she must have forgotten, that she herself had heard him tell Iris that he'd be away a couple of days. In the years to come Iris did not change her mind and wondered why her mother had lied. Iris knew now that her father was saying goodbye to her that morning on the stairs, that he had no plans to return, ever. She remembered screaming when her mother told them that her beloved father was dead, while Hazel stood rooted to the spot, uncomprehending. There would be no funeral. Their mother said that he would be buried in England near his family. She never mentioned him again and forbade the girls from asking about him. It was a loss that Iris had never recovered from and was even worse than the death of her mother less than three years later.

"Aunty Iris?" Jack said, waking her from her thoughts.

"I think it's cool if you can make something new from something old. It's like the wool gets a second chance to be something," he said, still unravelling an old Aran jumper.

Iris smiled. A second chance. If only . . .

Chapter 7

On Saturday morning, Hazel awoke feeling a bit better and wondered if she'd overreacted a little the night before. She was disappointed with how the night had gone as she had imagined a romantic night with Pete, with no kids and no responsibilities. After they ate their Chinese meal, Pete had returned to the television to watch a match while drinking can after can until he fell asleep on the sofa. She left him there and went to bed in the boys' room. She slept in Jack's lower bunk where she could smell the scent of her boys as she drifted off to sleep. She didn't want to sleep in her own room in case Pete came up later and tried it on with her. She wasn't in the mood.

But in the morning light Hazel knew that her life was never going to be all fantasy and good times and that she had to be happy with the little bit of enjoyment that was on offer. She went downstairs where Pete was waking slowly and cooked a fried breakfast which he ate silently on his lap in the sitting room, the noise of banging dishes too much for his hangover to cope with.

"Hazel?"

"Yeah?"

"Could you keep it down in there? Me head's lifting, for Christ's sake!"

"Sorry."

The rest of Saturday passed peacefully between them. They didn't actually go anywhere. Pete rented a couple of DVD's and they sat on the sofa, finishing off the last few cans in the fridge. That evening, Pete invited some friends around. Hazel hadn't wanted company but Pete thought it would be nice if she met a few of his friends.

As Hazel got ready, she could hear the noise of people arriving downstairs. She felt nervous and wished they could have had another quiet night together, their last before the boys returned the following day. Eventually she made her way downstairs and immediately felt like a stranger in her own home. There were about twenty people in her sitting room and she didn't know any of them. She walked across the room to where Pete was talking to two men and stood smiling at the trio waiting to be introduced. Pete ignored her except to ask her to get him a beer. Hazel turned quickly to hide her embarrassment and, as she turned, Pete slapped her on the bottom and laughed. She heard one of the men ask Pete if that was "his chick" but did not hear Pete's answer. She walked into the kitchen and stood alone, listening to the noise. She felt like a fool. No one knew who she was. The purpose of the party was not to introduce her to his friends as Pete had said it was. It was just a convenient place to have a party in. Someone turned the music up louder and she could hear Mrs Whelan knocking loudly on their adjoining sitting-room wall. Hazel hoped the old biddy would ring the police as she did before when one of Hazel's boyfriends got a bit rough. It would clear the freeloaders from her home, and she included Pete in that.

Hazel got herself a beer and didn't bother bringing one back for Pete. He could get his own. She stood in the sitting room and, when no one talked to her, she knocked back her beer quickly and got herself another. She stood on the outside of a group of women and pretended to laugh at their jokes until one or two of them looked at her strangely and she moved off. She wanted to say, "It's my house you're in, so have some manners," but hadn't got the nerve. She wasn't like Iris. She never would be. She was starting to miss the boys and wondered why she had left them with Iris for the likes of Pete. She hadn't enjoyed the weekend one bit and the anticipation turned out to be better than the reality. Iris was right. Pete was using her. Well, she was going to finish it tonight when everyone was gone, or maybe tomorrow before Iris dropped off the boys. She'd start afresh. A new beginning.

She sat on the sofa and listened to the music. She tried not to look embarrassed or isolated and tapped her foot as she sang along, hoping that no one was looking at her.

At the other end of the sofa a very drunk man was also singing quietly to himself. Hazel looked at him. She had no idea who he was but he was scruffy and she could smell his feet from where she was sitting. There was something about the scene that mesmerised her and she watched him closely. Even though the man started to retch, he still tried to drink the beer in his hand and it spilled onto his jacket. When he leaned forward and began to vomit down the side of the sofa, Hazel was instantly transported back in time. A memory resurfaced that she had somehow forgotten over the years. She could no longer see the man but was looking at herself and Iris in slow motion, trying to lift their mother's drooping head as red-streaked vomit poured from her mouth and nose. She remembered Iris shouting to run next door and get Mrs Whelan to ring an ambulance because their phone had been cut off. She did not move but stood horrified beside the sofa as her mother's vomit poured down her school uniform. Iris looked at her and said: "It'll be okay, Hazel, don't cry." She hadn't even realised that she was crying.

When the ambulance came and took their mother away, Mrs Whelan cleaned them up and brought them into her house where she gave them milk and biscuits while her six wild children stared at them from across the large orange Formica table. At bedtime, she put them into a single bed together in a room with her three girls who moved over and shared a double bed under the window. Iris and Hazel lay awake that night, their arms wrapped around each other. They had never slept anywhere other than home and had never been separated from their mother before. Iris whispered songs into Hazel's ears, her favourite ones from a television programme they liked to watch. Before dawn, the girls heard a solitary car driving up the narrow cul-de-sac, its headlights throwing shadows on the ceiling of the room they slept in. When the doorbell rang they held onto each other. Somehow, by instinct, they knew their mother was dead. Their world collapsed. They were alone.

A drunk woman banged into Hazel as she tried to make her way past the sofa, bringing her back to the present. She looked about the room where nobody seemed to notice the vomiting man. It had been a long time since she thought about that last night with her mother. Had it always been that bad? Had nights like that been a regular occurrence? She didn't remember and wondered how this was possible. Was this why Iris was so bitter?

Hazel felt a deep anger welling up from within her, surging forward like a burst dam. She looked back at the vomiting man who had begun to wipe his mouth in Jack's pyjama bottoms that had been lying at the end of the sofa.

She began to scream at him and hit him, pulling her son's clothes off him. "Get out, get fucking out! All of you! Get out of my house! *Now*!" Hazel rarely cursed and could see Pete looking at her as though she had gone mad. The room quietened and someone stopped the music.

"*I said out, now, all of you!*" she screamed.

People began to move toward the door while Pete began shouting at her to calm down. He moved to the door, apologising and asking people to stay. Hazel screamed at him. "You too, you using bastard! Get out and don't ever come back here!"

Pete flushed in front of his friends and made a run at her, punching her in the face and sending her flying into the fireplace. He tried to hit her again as she lay on the floor but the two men he'd been talking to held him back and moved him towards the door as the others drifted out slowly, collecting their beer from the kitchen first and staring in at Hazel as they left.

Within minutes Hazel was alone. She sat sobbing on the fireplace surround. She knew her lip was bleeding and that she'd probably have a black eye in the morning. Her first impulse was to phone Iris but she couldn't. She had lied to her sister, lied to her children, and for what? Hazel looked about the room at the empty beer cans and overflowing ashtrays and started weeping again but this time she was crying because suddenly everything seemed to change. Memories of how it really was with their mother came flooding back as though someone had replaced the reel in her head that played the same few happy memories over and over again. Her memories of a day at the cinema to see *Jungle Book* and the day her mother kept them from school to take them to the seaside were replaced with the time they set off for the Phoenix Park to see the deer but stopped at a pub in town and never made it. She remembered the day of her First Communion when her mother promised to take them to the zoo but started drinking in the house and fell asleep on the sofa. Hazel sat in her Communion dress all day watching her mother, hoping she'd wake up but when it got dark Iris made them scrambled eggs for tea and brushed out her ringlets as they watched telly.

Hazel wondered how she could have fooled herself for so long. Why was she remembering this now? What else would she recall? She didn't want to remember anything else. She was tired and her head hurt. She wanted to get up, to move from this horrible scene but every ounce of strength seemed to abandon her and she sat there, on the cold stone hearth, and stared into the nothingness that was her life.

Chapter 8

After the shop closed on Saturday, Iris brought the boys to the local chipper to buy fish and chips to eat back at her place with mugs of hot tea followed by apple tart and ice cream. "A party" the boys had called it and Iris wondered if the boys ever got treats and, if not, what did Hazel spend her One-Parent Family Payment on?

When the boys started to fall asleep, Iris put them both in her single bed and went to the sitting room to read.

Within a few minutes Luke returned to the sitting room and stood quietly by the doorway, his large brown eyes looking at his aunt who he guessed was hoping for a couple of hours' peace.

"Aunty Iris?"

She turned and smiled at him. "Thought you were asleep!"

"Can I sit up with you for a while?"

"Yeah, love. Come and sit here," she said as she patted the sofa.

Iris sensed that Luke had something to say, so remained quiet. Luke cuddled into her and she smoothed his hair as she continued reading.

"I'm in trouble in school," he said finally.

"Yeah, I know," Iris replied quietly while pretending to read. She knew her nephew better than he knew himself and knew that if she asked him any questions, he might change his mind and clam up.

"The kids call me a bastard," he said finally.

Iris pretended not to notice the tears that he wiped quickly with his pyjama sleeve.

"And what do you do when that happens?" she asked, hoping it wouldn't end their conversation.

He lowered his head. "I get into fights. I have a dad, everybody does. It's just that I never see him. If he could come to my school even once and let the other kids see him, I think they'd leave me alone."

Iris tried to think. Now more than ever she needed to say the right thing but knew this was something she wasn't very good at.

"There must be other kids in your school whose dads aren't around?"

Luke nodded.

"Well, do you play with these boys? Maybe they'd be better friends, you know? You'd have something in common."

Luke sighed. This wasn't the answer he wanted.

"Iris?"

"Yeah?"

"Can you tell me about my dad?"

Iris stopped pretending to read and looked into her nephew's serious face.

"Well, love, you're probably better off asking your mam about that."

"I did," he replied in a slightly raised voice.

His quickness to anger worried her.

"She said it made her too sad and to ask you about it."

Iris raised her eyebrows at him. He didn't appear to be lying but she could not imagine Hazel saying that. She had only met Gerry Henan a couple of times and she hadn't liked him.

"Well . . ." she said gingerly, "Gerry was good-looking. You look a lot like him – so does Jack." She tried to think of something else to say but couldn't.

Luke sensed this and worried that this was all the information his aunt would offer.

"Where was he from?"

"From here, love – Dublin. Why?"

"I just want to be able to say something about him, anything to

30

show the kids he's real," he said, blushing slightly. "I don't want to make stuff up any more." He'd never tell his mam any of this stuff. It would only worry her.

Iris's heart almost melted for the child. He was so vulnerable and he was hurting.

"What did he work at?" he asked.

"Well, he worked with your mam. She didn't tell you that?" Iris was becoming nervous. She didn't want to step on Hazel's toes but she could see that Luke needed some answers. He deserved them.

"In that restaurant in town?"

"Yes, love, but I doubt he still works there. It was a long time ago."

Iris could feel her heart quicken. It worried her that her nephew might go in search of his father, a search that would end in disappointment. She pulled him closer to her as they cuddled on the sofa.

"Aunty Iris?"

"Yes, Luke?"

"Why didn't my dad marry my mam?"

There was no way that Iris could tell him that it was because he was already married.

"I don't know, love. There are things that happen between a man and a woman that you can't understand yet."

"Like sex?"

Iris blushed. "That's one thing but there are other things. Life can be complicated. Do you know what complicated means?"

"Yeah, it means hard. But at least I'd have a different last name then, not Fay. Then people would know I had a dad."

"I understand, but you're alright with us, aren't you? Your mam loves you and so do I."

Luke nodded and cuddled closer into his aunt's warm body – although he would never admit this to his friends. It wasn't cool. Although Luke loved his mam, he felt safe with Iris. She always cooked a proper dinner and made sure they brushed their teeth. She fussed if they weren't wearing warm clothes and made sure Jack took his medication. Sometimes he wished that Iris was his mother

31

but he'd feel really guilty afterwards and do something special for his mam to make up for his bad thoughts.

"Will you ever have any babies, Iris?" he asked innocently.

Iris stiffened and hoped he didn't notice. A wave of nausea rose from the pit of her stomach. Memories best left alone were stirred.

"No, love, not now."

"Why not, Iris, you're a good mam."

Hot tears sprang to her eyes as she shushed him. She didn't want to cry.

"I wasn't cut out for it, Luke – not everyone is."

Luke looked at his aunt and noticed how sad she looked. He thought about what she had said even though it didn't make any sense to him. He wasn't exactly sure what a good mammy did but he was sure that Iris would know how to do it.

Chapter 9

On Sunday morning Iris woke early to hear Jack wheezing in his sleep. She jumped up and went into the small bedroom to find Luke pressing on the inhaler which he had lodged in his brother's mouth. She noticed Jack's swollen, watery eyes.

"Luke, get the nebuliser out of the bag your mam left."

Luke darted from the room.

"It's okay, Jack, big breaths, big breaths, love," she said calmly while Jack struggled to breathe.

Luke arrived back, panicked. "It's not there! It's not in the bag, Iris!"

Iris raced out into the kitchen and opened the plastic bag. The nebuliser that would ease Jack's breathing was not there. She took a deep breath. Jack was panicking and she needed to calm him down. She took a paper bag from the drawer and ran back into the bedroom.

"Jack, let's watch how big your breath is. First, take some more of the inhaler. Now, breathe into the bag. Look, good, see how big the bag gets? Come on, big breaths. Well done. Now more, again, keep it up – good boy!" Iris watched as Jack's breathing slowed and relaxed, his red eyes looking up at her. She wondered if unravelling the wool the day before had brought it on but thought the reaction would have happened sooner. She looked at the bed and remembered that her pillow was made of duck feathers and the boys normally slept on two foam pillows that she kept in a cupboard in the shop. Iris felt stupid that she hadn't thought of this and guilt enveloped her as Jack lay back on the bed, exhausted.

"Come on, love, we'll take you home early so you can use your nebuliser. I have a key and it'll be a nice surprise for your mam when she gets home, won't it?"

Both boys nodded.

"Iris, does that mean that we don't have to go to Mass?" The boys knew they always had to go to Mass when they stayed with Iris but their mam rarely made them go.

Iris laughed. "Yes, we'll have to miss Mass. I'm sure you're disappointed?"

"Hooray!" they shouted, laughing.

Iris threw them a mock-stern look.

Luke suddenly frowned. "Aunty Iris?"

"Yes, Luke?"

"You said you'd take us to Fairview Park before we went home."

"We'll see if Jack's up to it after breakfast. But don't forget, Luke," she admonished, "you're a Communion boy next May, so you shouldn't be missing Mass."

But the boys were still laughing.

Chapter 10

The key to Hazel's house was old and Iris rarely used it. As the boys stood by her side, red-faced and panting from chasing, Iris jiggled the key impatiently in the keyhole. The boys were cold and hungry after a long walk through the park and were pushing each other playfully on the doorstep, betting each other as to who would make it to the fridge first. It took several more tugs before the door finally opened. Iris pleaded with them to calm down as they raced each other down the hallway. As she stopped to pick up the bag on the doorstop, she noticed that the boys had suddenly gone quiet. She followed them down the hall slowly, her mouth dropping open at the sight of empty beer cans littering on the floor of both the hall and sitting room. The house reeked of cigarette smoke. She could see both boys standing at the kitchen door, staring in at what she did not know. There was no sound and she could hear every slow footstep she took on the linoleum floor as though she was walking through a large, empty room. She made her way to where the boys were and looked briefly at them before turning her head to see what they were looking at.

In a kitchen newly painted after the fire, with a gleaming new cooker, Hazel sat at the table. She was half-dressed and staring into space, in front of her an empty red wine bottle and half-eaten pizza. She looked towards them and then looked away slowly as though she did not see them. She did not speak. Her eye was bruised and her lip was swollen. Her hair was not brushed and fell around her shoulders in matted tufts. Mascara ran down her face in uneven lines and made her look like a sad circus clown. She wore a short cheap nightie, worn and faded, with no shoes despite the cold.

Iris walked towards her sister, one hundred questions racing through her mind. The boys stood transfixed, still staring at their mother.

"Hazel . . . what happened? What are you doing here?"

Hazel did not answer.

"Hazel, what happened to your face?" Iris asked gently. She could see that her sister was in a daze.

Again, her sister did not answer.

Luke spoke first, in a voice filled with rage that came out of nowhere and filled the silent room.

"You didn't go anywhere! You're a lying bitch! You were here. The whole time, you were here. I hate you. You're a useless mother. I wish you were dead!"

He ran towards Hazel and started hitting her with his fists. She grabbed at him and slapped him hard. Jack began to cry and hid under the table, his laboured breathing inaudible above Hazel's who had now come to life and had met Luke's anger with her own. Luke jumped back, stunned, rubbing his face. Tears appeared in his eyes but he did not cry. He would not allow it.

Iris jumped forward and grabbed her sister's arms, preventing her from lunging at Luke as he shouted more abuse at her.

"Hazel, that's enough. Don't hit him. He's just a child. He doesn't mean it."

"I do! I hate her! It's all her fault, everything is her fault!"

Hazel broke free from her sister's hold and slapped Luke so hard again that he spun around and hit his head off the kitchen table.

"I gave everything up for you, you ungrateful little bastard!" she screamed. Iris could see Luke crumble. His own mother was mouthing the words that taunted him in school. She could hear Jack's breathing quickening and glanced towards him to see if he was okay. His lip trembled and he remained under the table that his brother had smashed up against.

36

Rage flooded through Iris. "Stop it, for God's sake, Hazel, stop it!" she shrieked. "These are your children. What on earth is the matter with you?"

Hazel stood back and almost smiled at her sister, a creepy half-smile that made Iris's blood run cold. Hazel seemed mad, possessed.

"That's right, Iris. They are *my* children. Not yours. You've some nerve telling me how to handle my kids. What about your own son? Do you wonder what happened to him when you abandoned him? Do you ever wonder how an eight-month-old child felt when you suddenly disappeared?" Hazel threw her head back which made her smeared face look frightening.

Iris's mouth dropped open as did the boys'. Shock rooted her to the spot. She could not believe that her sister had uttered those cruel words. She reddened, shamed that the boys had heard what was her most private, most painful memory.

"How can you be so cruel, Hazel?" she said, her voice shaking. "I've lived with my mistakes every day. I pay for them every day. How can you say these things to me? How can you?" Tears began to flow and she sat down on the chair Hazel had vacated only minutes before. "Luke, take Jack upstairs, please," she pleaded through her tears. There were things she needed to say to her sister.

Luke gave her a venomous look that cut through her. He walked halfway down the hallway and when he was sure he was at a safe distance shouted, "You're both liars! Both of you!" before running upstairs with his little brother in tow.

Iris smoothed her skirt with her hands in long even strokes and took a deep breath.

"I don't know who you are, Hazel. I've done everything I could for you but you keep pulling away from me and from the boys, from the people who care about you. I don't know what you want, what it is that you are looking for, but I can tell you that it isn't out there – it's in here, it's your boys. No one knows it better than me."

Hazel turned her back on her sister and spoke quietly, in almost a whisper, tears running down her face too. "I'm lonely, Iris. Can you understand that? I always have been. Every day, I feel that there is something missing. I need people. I am not you, Iris, so don't berate me for that. I am not you . . ."

"Well, then, you are lucky, Hazel. You are lucky that you're not like me," Iris said sadly as she stood and walked towards the hall.

"Where are you going?" Hazel asked, suddenly frightened of being alone.

Iris did not answer. She walked to the front door and opened it as quietly as she closed it behind her. She walked down the narrow cul-de-sac and out onto Mobhi road which would lead her all the way to the Botanic Gardens. She rarely went there any more but it used to be her favourite place to sit and think. It was there that her father would take her to point out the various flowers that he loved. He tried to instil a love of gardening in both of his daughters but only Hazel had developed an interest, which Iris thought was odd, given that she was so young and couldn't possibly have remembered the visits.

In the Gardens, Iris found herself a seat and watched streams of people walk by her on their Sunday walk. She bought a newspaper at a nearby kiosk so that she wouldn't look odd sitting on her own in a place where people usually came with their families, and pretended to read while she cried quietly its pages. Hazel could be so very wrong about many things but she was right about Iris not needing people. She had no right to need anyone, not any more. She flushed thinking about how the boys now knew that she had a son. She'd had many disagreements with her sister over the years but this one was different. She couldn't take any more of Hazel's erratic behaviour. She had her own demons to fight.

Iris thought back to that day that changed her life. The day that she walked out on her baby son Kevin and her husband Mark.

In some ways, it seemed like it was yesterday and the pain of the memory often woke her like a recent wound. Other times it seemed like a lifetime ago. She was a different person then – "damaged but hopeful," she used to say to Mark when they talked about her past. When her mother died, her Aunt Eileen moved in and looked after them, and Iris used the words "looked after" loosely. Their grandmother, who had remained estranged from their mother, had died eighteen months before, and with no other relatives Eileen agreed to care for them "out of duty", as she said.

Eileen, a spinster, was completely different to their mother – she seemed so old to them, even though looking back she was only in her forties. Eileen was obsessed with cleanliness, mopping and scrubbing the house regularly. "Cleanliness is next to godliness," she used say to them if they were untidy. She cooked proper meals and made the girls go to bed at a regular time. The house was run in military style and although Iris was glad to have the pressure of caring for Hazel taken off her, she simultaneously resented her loss of power in the house. Even though their aunt was not cruel, there was coldness about her and she rarely hugged the girls or congratulated them on their achievements. Some evenings Eileen would bemoan the loss of her life in London where she had worked as a teacher and where, according to herself she had "loads of friends" which Iris and Hazel used to laugh about when out of earshot.

Then Eileen died two years later. Years later, Iris obtained Eileen's death certificate which said she had died of breast cancer. Iris wondered about this. Eileen must have known she was sick for a long time but hadn't said anything. She could never work out why Eileen had opted to care for them but was glad that she had, as it kept them in their own home.

At the time of Eileen's death Iris was fifteen and Hazel was eleven and the Health Board arranged for them to be fostered by a couple fifteen miles away. The house was closed up until such time as the girls were old enough to take responsibility for it.

Mr and Mrs O'Riordan had two children of their own and fostered two others who were siblings, brothers from inner-city Dublin who were always cheerful despite terrible childhoods that the girls' didn't even compare to. Each summer the couple would put all four of the fostered children into state facilities when they went on their annual holiday to Mayo for three weeks. Iris and Hazel both hated it and, while their foster home wasn't exactly a cosy, home-like environment, they ate well and there was no drinking or shouting between their foster parents.

Three years later, Iris's exceptional Leaving Certificate results got her accepted into a nursing training course in London. She didn't want to leave Hazel but knew that when she turned eighteen in December, she would have to leave her foster home in any case and move into an adult facility in inner-city Dublin – or face the ghosts in her mother's house. So, instead, she bought a ticket for the ferry and moved to England.

She still remembered Hazel screaming after her. It was the first time they were ever separated. "I'll be back to see you just as soon as I get a break from the school!" Iris bawled as her foster mother tore Hazel's fingers from the door. The neighbours were watching and she didn't want anyone thinking there was any trouble in her house.

Iris cried quietly for the first half-hour of the ferry trip to Holyhead in Wales while a young man sitting opposite her smiled sympathetically towards her. When he offered to buy her a cup of tea, she was relieved to have someone to talk to. She had never left the country before and was scared out of her wits. Mark turned out to be more than a listening ear and gave her his phone number and his address in London should she need someone to talk to. He said he was in his third year of medicine in London and that he knew what it was like to move to such a big city alone. She almost gave him the address of her digs in London but hesitated. She didn't know him and worried that he could be a nutter, dressed up as a polite medical student who was kind enough to buy her tea.

After three long lonely days in London, she phoned him and arranged to meet on Saturday, in the daytime which she thought would be safer. He brought her on a tour of the city, pointing out famous landmarks and explaining the tube system to her. They bought sandwiches which they ate at Trafalgar Square. She had a good time and, though she had attended an all-girls' school right up to Leaving Certificate and had never had a serious boyfriend, she felt so relaxed and safe around him that she allowed him to walk her all the way back to her digs.

Iris told Mark all about her sister and how she couldn't sleep at night thinking about her and had already written to Hazel twice in three days. Mark had lovely brown eyes and listened intently to her woes, reassuring her that the first term would fly by and that then she could return to Dublin to see Hazel.

The first term did go quickly, as did the first year, but each time Iris took the ferry home she grew more worried about her sister who was dressing in skimpy clothes she bought from the wages she earned in her weekend job. Hazel was also skipping school and her foster placement was under threat as the Health Board tried time and time again to smooth things over. Eventually, almost one year after Iris left for England, Hazel was moved to a girls' home where her every move was monitored. She ran away twice, once making it all the way to London where Iris tried to keep her until the UK police returned her to the police in Dublin. Hazel was not yet sixteen and the authorities didn't think Iris could care for her and complete her studies, so she was returned to care once again.

During this time Mark and Iris's relationship developed and he brought her to meet his family that Christmas during a visit to Dublin. Iris stayed in her mother's house during these visits. She was allowed to take Hazel out for Christmas and it was the best the girls had had for years. Iris took her sister with her to Mark's house in Cabra. His family were ordinary, down-to-earth people who were proud of their son and happy that he had Iris in London and wouldn't be lonely. If only Mark's parents had known what was to come, they would have thrown her out at first sight.

Iris and Mark married and the young doctor took up a permanent post in a nearby hospital. Iris was now twenty-two and had been disappointed that Hazel had not joined her in London as expected but had gone to live in the family home on her own. Iris knew that Hazel let boyfriends stay overnight and the availability of having somewhere to sleep meant that she was constantly attracting the wrong kind of men. She had turned into an attractive woman and had no shortage of admirers. Even though it was the early nineties, Hazel had developed a reputation that she couldn't shake off and the habit of picking up men who only wanted to use her. Even though she had obtained a decent Leaving Cert, she refused to go on to further training and enjoyed rebelling against whatever she felt people wanted her to do. She moved from one dead-end job to another just to get by and never seemed to have any money. During this time the sisters' relationship began to change as Iris spent more and more time telling Hazel what she shouldn't be doing which only served to make Hazel more defiant.

Iris had proved to be a highly efficient nurse but had soon begun to fear that she wasn't really cut out for the profession. She often wondered why she'd chosen a caring profession when she had already spent a big part of her life caring for people who should not have been her responsibility. Now that she was married, she promised herself that her life was going to be her own and set about enjoying it to the full. Mark earned a good salary and with her income they could afford a decent standard of living and a really comfortable flat. She finally felt free. She finally felt like there was hope that she could have a normal life, a good life, but that's when her life suddenly changed for the worse.

She still remembered the day that she found out she was pregnant. Mark's face lit up in their sitting room as she ran to the bathroom to vomit for the third time that day. She hoped it was just a stomach bug but when the test she bought on her way home from work was positive, she was filled with a sudden and incomprehensible feeling of utter dread. They hadn't talked about having children, which was unusual. Why hadn't they, she wondered. What would she have said to Mark if they had discussed children? Somehow it had never entered her mind, which she realised now was not normal for a woman, not normal at all.

Mark was thrilled, even if parenthood was coming a little earlier than he'd imagined, and phoned his parents immediately. He didn't notice Iris's anxiety which seemed to grow at the same speed as her stomach. Friends and work colleagues congratulated them wherever they went and soon Mark's mother, knowing that Iris's mother was long since dead, began to send over regular parcels of homemade cardigans and bootees in colours to suit either a boy or a girl. Mark's parents were so happy – their first grandchild.

In the months to come Iris learnt how to hide her true feelings, whatever they were, because she wasn't sure, and smiled along with company who talked excitedly about the new life that would be due in late December – another winter baby. When her son was born in early January, Iris held him in her arms and looked at his tiny squashed face. It had been a long, difficult labour and had almost ended in a Caesarean section. She sobbed loudly into the new baby's face while the nursing staff and Mark soothed her, thinking she was exhausted and overwhelmed with emotion, with love for the tiny baby, her first child. But Iris was overwhelmed by something else, by the responsibility that looked up at her with Mark's lovely eyes and a head of thick black hair.

Mark took photos and bent towards her, his face flushed with pride and joy. She had never seen him so happy. He kissed her gently and cupped her face between his large, gentle hands. "I love you," he whispered and it shamed her to her core.

When she came home from hospital, the months went by in a blur of sleep-deprivation and constant work. She walked the floors at night with Kevin who had colic and seemed to cry constantly. She became obsessed that there was something wrong with him and took him to two different paediatricians who both said he was healthy and scolded Iris for being over-protective. Mark was working more and more shifts at the hospital to make up for Iris's lost wage but when he was home he would stare at his son in wonderment. Iris felt a strange sort of jealously that embarrassed her. She resented the attention Mark paid the baby and they began to argue. Mark was patient and loving towards her. He suspected she had post-natal depression and brought her to a doctor who prescribed tablets that made her feel tired and numb, as if she was looking at life through a glass wall. In the mornings her speech was slightly slurred as though she'd been drinking. It scared her, brought back too many memories of her mother so she flushed the rest of the prescription down the toilet. What Iris really felt, what she couldn't tell anyone, was that she did not want this child. She did not want anyone to need her, to depend on her. She might let them down. She might fail. She might be just like her mother. She felt trapped, suffocated and inside she screamed silently as she moved through each day in a mist of fear and anxiety.

By the time Kevin was six months old, Mark was doing most of the housework and Iris spent as much time as she could in bed. She rarely slept during the night but would sleep during the day – exhausted, dreamless sleeps that did not seem to ease her fatigue or her mood.

A distance grew between the two. They rarely ate together or went out. Iris barely spoke to her husband who had stopped asking her what was wrong. She watched Mark take over the care of Kevin more and more until she felt obsolete, invisible. Perhaps he sensed her lack of love for the child or, on a deeper level, understood that this is what she wanted, to leave, to disappear and he made it easy for her without realising it.

On the morning of August 17th, she rose early and sat in her living room with a cup of coffee and gazed out of the window that faced a small, empty park. She had not slept and dark circles ran beneath her large blue eyes. Mark was still asleep and Kevin was sleeping soundly in his cot, having cried until four in the morning. Iris looked at the clock. It was half past six. She walked down the hallway to her bedroom and took a small bag from the top of the wardrobe. She threw a few things into it and turned to look at her husband who did not stir. A lump rose in her throat as her mind finally let her in on its plans. He looked so peaceful. Her kind husband who should have done better than her. She didn't deserve him. She moved towards the bed to kiss him but stopped. She was afraid he would wake and would try to stop her, would try to talk her out of it.

She crept quietly down the hallway to Kevin's room. A mobile of brightly coloured teddies moved gently above his cot. Iris inched over and looked in at her baby. He was awake and giggled when he saw her, kicking his legs excitedly. Iris let out a gulp and covered her mouth. She had no right to cry. Kevin raised his arms, hoping to be lifted up. He began to whimper and she rushed to place a soother in his mouth. He raised his hand and gently caressed his own head as his eyes slowly closed. Iris leant in and, as she kissed him on his soft cheek, his mouth turned upwards into a half-smile. She stood back and looked at him. He was so vulnerable. She started to cry and lifted a Babygro from the cot, raising it to her face. She closed her eyes and inhaled his lovely baby smell, already distancing herself from his body which was not more than four feet from her. She did not reopen her eyes but placed her arms out in front of her and made her way quickly from the room, shoving the Babygro into the small leather bag that waited for her in the hallway.

She left a simple note for Mark on the coffee table.

"I have to go away for a while. I tried to be a mother but I don't know how. I need some time to think. I love you. Don't hate me."

It was a memory she had replayed over and over in her head in the months and years to come as she lay awake in whatever place she called home. She didn't know why but over the years she would always send him her new address. She often wondered at this and wondered what she expected from it. Did she half-hope that he'd come and get her, beg her to come back? No, she neither wanted nor needed that. She just wanted him to know . . . to know that . . . she was alive.

When she left the apartment she'd walked three miles to the Tube and made her way, robotically and without conscious thought, to a friend's apartment in Maidenhead. Louise Nugent was from Cork and, though she had trained as a nurse with Iris, she had swapped bedpans for a more exotic life as an artist and was doing well. The friends were not in regular contact except for a card at Christmas and the occasional postcard. Maidenhead was over thirty miles from where Iris lived and she knew that Mark would never think of looking for her there. She had never talked to him about Louise – possibly had never even mentioned her.

It was there that she began her new life.

She got a job in a sewing factory – sewing was something she had been good at in school. When she had enough money, she moved into a rented room and lived an almost solitary life. In time she realised that the lonely life she chose was not something that she wanted . . . not something that she longed for . . . but was a sort of a punishment for a sin that she would never be able to forgive herself for.

In the evenings and during the long lonely nights she would torment herself: "Mothers don't leave, mothers don't leave . . ." Yet she knew that she'd had no option. She was dying there. She had to get away. It was best for everyone. And she couldn't tell Mark . . . couldn't say the words . . . that twice she had wanted to put her hand over Kevin's crying mouth and to silence him, to press down on his mouth until she smothered his cries forever and so she could sleep . . . sleep without worrying about all the awful things that could happen to him . . . all the awful things she might do to him. How could she tell her husband what a monster she was? On both occasions she'd locked the baby in his room and left the flat and sat on the stairwell with her hands over her ears so she could no longer hear his piercing cries.

Three weeks after she left, she phoned Mark. He sounded so . . . alone. She cried silently down the phone as he pleaded with her to return, promised that he'd get her help for postnatal depression – a psychiatrist – no pills – she would feel better . . . Even then she couldn't tell him that she didn't want this life . . . that she could not live it . . . that she had to be free.

Just before Christmas when she was sure Mark knew that she'd never return, she agreed to meet him in Trafalgar Square but begged him not to bring Kevin. She couldn't bear to see him. They sat by the fountain where the hundreds of pigeons that frequented the square were oddly sparse. An unbearable silence settled between them. She wished he'd scream, shout, hit her even but he just sat there with his big sad eyes. She hated him for loving her still. How could he? He didn't know the awful things she was capable of . . . those thoughts . . . horrible . . . burning . . . shameful.

"Is it another man?" he finally asked.

Her mouth dropped open in surprise. "No!" she said vehemently.

"Then . . . what?" he asked so quietly she felt he would break in two in front of her very eyes.

She stood and, without looking at him, pushed her address and a small present into his hands, a gift for Kevin, a tiny wooden framed photo of her holding him on the day he was born.

"Look after yourself . . . look after my . . . ba–" She stopped, the words cutting into her throat and choking her.

He stood up and stepped towards her.

She shivered and brought every ounce of strength within her to bear to make herself face him, make herself look into his pleading eyes. She moved backwards, slowly edging her small feet away.

"I can't do it, Mark . . . it's better . . . safer . . ." she whispered.

She backed further into the crowd. He moved toward her and put out his arms as if to grab her, to prevent her from leaving. She jumped backwards and her arms jerked forward, blocking his arms from her body.

"I can't, Mark . . . I . . . love you . . . and I love . . . I love . . ." She gulped, then raised her voice to a shout as if the volume of her voice would convince him: "I love *him*!"

She turned and disappeared into the crowd. She kept running, pushing through the crowds, bawling inconsolably as she shoved her way forward. She could hear him call her name, twice, maybe three times and then a quiet descended around her as if the crowds knew her secret, knew her worthlessness. She placed her hands over her ears and ran faster, blocking out the silence that was now deafening her, a silence that had since haunted her sleepless nights and her every waking moment.

She did not stop running until she arrived at the Tube station. She boarded her train and found a seat at the end of the carriage. Other passengers looked at her red, tear-stained face until she ran her sleeve roughly over her eyes and sniffed away her tears. She lowered her head and stared out of the window as she silently counted the number of stops to her flat. She knew she would never be the same again.

In the Botanic Gardens, Iris shook her head and tried to shake the awful memory away. She shivered and pulled her coat closer around her thin frame. She realised that she had turned out just like her father. She had known on that fateful morning that he was not coming back and she had hated him for it for many years. But for some reason she had done the same thing as he had, had abandoned a family who needed her. She knew that it was easy to regret things when you could no longer change them. Her son was almost a man now. He didn't need her any more. And she did regret it . . . every single day of her miserable life. She wondered if things could have been different . . . if she could have felt stronger . . . able . . . if she could have been someone different. But she knew these thoughts were useless. They didn't change anything. She was who she was and her parents were who they were. These things couldn't be changed. She wouldn't have been good . . . she saved him . . . her son . . . she might regret it but deep down she knew she had done the right thing.

Iris rose awkwardly from the bench and walked slowly towards the park gates. It was almost four and the park closed early in winter. It had been a clear bright day which delayed the late afternoon darkness that was normal for this time of year. She felt weary and walked slowly as though her muscles hurt. She did not recognise the gatekeeper and thought that he must be new. He tipped his cap and smiled a toothless grin at her.

As she walked out onto the main road, she could see in the distance the cemetery where her mother was buried. She turned and walked the other way, the long way home, as clouds slowly covered the setting winter sun.

Chapter 11

In the three weeks since the falling out with Iris, Hazel had twice phoned Pete's number but hung up when he answered. She didn't know why she was phoning him – after all, the last time she saw him he had left her with a black eye and split lip. But she wondered now how much of it had been her fault. She needed someone to talk to. The atmosphere in the house was killing her as Luke continued to sulk and Jack took his brother's lead by only talking to her when he had to, although the five-year-old wasn't sure what it was all about. Three days before, a letter from the school invited her to attend a meeting about Luke and stated that the board of management wanted to have Luke assessed because of his aggressive behaviour. She hadn't been able to sleep since and had not mentioned the letter to Luke although she felt like throttling him for bringing more trouble on her. She wanted to ask him why he was behaving like that in school when he never once hit his brother at home. It didn't make any sense to her but she knew that asking him would only end in another row and she didn't have the strength for that. There was also a part of her that was afraid he would say something to confirm her suspicions that she was to blame, that she was a terrible mother and had caused her older son to develop some sort of mental problem. Another part of her knew that wasn't true. She was doing the best she could and if that wasn't good enough then it was just tough.

When the doorbell rang later that evening, her mouth dropped open to find Pete standing there, grinning smugly at her.

"Missed me, did ya?" he asked in an arrogant, almost menacing tone.

"Pete" she said hoarsely, noticing the fear in her voice and wondering what on earth possessed her to call him at all.

"No, I em . . . I wasn't expecting you . . . em . . . what do you want?" she asked, trying to conceal how nervous she was.

The boys had been in bed but she could hear them come out of their room and stand on the landing, hopefully out of sight.

"Come on now, I know it was you ringing me and hanging up, wasn't it? Glad to see you've calmed down, Haze. Went on a bit of a mad one, didn't ya?" He leaned in towards her while keeping his feet outside the front door, waiting on the invitation he knew would be coming.

Hazel moved back and turned her face away from him. He smelt of beer and had a six-pack in a plastic bag under his arm. She saw the change of expression in his face as she moved away from him, a mix of surprise and anger, and her heart jumped, afraid that he would hit her again.

"Go away!" a voice ordered from the top of the stairs.

Hazel turned to see Luke standing with Jack on the landing.

Pete looked up, surprised, and shook a fist at the boys.

"Shu' up, ya little brat!" he shouted.

"Pete, maybe not tonight, eh?" Hazel said nervously. "It's been a long day, the boys are tired, you know? Maybe tomorrow night?" She tried to sound eager, pretending to be interested and wondering where she would go the following night to avoid him.

Luke moved forward on the landing but shoved Jack in behind him.

"My mam doesn't want you here. You better get out or I'll ring the guards," he said loudly although his heart beat fast in his narrow chest.

"Yeah!" Jack echoed from behind his brother. He needed to pee and crossed his legs as he peered under Luke's arm.

Pete looked towards Hazel, waiting for her to correct her brats, but she stood rooted in the doorway. He smiled strangely towards the boys then pushed his way into the house, banging the door behind him.

"I'll put some manners on your kids if you won't!" he said to Hazel as he took two steps at the time towards the boys.

Luke grabbed Jack and shoved him into their bedroom. He could hear his mother shouting "No!" as Pete's footsteps pounded on the thinly carpeted stairs. Luke locked the door and pushed Jack into the wardrobe before diving under the bottom bunk. The doorknob turned and then the door smashed open before he could get his legs hidden. He felt his legs being tugged as Pete pulled him from his hiding place. He could see his mother's feet enter the room, coming to save him and his brother whose breathing he could hear from the closed wardrobe.

"Pete," she said in a soft voice, "they don't mean anything, they're just playing, that's all. Come downstairs and we'll have a chat, eh?"

Luke looked up at her, stunned. His mind raced. His mother was actually going to let Pete stay even though he was going to beat him and Jack. He stared at her and watched her avoid his gaze as she wrung her hands nervously and shifted from foot to foot.

"Come on down, Pete, eh?" she said again.

Pete pulled Luke onto his feet roughly and shook him. "You're lucky your ma's so good-looking, ya little runt, otherwise I'd have half killed ya!" He dropped Luke onto the bunk and with a clenched fist banged the wardrobe door where he knew Jack was hiding, the noise of his loud, laboured breathing filling the tense room.

Hazel gently moved Pete towards the door and wondered what she would have to do to get him out of the house without him hurting her boys, or herself. She knew she'd have to play along with him tonight, at least until he passed out on her sofa which he usually did after a few beers. Hazel looked back at her older son whose mouth had dropped open like a drawbridge and whose eyes were opened wide, trying to digest what had just happened. She could not explain to him that this was the best way to make sure

Pete hurt no one that night. Tomorrow she might go to the police and get a barring order. She'd think of something. It hurt her to see how her son looked at her, as though she was dirt. As Pete begrudgingly walked downstairs, she quickly stepped back into the bedroom.

"Jack, come out, it's okay," she said softly but Jack did not answer. "I know you're in there, Jack. I can hear you breathing. It's okay. Pete's gone downstairs."

When Jack did not answer she sighed loudly and walked towards the door.

"Don't come downstairs," she said to Luke, "and keep Jack here. Do you hear me?"

Luke ignored her and lowered his head, his eyes refusing to meet hers.

When she was gone he opened the wardrobe door and helped Jack, who had turned as white as a sheet and had wet himself, out from his hiding place.

"It's okay, Jack."

Luke could see Jack's bottom lip begin to quiver and quickly began singing the silly chicken song that his little brother liked and that he himself wouldn't be caught dead singing in front of the kids at school. When Jack smiled weakly, Luke took off his brother's wet pyjamas and helped him into a clean pair. He sat Luke down on the bed and pushed the hair out of his eyes. Luke placed his hands on his brother's narrow shoulders, something his mother did when she wanted to get Jack's attention.

"Jack, there's something we need to do."

Chapter 12

Iris lay awake in her bed. Although she had gone to bed at eight o'clock, exhausted, she found herself still awake as the clock moved towards eleven. She had been feeling so tired lately that she found herself going to bed earlier and earlier, sometimes without even having any dinner. She wondered if it was because she was missing Hazel but she didn't think it was that – they had fallen out so many times before that it was a normal part of life. Hazel mentioning her son had brought her past to the front of her mind again, not that it was ever that far from her thoughts, and she knew that this too was preventing her from sleeping through the night. She had dreamed of Mark the previous night and in her dream he looked older which was strange as, although it was over sixteen years since she had seen him, she always imagined him as he was then, thin and good-looking with a mop of dark, dishevelled hair. She had only had one letter from him, some years back. He had written asking her to sign divorce papers and telling her that he intended to marry Miriam, another doctor at the hospital whom Iris had known and liked. Miriam was also divorced with a daughter, Anna. She was a few years older than Mark but Iris knew she would make him happy and, although it hurt when he wrote to tell her his news, she was happy for him and knew that Miriam would be a good mother to her son although she tried not to think about that too much. She remembered how she cried at the formal tone in Mark's letter, but what had she expected? Inside the envelope was a photo of Kevin in a school uniform. She gulped at the photo of the growing boy, the shock of him no longer being a baby startling her. He was smiling confidently into the camera. His hair, still a mop of dark curls, his eyes, the same deep brown as his father's. The day that letter arrived she closed the shop early and sat in the back, sobbing and staring at the photo of her beautiful son, but by nightfall she had dried her tears and signed the papers under the dim light of her table lamp. She stuck a stamp on a creased envelope she found in a drawer in her shop and walked out into the cold night air. She threw the letter into the post-box across the street and quickly turned to face home. When she returned to the shop she took one last look at the photo and placed it into an old wooden frame she had. She wrapped the frame in tissue paper and placed the photo under some clothes in her bedside locker. She wondered why Mark had sent it to her. Did he know how upset it would make her or was he saying, 'I am moving on, here's a photo of our son, that's all you're getting'? She doubted it. Mark was not cruel and she didn't believe that he would do anything to hurt her, despite what she had done. She spent hours thinking about this and decided that her husband was saying goodbye and that the photo was part of that message. She wondered about the other photos that were probably placed around Mark's flat in London. Photos of Kevin's first day at school, his First Communion, Confirmation, birthday parties. Photos that she would never see. It hurt, even though it was her fault. She knew she could have phoned Mark and asked to see Kevin at any point but too much water had passed under the bridge, too much time lost. It was too late. Her son had a mother now. He no longer needed her. He had grown up without her help and she had no right to ask to be part of a life that someone else had nurtured and cared for. No right at all. She tried to will her mind not to return to depressing thoughts but still they came.

A year after she had left Mark and Kevin, Iris moved to another town and found a job in a small dressmaker's. The owner was a widow who rented Iris a small flat at the other end of the town and who taught her everything she knew about the trade. She was a quiet, unassuming woman who didn't pry into Iris's life which suited her tenant just fine.

Iris wrote to Hazel from time to time but had only seen her sister twice in recent years, during the time when she was dating Luke's father whom she had begged her to finish with. They did not visit each other often back then, not even at Christmas. Even though Hazel said very little, Iris could sense that her sister was furious with her for leaving her son, especially after the childhood they had endured.

She sometimes wondered which of them had done the right thing: she who had left her son because she knew she couldn't be a good mother or her wayward sister who stumbled through life dragging her two boys with her. What she did not wonder about was how neither of them were good mothers. After all, what example had they been given? What did they know about motherhood? About parenthood? Iris knew that it was their father she resembled more than their mother. Like him, she had run away when the going got tough – backed off and left her responsibilities to someone else.

She knew that Hazel didn't realise that she thought about her son every minute of every day. In those early years before Mark remarried, she wondered who was looking after him while he was at work. Was the person kind to him? Did she lift him when he cried or was he in one of those awful crèches where rows of babies lined the walls, being picked up only when they cried or needed feeding. She doubted that. She knew Mark would have looked for someone to care for their son in their home, no matter what the cost. But still she worried. She wondered if the carer knew what his different cries meant. The only peace she got was when evening came and she was sure her son, now a toddler, would be sleeping soundly, Mark in the next room listening out for his cries. Those thoughts had almost driven her crazy during those early years and only mildly improved when she knew her son would be speaking, asking for things, making his needs known. When Miriam became Mark's wife a different kind of torment ensued. Her son now had a mother and, while she knew Miriam would be good to her son, she felt like the attachment she had to him, however imaginary, had been severed and that she had been somehow set adrift. She knew this feeling made little sense – after all, it was she who had chosen to set herself adrift years before. It was like all the thoughts and feelings that spun incessantly through her mind, one contradicting the other, in a never-ending circle.

Iris stayed with the dressmaker for several years and lived much the same way as she did now. She was content with her life and kept to herself. She had no friends to speak of, nor did she want any. She spent her evenings alone and worked long hours, becoming a skilled seamstress and attracting new business to her employer's shop.

When she received a frantic call from Hazel begging her to come and help and informing her that the boys' father had left her for good, she returned to Ireland for what was supposed to be a short stay. Hazel was in hospital after surgery having supposedly fallen down the stairs and broken her arm. The boys were in foster care and she needed to prove that she had someone to help her in order to get them back. When Iris saw what had become of her sister, she had reluctantly stayed.

The sudden wailing of a passing ambulance snapped Iris out of her painful thoughts. She tried to close her eyes and resented the fact that, despite how tired she was, it was probably going to be another one of her sleepless nights. She turned to face the wall to block out the streetlight that shone over the side alley that led to her back yard. She pulled the covers snugly around her and tried to will herself to sleep.

Then the phone rang loudly in the silent flat. She jumped up and ran to the sitting room, a feeling of dread sending a shiver down her spine.

"Hello?"

Iris could hear a woman's voice crying into the receiver.

"Hazel, is that you?" she asked.

"Iris. My boys . . . my babies . . . they're gone."

Chapter 13

Sergeant Bernard Keogh picked up the two photos of the boys in their school uniforms and stood by the fire in Hazel's sitting room. Iris sat on the sofa with her arms tightly around her sister who was in a daze and looking around her as though she had just woken up from a long dream.

"We'll get these distributed to some of the local stations. See if anyone has them. They ever do anything like this before?"

Hazel shook her head.

"Never," Iris answered.

"Did anything happen? Was there a row? Anything upset them?" he asked.

Hazel stiffened under Iris's embrace and looked sideways at her sister who instinctively knew that Hazel was well aware of the reason the boys had run away.

Hazel shook her shoulders to free herself from Iris and reddened slightly. There were two female guards in the room with the senior guard and Hazel was embarrassed discussing such private business in front of strangers.

"An old boyfriend called," she said nervously, looking more at her older sister than at the guards. "I tried to get rid of him but he barged in. He threatened the boys, but just in a kidding way. He wouldn't really hurt them."

Iris tensed up but remained silent. This was no time for a row.

"Where is he now?" Keogh asked sternly.

"He left as soon as I phoned the police about the boys," Hazel replied quietly. It hurt her that even though he was to blame for the boys running away, Pete hadn't even stayed with her to help find them. Instead he grabbed his jacket and began searching through it before running out the front door and cursing loudly as he made his exit. She knew he must have had a reason to avoid the police – another reason to stop seeing him, as if she needed one.

At about half ten, when Pete was busy watching football, she had gone to check on the boys. She had felt guilty all evening that she hadn't gone up to see if they were okay, but she knew that Pete would moan if he caught her checking on them. "They're not babies, ya know, Haze," he would say.

Now she wondered how long they had been gone by half ten and if she could have stopped them by simply going up to say goodnight. She hadn't heard them come downstairs and reddened, thinking they might have seen her with Pete.

"What did they take with them? Clothes, favourite toys, that kind of thing?" the sergeant asked.

"I don't know," Hazel replied, still blushing.

Iris went to the kitchen and returned quickly.

"They've taken the nebuliser," she said directly to Hazel.

"The what?" Keogh asked.

"The nebuliser," Iris replied. "It's for Jack. He has severe asthma. It helps him breathe but it needs to be plugged in so they must be planning on going to someone's house. Otherwise, they wouldn't have taken it. It's heavy."

"Have they friends around? Other relatives?"

"Just me. Hazel doesn't know what time they left but they would have got to me within an hour if they walked – sooner if they had the bus fare."

"Had they any money?" Keogh asked, aware that the children's mother wasn't being entirely helpful and that he had to drag every bit of information out of her.

Hazel heaved herself to the kitchen and opened her purse which she always left on top of the microwave. Her legs felt like they were made of lead. She knew she'd only had a fiver left. It was gone. She went back and told Keogh.

"Well," he said, "that won't get them far."

He stood thinking for a moment and looked at the children's mother.

"Ma'am, why didn't you ring the police when your boyfriend threatened your children?"

Hazel stared at Keogh, giving him a venomous look. She wet her lips and shifted her eyes from side to side like a rabbit in headlights.

"I – I didn't want to make a fuss," she replied.

Keogh took in a deep breath while the two female officers glanced at each other. "Well, it's certainly a fuss now, isn't it, ma'am?"

Hazel nodded and lowered her head. Iris returned to her side and put her arms around her. She knew the sergeant was right but it hurt her to see Hazel being tortured.

Iris thought back to the last time she spoke to Luke. It was the weekend she had looked after them which ended in a row back at Hazel's. She thought about how miserable he was and how much difficulty he was having in school. She remembered how Hazel had called him the very name he hated – *bastard*. She looked up at the police as her eyes widened.

"I know where they are."

Chapter 14

Barrett's restaurant on the corner of Green Street was an upmarket establishment whose tables were booked months in advance unless you were a celebrity or a high-profile politician. It was two bus journeys away from Hazel's house and she had pointed out her old workplace to the boys several times on their way to the children's hospital in Crumlin that Jack attended for asthma.

The boys had just got off their first bus which had seemed to take a lifetime to get into the city centre and were making their way to where they'd get the Number 50 bus in College Street. As the boys crossed O'Connell Bridge, they stopped for a rest and looked into the murky water. Luke had a backpack on his back and was carrying a big plastic bag. The bag contained a few clothes that would do them until their dad took them out for all new stuff and the backpack held Jack's asthma equipment which Luke knew was more important than any other running-away equipment they could have brought. He had packed in a hurry and even the medals Luke won for hurling, which he would have liked to show his father, and Jack's teddy were left behind. Luke felt that Jack was getting too big for that sort of toy anyway.

It was dark and Luke was a little afraid although he wouldn't admit it to his little brother. He worried that his dad would not be working that night but had a plan to get his address that he was sure would work. He felt bad that he had stolen his mam's last fiver because that was a sin, no matter how much you needed it for bus fares, but he was sure his dad would pay her back as soon as they had settled in.

They started to walk again.

"Luke?"

"Yeah?"

"Didn't Mam say that our dad lived in a different country, too far to visit us?"

"Yeah," Luke replied angrily. "She lied to us."

"Well," Jack replied breathlessly, "if our dad only lives two buses away, how come he doesn't come to see us?"

Luke frowned and thought hard to come up with an answer that Jack would find believable and, more importantly, that Luke himself could accept.

"Maybe Mam wouldn't let him see us? You know Adam in my class?"

Jack nodded. He was too out of breath to talk.

"Well, it's like him – his mam – she doesn't let him see his dad," Luke said.

"Well, I think that's very naughty," Jack said innocently.

"Mmm," Luke said, nodding, slightly worried that his mam hadn't stopped his dad from coming and that maybe, just maybe, their dad didn't want to see them. But he knew that couldn't be true. He knew now that his mam was a liar and that she had kept them from having a dad that could love them and take them to football matches.

Luke looked into the distance and saw the Number 50 revving up beside College Green.

"Run Jack! It's our bus!" he shouted above the din of traffic on D'Olier Street. "We're going to see our Dad, Jack! For real!"

Chapter 15

When the police car left the house, Hazel and Iris sat in the kitchen and waited. They had both wanted to go looking for the boys but Sergeant Keogh had insisted they stay behind because, he said, most kids return to the house within a few hours and someone would need to be there to let them in. Hazel didn't believe this and worried that the police felt the boys had come to some terrible end and that she would be identifying their bodies rather than hugging her boys.

She started to cry again as Iris held her tightly at the kitchen table.

"It's all my fault, Iris. I didn't know Luke felt that way. I didn't want to tell them about Gerry, for their own good. Please, God, don't let anything happen to them!"

"Shh, don't even think that, Hazel. They're probably on their way back here. Let the police do their job. It'll be alright, don't worry." Iris didn't believe a single word she had said and knew Hazel didn't believe it either.

Hazel dried her eyes and sniffed. Her face was red and blotchy from crying and her nose was running.

"I'm sorry for mentioning Kevin in front of the boys. I get so angry sometimes. I say things I don't mean."

"It's okay," Iris said quietly even though it wasn't okay. The boys were the only positive thing in Iris's life and Hazel had ruined that – but she couldn't think about that now.

Both women fell silent, burdened by their thoughts.

"Iris?"

"Mmm?"

"The night of the fire, I didn't want you thinking I messed up again. I was annoyed that Luke went to you for help when I should have been the one he came to."

"You were on your way to hospital," Iris said flatly.

"I know but, well, you always seem to do things right. I'm always the one messing things up."

"That's not exactly how I'd describe myself."

"It was Pete. He fell asleep. I left him in the sitting room and went to bed. He woke up and, drunk as he was, started to cook burgers and chips and dozed off again. He could have burned us all to death."

Iris remained silent. She was annoyed that Hazel continued to see Pete with all he had put her through but didn't want to argue with her sister. She was going through enough tonight.

"The night . . . the weekend I asked you to mind the boys?" Hazel said in a questioning tone.

Iris looked up. "Yes?" she said slowly, still annoyed at having being lied to.

"Something strange happened. Pete asked his friends around and they were all drinking and laughing. I was alone even though my sitting room was full of people."

"Full of strangers," Iris said quickly but instantly regretted it.

"Yeah," Hazel sighed. "Strangers."

"A fella started getting sick on the sofa. It was . . . disgusting but I couldn't look away and I . . . I remembered something. I remembered Mam vomiting onto my school uniform. It was like someone had stuck a memory back into my head that I had forgotten about. I just lost it, started screaming at everyone to get out. Pete went mad and hit me. It was . . . it frightened me." She shook her head and fell silent.

Iris reached over and put her hand on Hazel's arm.

Hazel wet her lips. "Did it happen often, Iris? Mam being sick from drink like that?" She could not look directly at her sister but stared out of the kitchen window into the darkness.

Iris remained silent, trying to decide how to answer.

"Yes," she said softly.

"Is that why we're . . ." Hazel tensed up – she didn't want to include Iris in this. "I'm . . . the way I am . . . is it why I'm . . .?" Her chin quivered and she broke down. "Jesus . . . I'm a useless mother! If only Dad was around . . . if only he didn't die . . . it would have been better, wouldn't it, sis?"

Iris looked into her sister's face. Hazel looked so innocent. She couldn't tell her the truth. She couldn't tell her about their father. She took a long deep breath and let it out in a slow sigh.

"Partly, I suppose," she said, "but it doesn't mean it has to be that way. You're . . . you're trying."

Hazel stood and began to pace backwards and forward. "Oh, why aren't they phoning? What's keeping them?" she asked nervously. She moved to the kitchen drawer, took out a white envelope and handed it to Iris. "I got this letter from the school."

Iris opened the letter and read it.

"They say Luke is disturbed," Hazel said. "Want him to see a shrink. It's my fault, Iris, my fault. He was such a lovely baby. Perfect. My . . . fault." She gulped and began to sob again.

Iris stood and hugged Hazel in the dimly lit kitchen. Then she pulled back.

"He's not disturbed, Hazel, listen to me," she said authoritatively. "He's just angry. That's all."

Hazel looked into her sister's eyes. "What do we do with all that anger, Iris? You, me and Luke. What do we do with it?"

Iris did not have an answer.

Chapter 16

Barrett's restaurant was the only building on Green Street to have Christmas lights up as it was still only mid-November. The lights from within the restaurant shone out onto the wet street and made it look warm and cosy inside.

"Is this it?" Jack asked, amazed that their dad worked in such a posh place.

"Yeah," Luke replied, smiling. The building looked so different at night.

As the boys walked inside the restaurant, a waiter all dressed up in a black suit approached them, frowning.

"Can I help you?" he asked in what struck Luke as a television accent.

"We're looking for Gerry," Luke said confidently even though he noticed people putting down their knives and forks and looking at him.

"Gerry?" the man in the wedding suit replied as though he didn't know who Luke was talking about. "Is he dining here?"

"No." Luke wasn't sure what 'dining' meant but he didn't think it sounded like part of his dad's job. "But he does work here," he said, amazed that this man didn't know his dad.

"What's his last name?" the waiter asked impatiently.

Luke looked at Jack. "We don't know," he said, embarrassed.

"I think they're looking for Romeo," a passing waitress said. "He doesn't work here any more, lads," she said kindly as the waiter looked crossly at her.

Luke felt as though he could cry. He was tired and he needed somewhere to plug Jack's nebuliser in by bedtime and it was way past that time now. He might even need to plug it in sooner if Jack got nervous which was very likely.

The woman bent down until she was face to face with Luke.

"What do you want him for?" she asked softly.

Tears welled in his eyes and he bit his lip. "He's our dad and we have to see him tonight. Our mam's sick . . ." He elbowed Jack when his brother turned and stared open-mouthed at him.

"How come you don't know where he works?" the woman asked. "He left here about four years ago."

"They're divorced," he lied. That's four things for confession if I count taking Pete's Panadol from his pocket, he thought. When he took money from his mam's purse he had also looked in Pete's jacket to see if he had any money but all he found was a small plastic bag with lots of Panadol in it. It was probably for Pete's head when he drank too much and Luke was delighted that Pete would have to put up with a headache the next day.

"Well," the woman said kindly, "he works on the ferry now." She looked at her watch. It was almost midnight. "It's gone for tonight but he might have worked on the one coming into Dublin. It docks at East Wall. Do you know Mac's pub?"

Both boys shook their heads.

"Well, it's facing the ferry terminal on East Wall. You walk down the quays and . . ." The woman stopped herself. It was dark and these boys were too young to walk the quays at night. "Look. Why don't you boys go home and look for your dad tomorrow? There's a ferry at ten in the morning and he'll probably be on it. Do you have any one looking after you tonight?"

Jack shook his head while Luke said, "Yes!" loudly, startling some customers. He was worried that they'd phone the guards or social services. He didn't remember it but he had heard his mam and Aunty Iris talking about the time he and Jack, who was only a few weeks old, had to go to a foster home for three whole days because Mam had hurt herself and Aunty Iris was still in England. Aunty Iris came home to help them after that.

"Get them out of here," the waiter said quietly into the waitress's ear.

"My aunt is looking after us," Luke said, putting on his best innocent face and smiling at the woman while Jack looked amazed that he didn't know this.

"Okay then. Well, go home. Your aunt shouldn't let you come into town at night," the waitress said while making frown-marks on her forehead and tossing Luke's hair.

Luke and Jack turned and made their way back to the front door.

"Hey, kids!" the waitress called.

They turned.

"It's Henan – your dad's name. Gerry Henan."

"Hennin?" asked Luke.

"H.E.N.A.N," she spelt. "Henan."

Luke smiled at her and waved as he held the heavy door open for his brother.

"Hear that, Jack? We're Luke and Jack Henan."

"I didn't know that," Jack said, realising that there seemed to be a lot of things that he didn't know.

By the time they had waited at the bus terminus for over half an hour, the boys realised that the Number 50 bus had finished for the night and that they would have to walk back to the city centre.

"How far is it?" Jack moaned. "I'm tired, Luke!" He wanted to go home and run away again the next morning but he didn't want to let his brother down and it was, after all, an adventure that they were on.

"Not far, Jack. Stop talking – you're using up your breath. Here, take this." Luke pushed the inhaler into his brother's mouth and pressed it twice.

As the boys walked down Harcourt Street it started to rain.

"Here, Jack, quick, let's shelter in the park," Luke suggested, grabbing his brother's hand and leading him across the road to St Stephen's Green.

"Can we feed the ducks, Luke?" Jack asked eagerly. It was his favourite thing to do.

"They're probably asleep," Luke replied even though he wasn't really sure if ducks slept and, anyway, they had nothing to feed them with.

"Ahhh!" Jack moaned.

"Well, we'll see. Maybe one or two of them are still up."

The boys made their way towards the water in the middle of the park and sat on a wet bench. Luke could hear men talking behind the trees and he wondered why anyone would visit a park at night when you couldn't see anything.

"Hello?" he called out, thinking somebody might have extra bread so Jack could feed the ducks which might keep his brother from moaning for a while. He heard someone running but it sounded like their steps were getting further away.

"Hello?" he called again.

"Maybe it's a ghost, Luke, and it'll come after us? I'm scared. I want to get out of the park. I want something to eat."

Luke dug down into his pockets. He had spent almost €3 on bus fares and had only enough for some chips and a coke to share between them.

"Okay, Jack. Let's get you something to eat."

On the way out of the park they met two men coming in. One of the men looked at the boys and shouted, "For Christ sake, lads, get out of the park! It's not safe. Where's your mother?" which made both boys run towards the crossing without looking back.

"Well, if it's not safe, then why are you going in there?" Luke shouted back when he was at a safe distance but the men had already disappeared out of sight.

Chapter 17

By the time the guards got to Barrett's restaurant, the boys had already left. They spoke to the waitress who directed them towards the port where Gerry Henan might be drinking but they hadn't shown up there. None of the regular drinkers knew where Henan lived, or at least wouldn't say. They phoned the boys' mother who told them she didn't know where else they might be as she cried loudly into the phone. With no more leads to go on they spread out and started a general search of the port area.

They were not the only ones looking for Luke and Jack though.

Pete Doyle drove his car through the city centre like a man possessed. He was supposed to offload the tablets and then meet his supplier with the cash in Dwyer's Pool Hall and now the little bastard Luke had made off with them. Jimmy Power wasn't the calmest of people and would make serious trouble for him if he didn't come up with the money. The only reason he had got involved with him is that he owed money through bad bets and it was the only way to pay him back. He was sure Luke wouldn't know that the tablets were ecstasy but, if he did, the little bastard might try to sell them. Pete swore to himself that when he caught up with him, he'd teach Luke Fay a lesson he'd never forget.

As Pete swung his car right into O'Connell Street, he unknowingly passed by the boys who were sitting in a doorway and looking out at the wonder of crowds of revellers.

"Luke?"

"Yeah?"

"Do you think our dad lives in a house with enough room for us? He might live in a flat and have no extra beds."

Luke's eyes opened wide. "We know his name now!" he exclaimed loudly.

"Yes," Jack replied, unsure why his brother was excited when he himself was tired and cold and was really only interested in how many beds his dad had.

"We could look him up in a phone book, couldn't we? Aunty Iris taught me how to do that!" Luke jumped up and grabbed the bags. "Come on, Jack, hurry up – we have to find a phone box."

Outside the GPO, Luke and Jack huddled in a battered phone box and Luke began to leaf through the book which was badly torn. He knew he must find the letter 'H' first because his dad's name began with a 'H'. Then he'd have to search for 'H.E.' because the waitress had spelt it H.E.N.A.N. He found the 'H' names and recited the alphabet loudly while he ran his dirty finger along the torn page past the names that began with 'H.A.' until he got to 'H.E.'. Then he carefully dragged his finger down one page after another until he found it: H.E.N.A.N.

Luke heaved a great breath of relief.

Luckily, there were only three Henans in the book. The last was G Henan. 'G' for 'Gerry'.

Luke tried to read the address. It was difficult. The only word he recognised was 'flats'. It said 'Seville Flats' but he didn't know that word 'Seville' or how to say it. He could feel himself becoming upset but he didn't want to worry Jack and so pretended everything was under control. He tore the page from the book, folded it and put it in his pocket.

"Did you find Dad?"

"I'm not sure, Jack. He lives in some flats but I can't exactly remember where they are," he lied. "We can ask someone to show us. We'll have to pick someone who won't care that we're out on our own."

Luke was beginning to feel like he had made a mistake and

wished he had gone to Aunty Iris instead. They could be wrapped up on her sofa bed now after getting hot chocolate and biscuits. He could plug in Jack's nebuliser which was worrying him most of all. But deep down he knew he had made the right decision to run away. They had to find somewhere safe to live where there would be no one like Pete Doyle and where they didn't have to worry about their mam who was an adult and should know better than to be friends with people like Pete.

About a hundred yards down O'Connell Street Luke noticed an old man who looked homeless sitting on the ground and wrapped in a filthy sleeping bag. He had an empty wine bottle under his arm and was stabbing a sharp-ended walking cane into the ground as he shouted out to passers-by for change.

Luke approached him.

"Mister?"

The old man ignored him. He was sick of young ones asking if he had the time and the running off with his meagre takings when he wasn't looking. He had even taken to paring down his walking stick and giving bowsies a good sharp jab of it when the need arose.

Luke put the plastic bag down at his feet and pulled the phone-book page out of his pocket. He held it out to the old man, pointing to his dad's name. "Mister . . . we're looking for that address there. Those flats. Do ya know where they are?"

The old man looked carefully at the boys. They didn't look too rough and the younger one was breathing very heavily.

"What have ya got in the bags?" he asked slowly.

Luke swallowed hard, worried that the old man might not be harmless even though he looked old.

"Just a few clothes," he said.

"What about the one on your back?"

"My brother's breathing machine," Luke replied nervously.

"A time machine?"

Luke and Jack looked at each other. They wondered if the man was drunk but they weren't sure. They had seen their mam drunk plenty of times and although her words got mixed up, she never thought that the nebuliser was a time machine.

"No, it's for asthma," Luke said, pushing the phone-book page back into his pocket. He picked up the plastic bag and stepped back, preparing to run.

The old man suddenly lunged forward and grabbed the bag. Luke tried to pull the bag away but the man hung on grimly. Then, as Jack too caught the bag and pulled as hard as he could, the old man moved his left arm backward and stabbed his cane into the younger boy's foot until he screamed in pain.

Luke let go of the bag and repeatedly kicked the man until he loosened the cane from his brother's foot.

"Run, Jack, run!" Luke screamed but Jack was in too much pain to respond.

Luke reached to the ground and began to stuff their belongings, which had fallen out, back into the bag.

The old man began to scream, "They're taking my things – help!"

Luke stood, dumbfounded, wondering why the man would say this when it wasn't true.

A passing couple halted and the man grabbed Luke who kicked and got free.

The woman had picked up the bag of clothes and was shaking the wet from the end of it. "Here you are," she said kindly to the old man.

He grabbed the bag and pretended to thank her sincerely.

Her husband let out a roar at the boys. "Get out of here! You ought to be ashamed of yourself!"

Luke took Jack by the hand. He didn't want to draw attention to them and had no choice but to walk away and hope that their dad had enough money to buy them new clothes. He was glad that he had put the nebuliser in the backpack. They walked away in silence, both wondering what they would do now.

They turned the corner at the top of O'Connell Street and sat on a wall facing the Rotunda Hospital where they had both been born. Luke put his arm around his brother who was whimpering with pain. He took Jack's shoe off and rubbed his foot which he could see was bleeding a lot through his sock.

"Shh, Jack. Don't cry. You'll be alright. I'll protect ya, won't I?"

Jack nodded through his sniffles and cuddled up into his brother.

"I just want to go home!" he cried.

Luke rubbed Jack's head as they sat on the damp wall. "We're nearly home, Jack. Tonight we'll be with our dad and we'll have a new life, you'll see," he said as confidently as he could.

He briefly wondered what his mam was doing right now. He wondered if she was looking for them or if she went straight to bed with Pete and still didn't know they were gone. He preferred to think that she had looked in their room and was now worried sick about them. Serves her right, he thought. She's a useless mam and she doesn't deserve to have kids.

Luke lowered his chin onto Jack's head and sighed as he wondered what they would do next. In the brightly lit windows of the hospital he could see mothers walking the wards with their newborn babies in their arms. He felt like crying but didn't know why. He could hear Jack begin to make short breathing sounds and turned him slightly.

"Jack?"

Jack opened his eyes, startled.

"Luke! I was at our dad's house and he wasn't home," he said, wide-eyed and worried. "We knocked and knocked and no one answered."

"It was just a dream, Jack. Come on, get up, we better keep walking." He placed his brother's shoe back on and pulled him to his feet.

"But it's sore, Luke," he whimpered.

"I know. We'll get it fixed soon. I promise." Luke suddenly remembered the packet of Panadol in his pocket. He pulled it out. "Here, Jack," he said, breaking a tablet in two. "Take this. A whole one's too big for your age. It'll make the pain better."

"But I can't without water!"

"Just try to swallow it with your spit."

Jack swallowed the white half-tablet with difficulty.

Luke looked down the street to Clery's clock. It was a quarter to one. He worried that even if he found their father's flat, it was already too late to knock and that they might have to wait until morning.

As they walked the length of O'Connell Street, he knew he must find somewhere safe for them to sleep for the night.

"Wait till you see, Jack. Tomorrow everything will be different."

Chapter 18

Hazel was tempted to smoke the few cigarettes that Pete had left behind in his mad rush out the door but resisted the temptation and sat staring out the kitchen window into the dark, never-ending night. Iris stood by the window, waiting on the kettle to boil to make what would be their umpteenth cup of tea that night. Hazel hated the silence that permeated the room and she wished that her sister would say something.

"I did some work in the garden a few weeks back," Hazel said suddenly.

Iris looked at her, surprised at the sudden conversation and also at the strange topic given the circumstances. "Oh," she replied, unsure what else to say.

"I had to rip up some of the plants. I was sure they were making Jack's asthma worse. I'll plant new ones in spring. He likes playing football out there and . . ." Hazel stopped talking. She could feel herself well up again and she had only stopped crying minutes before. She took a long, quiet breath. She often felt nervous around Iris and believed that her sister was always judging her. She put her hand to her mouth like a scolded schoolgirl even though Iris had said nothing and was making tea with her back turned to her.

"That's nice, Hazel," she finally said.

Hazel could detect no sarcasm in her voice. Maybe it was her own lack of confidence and Iris wasn't actually judging her at all.

"I'll help if you like," Iris said brightly. "We could make a day of it with the boys. They'd love it."

Hazel narrowed her eyes at her sister. Iris wasn't usually this enthusiastic about her sister's many projects, which made her worry that Iris was trying to placate her and that the boys would never be home planting shrubs . . . that they would never be home again.

Iris placed a hot cup of tea in Hazel's hand and stood behind her chair.

"Really?" Hazel replied weakly. She felt like a lost little girl around her sister.

"Really, Hazel," Iris said. She leant forward and put her hand on her sister's shoulder, squeezing it gently before abruptly leaving the room.

Hot tears fell down Hazel's face as she hugged her cup of tea to her chest. She briefly wondered at Iris's strength and stood to look out of the kitchen window, already planning a new garden.

Upstairs, Iris sat on the side of the cold bath and cried as silently as she could for the boys – Hazel's and her own.

Pete Doyle sat in the window of a dingy nightclub and wondered what he'd do next. He was glad of the loud, booming music which distracted him a little from the trouble he was in. He had driven all around the city centre and had even driven halfway down the docks but had to turn back as it was full of cops and he had no insurance on his car. He briefly wondered what was going on but shrugged and returned to his own problem of what he was going to tell Jimmy Power when he caught up with him.

As he lifted a pint to his lips he gazed out the window and couldn't believe his luck when he caught sight of Luke Fay almost carrying his little brother down the street. The younger one was limping and looked as though he was in pain. They were soaked and for a moment he almost felt sorry for them. He didn't mind the younger lad, he was pleasant enough, but he was always aware of Luke's eyes on him, sizing him up and giving him dirty looks if he stayed over.

He finished his drink quickly and, leaving the club, followed the pair down the crowded street. People were beginning to drift out of late-opening pubs and looking for another place to drink for a few hours. Taxis beeped their horns at careless pedestrians who ran across the road to escape the rain which had begun to pour down. Pete had to quicken his steps as people obscured his view of the kids and stopped for a moment when he could no longer see them. He climbed the three stone steps of the bank and scanned the street but could not see them.

"Luke! It's Pete! I'm with your mam here. We were worried about you!" he shouted into the crowd but received no reply.

Luke had heard him though and quickened his step, turning quickly into a long alleyway that led to a tall block of flats. He put his hand over Jack's mouth.

"Don't say anything. Don't tell him I gave you one of his tablets!" His heart raced and he could feel sweat run down his back even though it had become quite cold.

"You only gave me a half and it almost all came up when I got sick." Jack could hear his words run out of his mouth quickly and he felt like he could run a race and beat every junior infant in his class, even the tall ones.

"I know but don't tell him," Luke replied nervously as he looked out onto the crowded street from behind a row of bins. He looked down the alley behind him. There were several blocks of flats that looked black in the dark night and only a few windows were lighted. They looked a bit dangerous and there was no one around. He had no choice, though, but to stay hidden there.

"Come on, Jack," he said as he pulled his brother with him into the darkness. Luke was glad that Jack was walking faster and his foot appeared to be much better. He looked up at the solitary street light which shone down on the street sign. His mouth fell open.

It said: *Seville Flats.* That was the name in the phone book! He pulled the phone-book page out to compare. Yes! There it was! *23, Block D, Seville Flats.*

"Jack, it's here! I think these are Dad's flats," he whispered, the sound of relief audible in his voice.

Jack shouted "Hooray!" taking Luke by surprise. His voice echoed down the empty laneway.

"Shh, Jack! What are you shouting for? Pete's looking for us. Be quiet!"

The two made their way to Block D where the phone book said G Henan lived.

Luke could hear Jack grinding his teeth and wondered if he was as nervous as he was about meeting their dad after so long that neither of them could even remember what he looked like.

In Block D the stairs were full of rubbish and Luke stepped gingerly over two syringes that were on the bottom step. Jack lifted one up.

"Look, Luke, 'member I had to get these when I was in hospital?"

"Drop that, Jack. Mam said they carry germs. What's wrong with you? You're going crazy on me!"

The stairs were dark and Luke could just about make out broken bulbs on the landing. He hoped there were no rats on the steps. He hated rats and mice the same as his mam did. The flats smelt awful and Jack held his nose as they stepped over a used nappy.

They found Flat 23 in the middle of the second landing. There was a light on in a small window beside the door which was painted bright red. A gnome stood on guard outside and smiled a toothy grin into the darkness.

Luke and Jack looked at each other. Luke swallowed hard as he raised his finger to the doorbell which played a loud, merry tune.

"Gerard, get the door!" they heard a woman's voice shout from within the lighted room.

They did not hear any steps and jumped back when the door swung open quickly.

The tall young man who opened it stood silently and looked at the boys as if they had come from outer space.

"Yes?" he asked politely when neither of the kids, who were staring at him, spoke.

"Are you Gerry?"

"Yeah."

Luke and Jack looked at each other, bewildered, and then looked back to the skinny man who had the same dark hair and eyes as they had. They thought their dad would be a lot older.

"We're Luke and Jack," Luke offered, hoping to see some recognition in the man's face but the young man just stood open-mouthed and stared at them.

"Luke and Jack Henan, your sons," Luke replied, deflated. He had been hoping for one of the reunions you see on the telly where the dad is glad to have his child back safely when something bad happened.

The young man laughed out loud and opened the door wide.

"I think you'd better come in."

Chapter 19

It was over three years since Rose Henan had seen or heard from her husband. She knew he was still in Dublin and that he worked on the boats. A few of her friends had seen him around town, always with some young one, a different one each time. It used to bother her but she had grown up a lot since Gerry Henan had abandoned her with three children to raise. Her son Gerard Junior was then eighteen and her two daughters were almost grown, and she had to struggle to keep her son in college and the girls in school but she had managed. She had known over the years that her husband was unfaithful to her but, with three young children, she had no choice but to stay with him. Her mother would not take her in and her siblings had all emigrated so she put up with it, year after year. She wondered now why she hadn't just thrown him out and taken on extra work to keep the family going but she had wanted to avoid the shame attached to a broken marriage and, perhaps even more importantly, she had wanted to prove to her mother that she had made the right choice in Gerry Henan, a man her mother never approved of. Of course, her mother was right, but it was the way she handled it that had irked Rose over the years. She could never imagine saying such things to her girls. "I suppose you deserve nothing better than that waster," her mother used to say to her, even in front of the kids. She had always put her down and it was only when she died that Rose began to feel she was her own person.

When Gerry left, it was actually a relief. She didn't have to play happy families in front of her neighbours, who knew only too well what he was like in the claustrophobic flat complex they had lived in since their marriage. She just wished she had been the one to end it.

She looked at the two young boys in front of her and her heart broke for them. She remembered only too well how her son was affected by his father's constant absences when he'd pick up with another one. She smiled at her younger daughter, who had got out of bed on hearing the commotion, and was staring at the boys while they sat at the fire and drank hot milk. Her older girl was holding herself aloof.

Rose had known about the older boy. A friend had told her about Hazel Fay but she hadn't known there had been a second child. She reflected now on the awful legacy her handsome husband had left behind him. So many damaged souls. She did not feel any resentment towards them, only dismay at the man she had once loved. It was not the boys' fault. Neither was it their mother's. She was another victim of Gerry Henan's and God alone knew how many women there were and how many other children there were. She often wondered about the possibility of some of these children meeting up and, God forbid, marrying each other, not knowing they were actually half-brother and sister, and it worried her. She sat down in her pink, quilted dressing-gown and worn, matching slippers and touched Luke's knee, smiling warmly at him.

"So love, what's brought you here?"

"We're looking for our dad," he said. He had realised that the young man was not actually the Gerry Henan he was looking for.

A silence fell in the room as Rose searched for the right words. Her older daughter stood abruptly and left the room. Luke could hear her run up the stairs of the two-level apartment and turn her music on loud.

Rose cleared her throat. Although she had given up smoking years before, she had never got rid of the cough and her voice was raspy. She saw no point in lying to the boys and felt that happy stories of fathers in far-off lands would only come to tears, eventually.

"I was Gerry's wife. These are my kids – your half-brother and sisters."

Luke could see Gerard Junior looking at him but could not make out what his face was saying. The younger girl, who looked more like her mother, looked like this was an ordinary Saturday evening and did not seem concerned.

"Where is our dad?" Jack asked loudly.

Luke frowned at him and was worried that the Panadol was affecting him, even if he had vomited most of it up. Jack seemed to find it hard to sit still and was moving his head back and forth like it was on a spring.

Rose Henan put her cup down on the coffee table. The flat was spotlessly clean and at odds with the rundown building she lived in. There were plants all around the small well-lit room and the large patterned sofa looked new.

"He left," she said simply and waited for the boys to digest this information. She felt bad but knew the truth was better than a lie. It was always better, even if it hurt.

Luke looked at her and then lowered his head, thinking.

"Your dad was a good-looking man and women liked him a lot. He found it hard to stay in one place. It doesn't mean he's a bad man – it's just the way he is," she said softly as she watched closely for the boys' reaction. "But it does mean that people get hurt when he leaves." She could see Luke's eyes water but the younger lad sat stone-faced, grinding his teeth and breathing heavily.

She looked enquiringly at Luke.

"He's okay," he replied. "He has asthma. Can I plug his nebuliser in, please? It doesn't use much electricity."

"Yeah, sure, I have it too, don't I, Mam?" Gerard Junior said from the corner armchair. He stood and directed Luke to a socket.

Luke plugged it in and the machine buzzed loudly in the room. He slowly placed the mask over Jack's mouth, anxious to spend enough time on the task for his eyes to dry.

Rose smiled at him across the room. "But you have people who love you, don't you?" she said.

He nodded, embarrassed that his tears were noticeable. He was disappointed that he hadn't found his dad and didn't want to cry in front of his big half-brother who probably didn't cry when Gerry Henan left him. He knew what she meant, even though he was only nearly eight. He knew she meant that Gerry Henan would not want to see him.

"Your mammy is probably worried sick about you," she said softly. "Now, why don't we call her and get you boys safely home? Where do you live?"

"In Glasnevin. Bridge Street Crescent," he offered reluctantly. "Mrs. Henan?"

"Rose, love, call me Rose."

"We'd rather go home alone. Our mam doesn't know that we came here. She might be mad."

Rose smiled and her eyes watered. Luke was so much like her son when he was younger. "Your mam won't be angry. She'll just be happy that you're alright."

Luke wondered if this was true. If his mam would just be happy that he was alright. She might be angry that he got poor sick Jack into this. He was glad to be going home though. Maybe he'd get to meet his dad some other day.

"Alright," said Rose. "But I insist though on you getting a taxi, okay? I'll give you the money. You can come back and visit sometime if you like. If your mam says it's alright."

Luke looked enthusiastically at his half-brother who nodded.

Rose squeezed a twenty-euro note into Luke's hand after he put Jack's nebuliser away.

The taxi arrived and, as the boys walked out of the front door, Rose caught Luke gently by the arm.

"Luke, I meant what I said. Having a mam that loves you is better than having two rotten parents."

Luke nodded but could not look her in the eye. He didn't want to tell her that he did get two rotten parents. He knew that his mother was okay sometimes but he needed her to be okay all the time. Sometimes just isn't enough when you're a kid.

Pete Doyle had thought the little bastards would never come out of whichever flat they'd sneaked into as he waited in the cold. He did not see which block they entered but there was only one way out of the flats and he was waiting there in the shadows out of view. He had missed his delivery deadline and knew that when Jimmy Power caught up with him he was in for the hiding of his life.

He watched as the taxi turned down the laneway and stopped in the darkness. He moved a little closer and laughed when he saw the two little bastards getting in. He moved back out of view, anxious that the woman and young man standing beside the taxi shouldn't see him.

Then, as the taxi made its way out of the complex, he jumped out and stood in front of it.

The taxi ground to a halt and the irate driver wound down his window. "There's yis are, yis little messers!" Pete said jovially. "I was late to pick them up from their ma's," he explained apologetically to the driver. "She always does that – rings a taxi to show me up. She knows I won't be home before the taxi and the poor kids'll be on the doorstep. Dangerous carry-on. Women, eh?"

The elderly taxi driver turned and looked at his two frightened passengers in the back seat.

"He's not our dad!" Luke screamed as Jack continued to grind his teeth and pull strange, grimacing faces.

The taxi driver thought he'd seen it all but he had never come across anything like this. His mind raced. He wondered why anyone would say kids were theirs if they weren't – but there were all sorts of carry-on these days. Some of the things he read about in the paper made his hair stand on end and he was glad his four children were all raised. It was almost two o'clock – what time was that to collect two kids?

"Look, I have an address to take these kids to and, if you're their dad, I'll wait there for ya, okay?" he said nervously. He could see that Pete was a big bloke and didn't want any trouble.

"Look, I wasn't going straight home," Pete explained genially. "Was going to take them to my mother's, you know? They love to sleep at their granny's overnight, ya know what I mean?" he said, trying to play best buddies with the driver.

"No, I don't know what you mean – but I'll drive the kids to the nearest police station and you can sort it out there," the driver said bravely.

Pete looked at him and appeared to be thinking about this when he suddenly pulled the door open and grabbed hold of Luke, trying to drag him from the car. Jack screamed and hit out at Pete. He was amazed at his own energy and courage as he grabbed onto Pete's arm, biting down on his left wrist, trying to free his brother. He could hear the driver radio his base for the gardaí. Everything seemed to move in slow motion. He could see Pete's right hand swing towards him, felt it punch him in the mouth, making him release his grip. He could feel Pete pinning him to the seat with his free arm as he pushed Luke to the ground. Pete let go of Jack then and held Luke face down on the wet ground as he roughly searched his jacket pockets. Jack lunged forward again and threw himself out of the car on top of Pete who was now pulling furiously at Luke's trousers. He tore at Pete's face with his nails.

The elderly driver had got out. He was shouting for help.

The last thing Jack remembered was Pete's huge elbow coming back towards him and smashing into his face. And then nothing. He did not see the driver lunge at Pete with a wheel brace or see Pete run off, taking Luke screaming and crying with him as the police siren screamed in the distance.

Chapter 20

Hazel had just put the phone down on Gerry Henan's wife, a person she had never expected to hear from, still less hear telling her that her boys were alive and well and on their way home. Hazel and Iris hugged in the hallway as both sisters gave way to their tears.

It had been a long night, the longest of Hazel's life. Now that she knew her boys were well, she wasn't going to make any statements about turning over a new leaf. She knew she couldn't change on her own. She had tried, time and time again. But what she was going to do was to get some help, for all of them, but mostly for herself. She knew that if she didn't change, if she didn't learn how to be a good mother, her boys would turn out just like her and Iris. Damaged. She had prayed that she would get a second chance and it was here. A last chance perhaps and she thanked God for answering her.

In a matter of minutes the phone rang again. It was the police. Jack was on his way to hospital and Luke was missing. Hazel collapsed into a heap on the hall floor. She felt numb. In one sweep her hope was gone. She did not cry. It was too late. There wasn't going to be a second chance. There wasn't going to be any chance for her and, while she knew she deserved this, her boys didn't.

"Get up!" she heard Iris command and she looked up, stunned. "Get up and stop feeling sorry for yourself. You go to the hospital and be with Jack. I'll stay here and wait in case Luke comes back."

Hazel automatically stood at Iris's command and put her coat on. As she made her way to the door, she tried to say something to Iris.

"No!" Iris said, somehow anticipating that her sister would beg Iris to go in her place, that she would plead that she wasn't up to it.

"Just go, Hazel."

Less than three miles away, Pete Doyle stood open-mouthed as he looked through the packet of ecstasy that he had taken out of Luke's pocket. He picked out the half tablet and held it up. Luke cowered on the steps of the back-alley building where Pete had thrown him moments before.

"Did you take this?" he shouted.

"No. I didn't!" Luke cried. He was never as frightened in his life. All he wanted was to find his dad and have a normal life. Tears and snot ran down his chin. He badly needed to pee and could feel himself dribbling a bit. He was sure his brother was dead and, if he had it to go over again, he'd forget about having a dad and settle for having his brother alive and well.

"Please let me go. I didn't take it. Honest. I didn't!" he sobbed.

"I'll let ya go if you tell me what you did with the tablet. Deal?" Pete was beginning to feel a bit bad. He hadn't expected the kid to be this upset. He'd thought he was tougher than that. The scene kind of reminded him of when his old man came home at night drunk and had them all crying, his mother included.

Luke looked up suspiciously at Pete. "Will ya? Really?" he sniffed.

"Yeah, just tell me and I'll let you go."

"I gave it to Jack. For his sore foot."

"Ya did what? Ya stupid little fucker!" Pete shouted as he caught Luke by the shoulders and shook him.

Luke began to cry louder. "His foot hurt. I didn't have Calpol because we had run away so I gave him your headache tablet."

"They're not headache tablets, they're . . . ya little fuck! When did he take it? What time?"

"I don't know. An old man took our stuff and he hurt his foot and . . . I don't know what time . . . I don't know!" he sobbed. "Anyway, it wasn't much good because he got sick and some of it came up."

Pete stood back from the sobbing child and ran his fingers through his hair. He could feel the blood rushing through his ears. He never took E himself and had no idea what effect it would have on a small child, especially a skinny little bag of bones like Jack. But what he did know was that the hospital would have to know what the kid had taken and that if he told them, he'd surely do time for possession. He paced up and down trying to think of a Plan B. He couldn't go to jail. He just couldn't. But it would go worse for him if the kid died or was brain-damaged and he was caught for it.

"Here," he said at last, taking twenty euro from his jeans pocket and shoving it into Luke's hand. "Get a taxi straight to the hospital. Go to the emergency department. Tell them Jack took E. Remember *E for Elephant*, ya stupid little bastard!"

Luke nodded.

Pete grabbed Luke by the neck and squeezed until he hurt him.

"And remember, if you mention me, I'll come back and kill ya . . . *and* yer mam!" He pushed Luke towards the entrance to the alley.

Luke did not look back as he ran towards O'Connell Street and tried to hail a taxi. People were still dribbling out of the city's clubs, trying to get home. He knew where the nearest children's hospital was and knew that he could walk it but he didn't want to deviate from Pete's orders and worried that he was watching him.

Pete was already on his way to the docks. He phoned his brother en route and asked him to meet him at the port with some clothes and his passport. He'd have to lie low for a while and wait to see what happened to the kid. What worried him more was the fact that he had hidden his larger stash in Hazel's house. He couldn't risk leaving it in his mother's and Hazel's was a perfect place to use. He was worried that someone else would get to his stuff before he had a chance to return. He knew he had opened his big mouth on more than one drunken occasion about how he used Hazel's house to hide the gear and get a bit of action at the same time. His drinking buddies had thought it was hilarious but it crossed his mind that now that he was out of the way, someone might get to his supply. If he admitted where he hid the gear to Jimmy Power, Power would have no further use for him. He knew these guys were rough and that they were into all sorts of things. He decided that as soon as it was safe, he'd return and somehow get into Hazel's. He could hand over the gear, make his peace with Power and get out of this racket altogether.

When Luke ran into the A&E department and breathlessly gave the message to the nurse at the front desk, he heard a familiar voice.

His mother was coming towards him, white-faced and crying.

"Mam!" he cried and ran into her arms, sobbing.

Hazel cried as she had never cried before. "You're safe. God, you're safe!" she sobbed. "I'll never let you out of my sight again!"

"I'm sorry, Mam. Sorry I got Jack sick!" he cried, his voice muffled in her hair.

Hazel shushed him.

"I'm sorry I ran away looking for my dad when you were worried about me."

Hazel pulled back and looked into her son's eyes. "It's okay. I should have told you. I should have told you about him. It was upsetting for me to talk about your dad but I was wrong."

She hugged him again and smoothed his hair before pulling him close again. A few moments later a nurse came to call them to Jack's bedside. She led them down a long white corridor lined with trolleys laden with patients and chairs laden with their families. It looked to Hazel like some third-world scene. Some of the staff smiled sympathetically towards her while others avoided her gaze.

They came to a cubicle off the corridor where Jack lay unconscious, surrounded by buzzing machines and tense staff. They moved slowly over to the bedside and looked at him.

There was a strange tube going up his nostrils and also several large stickers on his chest. A needle fed a drip into a vein in his hand which Hazel thought looked sore. She wanted to pull it out, a mother's instinct.

Luke stared at his brother, scared and stricken with guilt.

They settled down on chairs beside the trolley, to wait.

Some time later she remembered to phone her sister and tell her that Luke was safe.

Twenty minutes later Iris joined them and they sat together as a family and dozed and prayed for Jack until the weak winter sun rose over Dublin city.

Chapter 21

As Hazel, Iris and Luke sat by Jack, Pete Doyle sat waiting for the bar on the Dublin-Liverpool ferry to open. Gerry Henan watched the worried-looking Dubliner as he polished glasses for the stormy ride across the Irish Sea.

"You look like you could do with a drink," Gerry said to Pete.

"Yeah, what time do ya open at?"

"Not till we're out to sea." He looked around him and leant in closer to Pete's ear. "Look," he whispered, "I'll put one in a teacup. No one will know, eh? What do you fancy?"

Pete looked up at the top shelf behind the bar. He didn't normally go for spirits but he needed something to take the edge off his nerves. He felt like everyone was watching him. He had bought the early morning paper at the ferry terminal to find Hazel's kids' photos splashed across the front page. Pete reasoned that it wasn't his fault. He wasn't to know that Luke would take the tablets or give one to Jack but he could still be got for possession with intent to sell.

Gerry waited patiently for an answer. He had seen this guy's type before, running from something, and he knew that it was easier to get away on the ferry. Even though it took longer, passport checks were random and he'd have to be awfully unlucky to be pulled.

"Whiskey," Pete answered flatly, rubbing his hands over his unshaven chin.

"Whiskey it is," said Gerry.

"Do you work the ferry all year round?" Pete asked, trying to change the subject. He was aware that the barman was interested in him and he didn't want to answer any awkward questions.

"Yeah, weather permitting," Gerry answered. He knew the other man didn't want to talk and was slightly irked that he wouldn't be getting much out of him. Getting a bit of gossip usually made the journey less boring.

"Must be a nice life," Pete said. "No responsibilities and that?"

"Yeah, getting away from it all, that's for sure." It had certainly been like that in the beginning when the younger waitresses were interested in him but now, at his age, they hardly gave him a second look. "Running away from the missus and kids, are ya?" he added with a grin.

"Something like that."

"Yeah, I know how it is alright," Gerry sighed, wiping the already clean counter. He did know how it was but things had changed for him now. He wasn't as young as he used to be and often, when he was alone in his bed-sit, he would think of Rose and the kids and wonder how they were doing. He had worked every Christmas since he walked out on her because he didn't like being alone at that time of year and none of the girlfriends he picked up ever lasted very long, even the ones that he had knocked up, and there were a few of them going around.

As the ferry pulled away from the port, the two men looked out towards the open sea. It was choppy under the heavy grey sky. There was nothing to see but the empty ocean as the land disappeared slowly from view.

In the hospital, Hazel, who was half-asleep on her chair, woke to find a middle-aged woman and uniformed garda standing over her.

"Ms Fay, can we have a word with you?" the woman said.

Hazel sat up and smoothed her unruly hair down. She looked at Iris who was awake and supporting Luke who was leaning against her and sleeping soundly. She looked back at the woman, puzzled.

"I'm Mary Lennon, the social worker here," the woman said quietly. "I'd like to speak with you. The police need to be present, of course."

Hazel looked at her sister and Luke who was snoring lightly.

"Your sister will look after your son," the social worker said, looking at Iris who nodded, her large eyes betraying her concern.

Hazel rose from her seat and groaned. Her back hurt and she limped slightly as she followed the social worker who led them down the corridor and into an office.

Mary Lennon sat down behind a desk and motioned for Hazel to take the seat facing her. The garda sat to Hazel's right and slightly behind her. Hazel could feel his eyes on her though and felt unnerved. Out of the corner of her eye she watched as he took out a small notebook and waited.

"Ms Fay, we have to interview you because your son came in here having taken MDMA," she said casually, as if she said those words every day to some worried parent who was going out of their mind wondering what was going to happen to their child.

"MDMA?" Hazel asked innocently.

"Ecstasy," the garda said.

Hazel looked at the two and the realisation of what they were thinking slowly dawned on her.

"I didn't have that in the house. I never would. I don't know where he got it, honestly."

Mary Lennon and the tired-looking garda looked at her as though she was lying.

"Your son said he took it out of your boyfriend's pocket," the social worker said matter of factly.

"How did your sons come to be walking around Dublin city alone at night?" the garda asked.

"I told the police last night. They ran away. There was a row . . . they were upset . . . I tried to . . . I . . ." Hazel broke down, overcome by a mixture of exhaustion and shame.

"Where is your boyfriend now?" the woman asked sharply.

Hazel could hear the disapproval in her voice. "I don't know," she said flatly. "And I don't care," she added. "As long as my boys are alright, I don't care about anything else any more, that's the truth. It took this to happen for me to see that."

"You put your children in danger," said the social worker. "There'll be an investigation. This is the second time in a matter of weeks that your younger son has been here. We have to make sure that your children are safe."

Hazel broke down again, the realisation of how much trouble she was in dawning on her and also the realisation that her children might be taken into care crashing down on her and arousing memories of her own time in foster care.

"I know I need help," she sobbed, "but please don't take my kids from me. They're all I have. I didn't know about the drugs, I swear. I didn't know!"

"That may be up to the courts to decide," Mary Lennon replied, feeling slightly sorry for this woman who didn't look like she could take care of herself, let alone two youngsters. "You'll be assigned a social worker. Right now, you need to be here for your son. Could your sister look after your older son?"

Hazel nodded. "Yes, she'll take good care of him," she gulped.

"The police will need to interview the older boy again," Mary Lennon said, "but in the meantime we suggest your sister takes him home."

"Is there any news on Jack's condition?" Hazel asked hopefully.

"I'll ask the doctor to come and speak with you," Mary Lennon curtly replied, before standing and walking abruptly out of the room, the loud clicking of her heels on the shiny corridor outside signalling her disapproval.

The garda nodded at Hazel and stood to open the door wider, indicating that the interview was over. She stood and edged her way slowly by him, avoiding his eyes.

Back in Jack's cubicle she gazed at him as he lay surrounded by wires and beeping machines. She thought he looked tiny, like a new infant, motionless in the bed. She sat down and wrung her hands in frustration and anger. She glanced sideways at her sister and quickly wiped the tears that had begun to flow down her face. She knew they weren't tears for Jack but for herself, for the shame she was feeling, the embarrassment, the cold hostile treatment that she'd received from the social worker who knew nothing about her or all that she had been through in her life.

Iris swallowed and tried to think of a question that wouldn't worsen her sister's mood.

"Are you alright?"

Hazel clenched her fists and screwed up her face. "That bitch . . . that one, she said . . . she's going to . . ." but she couldn't finish the sentence. She was talking to the wrong person. She knew Iris wasn't exactly on her side and, like the social worker, didn't exactly see Hazel as a victim in the awful situation she found herself in. No, she'd get no pity from her.

"She said you've got to take Luke home. Someone will ring to talk to him when he's rested."

Iris nodded and decided not to ask any more questions. "Okay. I'll take him home for a rest. I'll come back later and let you go home for a while."

Hazel shook her head violently. "No! I'm not leaving him, Iris. Not until I know he's okay."

Iris nodded. "I understand but Luke needs you too. He's been through a rough night. He'll need to talk when he's had a rest."

Hazel did not answer. She wanted to say that she, too, had been through a lot but why didn't anyone ever see her point of view? She looked at Luke and pulled him so tightly to her that he squirmed in her arms.

"I'll be back later," Iris said again. "Come on, Luke."

She could feel tears welling up for her sister but did not want to cry in front of her. Luke sensed it.

"It's okay to cry, Aunty Iris," he said confidentially as they made their way down the corridor, then added too calmly for Iris's liking, "I cried when Pete caught me last night."

"You must have been frightened, Luke," she said, looking at him, concern written all over her face.

"A little bit but I was happy as well because he didn't get Jack and that's all that mattered," he replied, in a voice and tone that was older than his years.

Iris hugged him close and wiped her own tears. "You're a very brave boy, Luke."

Luke pondered this, then shook his head. He knew he'd put Jack in danger last night. "Will he be alright, Iris?" he asked, premature frown-lines showing on his young face.

"Yes," she lied. "Of course. Jack is lucky to have you for a brother."

"And Mam is lucky to have you for a sister, Aunty Iris," he said, smiling up at her.

"Now, what's it to be? Hot chocolate or a milkshake?"

"Hot chocolate, Iris," he said, jumping slightly and showing his true age as the pair headed off towards Iris's flat.

"Iris?"

"Yes?"

"You mightn't need a dad if you have people who love you?" he said in a questioning tone.

"That's true, love. That's very true."

Chapter 22

"Ms Fay," a quiet voice said.

"Yes," Hazel replied wearily to the short, fair-haired nurse who was gently waking her. "Your son's beginning to come to. It'd be best if he saw your face first."

"He's awake?" Hazel asked incredulously.

"Yes," the nurse smiled.

Hazel jumped up from her seat. She hadn't even realised that she was dozing but had dreamed of herself walking through the house looking for Jack and finding only his teddy and a pair of old baby shoes.

Hazel leaned over her son as he looked up at her.

"Mam," he said drowsily.

Hazel gulped and dug her nails into her thighs.

"Yes, love. I'm here. You're safe now," she said and the irony of her words was not lost on her.

"Mam," he said again but appeared to be dreaming. He did not seem to be able to see her. His eyes closed again.

Hazel slumped into her hard chair again.

A little while later a doctor came to the bed and checked some of the machinery.

"What's wrong with him?" she asked the doctor.

"He's high, drugged," he said flatly. "It'll wear off. We're watching for kidney damage but so far he looks okay. There was very little MDMA in his blood. I understand he vomited most of the tablet up so the effects were less serious. Still, it could have been fatal. He could have died or been brain-damaged and you need to be aware of that." He threw her an unsympathetic look.

"I know," she said, lowering her head like a schoolgirl. "I know."

Hazel gazed at her little son. She knew Jack wasn't out of the woods yet but he spoke, he was awake, and if he pulled through this, she was going to ensure he never came to any danger again.

Iris put an exhausted Luke to bed after sponging him down in her cold bathroom. She could hear him toss and turn and occasionally shout out, dreaming she supposed of the awful night he had endured. She had yet to hear the full details of what Jack and Luke had been through but knew it was best they forgot about it. She hoped that in time they would but she doubted it. She could remember so many episodes from her early childhood, bad memories, and she wondered if these are more easily remembered than good ones. She knew there must have been some happy times with her mother but she could hardly remember more than a couple of occasions when she felt happy and secure, when she felt safe.

Iris wondered when things started to go wrong for her mother. She couldn't always have had a drink problem and she wondered how it started and why she didn't have the courage to face up to her weaknesses and get help. Iris was sure that this time Hazel would wake up and face her own demons. It had been a close call last night.

She remembered a night when her mother brought Hazel and herself to an inner-city pub to meet a "cousin". Iris's mam sat drinking in the snug with a man she introduced as Noel and Iris watched as he put his hand on her mother's knee and bought her lots of drink. Iris took Hazel outside and they played under the streetlight directly outside the pub. It was a school night and they both had their uniforms on as they played hopscotch and chasing. They seemed to be playing there for a long time when a man she had seen drinking in the pub approached them and asked them to come down the laneway that ran behind the pub. He said he had sweets for them. Hazel wanted to go. She was hungry and neither of them had eaten since lunch-time. Iris started to scream as loud as she could until he ran off. She even frightened Hazel who stood white-faced under the yellow street light. Iris didn't know how she knew what danger this man presented. When their mother eventually came out with Noel in tow Iris didn't even tell her what had happened as they savaged the chips and bun burgers that Noel bought them in the chipper beside the pub.

Iris shook her head thinking about it. In some ways these memories belonged to someone else, a stranger, another lifetime, but on days like today they were so close that they haunted her and made her feel like the vulnerable little girl she had been.

She finished a few repairs and then sat down and watched some mindless television for a while. When Luke woke up she would relieve Hazel at the hospital and let her go home and get some sleep. She knew she should catch some sleep herself but the memory of how close her nephews had come to harm or even death lay heavily on her mind and she knew she wouldn't sleep. She realised none of this would have happened if Hazel had been honest with the boys and told them, as gently as she could, that their dad did not want anything to do with them. Now Hazel might never have got the chance to tell them how much they meant to her, how sorry she was for everything she had done that was wrong. She sat a while longer and bit her fingernails, a habit she'd had since childhood. Eventually she stood and took some paper and a pen from the shop and sat down at her small table to write.

Dear Kevin

I am sure you'll be surprised to hear from me. I am posting this letter to your dad. If you're reading it, he'll have decided that he is happy for you to hear from me. (If not, Mark, I understand, really, I do.)

It is hard to know where to begin. I could start by saying I am sorry for the hurt I caused you and your father but those words aren't nearly enough to make things right. No words are.

I could explain or try to, even though I never really understood why I felt the way I did. Not fully anyway. I felt you were better off with me. I still do. But I imagine you don't think this. I didn't either when my father left me or when my mother died. I suppose that much of this will be hard for you to understand. One thing I can say is that I never stopped loving you and that I thought of you – I think of you every day of my life. I wanted to say this to you while there is still a chance to say it. We never know when there will be no more chances to say the things we want to say. Anyway, I love you and I want you to be happy, you and Mark. I hope that you are. I hope you forgive me. I always think of you. I hope you believe that.

    Love

    Iris

Iris bit down hard on her lip to stop her mouth from trembling. She put the letter into an envelope with a short note for the attention of Mark. She did not want to bypass the man who had been kind to her during their marriage. She put a stamp on it and before she had a chance to change her mind, she opened the door of the shop and ran across the road, throwing it into the post-box outside the newsagent's. Her heart was thumping and, when she returned to her seat in front of the television, she knew she had opened herself up for hurt and rejection. Deep down, she did not expect Mark to give the letter to Kevin and knew that if the tables were turned, she would do the same thing.

She didn't really expect her son to contact her. She just wanted to tell him that she loved him, that she had always loved him and had left because she felt he was better off without her.

She wondered what her son would make of the letter. He was now almost seventeen. She knew he might very well tear it up and rage at her for contacting him or he might understand why she did what she did. But he would know, at the very least, that she never stopped thinking about him.

When the phone rang and Hazel told her that Jack was awake and did not appear to have sustained any brain damage, Iris cried openly. Maybe there was hope for them all. Maybe it wasn't too late for explanations.

Hazel insisted that she leave Luke sleeping and that she would stay at the hospital with Jack.

When Iris put down the phone she saw Luke standing in the bedroom doorway.

"You're awake! You okay?" she asked gingerly.

"Yeah," he replied quietly.

He still looked tired and there were large dark circles under his eyes.

"Is there anything you want to tell me or to ask me?" she asked.

"No," he said sullenly.

She sat down and patted the sofa, inviting him to come and sit with her. She knew it was time they had a chat. She knew he must have questions about her son and she felt it was time to stop harbouring secrets.

"Are you angry that you didn't know about . . . me having a son?"

Luke nodded, his demeanour still sullen as he looked toward the ground.

"I understand, Luke. You have a right to feel that way. I didn't want you to think badly of me. You and your brother mean a lot to me."

"Didn't your son mean a lot to you? Didn't you love him?"

"Of course" Iris said as calmly as she could although she felt the sting of Luke's words.

"Then why did you leave him like my dad left Jack and me?" he asked.

Iris could see tears welling in his eyes. He looked away.

She pulled him towards her and he relented, allowing her to pull him close in to her chest.

"Luke, it's hard to understand when you are young. I was just like you once. I didn't understand my father . . . or my mother. I still don't in many ways, but life isn't as simple when you are older. It can be very hard."

Luke did not speak. She knew he wanted more, he needed more.

"I left my son because I didn't think I could be a good mother," she said, feeling her jaw tighten as the words came out of her mouth. "I was afraid of the responsibility. I was afraid I would do it wrong like my father. He . . ."

Iris stopped speaking, aware that Hazel herself didn't know the truth about their father. She realised that some secrets are best kept, after all, because the truth causes too much hurt. "He did love us . . . but . . . there were lots of problems, Luke. Things you are too young to understand. My mother didn't take good care of us, you see . . . So I was afraid that I'd neglect my son like my mother neglected Hazel and me . . . and I ran away."

Luke looked up at her. "You should have tried," he said flatly.

"I know," she said. "I know that now." She could feel her bottom lip tremble. She smoothed Luke's hair down and cuddled him closer. "Do you wish your dad had tried?" she asked, knowing that this more than her problems was foremost in his mind.

Luke took a deep breath while he gathered his thoughts. "He left his first family. He didn't want to look after them."

Iris waited and watched as her nephew moved his tongue around in his mouth. She knew he did this when he was finding it hard to formulate his sentences.

"He could have visited us if he'd wanted but he didn't," he said.

Iris could see him take his thoughts forward one step at a time.

"So he didn't want us," he concluded.

Iris could hear finality in his voice and the maturity of his tone saddened her. He'd had a rough eight years, a hard short life.

"Well, do you want to know what I think?" she asked.

He turned and eyed her suspiciously but nodded.

"I think that your dad missed out on having two amazing sons. And I think that your mam and I are so lucky to have the two of you. You mean everything to us. Do you believe that?"

He nodded but kept his lips pursed.

The two fell silent as Iris rubbed his arms under her own.

"What was your new brother like?" she asked.

She noticed his small face become brighter.

"He was big and nice. His mam said we could visit." A small smile appeared on his face.

"Really?" Iris said, surprised. "Would you like that?"

"I don't know."

Iris could see he was still exhausted and silence fell between them once more.

"I posted a letter today to my son," she said, taking herself unawares as she hadn't intended telling anyone, Hazel included. She hoped she wouldn't regret it but she was trying to reach out to her nephew, to tell him that everyone makes mistakes that they have to try to live with.

Luke looked at her, surprise written all over his face.

"Will he write back?" he asked innocently.

"I don't know," Iris smiled. "I doubt it but I just wanted to tell him that I was sorry." She felt slightly embarrassed to be talking so frankly to such a young child. She knew that Luke was older than his years but he wasn't yet eight and she needed to remember this, even if Hazel didn't.

"I hope he does, Aunty Iris," he said kindly as they cuddled together.

Iris squeezed his arm, unable to answer because she didn't know what she hoped for, she really didn't.

By the time they arrived at the hospital, Jack was sitting up and had even asked for food and something to drink. Hazel sat by his side and seemed to be looking at him as though she had never seen him before.

The same garda arrived to speak with Luke but the boy, who had chatted all the way to the hospital was struck dumb and refused to look at him, let alone speak. Iris could see his leg shaking as Hazel tried to cajole him into telling the officer what had happened. Instead the guard went to Jack's bedside with the same social worker while Hazel sat white-knuckled by Jack's side. Iris excused herself and took Luke outside for a drink to calm the child's nerves. Hazel listened with horror as Jack told how Luke took the tablets out of Pete's pocket and gave a half one to him for his sore foot. He told them about their adventure looking for his father and how they found a whole lot of other Henans who were nice to them. Finally, he told them about Pete stopping the taxi that was supposed to take them home and that Pete had hit him in the face when he dragged Luke out of the taxi. He told them that he didn't remember anything after that until he woke up in hospital. The guard then informed Hazel that there would be a warrant for Pete's arrest and that if he contacted her she should inform them of his whereabouts.

Overcome with emotion, Hazel left the room. She walked down the corridor and looked for her sister and Luke.

"The police have a warrant out for Pete's arrest, Iris. I have to tell them if he contacts me."

Iris noticed the blood draining out of Luke's face.

"No!" he suddenly screamed. "He'll kill me. He'll . . . no!"

Iris took him by the shoulders.

"Luke, you're safe now. He's gone. He won't be coming around any more. Will he, Hazel?" Iris stared hard at her sister.

"No, never. Luke, I promise you."

Iris sat Luke down on a bench and moved out of ear-shot with her sister.

"He's really afraid, Hazel. You'll . . . you'll have to stick to that. I mean . . . never see him again."

Hazel reddened with anger. Did people think she was a complete idiot? Iris touched her arm and she flinched, pulling herself away. She took a deep breath and reminded herself that this was all her fault.

"I think they believe me that I didn't know what he was up to but, still, I should never have had him in the house. They'll be keeping an eye on me."

"What about the social worker?" Iris asked.

"Someone is going to come to the house."

Iris could hear the shame in her voice but said nothing. She knew the authorities were right. Hazel did need supervision, at least for now.

"Go and get some rest, Hazel. We'll sit with Jack until you get back."

"Iris? I really am sorry. I really have changed. I know you've heard it before but this time it's true. No more boyfriends. No more drink."

"I know, Hazel," Iris said, trying to sound as reassured as Hazel wanted her to be. "I know."

Three days later Jack returned home to find the bedroom he shared with Luke newly painted in grown-up boys' colours with a new Manchester United duvet set for both boys' bunks. Hazel couldn't afford this but she wanted a surprise for Jack, a new start for both her boys.

That evening she invited Iris around for a dinner she cooked herself. She cleared the fridge of any leftover beer and poured, much to her own amazement, a quarter bottle of vodka down the sink. A social worker would be calling the following day but it wasn't because of that. She was starting afresh and she couldn't do that with reminders of her old life in the house.

At dinner, she lifted her glass of water and said, "A toast!" which made the boys giggle and tip each other in embarrassment. "To this family, that we stick together and be kind to each other always!" she announced.

Luke and Jack banged their glasses a little too loudly and spilled water on the table. Hazel looked at her sister who smiled serenely.

Iris hoped that Hazel would stick to her resolution but deep down she really didn't believe it. It was too good to be true and she had heard it all before. Many, many times before.

Chapter 23

Life returned to normal, except that Hazel appeared to be keeping her word and was working on her parenting skills. She had even attended a course the Health Board had sent her on, which she never stopped talking about and her new-found "good mammy routine" was starting to annoy Iris although she didn't know why. Wasn't that what she wanted? For Hazel to be a good mam to her boys and to stop the cycle of damaged children in their family? Somehow she felt she preferred the flawed Hazel, the one that perhaps made Iris feel good about herself. She never felt so bad about her inadequacies while she had Hazel to compare herself to.

Christmas had come and gone and, even though it was a happy time for them, Iris felt lonely which was something she hadn't felt for many years. She was also feeling even more tired of late but had kept up her routine of walking each morning.

One morning as she was returning from her walk, she could see a man waiting outside the shop. She looked at her watch. It was only ten to nine. God, she thought, can they not even wait till normal opening time? Iris had the occasional customer who, knowing she lived behind the shop would knock loudly in the evening to collect something that could easily have waited until morning and it annoyed her. As she approached him, she fumbled in her pockets for the keys. She couldn't see him clearly but he looked well-heeled and she put on her best smile. She could use all the well-off customers she could get.

"Hello!" she called to him. "Just opening up . . ." Iris did not get to finish her sentence and her mouth dropped open at the sight in front of her.

She hardly recognised her ex-husband. He wore an expensive suit and a brown overcoat. His black hair was greying slightly even though he was still only in his mid-forties. He had the same kind, rather sad-looking brown eyes. Iris felt her heart jump. She had not seen her husband since that day in Trafalgar Square over sixteen years ago. She was worried that he was annoyed with her for writing the letter. In truth, she had no idea how it would have made him feel. She wondered now if he viewed her letter as an unwelcome intrusion into the life she had forced him to lead and now had the cheek to want to be part of.

"Mark!" she said, louder than she intended, stirring interest in the few people waiting at the bus stop that was almost directly outside her shop.

He did not answer but looked at her from head to toe. First, staring into her eyes and then slowly moving his eyes from her head to her feet as if inspecting her, as if he was seeing her for the first time. It made her nervous. She moved nearer to him but avoided his gaze.

"What are you doing here?" she asked, quieter than before but yet revealing her surprise and nervousness.

"Your letter," he said curtly. "I came because of your letter."

Iris reddened and looked away from him. She began opening the cumbersome locks on her front door that usually annoyed her but she was glad on this occasion for the respite from his eyes. She couldn't quite place their expression and had no idea if he looked annoyed or surprised.

"Come in," she said quietly.

She led him through the shop and took him into the sitting room, which wasn't as tidy as she would have liked. She still hadn't taken down her tiny Christmas tree and it looked pathetic in the corner of her equally tiny sitting room. She could feel Mark's eyes scan the room which added to her embarrassment as he had done very well for himself and she was sure he lived a comfortable life in London. She never planned on Mark seeing her home and it worried her that he might feel sorry for her.

"How is Miriam?" she asked anxiously. It seemed a strange question when they both knew what she wanted to ask about was her son, their son. But she had no business, she knew. Mothers do not leave.

"Fine thanks," he said somewhat sternly.

Iris thought she sensed some sadness in his voice but did not ask. He seemed like an apparition to her. His large frame did not belong in her flat, in her world.

"You look well," he said.

Iris blushed. She knew she looked awful. She was much thinner than she used to be and she rarely wore make-up or had her hair done any more.

"You do too," she smiled. "It's nice to see you," she added shyly.

She looked at her feet but could sense him looking at her. She wished he would speak.

"What made you write now, Iris?" he asked finally.

Iris opened her mouth to speak. "Nothing. Honestly. I just . . . I just . . . Was it stupid to send it? That's why I sent it to you first, for you to make the decision. I was feeling . . . sort of low . . . I don't know what I was thinking really." She could hear the words spilling out of her mouth. She was nervous. She wanted, more than anything, to ask if he had given the letter to Kevin but dared not ask. It was too much. She had no right.

Iris heard the shop bell ring and looked towards the front. It was Mrs Ahern coming to collect some repairs.

"I'll be back in a moment," she said, leaving Mark to look around the dump she called home.

In the shop front, Mrs Ahern was in the mood to gossip which Iris was almost never interested in hearing. It took almost five minutes to get rid of her as Iris sweated under her brown wool cardigan.

"Sorry," she said as she returned to Mark who appeared to have stood still since she left. "I'll put the kettle on. Please sit down," she said, vying for more time.

How strange this situation was! From time to time she had thought about what their reunion would be like, if ever a reunion was to take place and while it was never romantic or even happy, it hadn't been this awkward, this tense.

"Iris," he said, catching her by the arm and preventing her from entering the kitchen. "Why did you write that letter? Is something wrong?"

He was searching her face as though he still knew her like he once did.

"No, Mark. I was . . . look . . . Hazel's boys ran away. They were alright in the end but it made me think about the danger they were in. About how Hazel might not have got to tell them how she felt and why she acted the way she did. It made me think about Kevin. I – I wondered what he thought of me. I just wanted to tell him why I did what I did, as best I could. Though I still don't understand it. Maybe I never will . . ." she trailed off. "I had no right, I know, Mark. I'm sorry." She bit her lip and looked towards him.

"I didn't give it to him," he said flatly.

Iris nodded. "Yes, you were right," she said, lowering her head and turning slightly to hide the tears that were beginning to surface.

"He's been through a lot, Iris. Too much. You can't expect . . ."

Iris turned quickly. She didn't want Mark to pity her. She couldn't stand that.

"I don't expect!" she said sharply before lowering her voice and taking a deep, calming breath. She did not want to fight with him. "I don't expect anything. I wanted to tell him so that he didn't feel that my leaving was anything to do with him. I wanted to explain that it was me. That it was me, that's all."

Mark moved toward her and put his arms out. She turned to him, somewhat ashamed, somewhat scorned, but refused his arms of comfort. He took a step back from her, his eyes still searching her face, looking for what she did not know.

"My father's been ill," he said, changing the subject. "I've been over a few times when he was in hospital. I would have called to see you but I didn't know if you wanted that. I felt you didn't."

"I'm sorry to hear that," she said genuinely. She had liked Mark's father but under the circumstances she had never visited the Careys since she returned to Ireland. She did not know if she would have liked Mark to visit her or not. Perhaps it would have stirred up too many memories, made her mistakes, her loss, seem more real.

"Your mother . . . is she . . .?" she asked.

"She's frail but she's managing. Now that Dad is so weak, it's obvious how much she depended on him. I'm sorting out some home help. John and Karen are in London so they're alone here." He paused. "Ke-Kevin is in London at school. I didn't bring him with me."

She wondered why he found it hard to mention their son's name. Perhaps he felt that by naming him, he was sharing him, and he wanted to deprive her of knowing anything about their son's life. Her ex-husband seemed so different. He seemed in pain, lost somehow, not the Mark she had known.

"Mark," she said gently, "I am not looking for anything. I know what I've done. I'm not looking to come into Kevin's life. I promise."

Mark looked towards his feet and dug his hands into his pockets. The flat was cold. Iris rarely turned the heating on until evening time and sat at a two-bar electric heater in the shop.

"You live here as well?" he asked. "I thought this was just your business address."

Iris looked around the room, acutely aware of how it would look to him.

"I don't mind it. I hadn't planned on living here but the house seemed, well, it had too many bad memories. Hazel lives there with her boys." She blushed again although she didn't know why.

"How is she?" Mark asked sincerely. He had liked Hazel even though she brought more than her fair share of worry on her sister.

"Oh, I should say the same but lately she's taken to . . . well, she's turned over yet another new leaf and let's just say that the boys never miss Mass on Sunday any more." Iris smiled. It was nice to have some cordial conversation with the man she had once loved, the only man she had ever loved.

Mark raised his eyebrows in mock surprise and laughed which made him look like his old self, the funny man Iris knew before she walked out on him and their son.

"Well, I should go," he said suddenly, taking her by surprise. "I'm flying back tonight."

He put out his hand to shake hers and she took it, thinking how strange, shaking the hand of someone you were once so intimate with, someone with whom you created a child. A million questions raced in her mind. She wasn't entirely sure why he had come. Was it simply to tell her that he hadn't given Kevin the letter? He could have done that by letter or by phone. She wondered if he wanted to see the look on her face when he told her that he didn't pass it on, to see how much that would hurt, like she had hurt him so badly all those years ago. Yet, he seemed upset at her obvious disappointment. She walked behind him as he made his way through the shop and towards her door.

"It was good to see you," was all she could say as she stood with one hand on the open door.

He smiled at her and handed her his business card.

"My new mobile number," he said before disappearing into the busy street.

She stood for a few minutes with her back to the shop door. Her heart was still thumping. She lifted the business card. *Dr Mark Carey – Paediatrician*. She locked the shop door in a daze. She walked into the flat and put Mark's business card on top of the television. She lay down on her single bed and felt tears fall down her face and onto her pillow until they turned to a torrent of sobs that racked her body. She cried in a way she hadn't for a very long time. It had hurt to see him. It opened up old memories that were best left alone. She had been a fool to write that letter. A selfish fool.

Iris lay there until the tears subsided. Eventually she lifted herself off the bed and washed her face in front of the broken mirror. She knew that she deserved his cool demeanour, his staring eyes. What had she expected? She walked back out to the shop and turned the "Closed" sign around.

She sat down on her stool behind the counter and pursed her lips as she stared out at life passing her by.

Chapter 24

Hazel had a renewed interest in life which put a spring in her step. She had completed the parenting programme that the Health Board had "suggested" she go on but she'd known it was more than a suggestion so she had agreed. She knew she needed it and the course hadn't felt like the boring lectures she was expecting. She had learnt all sorts of things about child development and about trying to see how life looks through younger eyes. She was getting on better with both the boys, especially Luke who had settled down at school. She had taken him to see a psychologist who decided that there was nothing wrong with him and that his behaviour was "normal" given the "abnormal" situation he was living in. Hazel was learning all sorts of new terminology.

She could sense that her sister was indifferent to her new life, which annoyed her. After all, Iris was the one who kept on at her about not being a good mother and, now that she was trying, she was not interested at all. In fact, Hazel had noticed that her sister was even quieter than usual, always appearing to be tired, and she wondered if Iris was depressed – she had learned a lot about the symptoms of that too. She wasn't sure if she should raise it with her sister. Hazel knew Iris hated people asking her personal questions.

For her own part, Hazel had decided to do a course to help her to get a decent job. She was tired of working in shops. None of the jobs she had lasted very long anyway as she wasn't exactly the customer-friendly type. As she leafed through the FÁS course booklet, she found exactly what she was looking for. Horticulture. Like her father, she loved plants and would love to work at this for a living. She needed a Leaving Cert for the course, which she had, and an interest in horticulture which she definitely had. The course ran for almost a year and was two bus journeys away. She knew she wouldn't be home in time to collect the boys from school but she'd work that out if she got a place. Hazel completed the application form and stuck her last stamp squarely on the envelope. She felt a surge of excitement run through her. She hadn't felt this good about life for ages.

The doorbell rang and she raced to open it. She expected it was Úna Jordan, the social worker assigned to her, who called twice a week now to check on things. So far Úna was pleased with the improvement in Hazel's parenting skills.

Hazel flung open the door and her jaw dropped when she saw a garda standing on her doorstep. It was Sergeant Keogh.

"What's wrong?" she asked loudly, the panic audible in her voice.

"Can I come in?" he asked flatly.

Hazel stood back to let him into the long narrow hallway. She could see Mrs Whelan looking over the hedge and gave her a wry smile. She did not ask the sergeant to sit down. She knew he didn't like her and that he had thought she was a bad mother, the night the boys had run away.

"Well?" she asked, irritated that he was ruining her good-mood day.

Keogh looked right through her. He had been almost thirty years working as a policeman and he was sick of the likes of Hazel Fay, the type who had an attitude even though you were trying to help them.

"We are following up on Pete Doyle's drug-pushing," he said matter of factly. He noticed how she squirmed in her shoes and it gave him a little bit of satisfaction. He didn't believe that she hadn't known what Doyle was up to. She didn't look that stupid.

"I don't know anything about it," she said coolly.

"Yes, so you've said," he retorted. "Have you seen Doyle?" He raised his large bushy eyebrows towards his cap.

"No," Hazel replied sourly. She hadn't seen or heard from Pete since the night he practically ran from her house. Bastard. She hoped she'd run into him so that she could give him a piece of her mind. She'd had no idea that he was involved in that sort of thing and still felt like a fool.

"Well, we have reason to believe that his supplier is pretty vexed at his disappearance, Doyle owing him a lot of cash and so forth. He might come here thinking you've seen him."

Keogh watched as Hazel gulped.

She hadn't thought of that. Oh, why do these things have to happen when life is looking up for me? she thought.

"No one has called here, Sergeant," she replied nervously. "Who is the supplier?" If she knew who it was, she could be looking out for him.

"You don't know?"

"No!" she replied angrily. "I don't. I haven't a clue, whether you believe me or not."

Keogh watched her closely. She almost looked as if she was telling the truth. This worried him. Power was a nasty piece of work and could come knocking when he felt things had cooled down. She might be in danger.

"You do know a man named Jimmy Power?"

Hazel shook her head.

"He's about six foot, late forties, receding brown hair. Small scar on his upper lip?"

"No," Hazel replied. The description didn't sound like any of the losers Pete had invited to her house. "Is he the . . . was Pete selling for him?"

"We believe so. Well, don't let anyone you're not familiar with into the house. In fact, don't even open the door unless you're familiar with the caller."

Hazel felt he must think she was an idiot. "I won't," she said crossly as she opened the door and saw Keogh out.

He stopped just outside the door and looked closely at the acerbic woman.

114

"If you notice anything suspicious, someone hanging around the street, someone hanging up when you answer the phone – that'll be someone checking whether you're in or not – ring this number." He shoved a small card into her hand.

Hazel was annoyed. The sergeant's visit had lowered her mood. As bad as Pete was, she didn't believe he'd tell Power where she lived. And why would they come looking for her anyway? She didn't know anything. She looked at the envelope on the kitchen table and tried to raise her spirits. A new life awaited her, a life without the likes of Pete Doyle. She knew she'd miss the company but perhaps she'd meet someone new in time. For now, she had to focus on the boys and herself. Úna had explained that to her. She had to feel strong on her own before she could pick a good partner. It made sense.

She put the kettle on to boil and looked at the clock. It was almost nine and she wondered what Iris was doing. She walked to the phone, sat down on the sofa and rang her number. When Iris eventually answered, Hazel prepared to launch into her woes but Iris stopped her in her tracks.

"Hazel!" she cried. "I've found a lump in my breast."

Iris listened as Dr Walsh explained the tests that would be done over the next few days. She had only been to this GP on a couple of occasions since she had come home. She was surprised to realise she had hardly been sick in years.

Hazel sat beside her, white-faced, and Iris realised that the tables had turned, that her helpless sister was now supporting her for a change. Iris didn't like this one little bit. She had always been in charge, always the one who knew what to do but now she was going to depend on Hazel and it filled her with dread. She didn't think her younger sister was up to the challenge. Hazel had enough difficulty looking after herself and the boys.

The GP assured her that many lumps prove to be simple cysts, that a lump can be benign and that she shouldn't worry until the results came back. She knew all this, of course, from her nursing training but she listened patiently. He said he didn't think the tiredness she had felt lately was any indication of a serious problem, he thought that she was merely run down. But Iris couldn't shake off the feeling that she was seriously ill.

Two days later Iris presented herself at the local hospital for a mammogram. As the machine pressed down on her right breast she grimaced with pain. She knew benign lumps were more likely to hurt and that this was probably a good sign. She tried to be positive.

When she got a call a fortnight later to come back to the hospital for a biopsy, she knew that something was wrong. She had to wait another gruelling ten days for the biopsy results and another sleepless week before her suspicions were confirmed. She had breast cancer.

She had thought that she would cry or even scream but instead she felt numb. There was something about this news that seemed natural to her, as if she somehow knew that this was coming.

She walked with Hazel to the home where they had grown up. On Thursday she would be admitted to hospital for surgery to remove the lump. She knew she would have to stay with Hazel for a couple of weeks afterwards. She had no one else.

Over the next few days she relinquished her power to her sister who seemed to adapt well to her new role as carer. Iris found she had little to say and sat on the sofa, staring out of the window, waiting for her surgery day. The boys were great and sat with her while Hazel cooked meals to try to put some weight on her sister. On Thursday morning, Hazel reluctantly asked Mrs Whelan to drop the boys to school while she organised a taxi to take Iris to hospital. She sat with her sister as they waited in the ward. Iris was dressed in a hospital gown with her hair hidden underneath a blue cap. She looked gaunt and Hazel wondered if Iris would lose her hair from the treatment that she might need to have following surgery.

"You alright, Iris?" Hazel asked gingerly. She wasn't used to this role and was feeling more nervous than usual at her sister's change of personality. Iris had rarely spoken over the past few days and it worried Hazel.

Iris looked up at her sister as though she hadn't known she was there. Her eyes widened and then shrank, a dead expression making her tiny face appear more ghostly as though she was already gone.

"Yes," she replied so quietly that Hazel had to strain to hear her.

Hazel fought back her tears. What would she do if her sister died? Who would look out for her? She didn't want to be selfish and was trying her best to care for Iris. She owed it to her after all, but it was hard. She wanted the old Iris back, the one who would tell her what to do and when to do it, even if she ignored the advice and did what she wanted to do anyway.

When the trolley finally came to bring Iris to theatre, Hazel breathed a sigh of relief. She felt useless sitting in the ward and was starting to feel the cold white walls closing in on her. She kissed Iris awkwardly and waved as the orderlies wheeled her away.

"I'll drop around to your place to collect your things," Hazel called after her but Iris did not respond. Hazel stood and watched until the trolley disappeared from view and felt an emptiness she had never experienced before. She walked out of the hospital. Although the air still had the familiar sting of winter, the sun shone brightly in the clear blue sky. Hazel sat down on the corner of a small grey wall that surrounded the hospital grounds. She pulled her hood up to shield herself from a cold wind that had begun to blow around the side of the hospital. She watched the passing traffic and ordinary people walking by, leading their ordinary lives. She wished for a moment that she could be one of those people, could be anyone other than herself right now. She sighed as she stared into the passing crowd as she waited for news.

Chapter 25

Four hours after Iris had been wheeled away, Hazel decided to ring the hospital and was told that her sister was now in recovery. She had not left the hospital but had wandered around the grounds, thinking of everything Iris had done for her over the years. She wanted more than anything to find the strength to repay her sister. Hazel felt she should have been the one to be ill. Iris didn't drink or smoke while she did both, sometimes to excess. It wasn't fair.

The staff in recovery allowed her in for a few minutes. Iris was still asleep but twice she put her hand to her breast to feel if it was still there. It upset Hazel but she bit her lip. She had to be strong.

"It's alright, Iris. Can you hear me?" she whispered, trying to conceal the shakiness in her voice. "It's all over. You're fine. They just removed the lump." Hazel didn't know if the hospital staff knew any more at the moment and prayed that Iris didn't need any further surgery. She looked so frail in the bed, like a child. Hazel had never noticed just how tiny her sister was and yet she was the strong one. She wondered why it had turned out that way.

A nurse approached Hazel.

"She won't be fully awake for hours. Perhaps you should go home and get some rest?" she said kindly.

Hazel nodded. She leant towards her sister.

"I'll be back tomorrow, sis," she said.

She squeezed Iris's hand and turned quickly to leave. She wanted to scoop her up and take her with her. It was a new feeling, a change from the old Hazel who was used to being looked after. Instead, she was now doing the caring and she was adamant that she was going to do it right.

She walked out of the hospital and into the fresh cold spring air. She took a deep breath in and walked towards the bus stop. The boys would be home soon. She had asked Mrs Whelan to collect them. She hated asking the old bat but she was stuck and the boys seemed to like her, nosy and all as she was. As the bus passed the cemetery where her mother was buried, she wondered what her mother would have done in this situation. Would she have been a help? Would she be sitting now in the hospital holding Iris's hand? She didn't think so and the thought of this made her angry.

Hazel got off two stops early and went into the small garden centre. Although she couldn't afford it, she bought a tray of peonies. It was too late to plant them now but they would make a good border for her new garden and would give her something to look forward to. She hadn't heard anything from FÁS and hoped she'd get a place on the course, which was due to start in May but, for now, Iris was her main concern.

After she fed the boys and ensured they'd done their homework, they made their way to Iris's flat to feed the cat and pack a few more things for her. The flat seemed cold and abandoned. Hazel looked around the sitting room and wondered how Iris lived in this dump. It was damp and hadn't been painted in years. There were many things she didn't understand about her sister. She knew she didn't need to live like this.

The nurse had said that Iris would be in a while longer than she had originally anticipated so Hazel packed up some extra nighties and opened the top drawer in Iris's bedroom to see if there was anything else she should take. In a small wooden frame was a photo of Iris's son, Kevin. It was roughly wrapped in tissue paper. Hazel undid the wrapping and stared sadly at the photo. She wondered if her sister looked at the photo each night before she went to sleep. She put the photo into the bag, unsure if Iris would be angry with her for bringing it.

As she roused the boys from watching cartoons on Iris's TV, she noticed a card on top of the television. She took it down and read the name aloud: "Dr Mark Carey."

"Who is that, Mam?" Jack asked.

"Mmm . . ." she said, wondering what was best to say. "He was Iris's husband. He . . . he must have sent this card to her recently. Funny she never mentioned it."

"It probably came in a letter from her son," Luke said loudly, suddenly more interested in the conversation than the television.

"Why would you say that?" Hazel asked.

"'Cos she wrote to him. She told me!" Luke was delighted to have information that no one else knew.

"Really?" Hazel asked, amazed at this.

"Yeah. 'Cos she's sorry, Mam."

Hazel shook her head in amazement. She put the card in her bag in case she needed to contact Mark.

"Right, boys, school night. Let's go," she said authoritatively, still enjoying her new parenting skills.

As they reached the house, Hazel was preoccupied. She needed to call the hospital and see how Iris was, but she had no credit left on her mobile and her One-Parent Family Payment was already spent. As she opened her bag to search for the key, she heard Luke gasp.

"Mam! The door's broken!"

Hazel's jaw dropped open. Someone had broken in and a long narrow piece of the front door was missing. She pushed the door open fully and saw that someone had ransacked the house. The hall table was overturned and the phone had been pulled from the socket. She could see into the sitting room. The drawers of her mother's sideboard lay on the floor, their contents thrown about the room. Her sofa was ripped and lying on its side in the middle of the sitting room. There was a smell of urine emanating from the hall. She could not hear anything and was sure that whoever had broken in was gone.

"Luke, run next door and get Mrs Whelan to ring the guards," she said as calmly as she could.

Luke looked at her.

"Go! And take Jack with you," she ordered when there was no sign of her older son obeying her.

When the guards arrived, Hazel was glad that it was two younger men and not Keogh who she knew had taken a severe dislike to her. They took statements and another man in plain clothes took photos and dusted for fingerprints.

"Is anything missing?" one of the men asked.

Hazel looked around the room. It was impossible to tell.

"I don't know," she said. She was exhausted. It had been a very stressful day.

"If there isn't, it could be that someone is trying to send you a message – especially urinating in the hall like that," the taller policeman warned.

Hazel sighed. She knew she wasn't a very good judge of character but it seemed unbelievable that Pete would do this to her. She knew it must be the man Sergeant Keogh warned her against – Jimmy Power – or, if not him, then one of his cronies. She thought it must be a message for her to keep quiet. They were wasting their time. She didn't know anything.

Hazel shut the door after the guards left and stared at the mess. Tears sprang to her eyes. She took a deep breath and sent the boys straight to bed before making herself a strong coffee. On a night like tonight, she would have loved a large vodka and Coke. She thought about running down to the off-licence to buy a small bottle but she was already broke and anyway she was definitely not going back to that way of life.

Hazel went to the kitchen sink and pulled a pair of rubber gloves on before scrubbing the carpet. Her stomach lurched and she wondered who would do such a filthy thing. Despite her best efforts, it still stank of urine when she had finished. She sat on the stairs. The quiet of the house made her nervous. She needed someone to talk to.

Hazel went to the phone and dialled the hospital number. The nurse informed her that Iris was still groggy. They had given her something for pain and she had gone straight back to sleep. She'd tell her that her sister had phoned and that she'd be back in the morning.

121

When Hazel replaced the receiver, she immediately broke down. She would have loved to be able to tell Iris about the break-in, to share her problem. She felt alone and the burden of what had happened tonight hung over her like a black cloud.

Hazel knew she'd had no choice but to inform the police but she was worried now that the social worker would get wind of it. She was trying hard to be a good mother. She noticed her hands shaking. The pressure of everything that had happened over the past few weeks was taking its toll on her. She opened her handbag to search for the half-empty packet of cigarettes she left there for emergencies. She took out a cigarette and searched in the bottom of her bag for a lighter. She fingers closed on something unfamiliar. She pulled out Mark's card. She looked at it. He was a paediatrician now. She smiled. He'd be good at that. She'd liked Mark and it always saddened her that things hadn't worked out between Iris and him. She realised that she didn't have a lighter and sat there fuming. She stood and began to pace the floor, aware that she was rubbing her hands together nervously. What if Pete came back in the middle on the night? Maybe she'd ring the hospital again. Maybe Iris would be awake now and she could talk to her, tell her what had happened. No, she couldn't do that. Iris wouldn't be awake anyway. Hazel reached for the phone and dialled a number.

"Hello, Mark? It's Hazel."

Chapter 26

When Iris opened her eyes she thought that she must be dead. She could see Mark standing over her, his big sad eyes searching her face. She did not know that two days had passed since her operation and that a high temperature had raged within her, bringing her in and out of a dream-like state. She had vague memories of seeing Hazel sitting on the end of her bed and of Luke and Jack sitting quietly on two chairs beside her. She remembered talking to them and then opening her eyes again to find them gone and the ward enveloped in darkness. She thought she saw her father in his garden but when she tried to talk to him, he disappeared and was replaced with an old garden rake that she knew still stood in Hazel's small garden shed. She remembered waking several times to see a doctor or a nurse standing over her, lifting her dressings and speaking in low hushed tones.

She knew she must still be dreaming. Yes, she decided, this was another dream. She wondered when she might wake from it.

Now Luke and Jack were looking down at her, with Hazel standing behind them. Luke had a frown on his face and Jack just stared.

"Are you real?" she asked her visitors.

Hazel looked at Mark and started laughing.

"Look who's come to see you, Iris!" she said in a childlike voice.

Mark leant forward again, concern showing on his face.

"Mark?" she said weakly. Her throat hurt.

"You have an infection," he said calmly. "They've been giving you antibiotics. You'll be fine."

"What are you . . . why are you . . . ?"

"Shh," he said, putting his hand over hers. "Hazel phoned me."

Iris looked at her sister, a frown developing on her forehead. Hazel ducked her sister's eyes and pretended to smooth out the bedclothes.

Iris cleared her throat. "The cancer?" she asked.

Hazel looked at Mark, waiting for him to reply.

"There was a healthy margin," he explained, knowing that Iris would understand the terminology from her nurse training. "They got it all but you'll need some radiotherapy, just as a precaution."

Iris felt her shoulders relax into the bed as a sense of relief flooded over her. She wondered if Mark had brought Kevin with him but didn't dare to ask. He seemed to want to say something but closed his lips and smiled one of those pitying smiles. Iris cringed.

"Are you in pain?" Hazel asked, concerned.

"Yes," Iris lied.

"I'll get a nurse. Come on, boys," Hazel said, "help me find that nice blonde nurse."

The three made for the door of the ward. Hazel looked back at her sister. It had touched her that Mark had flown over the day after she phoned him and she was also moved by the way he looked at her sister as her fever raged. Iris had called his name twice as her temperature soared and Hazel was glad he was there to hear it. She knew he was married now but she couldn't help but notice that he still had feelings for her sister.

Mark looked down the ward and then back to Iris. He felt awkward now that they were alone and wondered why he had come. He hadn't even given it a second thought. As soon as he put the phone down on Hazel he organised a flight for the following morning. Kevin was at boarding school so all he had to do was cancel his appointments for a few days. He worked privately now so there was no problem.

There was an awkward silence between them, neither knowing what to say.

Mark knew she had questions. He had felt angry with her for writing to Kevin and it had taken him by surprise. He had always been willing to keep her informed about their son and even though she had not seemed to want that, he had never allowed resentment to develop between them. But, when Miriam left him, that changed. It shocked him that this could happen to him twice. He knew colleagues at work who were caught cheating on their wives with other hospital staff and whose wives had stuck by them. He had never been unfaithful to either Iris or Miriam and yet both women had abandoned him. But he couldn't afford to think about this now, not when she was so ill.

"I'm – glad – you – are – here," she said slowly, taking a breath between every word. "Hazel . . . is . . . well, she is trying but she gets . . . so worked up . . ." Iris tried to finish her sentence until the breathlessness became too much.

Mark rolled back his head and laughed. "Nothing changes," he declared just as Hazel returned from her search for a nurse.

"What doesn't change?" she asked, putting her head to one side.

Iris started to laugh also until a fit of coughing racked her body.

"Okay, that's enough excitement for today, folks," a nurse ordered.

Mark leant towards Iris and kissed her gently on the cheek.

He smelt familiar, safe, and Iris tried to remember that smell for when she drifted off to sleep again.

Hazel and the boys waved.

"We'll be back tomorrow!" the boys chorused as Iris slid away again to her dreams.

This time they were of her mother. She was calling her over and over, telling her to look after Hazel, and her son and Mark waving at her as they faded into the distance.

Nine days after Iris's surgery, she was allowed to go home to Hazel's house where she was under strict instructions to get as much rest as possible. She had one radiotherapy treatment before she was discharged and would have to return to hospital for further treatment.

It was strange staying with her sister. Iris could sense that Hazel was trying to be the best nurse ever but she was overdoing it. She was trying too hard and it was making Iris nervous.

Hazel had not told her about the break-in and had managed to find a local carpenter who repaired the door cheaply for her. She had sworn the boys to secrecy, mostly because she didn't want Iris worrying about anything but partly because she didn't want Iris to know that her old life was still causing problems.

Mark had remained at the hospital for four days where he regularly harassed the doctors for medical updates and Hazel was delighted to have him there. She felt overwhelmed by the responsibility and didn't want to shoulder it alone. The day he flew back to London he had held Iris's hand tightly and told her he'd be back in a couple of weeks to see how she was. Hazel noticed Iris becoming quieter after he left and she wondered if her sister still had feelings for her ex-husband. She tried to ask her but Iris got annoyed so Hazel hadn't raised it again.

Some evenings after she'd put the boys to bed, Hazel would sit in her bedroom for a while and pretend to have things to do. She found it difficult to be alone all the time with Iris who had become quite sullen and was not coping with her illness as well as Hazel had expected her to. The radiotherapy was making her weak. Hazel had to travel with her to the hospital every second day for three weeks. Iris had developed an awful cough and the breathlessness she had developed in the hospital seemed to get worse when she started the radiotherapy. Hazel was still worried that Iris wouldn't survive.

The boys seemed to be coping well with it though and were delighted to have their aunt around full time. Luke was working on a school project about family history and had brought down old photo albums and papers from the attic to show Iris. Each afternoon she would go through them with him as he put together his project. He was also delighted that his older half-brother, Gerard, seemed to have taken a shine to him and Jack and had phoned them a couple of times. Hazel had mixed feelings about it at first but, when she saw how much it meant to Luke in particular, she agreed that they could see each other. Gerard had even picked the boys up from school one day for her. He had no lectures that afternoon and was glad to do it. Luke never stopped smiling to himself that night. He said the boys in his class thought Gerard was his dad and he let them believe it. Poor Luke, she thought. He was so vulnerable and cared so much what other people thought.

One evening, when Hazel finally mustered up the courage to join her sister in the living room, she found Iris sitting in the armchair with a thick wool blanket around her shoulders. She was either freezing or roasting and nothing in between, Hazel noticed.

"You need anything, Iris?" she asked. "I'm going to make a cup of tea."

Iris smiled weakly and shook her head. She had nausea most of the time now and the tablets the hospital gave her didn't really help. She knew she had to keep her weight up but it was hard when she felt like throwing up all the time. Secretly, she wondered if her illness was punishment for leaving her son. She had begun to believe that everything bad that happened was a punishment for the bad things people had done. But she didn't dare voice this to anyone. She could see the way Mark and Hazel had looked at her and it drove her crazy. She didn't want pity. She probably deserved this illness.

"I'm knackered!" Hazel said, throwing herself onto the sofa. "Anything on telly tonight?"

"You do too much," Iris said breathlessly. "You should take it easier."

Hazel gave her sister a wry smile. Take it easy! she thought to herself. Fat chance of that looking after the kids and you all day!

Iris read her thoughts. She always knew what her selfish sister was thinking.

"As soon as the treatments are over I'll move back to my place," she said slowly.

Hazel looked up from the TV guide and reddened. "There's no rush, Iris. You need looking after. I'd prefer you to stay here until you're completely better." Hazel meant it. She found it hard to play nursemaid to her fussy sister but at the same time she knew it was the right thing to do and she hadn't done the right thing by anyone for a very long time, if ever.

Iris did not answer and looked away. She felt imprisoned and couldn't wait until she was well enough to look after herself. Even though her wound looked red and angry, it was healing slowly and as soon as the radiotherapy was over she was going back to her flat, back to her comfort zone. She knew it would be a while before she could work and the bills were piling up. Mark had left money with Hazel to cover any expenses they had and it had embarrassed Iris to the core.

The two sisters fell into an uncomfortable silence. It saddened Iris that, after all she had done for Hazel, her sister was put out by the responsibility of caring for her. She realised that although they depended on each other for different reasons, they were not close. They were two sisters who had endured a disrupted childhood which bound them together for life. She looked at her sister and felt slightly sorry for her. She knew Hazel was doing the best she could. She knew she was never going to change and that she was already trying hard to do what "normal" sisters would do for each other. She could see that Hazel was struggling and realised that she had no choice but to accept her as she was – but it made her feel lonely and vulnerable.

Iris squirmed in her armchair and felt another rush of heat overcome her. Her face reddened and sweat trickled down her back.

"You alright?" Hazel said, looking up from her magazine.

"Yeah," she replied breathlessly. "Think I'll go to bed. I have treatment tomorrow."

Hazel stood up to help her weakened sister up the stairs, taking one step at a time as Iris's cough racked her body.

"Hope I don't wake the boys," Iris wheezed.

"They're grand," Hazel said, turning her face away from her sister. Tears had formed in her eyes and she didn't want Iris to see them.

"I remember helping you up these stairs when you were learning to walk," Iris said slowly.

"Yeah?" Hazel said, glad to have something else to focus on.

"You kept falling down," Iris smiled, reminiscing.

Hazel gripped Iris tighter. She wanted to cry but held back.

"Well, now, big sis, I'm helping you!" she replied, trying to negotiate each step slowly.

Hazel sat her sister down on the single bed in the spare room and pulled back the covers.

"It's grand, Hazel. I can do that," Iris said, trying to hide the irritation in her voice.

Hazel nodded and left the room quickly. "Night then," she said as she closed the door behind her.

She moved as quickly as she could down the stairs, trying to put distance between her and these feelings, this situation that was becoming unbearable. She turned off the telly and turned on the radio as loud as she could without waking the boys. She sat on the sofa and curled her long legs underneath her, wrapping her arms around herself.

The music thumped through the floor of Iris's room as she lay on the bed, fully dressed and facing another sleepless night.

Chapter 27

"Wake up!" Hazel demanded as she shook Luke and Jack.

It was nine thirty and they were late for school. Hazel had lain awake until the early hours and had drifted into a deep, late sleep. She was surprised that Iris hadn't woken her. Ever since her sister had moved in, she had taken on the role of getting everyone up. Iris was always a poor sleeper and was usually awake before the dawn. When Hazel was sure the boys were getting dressed she ran to Iris's bedroom. Her treatment was due at ten thirty and they had planned on travelling there by taxi after Hazel dropped the boys to school.

"Iris! It's half nine. We've slept in," Hazel said, peering into her sister's face as she slept soundly. She could hear Iris's laboured breathing and frowned when her sister didn't answer her.

"Iris!" she said, slightly louder. "Iris?"

She started shaking her sister but she did not respond. She ran to the window and pulled back the heavy lined curtains, letting the bright early-spring sunshine flood the room. She noticed that her sister's face was bright red. She was burning up.

"Iris!" she screamed, bringing Luke and Jack running into the room.

"Luke, Luke, ring an ambulance! Quick!" she cried.

Luke ran down the stairs as Jack started to cry in the doorway.

"Stop it, Jack," Hazel screamed. "Go downstairs!"

Hazel pulled Iris's shoulders up from the mattress. "Breathe, Iris, please breathe!" she pleaded but Iris's head dropped backward. Hazel could hear her wheezing.

"Will I get my nebuliser?" Jack whimpered from the doorway.

Hazel softened. "No, Jack. It's not asthma. Go downstairs, love, and look out the window for the ambulance. There's a good boy."

Hazel sat alone by her sister's side and began to sob.

"Please don't leave me. I can't manage on my own. I need you, Iris. Please don't leave me," she pleaded but she knew her sister could not hear her.

When the ambulance arrived, Hazel moved out of the room to make way for the paramedics. Looking down the stairs she saw Mrs Whelan step through the open doorway and stand in the hallway. They didn't like each other but she was always willing to help. She had known Hazel's mother well.

"Hazel?"

Hazel came out onto the landing and peered over as the ambulance men saw to Iris.

"I'll take the boys to school and collect them. Don't worry about them. Go with the ambulance and I'll keep them until you're back," she said kindly. Hazel nodded. "Thanks, Mrs Whelan," she said, suddenly feeling sorry for all the bad thoughts she'd had about her neighbour.

In the Intensive Care Unit, doctors explained that Iris's bout of pneumonia wasn't responding to treatment and that she now had a secondary infection to cope with as well.

"Well, what are you going to do?" Hazel asked. She couldn't think of a more intelligent question and wished Mark was here. She had left messages for him throughout the day. She hoped he wasn't away. She needed him.

"We're suspending the radiotherapy for now. She's too weak. We need to fight the infection and see what happens from there," the doctor said matter of factly.

"But . . . but . . . she'll die if she doesn't have treatment!" Hazel could hear the desperation in her voice which sounded almost childlike. It embarrassed her. The doctor looked directly at her. She could not read his face.

"We don't know that. The radiotherapy is precautionary. We'll just have to wait," he replied coolly. "I'll be back later to check on her and see if she's responding to the antibiotics."

Hazel went to the small waiting room beside the intensive care unit and sat down on one of the hard plastic chairs that were strewn about the room. Iris was unconscious and her temperature was making her thrash about the bed as though she was having nightmares. Hazel wondered what she was dreaming about. She phoned Mrs Whelan who agreed to collect the boys after school. She had a key and told Hazel to stay where she was, that she would put them to bed later and wait there for Hazel to return. She told Hazel that she would pray for Iris. Hazel thanked her even though she didn't really believe that praying made any difference.

At ten that night, Iris's temperature started to fall. An exhausted Hazel felt a flood of relief and hoped that this meant that she was going to be okay. When the nurse on duty suggested she go home, Hazel was relieved. She didn't want to leave without their say-so. She was tired and hungry and badly needed a shower. She had got an awful shock that morning and had almost lost her sister. She could feel her hands shake with nervousness and was amazed that she had got through it on her own. She was pleased that it was still early enough to get a bus home as she didn't want to splash out on a taxi and was glad of the money Mark had given her. Iris usually supplemented Hazel's meagre income but, with the shop being closed, Iris had nothing to spare.

She got off two stops early and went into the off-licence, feeling the twenty-euro note in her jeans pocket. She bought herself a bottle of red wine and walked the rest of the way home. She was looking forward to relaxing with a glass by the telly. It had been an awful day and she deserved a treat. I'll start my clean living programme again tomorrow, she reasoned.

When Mrs Whelan left for the night, she slumped down on the sofa, exhausted, and stared around the empty room. She noticed an old biscuit tin on the floor. It had a little girl on the lid dressed in a red dress. It seemed to bring happy memories to her and she lifted it.

Where did this come from? she wondered. "Probably from Luke's family-history thing," she said aloud to herself as she opened the rusted lid. Inside were a stack of old letters, carefully folded and tied together with elastic bands. She undid one of the letters and peered at it. The writing was beautiful and she didn't recognise it. She stood and turned on the lamp beside her. It was dated June 1971 and was addressed to her mother, written by a woman named Grace Mooney living in Balcombe, Sussex. Hazel was amazed. She didn't know who this woman was and never knew the letters were in the attic. She shook her head and tutted to herself. She poured herself a generous glass of wine and sat down to read the letter.

Dear Elizabeth,
I was so glad to hear that you are expecting and that all is going well. Jack must be delighted that he is going to be a dad. It must have been hard to return to Ireland after your freedom in England but I'm sure you are doing the right thing. Your mam won't be alive forever and it's right that you are near her to help out. We miss you here in Jack's hometown although nothing much has changed. I wonder how he is coping with living in Ireland. Still, he wasn't exactly close to his parents so perhaps he is settling in well? John is fine. Working mostly away but I've got used to it now. He's nearly in my way now when he returns. The girls are grand. Molly will be starting school in September. She's a real handful, I can tell you. I can't believe she is five. The years have gone so fast. In a way I envy you. At times I think I'd like to come home but I know John never would. Anyway, I put a few knitted cardigans in for your new arrival, mint green so it doesn't matter what you have but I expect Jack wants a boy to carry on the gardening! Ha!
Write soon.
Love,
Grace

Hazel read the letter twice more before folding it and putting it back in the tin box. It must have been written when her mother was expecting Iris. Even though she didn't have the letter her mother wrote, the response was so positive and cheerful that she felt her mother must have been looking forward to the birth. She wondered what then, in the intervening years, had gone wrong. The letters seemed to have been filed neatly. Hazel lifted another letter and opened it slowly.

Dear Elizabeth

It was great to hear from you and to hear that you had a healthy baby girl. Trust Jack to name her after a flower! I was worried that I hadn't heard from you since my last letter and I'm sorry to hear that you've got a bad case of the baby blues. Don't worry. It'll pass. I had it myself. I was annoyed to hear that your mam is causing trouble about you and Jack. She hasn't changed, has she? Don't pay any attention. Religion isn't everything. At least Jack's agreed to raise the kids as Catholics. He told me one time that his own dad was Catholic with Irish roots but his mum raised them as C of E. Anyway, you'd better nip it in the bud and tell her that if she keeps it up, you'll go back to England. That'd show her. Hey, tell her Eileen will end up looking after her. It'd serve her right to have your cranky sister fussing about her. I saw Eileen last week in town with a new gentleman friend on her arm. I wonder if it's serious. She hardly spoke to me but you know how she is. She seemed surprised that you'd had the baby so I wondered if you two have fallen out again. Well, at least she can't steal any more men from you! You were better off without him and if it hadn't happened, you'd never have met Jack so all's well that ends well, eh?

Well, better go, washing, cooking, etc. Welcome to the world of motherhood!

Love,
Grace

Hazel closed the letter and sighed. So her mother hadn't got along with her grandmother. She didn't really remember her grandmother very well. They didn't see much of her over the years. She passed her house on the bus sometimes but someone else lived there now. She was also amazed that stuffy Aunt Eileen had stolen a boyfriend from her mother. She did remember that her mother and Eileen were not close and could remember them fighting when Eileen visited. It was amazing having this porthole into the past.

Hazel stretched and yawned. She was worn out.

She returned the letter to the tin box and turned off the lights. She walked into the hall and quietly phoned Intensive Care to see how Iris was before looking in on the boys. Instead of sleeping in their separate bunks, Luke and Jack were wrapped around each other in Luke's bed. She smiled. It was good that they were close but it worried her that Luke thought he was responsible for Jack. She had never intended that to happen but it had. Somehow her son had picked up on her inadequacies and had assumed responsibility for his younger brother.

She closed their door and looked at herself in the mirror on the landing. Her face was flushed from the wine and she regretted drinking it. She hadn't had a drink since Jack was hospitalised and had been very proud of herself. Mind you, she thought, she would usually have drunk the whole bottle on one night whereas she had only drunk one glass, albeit a large one.

In her room she eased her tired body into bed and turned off the light. She drifted off immediately but tossed all night as she dreamt of hearing Iris calling her. In her dream, no matter where she looked she couldn't find her sister but continued to hear her voice calling into the night.

Chapter 28

Hazel sat up in her bed as she heard the phone ring. She looked quickly at the clock. It was eight o'clock. She jumped out of bed, ran downstairs and grabbed the phone.

"Hello?" she said nervously, expecting someone to tell her the worst, expecting someone to tell her that her sister was dead.

"Hazel?"

"Mark! Did you get my messages?"

"Yes. I'm at a conference in . . ."

Hazel couldn't hear the end of his sentence. "Where?"

"New York," he said, clearer this time.

Hazel could feel herself go limp. She had hoped he was in London and could come over, but New York was hours away.

"I contacted the airlines and the best they can do is a flight in two days into Dublin." The phone crackled. "Kevin's with me," he added.

Hazel took in a deep breath.

"Hazel, I spoke to the doctors last night and again early this morning. They're doing everything right," he assured her.

Hazel didn't answer.

"Hazel, are you alright?"

She bit her lip. "I'm okay. I just wish . . . I wish . . ." She didn't finish her sentence.

"I told them I was Iris's husband. I hope you don't mind. It was a different doctor to the last time and he wouldn't have given me any information otherwise."

Hazel smiled through her tears. "I don't mind at all – but I hope your wife doesn't mind!" She laughed but noticed that he had gone quiet. "Mark?"

"Yes?"

"The line's awful but if you can hear me, thanks, thanks for everything. I couldn't have got through this without you."

"You're welcome."

"Mark, what can I do?" She sounded lost.

"Talk to her, read to her."

"Can she hear me?" Hazel asked, surprised.

"I think so," he said. "I'll ring you as often as I can until my flight."

Mark had suggested talking or reading to Iris because he had to think of something to occupy Hazel. He knew it was possible that Iris could hear although it was unlikely.

It was only six weeks since he had visited Iris at her flat after so many years apart and he was amazed at how quickly he had become part of her and Hazel's life again. He was glad that Hazel appreciated his help but he wanted to be there. He wanted to be with Iris but something was niggling at the back of his mind, warning him. He was trying to ignore it. He didn't want to leave himself open to rejection and he definitely didn't want to expose Kevin to any more loss . . . yet he couldn't stay away. She needed him and he was somehow drawn to her. He knew the news was not good from the hospital and that Iris had not regained consciousness and he worried that she might not make it. The ICU doctor had informed him that in her weakened state she was not fighting as well as they had hoped.

Hazel was pleased when Mrs Whelan dropped in and kindly offered to walk the boys to school again, enabling Hazel to go directly to the hospital. She also offered to pick them up after school and take them to her house but Hazel said she would make it back from the hospital to pick them up herself. She really couldn't impose on Mrs Whelan to that extent – the woman was doing so much for her these days. She also appreciated the offer Gerard Junior had made to take the boys to his house any time it would help, but there was no way she could do that. She couldn't imagine herself knocking at Rose Henan's door to collect the kids she'd had with her husband while they were still married, and reddened even thinking about it.

Before she left the house, she swept up the box of letters and put them in a plastic bag. She knew she couldn't think of things to talk to Iris about all day but she could read her these letters.

Hazel locked the door and made her way to the bus. She felt her normal energy levels returning to her bones. She had something to focus on until Mark was able to get back and take over. She felt useful which was a feeling she had rarely experienced in her life.

At the hospital bed, a machine that hadn't been there last night was now helping Iris to breathe. Hazel was afraid to ask if this was a bad sign and decided not to ask. She didn't want to know. It was better if she didn't understand how bad things might be.

She settled into a chair next to the bed, then opened her bag and took out the next letter. With a slight quiver in her voice, she read aloud quietly.

Dear Elizabeth,

Sorry for not replying sooner but Molly had her appendix out so I was up and down to the hospital like a yo-yo. I wouldn't mind but I had her at the doctor twice with pain in her stomach but he kept saying it was nothing to worry about. You'd wonder about these so-called professionals! Anyway, things don't seem any better for you. You didn't say why your mam has fallen out with you. What happened? About you saying you're not a good mother, I'm sure that's not true. You seem to be worrying for nothing. Everyone goes through that. Have you spoken to the doctor about your mood? The baby's almost a year old now so that should have passed. Work seems to be going well for Jack but I know what you mean. It's hard when they work long hours and you're on your own all day. Must be nice for Jack working in such a fancy house though. Are the gardens that he looks after very big? Bet he's

in his element. Glad to hear that little Iris is doing well. Will
you be giving her a little sister or brother?

I haven't much news. We're coming home in July for a week.
I'm dying for it. I haven't seen my mam for over two years. I'll
be sure to drop in to see you. Say hello to Jack (whenever you
see him, that is!)

Love,
Grace

Hazel looked up from her letter and stared at her sister. Images and thoughts flooded her mind, making comparisons between her mother and Iris. The depression after the birth, the feelings of inadequacy. It was strange how alike they were. She wondered if her sister could hear her and if she could, what she was thinking. She got up and went to the vending machine for a cup of their awful coffee. She hated sitting in the hospital all day but if Iris was aware and listening, it was worth it.

When she returned, she opened another letter. It was dated the year before she was born so Iris must have been about three. There didn't seem to be any letters in between so she wondered if her mother hadn't saved them. She leant towards Iris's bed and spoke quietly into her sister's ear.

Dear Elizabeth,
I got two letters at once from you so they must have been
delayed in the postal strike. I'm not sure if you got my last letter
as you didn't mention my pool winnings. £200! I was delighted
as you can imagine. John has been out of work for two months
now and the bills are piling up. I'm a bit worried about him. He
seems down and goes to the pub most evenings even though we
can't afford it. Anyway, enough of my moaning. Jack's job seems
great with good money. You must be living the life of Riley. I
can't believe the lady of the house gives him wine to bring home
to you! She sounds nice. I wouldn't mind that myself although
I've never tasted wine. I like an odd brandy but who has the
money for that? You didn't mention if you were feeling a bit

better these days and whether you took my advice and saw the doctor about it. I hope that means you are over it. Are you sleeping any better? The kids of course are driving me mad. John wants another one so I do all I can to stay out of his way if you know what I mean. Three is enough. I don't know how my mam raised thirteen kids in our little house. God help her, she had a hard life.

Well, that's all from here. Don't take so long to reply this time, you had me worried!

Love
Grace

Hazel looked at her sister who seemed to stir in the bed. She thought she heard her make a moaning sound. She felt Iris's head. She didn't feel half as hot as she had done earlier.

Hazel sat back in her chair, deciding that she should let her sister rest in peace for a while, but she couldn't seem to resist the letters and, before she knew it, she had lifted another one from the neat pile. It was dated May 1975. She realised her mother would have just been pregnant with her.

Dear Elizabeth,
Where do I start? Your letter was so sad I wanted to get on the next boat and come over to you. I'm sorry that you are not happy to be expecting. Iris is three now so at least you won't have two in nappies.

Hazel paused, staring at those sentences, her face flushing, her heart thumping. Her mother hadn't wanted her. She forced herself to go on.

I'm trying to cheer you up and maybe not making a good job of it. It's not so bad. Maybe it'll be a boy and things will be better between you and Jack? I'm sure you are imagining that he is having a thing with his boss's wife. He doesn't seem the type. What about this row with your mam? I can't believe she threw you out on Easter Sunday! What's wrong with having a few glasses of wine? I wish I knew exactly what happened. Why wasn't Jack with you? He couldn't have been working. I wish you had a phone so we could talk properly. I got one in although it costs a fortune. It's good for my mam. I ring her when I can although John always moans about the cost. I think she gets lonely. That's how you sound in your letters, lonely. I know money isn't tight with you so maybe you could come over and spend a few days here? I'd love to see Iris again. She was such a tiny little thing. Like a doll.

My sister-in-law said Eileen got engaged but not to the chap I thought she was seeing. She's some dame, isn't she? I wouldn't mind if she had your looks. Can't imagine what they see in her, no offence. She's teaching in London now so I never see her. God help the poor kids! Does she ever come home? I know your mam always doted on her. Maybe she still does? It must still annoy you, even after all these years.

Look, try to look forward to the new baby and see it as a blessing. I know it's hard but when they put him or her into your arms, you'll feel different. Anyway, won't it be good for Iris? She's such a serious little girl. It'll be nice for her to have a baby brother or sister. I don't know what else to say. Try to cheer up. It does no good to mope.

Write back soon.

Love

Grace

Hazel put the letter on Iris's bed and tried to get control of her feelings. Her mother hadn't wanted her. Is this when her drinking began? Was her father really having an affair with his employer's wife? She had no idea. Was her grandmother angry with her for drinking when she was pregnant? Who knew? She had one memory of her grandmother's door being slammed in their faces. She was about four or so and they went and sat in the graveyard by her grandfather's grave. Her mother had wept for what seemed to the girls like hours and they just sat there, waiting for her to stop so they could go home. They were strange kids, her and Iris. Most kids would have wailed that they'd had enough and wanted to go but they always seemed dumbstruck by their mother's strange moods and waited it out, patiently and without protest.

Hazel wondered if it was such a good idea to read these letters. Although it was giving her an opportunity to understand her parents a little better, she had tried over the years not to think about her mother. She couldn't face up to her feelings of resentment that her mother had not cared for Iris and her properly. It hurt to think about it. Now, as she read each letter she could see her mother slipping into a deep depression, knowing that there was no happy ending, no life-changing event to put things right.

She put the letters into her bag and looked at her sister. The ward was now full, with beeping machines all around. She stood and leant over and touched Iris's face, pushing back her dark hair.

"You do look like a doll," she said to her unconscious sister. Then added softly, "If you can hear me, sis, I'll be back tomorrow."

Hazel put on her coat and walked the long shiny corridor towards the door.

She couldn't identify what she was feeling about the letters. Hurt? Confused? Lonely? Maybe all of them. She wished she had made friends in school but she was always shy which made her a lonely little girl. By the time she returned home from foster care, she didn't know anyone in her local area and felt isolated. She could have gone to England to Iris but she didn't want to leave the house. The entire time she spent in foster care, she dreamt of coming back to her childhood home. Hazel wondered now if that's why she got pregnant: loneliness and the desire to feel needed by someone. Yet, when the boys were born the feeling hadn't gone away and in some way she resented them needing her, resented the responsibility they brought to her life. She knew there was a part of her that would always feel lonely and abandoned.

When she left the warm hospital, a cold breeze blew on the main street where she would normally wait for her bus. She still had plenty of the money Mark had left so she hailed a taxi and got it to stop at the off-licence on the way home. She bought a bottle of wine and hid it in the large bag beside the letters.

Last one, she thought to herself as she headed for home.

Chapter 29

Dear Elizabeth,

It was lovely to see you at Christmas. I was delighted to get home to see my mam and of course to see you and your two lovely little girls. My mam seems to have got over the stroke well enough but I'm not sure she likes living with my brother and his wife. She misses her independence. I asked her to come here but she'd never leave Ireland.

I can't believe Hazel is now four. Where does it go? God, they are so different. Hazel is the image of you but I don't know where you got Iris from. She's all eyes and seems a worried little thing. You'd never even think they were sisters. You say your mam is comparing them already. History repeating itself. You're right to stamp that out. Either way, Jack's smitten with them. I thought you said he wanted a boy? He doesn't seem to mind at all. I see what you mean about how distant he is and maybe you are right that he is seeing someone but I still cannot see it being the boss's wife. Would there be anyone else in work? I'm sorry to hear you two fight a lot now. It's not good for the kids. I know from experience. You said he's worried about you drinking during the week. I have to say I agree with him. You don't want to make a habit of that, Liz. He is trying to cut down on the

143

hours and spend more time with you and the girls so try and enjoy that. A bit of company is all you need. I don't know why you don't mix with any of the women on the road. That Mary Whelan next door seems nice.

Well, Molly is doing well in secondary school. Kate will be going in next year. I never see Seán, always out with his mates. Before I know it they'll be gone and it'll be just me and John. I dread it. We won't know what to say to each other after all the years of kids crying in our faces. I am thinking of going back to work, just a few hours a day in a shop or something. It'll be good for me. You lose your confidence being at home all day. Maybe you should try it when Hazel goes to school? You were a fast typist in your day! You're bound to get something.

We might be going to France on the ferry this summer. It'll be our first holiday if you don't count trips home. To tell you the truth, I'm a bit nervous about it. I've never been further than Wales since I came to England and that was only to get the ferry home.

Anyway, I hope you take Jack's and my advice and cut down on the vino, Liz. Enjoy the girls when they are small because in a flash they are all grown up and don't need you. I never thought I'd say it but I preferred when they were little. I miss the hugs.

Write soon and try getting Iris to smile! Ha.

Love,

Grace

Hazel sat at Iris's bedside for the third day in a row and although her sister mouthed the odd word in her sleep, she had not regained consciousness. The night staff said she had opened her eyes briefly and Hazel wished she had been there to see it. She couldn't help but feel that she was sitting there each day watching her sister slip away and she was losing hope of her ever recovering. Hazel had finished an entire bottle of wine the night before and her head hurt which surprised her. She had often drunk a whole bottle on her own and it seemed like these days, the less she drank the worse it affected her the next day. She felt like vomiting and wished she could but the nausea she woke up with haunted her for the day. Thankfully, the social worker hadn't called lately. After learning about Iris's illness, she was obviously giving Hazel some space.

When she started reading the letters first, Hazel thought that Iris was like her mother but now she was beginning to see similarities between her own life and her mother's and it frightened her. She knew she wasn't an alcoholic, that she could give up the drink no problem. She only drank when she was upset or worried which was proof, wasn't it? Still, she knew that that was how her mother started drinking, to ease the loneliness and drown out her feelings. She decided that she wouldn't buy any wine on her way home tonight. Mark was flying into Dublin later and she would see him tomorrow. Knowing there would be someone around would make her stronger. It always did. She remembered something the social worker said about making herself stronger but she didn't know how to do this. She needed people. She wondered if she should use some of her parenting skills on herself and say no to herself from time to time. She smiled thinking of how the boys did what she said these days. The transformation in them was amazing. She had learned that they needed boundaries, they needed to know what was acceptable and what was not and it was up to her to teach them. If only she could stick to some boundaries herself and not buy any drink when she was feeling low. She was going to try because if she didn't, her kids would be reading about how their own mother lost control and gave up on herself as well as them, just like her mother had.

When she arrived home, Luke met her in the doorway with news of school and homework and football scores. She wanted to scream at him – sitting by her sister's bedside was tiring and had worn on her nerves. But she resisted and listened to his news. She sat down and, as Jack sat on her lap and cuddled into her, she remembered Grace's words: *"Enjoy it when they are small because in a flash they are all grown up and don't need you."* She hugged her younger son tightly and smiled warmly at Luke who was sitting on the floor, half-doing homework and half-watching TV. Hazel relaxed back into the armchair and took a deep satisfying breath.

"Mam?" Jack asked.

"Yes, love?"

"I like it when you are happy," he replied innocently.

"I'm always happy," she said. She was taken by surprise. Luke was usually the one to make comments on her moods.

"Well," he said, "I like it when you are more happy."

Hazel looked away from her son, trying to think of an answer. How close she had come to being her mother, to losing the love of her children permanently! She had been a reluctant mother to them and yet they loved her. She wondered how she really felt about her own mother and did not have an answer. Partly she felt pity, especially since she began reading into her mother's life. She also felt angry. Hazel never drank during the day and wondered how her mother looked after her kids if she was drunk. No wonder Iris was such a worried little girl. She felt she understood her sister better, even if her sister didn't understand herself. Iris obviously felt responsible for Hazel and looked after her little sister. She wished she had the letters her mother had sent to Grace and wondered if she was still alive. Maybe she still lived at the same address and she could write to her? It was all very sad, too many lives hurt by the action of one person.

"I think we all deserve a treat, boys!" she exclaimed loudly, surprising even herself.

Luke looked up from the TV. He didn't know what surprise there was in the house for him and Jack but he knew his mother had no more wine which was her favourite treat. He said nothing. He did not want to spoil the extra good mood she seemed to be in.

"What treat?" Jack asked excitedly.

"Ice cream!" she replied. "Let's walk to the shop for ice cream."

Luke didn't say anything about it being a school night or about it being cold outside because he really wanted an ice cream. He helped Jack into his coat and watched as his mother counted out just enough money for ice cream and then put her purse back on top of the microwave. He eyed her suspiciously.

"Is that all we're buying?"

"Yes, Luke," she smiled. "That's all we need."

Chapter 30

When Iris opened her eyes the ward was dark and quiet. She didn't know where she was or how long she had been there. Her last memory was going to bed in Hazel's and falling into a deep sleep. She remembered hearing her mother calling her. In her dream, she followed her mother down unfamiliar roads but every time she caught up with her, she could hear Hazel screaming for her to come back, begging her not to leave her.

Iris turned her head slightly. She could hear voices whispering in the distance but when she tried to turn her head, a sharp pain ripped through her chest, causing her to cough painfully. A light shone at the end of the room she was in. She tried to call out and found her voice was raspy and her throat felt like it was filled with broken glass. She raised her arm and waved towards the voices until a machine beside her started beeping loudly in the silent ward. She closed her eyes, exhausted from the slight exertion. A head came into view, a nurse she recognised from her previous stay.

"You're awake, Iris, that's brilliant. How are you feeling? Any pain?"

Iris tried to speak. She wet her lips and simply shook her head.

"Well, your husband will be delighted. I'll get him," the nurse said, smiling.

Iris frowned, confused. Husband? Perhaps she was dreaming after all.

When Mark came quietly to her bedside her heart lurched. He was here. An urge to cry overwhelmed her but she bit down on her lip, surprised at how vulnerable she had become, how needy. He took her hand and smiled sadly at her. She could see deep laughter-lines around his eyes and worry-lines on his forehead. He looked even more handsome than he was as a younger man.

"You gave us a bit of a fright," he said softly.

"When did you come?" she asked hoarsely. "What happened?"

"I arrived tonight. I was in New York so couldn't get here till now. You've been here for four days."

"Four days!" she said incredulously.

"You developed a secondary infection after the pneumonia. Your wound is infected as well so your body went into shock. It happens occasionally."

Iris took a deep breath. She couldn't believe she had been here for four days and couldn't remember a thing about it. Then a memory hit her or perhaps a strange dream.

"I heard Hazel reading letters to me, or maybe I dreamt it. I'm not sure," she frowned.

Mark smiled. "I told her to read to you. Apparently she found old letters a friend sent to your mother and read them to you. I'm surprised you didn't wake up and throttle her!" he laughed.

Iris smiled back at him. She felt so weak and helpless.

"I appreciate you being here," she said. "I don't expect it though. Not after . . . well . . ." Tears were welling in her eyes and she wondered if the drugs they had given her were causing her to be more tearful than she normally would be.

Mark stopped her. He put his fingers to her lips "Shh. It's okay. I want to be here."

He leant in and lifted her shoulders off the bed, sitting her up. He gasped at how thin she was but tried to hide it and hugged her tightly. He knew she was going to need a lot of care if she was going to recover.

"I have someone here who wants to see you," he said when he was sure she was no longer going to cry.

He knew she would not like to see her son while in such a state. Iris's eyes opened wide.

"K-Ke . . .?" she could not finish the word. She dared not think it could be true, that he was here, her son.

Mark nodded and slowly left her bedside. She could hear his footsteps moving away from her bed, making a loud sound on the cold linoleum floor and then disappearing.

Iris lay back on the mound of pillows that Mark had placed behind her. Her heart thumped and she could hear the monitor beside her speed up. It was making her more nervous.

A pain shot through her chest and made her cough loudly. She had turned to her right to press the bell, hoping a nurse would come and help, when she saw him, standing there nervously.

Her mouth dropped open.

"Kevin?"

He nodded. Her son was a man, almost unrecognisable to her except for his father's deep brown eyes and sallow skin. He was now seventeen and was about six feet tall with his father's thick mass of black curly hair. He stood awkwardly at the bottom of her bed and then looked down at his shoes. A large lump rose in Iris's throat and tears fell quickly down her face. She wanted to put her arms around him, to hold him. He was here standing less than six feet from her and yet it felt like he was a million miles away.

"Kevin . . ." She could not speak. There was much to say. Where would she start?

He moved closer to her, his father's same kind expression moving over his face. He sat on the bed and looked at her. He seemed to be examining her, his eyes moving from her face to her arms and back, wishing perhaps that he had memories of this woman who had given birth to him.

Iris cleared her throat. "I never thought I'd see you again," she said finally. "There's so much I want to tell you . . . if you'll listen . . ."

Kevin nodded and smiled. He seemed shy. She didn't know what to expect because she had never thought about this moment. When she imagined him he was a little baby and now he was a man.

"My dad said you've been very sick," he finally said in his posh English accent.

Iris nodded. "Is that why you've come?" she asked, unsure what answer she wanted to hear.

"I was worried we wouldn't get to see each other," he admitted. "I know you sent me a letter. My dad told me when we were in America. He's going to give it to me when we get home."

Iris noticed how Kevin referred to Mark as 'my dad', not just 'Dad' and it made her feel as if she was on the outside of this family . . . but what did she expect? She was a stranger to him.

"I wanted to tell you why I left. Not to look for forgiveness because I never expected that, but to make sure you didn't think it was anything to do with you. You were a perfect little baby and I loved you." Her lips quivered. She was trying hard not to cry. Talking was taking all of her energy. She was amazed at how weak she was but she had to tell him everything now. She might not get another chance. "My mother died when I was eleven. She was an alcoholic and, well, she didn't look after us. She put herself first. She ruined her health. I suppose a part of me always wondered if it was my fault. If there was something I could have done to prevent it . . . but what I should have realised was that I was just a child and that nothing was my fault. I didn't want you carrying those same thoughts around with you. I didn't want you to think that my leaving had anything to do with you. I should have done it sooner but I felt I had no right to contact you."

"I didn't think that. I never thought it was about me," he replied softly. "Dad explained that you had a severe depression but that you couldn't see that at the time."

Iris sobbed. This child that she had abandoned was so understanding, so mature that it almost hurt. She wondered if she would have preferred if he was angry – but he wasn't and it was not what she expected. She didn't know how to react.

She opened her locker drawer and took out the photo of Kevin that Hazel had put into her bag. She was glad to have it near. She handed it to him and he smiled.

"I have that photo at home," he beamed. "You left it for me."

Iris nodded. "I never forgot about you, Kevin. I've thought about you every single day. I just didn't know how to be a mother. I was afraid I'd do it wrong and you'd be damaged as a result."

As she finally broke down Kevin moved to her and held her awkwardly in his long, thin arms.

"Thank you," she sobbed. "Thank you."

Mark returned and sat on the other side of the bed and the three held each other in a tender embrace. She weakened between the two large men and slumped between them, exhausted. Mark moved her back gently towards the pillow.

"You need some rest," he said. "We're here for a few days and we'll be back tomorrow to see you."

Iris nodded and stared up at her son who still held onto her hand.

"I look forward to it," she replied.

As the two men walked down the long ward, Iris watched until they disappeared from view. A nurse, who couldn't help but overhear, walked over to her. There were tears in her eyes. She did not speak but squeezed Iris's hand gently. She mostly saw despair on this ward and was glad to witness some happiness. She knew that if Iris didn't make it, at least she had made her peace with her son.

As the nurse walked away, Iris closed her eyes and slowly fell into a deep satisfying sleep, a small smile remaining on her ghostly white face.

Chapter 31

Hazel couldn't stop thinking about the letters from her mother's friend. Before she began working on her new garden, she had finished a letter to Grace Mooney who she hoped was living at the same address. She put her phone number in it and some information about how she and Iris were doing. Hazel hoped that Grace had kept the letters that her mother had written. Now that Mark was in town for a few days she spent less time at the hospital. Iris seemed happier than she had been for a long, long time and her reunion with Kevin, however brief, had brought a brightness to her sister's eyes that she hadn't seen for years.

Hazel had borrowed two large books on plants from the library and set about designing a new garden. She intended to leave most of her father's small trees and some of the shrubs which had become overgrown but she wanted to add her own touch to the garden which was large and had a good aspect, enjoying sunshine whenever the sun actually shone. More than anything, Hazel wanted it to be an all-year-round garden, not just the spring or summer garden that most people went for. She had hoped that Iris would be well enough to help her with it but it would be a while before she would be strong enough to even leave the hospital. Instead Hazel had meticulously planned the garden on paper and today had bribed the boys to help dig the new border, with the promise of pizza for lunch. In her new design, she would have hebes and violas which would be beautiful all year around. In early spring she would have thick rows of daffodils and snowdrops. When summer came they could enjoy tulips, poppies and lilies. Then rows of colourful geraniums for autumn. She would replace the winter irises that had died off some years back. As the boys dug she was aware that a cold wind had blown up in the yard. She looked at Jack who was sniffing. She hadn't bought many of the new plants yet but had made sure that the ones she'd chosen wouldn't affect his asthma.

"You alright, love?" she asked him.

"Yes, Mam. I can't wait to show the garden to Iris."

Hazel smiled and patted his head.

The doorbell rang loudly through the back door which had been left open in case the hospital rang.

"Pizza!" she announced but her two co-workers, engrossed in their digging, didn't even look up.

Hazel picked her purse up from the kitchen and walked down the long hallway. She could see a tall figure through the glass panel at the top of the door as she opened her purse.

"How much?" she asked as she swung open the door. She looked up, her jaw dropped and fear choked her. She tried to step back and close the door but Pete Doyle pushed inside.

"Pete!" she gasped.

"I don't want to hurt ya, Hazel. I just want the gear," he said, dragging her into the sitting room.

"What gear?" she asked. She could hear the fear in her own voice and knew that Pete realised just how scared she was.

"Where are the kids?"

"They're not here – they're with Iris," she replied quickly, glancing at the half-open patio door and praying that they stayed in the garden until he left.

"Didn't expect you to know where it is. I hid it and you're going to stay very quiet while I get it."

Hazel gave him a look of disgust. It sickened her that he had used her house to hide drugs in, drugs that had almost killed Jack.

She could feel anger rising inside her. Pete caught her look and gripped her by the hair, dragging her towards the ground.

"Don't look at me like that," he snarled. "You don't know what'll happen to me if I don't return the stuff."

Still hanging on to her hair, he overturned the sofa and ripped the lining. Hazel's eyes were bulging and she could feel tears welling in them. She screamed from the pain. Pete let her go, then put his large hand over her mouth and stuck something hard into her ribs.

Oh God, she thought. He has a gun.

"Shut up with the screaming," he said menacingly.

She went limp against him and after a moment she felt the pressure on her ribs disappear.

With one hand still covering her mouth, Pete rummaged inside the sofa. Hazel could feel the urgency in his movements, the tension. He didn't seem to be able to find his treasure which alarmed her even more.

Perhaps whoever had broken in had found it? Perhaps someone else knew Pete hid it there. Hazel remembered how her intruder had overturned the sofa and ripped the lining. She had thought it was strange at the time but so was urinating in the hall so she forgot about it. It had taken her ages to sew it and she hadn't even finished paying for the sofa on hire purchase. She felt him loosen his grip on her as his search become more frantic. She tried to move away from him.

"Not so fast," he said threateningly.

Hazel looked into his sneering face and wondered what she had ever seen in him. He repulsed her. She could feel him deflate as he realised that someone had beat him to it. He looked at her, his teeth bared, his eyes bulging open. Slowly, she realised what he was thinking.

"No, Pete, I didn't even know it was there. There was a break-in. I swear. They must have taken it."

She pulled away, knowing Pete was about to rain blows upon her. She tried to free herself but he grabbed her shoulders and shook her until her teeth rattled.

"Who broke in?" he roared. "Come on, who? Who've you been talking to?"

"What? Pete, honestly, I don't know what you're talking about. I had to get the police. They even pissed on the floor!"

Pete shook her hard. He knew she was probably telling the truth but a deep anger was rising from him, born from the fear of what was going to happen to him if he didn't return the drugs. But he had to be sure that there was nothing she could tell him. He threw her onto her back and pinned her to the ground.

"Who . . .?" he started to ask but stopped suddenly with a sharp gasp. The colour drained from his face until all she was facing was two staring eyes. Then he slumped on top of her.

"Pete?" she said shakily, wondering if he was having a heart attack or something. She fought for breath, his shoulder covering her face, as she tried to push him off her. His weight was crushing her. She put her arms around his back and tried to roll him over but failed. She brought her hands around to his shoulders again to try to lever him off.

Her hands were covered in blood.

Hazel screamed, fear releasing strength she did not know she had as she pushed him off her and that's when she understood what had happened. Standing behind Pete Doyle was Luke, frozen and staring, a large bloodied kitchen knife in his hand.

Hazel was oblivious to the three garda cars and ambulance outside her front door as she sat in a daze in the living room. Mrs Whelan sat with her as a doctor examined Luke who was in shock and had not said one word since he plunged a knife into Pete Doyle.

Pete was alive and on his way to hospital.

The gardaí said that the gun was not loaded.

It turned out that Luke had the good sense to put his younger brother in the wheelie bin before entering the house. A search was about to be launched for Jack when someone heard whimpering in the back garden and followed the sound to the bin. He said Luke had put him in there when they heard their mother scream, telling him to be quiet and not to get out for any reason.

Hazel could hear people asking her if she was alright but all she could think of was "Why me?" She felt that there was no turning back from this now. There was no way she could ever put the pieces of this together and get on with life. What had happened to her and Luke today was far worse than anything she'd ever experienced before. Whether Pete died or not, she knew that Luke would be taken to a detention centre. If he lived, she worried that he might come after them. Hazel knew she was beaten. She laughed softly to herself and raised up her hands, saying "I surrender!" A doctor was called and gave her an injection.

Two social workers arrived with a female garda and tried to take the boys, kicking and screaming, out to a waiting car. It was clear to the authorities that Hazel Fay could not provide a safe environment for her children and that the older one was now showing signs of extreme violent behaviour. Mrs Whelan spoke with police officers and begged them to leave the boys with her. She told them a little about the girls' own traumatic upbringing and said that taking the children away would devastate Hazel but they informed her that as there were no immediate family members to care for the younger boy, a registered foster home would have to be found.

As Hazel slumped into the armchair, the last thing she saw and heard was her sons screaming for her as two guards tried to prise their fingers from the living-room door.

"I've ruined my children's lives," was the last thing she heard herself say as she drifted into unconsciousness.

At the hospital, Iris was propped up in bed, chatting to her son and Mark and oblivious to what had happened at Hazel's house. The atmosphere wasn't exactly comfortable and there were lots of long silences when neither Iris nor Kevin could think of anything to say. She was grateful for Mark who filled the silences with stories of their courting days in London when Iris was a green trainee nurse in the large city. While she knew that they were both leaving the following day, she was glad to have them here right now and refused to think about tomorrow. Mark promised to come back soon and had spoken about moving her to a private convalescent home until she was strong enough to return home. He knew Hazel wasn't able to care properly for Iris and he wanted to pay for private care. Iris surprised herself by saying that she would think about it. She was normally so proud.

When Hazel did not show up at the hospital by evening, Mark phoned her house and returned white-faced to Iris's bed.

"She's got the flu," he lied. "They won't be in for a few days." He could see Iris deflate. She was looking forward to seeing the boys.

"She's never sick," Iris said in a concerned, gravelly voice.

"Well, she wanted to come in but when I heard her coughing I asked her not to. You cannot afford to have anyone sick around you right now."

Iris smiled an appreciative smile towards him and there was a moment when there was a warm exchange between them, a moment when they seemed transported back to the early days of their relationship. She was enjoying having someone care for her so much. Kevin noticed it and wondered if his mother still had feelings for his dad. It made him feel uncomfortable but he didn't know why. He knew his dad had gone through hell when his stepmother left. They both did. He didn't want him to get hurt again and Iris was very ill after all. If she did not pull through this and Mark had fallen in love with her all over again, he'd never get over it.

But there was another reason. Kevin was glad to have met Iris and knew seeing her would heal some of the hurt he had felt growing up without her, but he had grown into a sensible, mature boy for his age and felt he had come through a lot with his dad's help. He wasn't sure if he wanted Iris to be a regular part of his life. He had managed without her and there was a fear attached to letting her in, a vulnerability that he wasn't sure he could expose himself to.

The two men eventually said goodbye to her and Iris settled into a long evening without a visitor. She couldn't wait to get out and wondered if Mark was right, if she did need to go somewhere to recuperate. If she did, she doubted she'd ever be able to repay him. Her shop had been closed for weeks now and her regular customers would by now have found themselves a new seamstress. She wondered what she would do for money and also wondered how Hazel was coping financially as she usually helped her sister out. She lay back in bed and tried not to let these worries get to her. She had to get better. She had to remain positive. It would be alright. She was sure of it.

In the middle of the night, unable to sleep, Iris sat up in bed and tried to read. She could hear the nurses talking about how someone had been rushed into surgery after being stabbed by a child.

Good God she thought to herself. What is Dublin coming to?

An orderly joined in on the conversation and told the nurses he knew the man, that he had grown up with Pete Doyle and lived on the same road as him even now.

Iris felt a shiver run down her spine. Could it be the same Pete Doyle, she wondered as a feeling of dread came over her.

"Nurse?" she called.

The nurse walked over to her.

"You say that a man was stabbed?"

The nurse nodded.

"Yes, but you shouldn't be listening, Iris. You should be asleep," she scolded gently.

"Who stabbed him? Please tell me. I think I know him," Iris pleaded. Her heart was thumping. It was unlike Hazel not to phone and she now had a sinking feeling in her stomach that something was horribly wrong. She could feel the fear rise up in her throat.

The nurse moved closer, ensuring that she could not be heard.

"A child, would you believe. Apparently," she whispered, "the man attacked the child's mother. I heard that they were alright. The kid just tried to protect her. Frightening what some children are exposed to, isn't it?"

Iris let out a loud cry, scaring the nurse.

"Oh God, no, I think it's my sister. Please let me use the phone, please!" She threw the covers off herself and tried to move her thin, weak legs over the side of the bed.

The nurse looked closely at her patient. She knew that if Iris didn't find out whether her family were alright it wouldn't do her failing health any good. At the same time, if any of her family were hurt, it could also set her back. Either way, it would be all over the papers tomorrow so she might as well find out now.

"I'll get you a wheelchair," she replied and marched off in search of one.

Mrs Whelan spoke softly to Iris over the phone, assuring her that Hazel was alright. She told her that she begged the guards to let her keep the boys but that they wouldn't hear of it. She swallowed when Iris began to cry loudly into the phone. She told her that Hazel was still asleep from the injection the doctor had given her but that she would take her to her house tonight where she could stay until she felt able to return home. Mrs Whelan assured her that she'd get her to call tomorrow and begged her not to worry, ridiculously claiming that everything would be just fine.

Iris put down the phone and continued to cry for the boys who would surely be separated tonight and would be cared for by strangers. She could not help but hope that, if Doyle survived the attack, he be put in her ward where she could smother him in his sleep, but she immediately felt guilty for thinking of doing something so awful. Doyle would one day get his comeuppance. She knew that, sooner or later, you had to pay your bill and that Pete Doyle's bill would be very costly. She knew because she felt that she was paying hers now and, if she survived this illness, she would probably be paying for her mistakes for the rest of her life.

Chapter 32

When Mark arrived the following morning alone, Iris was disappointed not to have a chance to say goodbye to her son.

"You found out about Hazel?" he asked. The nurse had had a word with him as he entered the ward.

"Yes," she said quietly.

Mark had noticed the change in her as soon as he sat on her bed and knew it was not all about Hazel. She was going to miss Kevin.

"I tried to speak with Hazel this morning but the phone rang out," said Mark. "I phoned the guards and I told them I was family. They said Luke . . . is in a juvenile detention centre and Jack's been placed with a family in Dublin."

Iris felt she just couldn't bear it.

"Sorry Kevin's not here," Mark continued. "I had to get him to stay with my parents. The home help cancelled this morning. Want to know what her reason was?"

Iris nodded even though she wasn't remotely interested.

"Her brother was stabbed yesterday and she had to stay at the hospital."

Iris looked up, amazed at this.

"No! You don't mean . . .?"

He nodded. "Yes, their home help is Doyle's sister."

It was certainly a small world.

"And then he ends up in the same hospital as me!" Iris added, even more amazed at how lives cross and paths sometimes collide.

"Speaking of hospitals . . ." Mark started.

"Yes," Iris said.

"Yes?"

"Yes. I'll go to the convalescent home. I know I can't go home and I can't go to Hazel's. She has enough on her plate without looking after me." She added softly, "I appreciate what you're doing for me." She looked down. She didn't want to be upset, not today when they were leaving.

Mark smiled. He knew he wouldn't rest easy when he returned to London unless he was sure that Iris was being properly cared for.

"Mark?"

"Yes?"

"Why are you doing all of this for me?"

Mark was taken by surprise. He had not expected her to ask this question. He didn't have an answer for it, at least not an answer he thought she'd want to hear. He took a deep breath, stalling for time and rubbed his hands together.

"Why not?" was all he could think of.

She frowned and gave him a look that said she wasn't falling for it.

He blushed slightly. He leant forward and took her hand, smoothing it gently.

"Because I care about you," he said so quickly she almost thought she'd imagined it.

"You . . . you still care for me?" she asked.

"Of course I do. We were once married. We have a son. We're still friends. Aren't we?"

Iris almost felt disappointed. A part of her was enjoying having Mark around. But he was married now and she knew that she would have to keep her feelings to herself. She had not stopped thinking about him since he had re-entered her life and realised that she still loved him, that perhaps she had never stopped loving him. But it was too late, for both of them.

"I'll go to the convalescent home on one condition!"

"Yes?"

"That I pay you back when I can."

Mark nodded. "Deal," he said, even though he knew Iris had no idea just how much it cost to stay in one of those places. But the money didn't matter.

Up until a couple of days ago he hadn't thought that she would survive but, looking at her now, despite the disappointment in her eyes that they were leaving again, she looked healthier.

"I'll arrange it today," he said smiling.

He stood and dug his hands into his overcoat pockets. He hated saying goodbye to her.

"Iris?"

"Mmm?" She was dreading this part. She was never good at goodbyes and always cried. She even cried saying goodbye to people she hardly knew. She'd been like that her whole life and could never figure out why.

"Kevin is graduating from school in May. It's nothing too formal, just some prizes and suchlike, a winding-up of the school year before they plunge into the exams. I . . . we'd like you to come, and Hazel if she'd like. You should be much stronger by then."

Iris's eyes widened. "Miriam wouldn't mind?"

"No," he said softly.

"And Kevin asked, did he?"

"Yes, he'd like you to come." This wasn't exactly true. It was Mark's idea that Iris be invited and Kevin was happy to do so if it was important to his dad.

"I – I'd love to come . . . if you're sure . . ." Iris was choked up. She didn't know what else to say.

"Good!"

He leant in and kissed her on the cheek, then moved back from her bed. She looked so vulnerable it almost broke his heart. If she'd been strong enough he would have liked to take her to England to a hospital there where he could keep an eye on her. He moved towards her again and kissed her softly on the lips.

"Bye," he said. "I'll phone you tomorrow."

Iris touched her lips as he turned and walked away. She didn't know what the kiss meant but smiled as she waved him off. She watched until he was out of view and slid down into the bed, still touching her lips, savouring the moment he touched her. A voice in her head tried to warn her – "He is no longer yours" – but she banished it and smiled serenely to herself. It was enough that he cared for her. It would have to be.

Hazel finished answering questions from the guards who had called to Mrs Whelan's house to go over her statement from the previous evening.

Before that the social worker had visited, informing her of the action the Health and Safety Executive had taken to provide care for her younger son. She could visit Jack tomorrow when he had settled in at the foster home the HSE had taken him to. The guards, she said, would update her on Luke's placement as it was out of the HSE's hands.

It had been fourteen hours since the incident and a deep physical pain at being separated from her boys had begun to permeate her body. She couldn't bear to think of Luke locked up in some place with delinquents. Her son was not violent. He was simply protecting his mother from Pete Doyle. It was she, the child's mother, who had brought violence into their home. She, who had brought Pete Doyle into her sons' lives with his beer-swilling and drug-selling lifestyle. And even if she hadn't know about his drug-pushing, he had hit her, more than once if she was to be truthful, and she had exposed her boys, her precious babies to that lifestyle. For what? She couldn't understand why she did not put them first. She didn't know why she made those choices when every ounce of her knew they were the wrong ones. Yet she kept doing it. Doyle was simply the last in a long line of losers she had taken up with. And her baby. Sweet innocent Jack who loved her so much, sitting in God knows whose kitchen this morning eating breakfast with a family he didn't know. Strangers. Would they be kind or would they be like the foster mother she and Iris had? Aunty Joan, as they had been made to call her, had met all of their needs, saw to it that they ate well and had clean clothes and school books but she did not hug them or tell them how good they were. She did not sit them on her knee and read stories or ask how their day was. Foster work was a business for her, a way to make extra money and she made that very clear to Iris and Hazel and all of the other poor unfortunates who passed through her door. Hazel couldn't bring herself to think about how she would get her boys back because deep down she believed that she would never get them back, that this time the authorities would see to it that the boys got a proper long-term home. They would have her file of course, detailing how she herself had been the long-term foster child of an alcoholic mother. It would detail her own battle with drink and her long list of abusive relationships. It would have a detailed record of the boys being taken into care when their married father put her in the hospital. She had got them back then, had pleaded and promised and had won. She did not think she would win now. Her drink problem had persisted and she had continued to expose her children to what they would call "inappropriate adults". She would not see her boys again except in a grotty little green-painted room with a social worker sitting in the background, staring at her, disapproving, looking down her little toffee nose at her.

Mrs Whelan saw the guards out and Hazel roughly brushed her hair and left the house to go and see Iris. She needed to see her. She needed to ask Iris for her help, despite how ill her sister was.

When she arrived at the hospital Iris was sitting up in a chair with blankets wrapped around her. She looked pale and there were deep lines underneath her eyes. Hazel knew her sister hadn't slept a wink with worry. As Hazel recounted the whole episode through sobs, Iris looked like the life had drained out of her. Hazel knew her sister wanted to say "I told you this would happen – I warned you" but that she was too ill to say anything, too weak. She had never seen Iris look so defeated before.

When she had finished recounting the night's events in as much detail as she could bear, Iris looked towards the ground and Hazel thought she wasn't going to say anything, wasn't going to offer the advice she so badly needed, the words of reassurance, the comfort.

"Iris?" she said.

Iris looked up and opened her eyes wider as though she had been sleeping.

"Yes?"

"What am I going to do?"

Iris had been thinking of this very thing all night long. Images of her son, so well-reared, a product of a functional upbringing with a father who loved him had flashed through her mind throughout the night. She thought of Luke, of the awful thing he went through and how this would scar him for the rest of his life. She couldn't imagine what he was going through right now, what he was thinking, feeling. It brought hot tears to her eyes. She knew the boys deserved the same life that her son had known. Her mind had raced all night with memories of all the stupid and dangerous things Hazel had done throughout the boys' short lives, the men, the drinking. It was time to face up to it. Hazel was never going to be a good mother to her sons. Iris knew her sister loved the boys but that wasn't enough. They needed to be safe and she knew that wherever they were today, they were safe. She did not want to think of them being separated from her, of her not being able to see them, visit them, hug them, but she also knew that the boys deserved a chance for a normal life, if it wasn't already too late for them to know what that was. Iris wiped the sweat from her brow and breathed out slowly. She knew her sister wouldn't be happy with what she had to say.

"You're going to leave them where they are. You have no choice. You have to put them first, Hazel. Give them the chance of a life. If it's the last thing you do for them."

Huge tears sprang to Hazel's eyes in anger.

"You want me to walk away? Like you? No! My boys need to be with me. I am their mother! I will get them back. I expected . . ." Hazel swallowed hard. She couldn't believe her sister wasn't standing in her corner. She had always supported her. Even when they were fighting she knew she could depend on Iris for help but now her sister was siding with the authorities.

"I expected you to understand," she said, standing and moving slightly away from her sister.

Iris reached out and grabbed her sister's forearm. Hazel recoiled. Iris's hand was icy cold despite the sweat that she could see dripping down her forehead.

Iris released her arm. "Hazel, please. Do what is best for them. Think about it, please."

Hazel stared over her sister's head and did not look at her. She focused on the window and looked at the sky.

"I'll be back tomorrow," she said sharply as she turned and walked down the long ward.

Hazel stood across the street from the house at which the social worker had told her Jack would now be staying. It was a nice two-storey mock-Tudor house in an ordinary housing estate. Bikes were strewn around the neatly cut lawn and a small doll's pram was parked outside the front door. The social worker had matter-of-factly told her that she could appeal the HSE decision and arrange for her case to be heard. As if Hazel would consider doing anything else. Damn right she would appeal. Who did they think they were? In the meantime, Jack would be living here and she could visit him twice a week. She looked at the card the social worker had given her. Vincent and May Egan were the foster parents. Hazel swallowed hard. She hadn't been into one of these places since she was a teenager. She could feel her chest tighten and her breathing become laboured. She opened the gate and walked up the long path to the front door.

Hazel pressed the bell once and listened as a musical tone rang loudly inside the house. She straightened her T-shirt and jacket and smoothed down her hair. She pushed back her shoulders and gritted her teeth, anxious to come across as confident and assertive rather than the bag of nerves she really was. When the door swung open, a slightly overweight man greeted her. He was smiling like a Cheshire cat and in an instant she recognised him. Vinnie Egan. He had been in foster care with her. She remembered his younger brother Joe whom she had allowed to kiss her once in the back garden of their foster home. They were both only fifteen at the time and even then she knew he wasn't her type. He was quiet and shy whereas his brother Vinnie was always laughing and joking. She remembered how much he annoyed her when he'd come home from school every day smiling and was always thanking Aunty Joan and her husband for everything they did for him. What he had to be thankful for she could never understand. She knew his parents had both been alcoholics and that he and Joe had suffered terrible neglect, much worse than she or Iris had endured before they were taken into permanent foster care. She hoped he didn't remember her. It would be too embarrassing, and not only because he had made a success of his life and was now fostering *her* child. He watched as her embarrassment deepened. He held out his hand and put his arm gently around her back.

"Hazel," he said warmly. "I thought it was too much of a coincidence. When I saw your name on Jack's paperwork, I wondered if it was the same Hazel Fay. I'm so glad you are here." He said it as if he meant it, as if she had dropped in for a coffee and wasn't here to see her child who had arrived suddenly on his doorstep not even 24 hours ago. No doubt he would have been informed of the history, the whole sordid story of how her older boy had tried to stab her violent, drug-pushing boyfriend and was now locked up in a juvenile detention centre at only eight years of age. Christ! Tears sprang back into her eyes and she fought them. She was not going to cry. But she could feel herself weaken under the weight of his arm, strong yet gentle against her back. He led her down a brightly painted hallway and sat her down in a cosy kitchen.

"It's okay," he said so quietly that she almost felt as if she was alone in the room.

She leant forward and sobbed into her hands. She felt a tissue being shoved into her hand. She blew her nose loudly into it and tried to regain her composure.

"I'll fight it," she said. "I won't let them away with it. I'll go to court and I'll – I'll win!"

Vinnie smiled sympathetically at her. "Look, it may not come to that. There's a process. If the social workers feel you've made adequate changes to your life, they may return the boys to you but it'll be slow. They'll meet with you every week, supervise you with the boys and then maybe they'll allow overnight visits."

"Maybe? *They'll allow*! They're *my* kids!" she bellowed.

Vinnie sighed and looked at the door where a small, somewhat plump woman had appeared. Hazel could hear the sounds of children playing and laughing in the garden. She recognised one of the voices. It was Jack and he was laughing. She stood and looked out but the kitchen faced out onto the side of the house and she could not see him.

"I'll bring him in when you're feeling better," Vinnie said. "This is my wife, May," he added as the woman extended her small hand to Hazel.

Hazel could see the deep laughter lines in the woman's face and her kind eyes. Long, narrow eyes that looked like they were smiling. She looked back at Vinnie and thought how suited he and his wife were and how she knew this must be a happy home. May excused herself and Hazel blew her nose loudly into the tissue and rubbed her eyes. She was afraid that she had made a show of herself and had got angry at the wrong people, people who were trying to help.

"It's . . . I didn't know . . . this is awkward," she finally said.

"When I saw your name I said to May 'I know this woman'. I told her we were like brother and sister."

Hazel cringed slightly. That wasn't how she remembered it. She knew Iris liked the brothers well enough but Vinnie never seemed to have paid Hazel the slightest bit of attention.

"You kept to yourself, but I remember you well. I remember the dagger's looks at anyone if they got in your way. Ha! Ah well, you liked your space, Hazel, that's all!" he laughed, as if reading her thoughts.

Hazel squirmed and decided that Vinnie Egan hadn't changed one bit. He was still the same gombeen he always was. Laughing when there was absolutely nothing to be laughing about.

"How come you were allowed . . . I mean . . . being a foster child and all . . . I mean, what would you know . . . why would they allow you to foster children?" She intended to hurt him even though she knew this was childish and probably foolish. The man was looking after her child after all. This man had power over her. He could tell the HSE anything, say she wasn't ready to get Jack back. She looked into his face and could see that he had not taken any offence which annoyed her.

"When I finished college – that's where May and I met – I began working as an accountant but I didn't really like it. I wanted to do more. To give something back. But, you know, the years drifted by – mortgage, financial commitments, everyday life got in the way of me thinking about what I really wanted to do. When we tried to have children we found it wasn't going to happen, not naturally anyway, so we adopted two boys, biological brothers. They are fifteen and sixteen now, at school and doing well. It reminded me of Joe and me and . . . well, it got me thinking about how lucky I had been. May and I decided to foster and now, apart from our own two, we have Nicholas who is eight and Lisa who's five. They'll both be with us long term. From time to time we get short-term placements, like Jack. Unless there's good reason not to, the HSE tries to place children as near to their own community as possible. That way they can keep going to their own school and it causes the least disruption to their lives."

"You'll be taking Jack to his own school?"

Hazel reddened again. The thought of Mrs Malone knowing that her child was in foster care made her feel nauseous. She already knew that her son's infant-class teacher didn't think much of her. She would have preferred that Jack didn't go to school until the court case was over. He was only five and she felt he wouldn't miss much in a few weeks.

"May will take him every morning. Lisa's school isn't far from there. I still work but I retrained as a juvenile liaison officer."

"And they'll know that . . . ?" Hazel began but she could not finish the sentence.

"Yes. I'm afraid so, Hazel. We have to tell the school who'll be picking Jack up, show them the order and that."

She looked around the neat, homely house and the success Vinnie had made of his life. Yet he had an even worse start in life than she had. Where had she gone wrong? Why did he succeed where she hadn't?

"You . . . you probably think badly of me," she said. It was a statement, not a question.

Vinnie did not answer her. "The important thing is that Jack is here and he is safe. Things might work or – or they might not," he said, rather too matter-of-factly for her liking. "But while you sort things out, you'll know your son is being well cared for."

The last sentence stung but she accepted it. She realised that the whole time she had been here she had not asked about how her son had settled in. If he had cried last night, if he'd eaten, if he understood what was happening and she knew that this was the difference between Vinnie Egan and her. She was always thinking about how things affected *her* or reflected on *her*. How was she going to change this? She did love her boys but she always saw things from her own point of view first. Maybe Iris was right. Maybe she should walk away and leave her boys to live in places like this. Good homes where they would be safe. But she couldn't do that. She needed them. They were all she had and if she wasn't their mother, what was she?

"I intend to get them back," she said curtly as if Vinnie himself was responsible for her losing her children. She knew she was behaving childishly but she couldn't help it. She was hurt and she was going to hurt someone in return.

He said nothing and slowly heaved his body off the kitchen chair.

"I'll get Jack. He'll be thrilled to see you. What he knows is that he will stay with us for while. That's about it. I'd be careful what you say to him Hazel. He's only five. Thankfully, he doesn't know all the details of what happened last night. He might ask where Luke is. We have told him we don't know but that we think he's probably in a very nice place."

Hazel did not respond. She stood and waited while Vinnie left the room through a door on the right. He came back within minutes with Jack close behind him.

"Mam!" he shouted when he saw her.

She bit her lip as the urge to cry returned. She decided that she would be strong, that she would not cry.

Vinnie left them alone and went through the door that led into the hallway. She could imagine him or his wife waiting outside, making sure that she didn't try to run away with Jack. She smoothed his hair as he squirmed with excitement, dashing from one story to another.

"Yes, Jack, Mammy's listening."

A week passed and Hazel had been to see Jack once more. She didn't like to admit it to Iris but seeing her baby so settled and happy had angered her. She wanted to shake him and ask why he wasn't missing her. She knew he was only five and that he thought he was on holiday but still she had wanted him to pine for her, to plead with her to take him with her. What also worried her was that he seemed to be missing his brother more and spent much of their visit asking where Luke was and why they couldn't go on a holiday to the same place.

Only once had she been allowed to see Luke. When she arrived at the detention centre, she was brought through a maze of locked rooms with window grills and security cameras on each wall. When they finally brought her to the visiting area, Luke was sitting alone on a hard plastic orange chair. He was dressed in newish-looking clothes. He looked down when she entered the room and would not raise his eyes to meet hers. She hugged him but he didn't respond so she sat down next to him and put an arm around his shoulders. She asked him if he was okay. When he didn't answer she gently continued to question him, trying to coax him to speak to her, but he stayed mulishly silent.

A social worker sat in one corner of the huge sparsely furnished room and looked out of the window, feigning disinterest, but Hazel could tell that she was listening to her every word and would spend the afternoon busily typing up her report on the inadequacies of Ms Hazel Fay, mother of two.

"Luke, please talk to me," Hazel begged at last. She desperately wanted to know if he was alright. If the staff were kind. If there were other kids to play with here. Nice kids. But he sat there, silent, his eyes fixed on the red linoleum. The social worker stood and shook her head, then beckoned for Hazel to walk with her towards the door. Hazel wanted to refuse, to say her time wasn't up but she knew that it was for Luke's sake that the woman was cutting the visit short. The social worker spoke briefly on her phone and almost immediately another woman arrived who went and told Luke to come with her. Hazel went back and gave him a brief hug, then he was led through another door on the far side of the room. Hazel called "Bye, love!" after him but he did not turn back as he left.

"He hasn't spoken since he's been here," the social worker said.

"We were hoping he'd speak to you, but no matter. I'm Gillian and I've been dealing with Luke since he arrived. Our psychologist, George Kane, is seeing him every day. Progress has been slow but Luke will talk when he wants to. Mr Kane asked for you to come here tomorrow at ten to speak with him if that suits."

Hazel nodded and silently followed the woman back through the maze of corridors.

When she finally stepped outside the main door she took a huge breath, drawing the crisp air into her lungs. She stood then quietly outside the dark and dismal building for what seemed like an eternity. Her child was in there. Locked up and refusing to speak to anyone and yet she felt strangely numb as though none of it was real, as if any time soon she would wake up and find it was all a dream. She felt cut off from Luke as though the child in that building was not her own but that he was out there somewhere, hiding from her, her cheeky, mischievous, older-than-his-years son.

She walked on wobbly legs towards the bus stop and made her way to the hospital to see Iris. Her life and the whereabouts of her loved ones were as fragmented as she felt. Iris in the hospital and Jack and Luke at different ends of the city – one within minutes of her, painfully close and happy in his new home, and the other now on the other side of the city, out of reach, in every sense of the word.

When she arrived at Iris's bedside she found her sitting up in a large chair that made her look even smaller than she was. Hazel slumped down on the end of the bed and looked at her. An uneasy silence had settled between them since their conflict about the boys, neither knowing exactly what to say.

"How's Mark?" she asked, trying to find something different to talk about.

Iris raised her eyebrows but understood that her sister wasn't ready to update her on her nephew's wellbeing.

"He's insisted on paying for me to go to a convalescent home and he's . . ."

Iris stopped speaking, afraid at how her sister would react to the next bit of news she had. "He's invited us all to Kevin's graduation in May."

"And you're going?" Hazel asked, amazed at how quickly the three seemed to have put the past to rest.

"Why not?" Iris asked sharply.

"No reason," Hazel replied nervously. She was always uncomfortable when Iris got annoyed. Her sister's blue eyes could cut through her.

"He'd like you to come too. And the boys . . . if . . . well . . ."

Hazel seemed to brighten up.

"Did he? Oh, yes, it's exactly what we need. By then they'll be back with me and oh, it'll be lovely. The four of us. We could get the ferry – you know I won't fly, Iris. Oh, yes," she said, beaming. "Do you think you'll be well enough?"

"Yes," Iris nodded. "It's months away and I . . . I wouldn't miss it for the world."

Hazel stared off into the distance, imagining herself, with her boys on their very first overseas holiday, even if it was only across the water. This was just what she needed, a goal, something to focus on. Something good.

"Oh, maybe we could go and see that friend of Mam's in Sussex? It's only about an hour from London. We could get a train."

Iris's eyes opened wide. "Oh no, I don't think it's a good idea, Hazel. It'd drag up too much from the past. Some things are better left alone." She watched her sister's face crumble and crease.

"Well, I'd like to see her. She might be able to tell us things about Mam and Dad that we didn't know. I'd like to see where he is buried. I've always wanted to do that. Put some flowers down, something he'd like. And you know, I've learnt a lot about Mam from those letters. I think it'd help me understand her better. Some of the things in it remind me of . . . of us, you know? How things turned out for us." Hazel swallowed.

Iris looked away, trying to think.

"I'm not interested, Hazel," she finally replied, knowing her younger sister wouldn't go anywhere without her. She wouldn't have the courage.

"Well, maybe while you're with Mark and Kevin, I'll take the boys by train," Hazel said authoritatively, taking Iris by surprise.

Iris frowned. She knew there was no point in trying to talk Hazel out of this right now.

Luke sat across from the man who told him to call him George even though his mother said he should always call grown-ups by their last names. The only adult he had ever called by their first name was Pete and he never wanted to think about him ever again. But he knew that he would never stop thinking about Pete Doyle and that he would not sleep tonight and or any other night for the rest of his life because every time he tried to close his eyes he could see a long knife sticking out of Pete Doyle's back and it scared him. He hadn't meant to do it. He didn't even remember deciding to do it. He just saw Pete Doyle on top of his mam on the floor through the patio door. Pete had told him that he'd come back and kill his mam and then kill him. Maybe he'd even kill Jack, he thought. So he hid his brother in the bin and before he knew it he stuck the knife into Pete's back. He was glad Pete wasn't dead because if he was, he'd be able to haunt him and he'd never have any peace from a ghost because they could go anywhere. He couldn't speak because all he wanted to do was scream and he knew if he didn't speak, he could control the screaming and no one would know how frightened he was.

That night, the gardaí, Mrs Whelan and that social worker who held him so close to her that he could feel her heart beating, they all said how very brave he was and how proud of him they were but this just made matters worse. He didn't feel brave. He was frightened and now he was never going to be able to tell anyone this.

He watched as George eyed him closely and waited patiently for him to answer his question. He was wasting his time, Luke thought, because he was never going to be able to speak again, not ever.

Chapter 33

Four days after Iris moved to the convalescent home, Hazel, who had moved into Iris's temporarily, returned to her house to collect her mail. She heard from a woman at the school that Pete would be out of hospital soon. That was the problem in Ireland: everyone knew what was happening and loved telling you even if you didn't want to know. She hoped Luke wouldn't get to hear about it but she knew he couldn't, not where he was. He had still not said one word to any staff member in the centre and while Jack was happy enough in his new home, he had begun to ask questions about when he could see Luke and when they could go home. She was hopeful that Pete wouldn't bother her as the police would surely be watching him and he was in enough trouble already – but she also knew that her ex-boyfriend wasn't very bright and would be more interested in settling a score than reducing his prison time.

She stepped over a bundle of junk mail and walked to the kitchen to check that everything was alright. The house seemed so deserted, so silent. She almost felt as if it resented her leaving and that it was watching her as she moved about checking windows and doors. As she checked the kitchen she looked out at the half-dug border. A lump rose in her throat. They had been so happy that day, the three of them, laughing and planning. Why was it, she wondered, that every time happiness and normality seemed within her grasp it was suddenly snatched away? Hazel sighed and opened the fridge to make a cup of tea. She switched the kettle on but unplugged it when she realised that the milk was sour. She opened a cupboard to get a glass for water and noticed a half bottle of wine on the top shelf. She imagined herself pouring a glass but snatched the bottle out and quickly poured it down the sink before she had time to change her mind. She walked into the hall and picked up the post which consisted of two utility bills, several advertising leaflets and two large letters. She lifted the first one. It was from FÁS. She opened the two-page letter and scanned it, expecting a refusal, such was her luck of late. She couldn't believe her eyes. She had a place on the course. The second page gave directions to the centre as well as information on what to bring with her when the course started in May. Hazel felt her spirits rise. Perhaps things were going to be alright after all? Iris was getting better and if she could get Luke to talk to her, she would be happy enough with her lot. The other letter was a thick one in a hard cardboard envelope. She looked at the stamp. It was from England, from Grace Mooney. Her heart jumped. This was even better than her letter about the course. She opened it quickly. Inside was a separate letter on top of a folded pile of old letters which were tied together in an old green ribbon. Hazel quickly read the letter and instantly recognised the handwriting even though it looked a little shakier.

Dear Hazel,

I can't tell you how much it meant to get your letter. I was a good friend of your mam's, her only friend, I think, Lord rest her. But of course you already knew that. Well, about your mam, I didn't hear from her for a couple of years before she died. I was very upset when I heard through a friend from Dublin who was home when it happened. Months had passed by then so I didn't even get to the funeral. Mind you, times were tough then so I probably wouldn't have been able to afford it anyway. The last few years of her life were rough on her and she didn't answer my letters. You were very young then. I only met you twice, when you were really little. I am glad you and Iris are well. I put in the letters that I kept. Some of them got lost over the

*years so I hope you can piece them together and that they don't
upset you. She was very down, you know.*

*Some things are better left alone, I often think, but I
understand that you want to know more about her. My
daughter lives with me now. My husband died a few years
back so she moved in to help me. I have arthritis. I was older
than your mam even though we were in the same class at
school. I was a bit thick, got kept back. Ha. That brings back
funny memories. Your mam was gas back then. She was shy
in crowds but when we were on our own, she was always
laughing and never getting upset at her cranky mother. I don't
know if you remember your grandmother? Anyway, if you
are ever over this way, I'd love to see you and Iris too. It
would do me good to see Liz's girls all grown up and happy.*

Love
Grace

"All grown up and happy," Hazel repeated slowly. She was neither
of those things. She put the letter down and opened the first letter
in the pile. It was not dated. She read it slowly and noticed the
terrible handwriting. She had never seen her mother's handwriting
and wondered if she always wrote like this. Surely not – she had
been a secretary once, after all. It crossed Hazel's mind that her
mother was drunk when she wrote this letter and she suddenly
remembered Iris's words, words echoed by her mother's friend:
"*Some things are better left alone.*" But Hazel didn't want to
believe that this was true. This was her opportunity to find out
about her parents, her only chance, and no one was going to tell her
otherwise. She opened the two-page letter and suddenly felt so
nervous that she felt she would love to have a drink while reading
them. She briefly regretted pouring the wine down the sink.

Dear Grace
*How are things? I hope you and the kids are well and of
course John. Nothing has changed here. My mother still isn't
speaking to me and Jack now refuses to go to see her. I don't*

think they'll ever get along although I admit he has tried. I don't know why she doesn't like him. I have to admit I'm finding it a bit lonely. I seem to have had more friends in England and haven't got the know any of the women around the place. I know a few of them think I'm too big for my boots because Jack earns good money and we have a car. Some days I feel very low and wish I was dead although I look at my two girls and feel bad for thinking it. Jack takes me to these fancy do's where he works but I feel even less at home there. The people are snobs and Jack thinks they are his friends and that he is not the humble gardener. That, of course, annoys him and we fight. We fight about everything. He goes on about my drinking but when I am alone, I need a glass or two to ease my nerves. I don't know why I feel so nervous. I haven't been right since Iris was born. The doctor gave me pills but they made me so drowsy that I stopped taking them. I'd take a job to get out for a while except I'd have to pay someone to look after the girls. There's no way I'd let my mother look after them. She's already making favourites between the girls. I won't have that. She did that to me and Eileen. I want the girls to be close. Jack is still spending more time at work than he needs. Sometimes I think he's having a thing with the boss's stuck-up wife. Her husband is away most of the time in France so she invites Jack in for a drink at the end of the day. She sends a bottle of wine home to me, scraps from the table. The leftovers for Liz. Story of my life.

Most days now I can't get myself up out of bed in the mornings. You wouldn't believe what Iris is capable of. She's a great girl. She's only eight but she dresses Hazel, gets her breakfast and then takes her to school. Hazel's just started junior infants and so far she seems to like it. Anyway, as usual, I am moaning. Life just seems so monotonous. Same thing every day. I hope things are more upbeat for you. Thank God I have you to write to.

Christmas will be here before we know it.

Write soon.

Elizabeth

Hazel reread the letter and tried to digest the contents. Her mother sounded so alone in the world. In many ways, she felt that Iris and herself were like their mother in that they did not make friends easily. She wondered at how similar you could be to someone you hardly spent any time with. Genetics, she reasoned.

She went to the sink and poured herself a glass of water. She wondered what her mother meant by "leftovers for Liz". She doubted that her father was having an affair with the boss's wife. Perhaps her mother's loneliness caused her to imagine things?

She looked at the clock. Jack would be leaving school for the day. She pictured May Egan smiling at him and waving and Hazel's neighbours looking at each other, wondering. A few times since he was taken into care she had wanted to stand in the background at the school, just to see him, but the thought of running into her neighbours was too much to bear. Besides, she was afraid that May would see her and would come to the wrong conclusion: that Hazel was considering abducting her son. She wouldn't do that because she knew she was going to get her boys back and she wasn't going to do anything to jeopardise that – she wouldn't give the authorities the satisfaction.

She had called to the detention centre earlier and had met with George Kane. She thought that he was going to tell her what was going on in her son's head and tell her not to worry, that they'd soon have him chatting like before, but George Kane had simply asked her question after question and scribbled her answers down in what looked like a child's school copybook.

Before she left, a juvenile-liaison officer informed her that the team were discussing moving Luke to the same foster home as his brother but that he was some weeks off being ready for that and that he'd keep her informed. They had even taken her son to court without telling her and informed her that the judge had ruled a "community sanction" in Luke's case, recommending that he continue to reside in a suitable residential placement where he could receive the appropriate treatment. Hazel was irritated by her lack of control and by the way no one asked her what she thought. Decisions were made without her, decisions made by other people about her children.

But she said nothing and simply nodded. What surprised her

most was Mr Kane's insistence that she meet with him once a week to discuss Luke's childhood because he needed some leverage to develop a bond with him, some vital information about the types of things he had experienced in his short life. As she got up to leave he held onto her hand a little too long for her liking and told her that their talks might also do her good, that she might benefit from having someone to listen to what she went through. She briefly thought it was a trick, a way for the HSE to get information on what a rotten mother she had been and she almost told him where to put his talks. But there was something about the man, something kind, gentle and sincere, so she found herself accepting his offer and agreeing to meet him the following week.

When she arrived at Iris's new convalescent centre, her sister had just returned to bed having taken a call from Mark at the nurses' station. She was smiling and even appeared to have put on some weight. The place was like a five-star hotel and Hazel would have given anything to stay even one night, but without being ill.

"You look happy," she said to her sister, a hint of envy in her voice.

"Mark said he might get over before the graduation," Iris said. "His mother is ill and he needs to find someone to look after her full time."

"I wonder what his wife thinks of all his visits to you?" Hazel said snidely.

Iris tensed, hurt by her sister's comment. She couldn't even let me have this one little bit of happiness, she thought. She knew she shouldn't be thinking of Mark in the way that she was but it brightened her days and she had little else to look forward to.

"Sorry," Hazel said suddenly.

Iris raised her eyebrows. It was unlike her sister to apologise for anything.

"What's wrong?" she asked intuitively.

"Luke might be transferred to the same care home as Jack."

Iris smiled. "Well, that's good isn't it? You said Jack's been looking for him and Luke will be out of that place. You said it was awful there."

Hazel sighed and ran her fingers up and down her cheek.

"I . . . I just thought they'd be home sooner than this. I've had it up to here with social-work meetings, psychologist meetings, care-home meetings, HSE interviews. I thought it'd be easier. I thought they'd see I was doing everything right now. I think Luke is . . . I think his not talking is . . . a way to punish me."

Iris clenched her fists on her lap and took a deep breath. "I doubt it has anything to do with you. I think he's scared."

Hazel turned her face away from her sister. She could feel tears begin to well in her eyes. She couldn't get over how quick she was to cry these days. She almost never cried. Rarely anyway.

"It'll be alright, Hazel," Iris finally said.

"I got offered that course," Hazel said suddenly, trying to change the subject and shaking her head to dry the few errant tears that had made their way down her face.

"Oh, that's great!" Iris said enthusiastically.

"Really?" Hazel had thought Iris wasn't that keen on the idea of a gardening course. Sometimes she thought she'd never work her sister out.

"Yes. You'd be great at it, Hazel," Iris said sincerely.

"Why?" Hazel asked suspiciously. Iris was rarely supportive of her ideas and that often suited her fine. She wasn't sure if she felt comfortable with her sister's enthusiasm. If Iris liked the idea, maybe it wasn't such a good choice after all?

"Because you love gardening," Iris answered simply and with sincerity. She would not be drawn into an argument with her sister whom she could see was itching for one. Iris knew her sister better than she knew herself and she knew that defiance was her middle name. She even knew that Hazel would be reconsidering her choice of course right at that moment because she had said it was a good idea. Their relationship was exhausting and she wondered if it would ever be any different, if Hazel would ever grow up and become her own keeper.

"Oh right," Hazel replied slowly. The visit to the detention centre had her nerves fraught and she felt angry with Luke. She knew she shouldn't be taking it out on her sister but she couldn't help it. "I got these letters in the post as well."

"From who?"

"Grace Mooney. Look, there's Mam's handwriting." Hazel was enjoying watching Iris's face frown at her. She knew her sister was not in favour of bringing up the past and that it would annoy her.

"Oh," Iris said. Her heart thumped. She had to know what was in those letters. She had to read them before Hazel did.

"Could you leave them with me?" she asked.

Hazel raised her eyebrows. She'd been sure that Iris would get annoyed about the letters but now she actually wanted to read them. She thought she'd never work her sister out.

"You'll read them?"

"Yes, sure," Iris replied, smiling. "It'll pass the time."

"We'll split them," Hazel said, narrowing her eyes at her sister.

"Right – give me the more recent ones, please."

Hazel stood and split the letters in two even piles, throwing the newer ones into Iris's bedside locker. She knew her sister had got the better of her again and she didn't like it one bit.

"See you tomorrow," she said gruffly.

When Hazel arrived back at Iris's flat that evening, she picked up her bag and took out the letter from FÁS. It hadn't sunk in yet that she was actually going to train as a gardener and a shiver ran through her. She had never done any further training after school, even though her teachers tried to encourage her. She knew she was bright but she had always been afraid to try things, always afraid of failure. But she already knew so much about gardening, how could she fail? Even Iris encouraged her although that had taken her by surprise and she still wasn't sure about her sister's reaction. Maybe she'd have a look through the brochure again and see what else interested her, just in case? Hazel picked up her mother's letters to Grace Mooney and pulled another one from the pile.

A few miles away, Iris was also taking out one of the letters.

Dear Grace,
I'm sorry that I have not been in touch. Things have been
very hard here as I am sure you know. I got your sympathy

card. Thank you. I know you ran into Eileen, she told me.
She couldn't wait to come here and "save me" and of course
tell me how incapable I am. Jack blames me. He thinks it was
the drinking. He cried. It broke my heart to see that. I never
saw him cry before. They said he had a heart problem, that it
was not my fault. I knew it wasn't anyway. He was lovely, a
perfect little boy. We buried him with my father. My mother just
stood at the grave with her disapproving face and stared at me
while Eileen put her arm around Jack. It was my baby and I felt
all alone. I feel like no one cares about me and that I am
invisible. I saw the way Eileen looked at Jack after the funeral.
She hung around for weeks, asking me if I was okay and making
eyes at him over the dinner table. I confronted her and she said
I am mad, that I am imagining it and that I should go back on
the happy pills. She thinks I'm a fool. Leopards do not change
their spots. Jack now spends every minute in the garden. He
planted a tree in the garden in memory of our son even though
I asked him not to. There is no marriage now and I have tried
to tell him that this is his fault, that he cared more for his work
than for me and left me alone to care for the kids when I didn't
feel able to. He watched me drown and now blames me for how
things have turned out. It's hopeless. If it wasn't for Iris I would
have driven myself into the ocean ages ago. She looks after Hazel
for me. She will make a good mother some day, not like me, eh?

Grace, I have nothing else to say. I hope I haven't depressed
you.

Liz

Iris put the letter down. She tried to imagine her mother speaking
those words but she could no longer remember her voice. Her
mother seemed more lucid in the letter than how she remembered
her but so much changed after the baby died. It must have been the
beginning of the end. Her mother seemed to have been suffering
from irrational fears and Iris wondered if she'd been mentally ill
all along and that no one knew. She remembered her father as a kind
man and she had tried to hang onto these early memories. She knew

that no matter how many letters she read, much of what happened between her parents would never be known and that perhaps it didn't matter. Knowing who was at fault would not change anything for her or her sister. She reread the part where her mother said that Iris would one day make a good mother and it brought tears to her eyes.

"How wrong you were, Mam," she said to the letter.

She looked around the room and inhaled deeply. She would soon be able to leave this place. Her last scan went well and doctors said she could expect a full recovery. Even though it was only a couple of months since she had been diagnosed, a lot had happened since then and she strangely could not remember what her daily life had been like before and felt apprehensive returning to it. Running the shop and living in her poky little flat seemed like a long time ago and she wondered how she'd fit back into it, or if she even wanted to. Hazel was living there now but she hoped her sister would return to her own house by the time she was discharged as there was no way they could share such a tiny space and not kill each other.

Each night she thought about Kevin's graduation, about what she'd wear, how Mark would look. She tried to blot Miriam out of the picture which she knew was ridiculous but she couldn't help herself. Hazel had already booked them into a hotel which was only a few minutes from Mark's house. He didn't offer to put them up and Iris didn't expect it. It would be too hard, watching Mark and Miriam together as man and wife and Miriam acting out her role as Kevin's mother. Iris looked at the clock: it was only nine thirty. She picked up another letter.

Dear Grace
I know it has been a long time since I last wrote. I got your letters. I am three weeks off the drink now and am trying to be strong. It's hard. My hands shake and now I think maybe I did have a problem – but no more. I won't ever touch another drop. I'm sure you've heard that Jack is . . .

Iris jumped from her bed and tore the letter up. She could not risk Hazel seeing it. She had no idea how much time passed between the last letter she read and this one but the deterioration in her mother was obvious. Iris knew only too well that her mother drank plenty after this time and that, rather than start afresh as she suggested in her letter, this was when she began drinking more heavily. She lifted the other letters and decided to read them all immediately to ensure that there was nothing in them. It was going to be a long night but it would be worth it. She had to protect Hazel from the truth: a truth she knew would send her vulnerable sister over the edge.

Chapter 34

Seven weeks had passed and Hazel continued her round of visiting Jack at the Egans' foster home and visiting her sister who was now almost like her old self and could easily have already have left the convalescent home if it weren't for Mark's insistence that she stay until she had put on more weight. She had also kept her promise to meet with George Kane and found herself telling the psychologist things that she didn't even know had bothered her. Things that she didn't even think she remembered. Some days she'd leave his office sobbing about a childhood memory or a break-up with a violent boyfriend and as the weeks passed she found herself becoming less angry, albeit a little sad. It was hard to remember things that had been hurtful but she knew that in the long term, these sessions would help her to be the mother she longed to be. The visits from the social worker were going well and, although Luke still wasn't speaking, he was due to be transferred to Vincent Egan's as soon as George Kane felt he was ready.

On Tuesday morning, Hazel made her way to the local community centre to attend a parents' group that George Kane had suggested she join. She was dreading it and could feel sweat trickling down her back. For two nights running she had the most awful dream where she walked into the crowded meeting and took a seat quickly. When people began pointing and laughing, she realised that she had no outer clothes on and was sitting in her underwear. The dream ended with her running out of the room as the group fell about laughing. Hazel knew that on the outside she seemed brash and confident to people but it was an act she had perfected over the years. Even though she knew she was good-looking and that other girls envied her, it did not give her any of the confidence she needed. In reality, Hazel knew that she was probably as shy as Iris but she had developed a tough exterior and it had served her well. Even though she really didn't want to go, she had forced herself to come to the group. She wanted people to know she was trying. She had decided to sit there and listen rather than speak. She didn't want everyone knowing her business after all.

In the small room, three people were arranging chairs in a circle. Hazel gulped. She thought it might be more like a classroom with rows of seats where she could hide from view and hopefully go unnoticed.

"Hiya," said an older man who seemed to be the organiser.

Hazel smiled self-consciously and took a seat.

She knew the two other people vaguely. Sharon McCann was in Iris's class in school and Tina Lawler was a couple of years younger. They had both aged terribly and were overweight. Hazel couldn't understand how anyone would let themselves go like that. It disgusted her although she admitted to never having any problem with weight. She could eat whatever she liked and never put on a pound.

Over the next few minutes, eight more people arrived, mostly strangers who sat around smiling and shaking hands with each other. Hazel felt like she was at an AA meeting, not that she was terribly sure how they went but it all seemed like a support group from a rehab TV show or something. She felt agonisingly uncomfortable. When the moment came for her to introduce herself, she could feel herself turn bright red. She heard her voice shake even though she said her name as quickly as she could.

She was relieved when the meeting officially started and Tina Lawler started filling the others in on the problems with her drug-taking daughter who was only fifteen. Hazel couldn't believe Tina would tell such personal stuff in front of these people and cringed with embarrassment. But by the time the third person told their woes, Hazel found herself listening intently. These people had similar problems to her: a difficult childhood and then the problems raising

187

children who also had difficulties in one sense or another. She felt something awaken in her, an interest in others whose lives she would never have thought bore any resemblance to her own. Perhaps her hopes for a normal life were unobtainable. Perhaps this was a normal life. Everyone at the meeting had problems. Some had problems much more serious that anything Hazel had to contend with. It made her feel that things were not so bad after all. She listened as some people gave others advice. She could see the short man who had introduced himself as Tony looking at her, weighing her up. She moved uncomfortably on her seat and pulled her skirt down lower over her knees in case he was looking. She was used to this. It happened almost everywhere she went. When everyone had spoken Tony looked directly at her.

"Would you like to contribute anything today, Hazel?"

Again, she reddened. She could feel all eyes on her.

"No," was all she could say in a voice so small she almost didn't recognise it.

"That's fine. There's no pressure here," he said.

An hour later, everyone stood around a small worn table and had tea and biscuits. The conversation was less formal as people spoke in small groups. As Tony approached, Hazel could feel herself becoming nervous.

"You seem anxious. Is there anything I can do to help you?" he asked kindly.

"No," Hazel replied quickly, knowing exactly what kind of help he had in mind. She tried to think of something to say. "Em . . . are your kids going to school here?"

"Oh, I'm not a parent. Well, not a local parent. I'm the counsellor," he said softly. "I come to the group a couple of times a month if parents want to talk to me. I counsel some of the children here so it helps to keep in touch with the parents also. You'll get a lot of support here, Hazel. Don't be afraid of it. Accept it. Will we see you next week?"

"Am I free to go then?"

Tony smiled. "Yes, Hazel. Of course. The meeting is over but some people stay around for a chat afterwards."

Hazel thanked him and waved quickly to the group who were now huddled in a corner and listening intently to Tina telling a joke. Something filthy, Hazel surmised.

She walked out into the fresh air and breathed it in. As she made her way home she began recounting some of the stories the people told today. Awful situations of wife and child-beating, alcohol and drug abuse, poverty where there wasn't even food in the house. She had no idea that things were this bad for people on her doorstep and it had opened her eyes. It was only twelve o'clock so she caught the bus to see Iris.

Iris was intent on preventing Hazel from reading the letters but she knew she had to be careful how she went about it.

"I enjoyed those letters, Hazel," she lied. "They passed a few hours for me last night but I read them all. You wouldn't let me have the rest of them, would you?"

Hazel raised her eyebrows in surprise. "Yes," she said, smiling, delighted that her sister was showing an interest. "I'll bring them in later then. I can read them when you're finished."

Hazel sat for another hour while they planned their trip to London which was now only weeks away. She didn't tell Iris that she had already bought the tickets, which included two for the boys as she knew her sister would look at her in a pitying way and maybe even tell her that the boys would not be with them and that she needed to accept that. But she was working hard at getting them back and her meetings with social services seemed to be going very well. Mark hadn't managed to get back over which had disappointed Iris but she was still excited about the trip. Hazel was even more excited but for different reasons. The day after the graduation, she was going to get the train to Sussex to meet Grace Mooney. She had it all arranged and couldn't wait to sit down with someone who had known her parents well. She wasn't going to tell Iris as she knew her sister would try to dissuade her. She had so many questions to ask Grace and had even made a list in case she forgot one. She was finally going to be able to piece together her parents' lives and might even find out where her dad was buried, which she felt would bring some peace to her troubled mind.

Chapter 35

George Kane was sitting at a small wooden table, watching with interest as Luke drew pictures with coloured pencils.

"Not bad. I was a bit of an artist myself when I was your age," he said without looking directly at Luke.

Luke looked up.

"Are you good at anything else?" George asked.

Luke did not answer. He knew why he was seeing George and he also knew that his mother was outside, waiting to speak to him and he wasn't falling for it. No one was going to make him speak if he didn't want to.

George picked up a piece of paper and began to draw a horse. The boy looked on with interest. It was good and he almost said so.

"Luke, do you know how worried your mam is about you?"

Luke nodded.

"Is there anything you'd like to talk to me about? I won't discuss it with your mam if you don't want me to."

Luke thought about this for a moment. He liked the look of George. He had grey hair and lines on his face. He was like a granddad. Luke never had a granddad. He didn't even have a dad. But the thought of screaming came to him and he knew he could not speak. The only way he could stay in control was if he didn't allow any sound to come out.

George was unperturbed. He knew this was going to be a difficult case and that progress would be very slow.

"Okay, Luke. Well, I think I'll have a short chat with your mam and I'll see you next week, okay?"

Luke was deflated. He was enjoying the drawing and he knew when the session was over he had to go back to the centre's small school which had lads of all ages, one of whom was fifteen and threatened to beat him every time that staff weren't looking.

Hazel was sitting outside the room, waiting. The magazines were ancient and she had flicked though almost all of them in the hour that Luke was inside. She couldn't hear anything and hoped the room was soundproof and that her son was talking. She hoped George Kane knew what he was doing.

She was glad she had taken his advice and gone to the parents' meeting. She had gone again the day before and had enjoyed it. She'd even told the group a little about Luke. Her face burned throughout but it was a start. She could see that Tony, the group leader, was a nice man who genuinely cared about people. Tina had told her that he didn't get paid to attend the parents' group but came voluntarily to offer some support.

When the door suddenly swung open, she was startled.

"Oh," she said, jumping to her feet. "It's over?"

George gestured to her to come in and then put his hand on Luke's shoulder and moved him gently from the room.

"I just want to talk to your mam for a few minutes, Luke, so you sit here, okay?"

Hazel sat down with her bag held tightly on her lap.

"Well?" she asked nervously. "Did he talk?"

"No. It could take some time."

"How long?" She hoped this wasn't going to drag on for weeks. Her course was starting on Monday and she'd have to ask them for time off for these sessions.

"There's no way to tell but it can't be rushed," he said calmly. "He hasn't known me very long. He needs time for us to develop a trusting relationship."

Hazel sighed. "How will you get him to talk? I've tried everything. Nothing works."

George leant forward, a look of concern on his face. "Different strategies work with different children. I have to get to know him and to find out what will encourage him to speak again."

"So you've known other kids to do this?" Hazel asked, amazed.

"Yes, I have."

She leant forward, cupped her head in her hands and sighed loudly. She eyed George. He hadn't a lot to say. He was nice but she wondered if he actually knew what he was doing.

"Did you . . . I mean . . . did you have a difficult childhood?"

"No," he replied. "I had a normal childhood."

"Then how can you help my son?"

"For exactly that reason. I can help your son. You need to believe that. Will you come back next week?"

Hazel knew the session was over and stood. "Okay, I suppose so."

George put out his hand and shook hers firmly.

Hazel walked out of the office and took Luke back to his classroom at the back of the centre. As she hugged him goodbye at the door, she thought she saw a glimmer in his eye, a flicker of emotion, but he turned his back quickly and opened the door to go inside.

"I love you," she said after him.

He stopped suddenly and she saw his shoulders rise up.

He had only heard her say this a few times in his entire life and it was usually when she was really sad. He felt sorry for his mam but he knew she wouldn't understand if he told her. She'd tell him to get sense and to get over whatever was on his mind like she usually did when he was worried about something. He turned and gave her a small wave and quickly went into his class.

Hazel's heart lurched. He had communicated with her. He hadn't spoken but it was a start. She turned and noticed that George Kane was standing in the corridor. He had been watching the whole scene and was nodding thoughtfully.

She left the centre and, on the entire bus journey to collect Iris she replayed George's words in her mind: "*I had a normal childhood.*"

This was something she had rarely heard in her life. It was something that most people were probably familiar with but that had no meaning in her life and she wondered what meaning it would have for Luke and Jack and for their children and the role she would have to play in this.

Chapter 36

When Hazel and Iris arrived at the flat, it was cold and dark inside. The cat was pleased to see Iris and purred into her face as she sat for a moment on the sofa. She looked around the empty room and felt an urge to cry. She opened the fridge and found that Hazel, who had decided to return to her own house that night, had not bought any food for the flat. She said nothing and sat over a cup of tea with her sister who ranted on about what a lovely man this George was and nattered on for what seemed like an eternity about her parents' group run by someone called Tony, all people that Iris had never met, people who were new in her sister's life. After a while she made enough yawning sounds to encourage her sister to leave her in peace.

The short trip home had exhausted her so, when Hazel left, she went to her room and lay fully clothed on the bed.

When she awoke some hours later, after a deep, dreamless sleep, Hazel was standing over her. She had let herself in and had brought ingredients to make Iris dinner.

"You alright?" she asked her sister.

"Yeah, I was just a bit tired so I lay down. What time is it?"

"Almost six," Hazel replied. "I'm going to subject you to my cooking," she said, laughing.

Iris was amused. She could count the number of meals Hazel had cooked for her on one hand. She seemed in a good mood and Iris wondered what the reason was because Hazel had to have a reason. She was either high as a kite or in the depths of depression.

Hazel beckoned Iris to follow her into the scullery.

"Did you go to see Jack?" Iris asked.

"Yeah. Remember I told you that Vinnie Egan was the foster parent?"

Iris nodded. She was pleased that the Egan brothers seemed to have done well for themselves.

"Well, the younger brother, Joe, he was there and, you know, I think he has a thing for me."

Iris let out a long, loud sigh.

"He's a lovely man, Iris, very kind. He calls in there every week and plays football with the boys . . . helps Vinnie out . . . you know how Jack absolutely loves football. He's really interested in Jack."

"No, Hazel, you can't be serious!"

"I didn't say I was interested in him. I just said he was nice."

"That's the problem with you, Hazel. 'Nice' equals 'interested'. Can't you just be happy Jack has found a good role model without wanting to . . . to . . ."

"You've got it wrong, Iris. He's just nice. Why do you always have to think the wrong thing?"

"Because I know you, Hazel. Is he married?"

"No . . . I don't know. No. He'd have said . . . surely?"

Iris shook her head and stormed off into the sitting room and put on the TV, leaving her sister to bang dishes around louder than she needed to.

When Hazel left, Iris put on a nightdress on and unpacked the bags from the hospital. Then she went back out into her sitting room and sat down with a cup of tea. She opened her mother's letters. She had read through them quickly in hospital to make sure her mother didn't say anything significant about her father but she wanted to read them again. Hazel hadn't asked for them back yet so she had time to read them properly now.

Dear Grace,

Thanks for the few bob. I appreciate it. I know you cannot spare it but I have no one to ask here. Iris needs Irish dancing shoes and I hate to let her down. I am trying to make her and Hazel join things. Neither of them are good mixers and it worries me. I blame Jack for the way they are.

I met a nice man, John, and we've had a couple of nights out. He's a bit of fun and it gets me out of the house for a couple of hours and he has no problem with me having a few drinks, unlike Jack. My allowance doesn't go far so if it wasn't for John, I'd never have any fun.

Hope all is well with you.

Liz

PS He's a one-woman man – so again, not like Jack . . .

Iris wondered how her mother considered this a proper letter to a friend. Once her mother thanked her friend for the loan, she went on about herself and never asked about Grace's life. As for the dancing shoes, Iris never got them and it was she who wanted to join the classes. She didn't have to think too much to realise what the money had been spent on. As for John, there were lots of Johns and Iris couldn't remember any of them in great detail. She wondered about her mother's comments about her father's womanising. Was it true? Was she so angry and bitter now that she was taking any kind of happiness she could find, even if it meant her kids went without? The letters only worsened her resentment towards her mother and she could not, for even one moment, see what comfort Hazel got from reading them.

The phone rang loudly and startled her. Iris lifted the receiver, expecting Hazel to launch into more exciting titbits about Joe Egan.

"Hi. It's Mark. Just wondered how you are getting on, your first night home."

This was the first time Iris had spoken to him on the phone from this flat and it seemed strange to hear his voice. She could feel herself becoming slightly irritated and couldn't understand why she felt this way. She was disappointed that he hadn't been able to come over to see her again but she was also trying to protect herself. There was no point in becoming dependent on him. Now that she was home she knew that she had to stand on her own two feet and that she had been vulnerable during her illness.

"I . . . I'm fine," she answered meekly. "I . . . Hazel offered to stay but, really, I'm fine on my own." She didn't want him to think she couldn't cope on her own. Mark had been so good to her but she didn't want pity either.

"Oh, that's good," he said.

Iris could hear the sincerity in his voice and it choked her.

"I'm looking forward to seeing you in London," he said. "It'll be like old times."

If only, Iris thought to herself. She knew it would be nothing like the old times when they were young and single, enjoying life in the big city – or after, in the early part of their marriage, before Kevin was born and she became dogged with feelings of helplessness and isolation. If only someone had been able to wave a magic wand and cure her of those feelings. Things could have been very different.

"Yes," Iris replied sadly. "Like old times."

"Iris?"

"Yes?"

"Are you alright. You sound . . . low."

Iris took a deep breath. She did not want to cry but being home made her realise just how lonely she was.

"I'm okay. Just tired," she replied, biting her lip.

"Well, rest as much as you can. I've arranged a couple of days off when you come over. I'm going to take you around all the old places, all our old haunts."

Iris smiled broadly. Memories of those days flashed in front of her.

"That'll be nice but I don't want to take up too much of your and Miriam's time."

He didn't respond and there was a silence.

"Mark. Are you still there?"

"Yes. Sorry. Iris . . . Miri . . . Miriam . . ."

"Yes?"

Mark hesitated. If he told Iris about his divorce from Miriam she might not go through with the visit. She might worry that he wanted more from her than she was prepared to give. From the moment he saw her outside her shop in January, he knew that he still loved her but he couldn't take the chance of scaring her. His feelings for her had taken him by surprise but they were growing day by day and he knew that he wanted to be with her, to spend his life with her. He felt that he had to get her here where it all began, to where they had fallen in love. He hoped being in London could restore the feelings they had for each other back then.

"Miriam's looking forward to it," he said quickly.

"Good," Iris replied even though she knew she did not mean it and hoped Mark did not pick up on her tone.

"Well, goodnight, Iris. I'm looking forward to seeing you."

Iris replaced the receiver and replayed that line over and over in her head. She knew it was silly but why not dream about it? She had precious little else to do.

Chapter 37

As Hazel walked to the bus stop to go to her appointment with George, she could see Tina Lawler frog-marching her teenage daughter into the secondary school that was adjacent to the boys' primary school. She watched with interest as the girl screamed profanities at her mother which Tina ignored. When the girl disappeared into school, Hazel turned her back, pretending not to have been watching the spectacle which other people seemed to be enjoying.

"Hi, Hazel!" Tina shouted.

Hazel was in awe of the woman. If it was her daughter that had made such a scene, she would have been embarrassed and crept away quietly.

"Hi," Hazel replied. She wasn't sure if she wanted to be seen with Tina. She had heard that she regularly got involved in fights with neighbours and that people generally steered clear of her.

"Do you want to go for a cuppa?" Tina asked smiling.

"Em . . . yeah," Hazel replied. She didn't want to turn Tina down and anyway, she was early for her appointment and her bus wouldn't be here for another half hour. She had left early hoping to see Jack from a distance but there was no sign of him in the crowd of infants.

As they ordered a pot of tea and scones, Tina filled Hazel in on her life. She had fallen pregnant at eighteen and her boyfriend at the time had disappeared as fast as he possibly could. Five years later she married a local lad who Hazel remembered but the marriage hadn't lasted long and left her as sole parent to a troubled daughter and a younger girl whom she referred to as her "angel". She also told Hazel that she had a few bad years where she spent time in women's shelters as well as frequent visits to her mother in the middle of the night but that she had come through it with Tony's help.

Hazel listened to Tina and was impressed by her resilience. She was strong and didn't care what anyone thought about her.

"Well, what about you, Hazel? Never thought I'd see the likes of you at the group."

Hazel winced but did not sense any maliciousness in Tina's words. "Why?" she asked. She was genuinely interested in why anyone would think she didn't need help.

"Well, your family, they were well off, weren't they?"

Hazel knew what Tina meant. Her family had a car, owned their home and when her dad was there he had earned a good wage, but that didn't mean things were good, or that her parents were good parents.

"There's more to being happy than having money," Hazel said more to herself than to Tina. "Anyway, when my dad died, money was tight alright."

Tina looked at her. Even though everyone knew that Hazel's mother was a raging alcoholic, she had envied her in school for her long blonde hair and huge blue eyes. Tina wasn't as overweight then as she was now but she was never considered pretty and had taken the first boyfriend that showed interest in her while Hazel Fay could have had any boy. Rumour had it that she was even involved with that roughneck Pete Doyle. It didn't make any sense to her. Hazel had had choices that she hadn't ever had, at least not until now.

"Tina, that group, is it really confidential?" Hazel was still worried that people at the group would be talking to others about what was said.

"Yes. Don't forget everyone is there for the same reason. We want to give our kids a different life from what we had. No one talks. I know, I've been going there for three years now."

"Do you think it helps?"

Tina thought about this and took a loud slurp of her tea which embarrassed Hazel in the busy tea room.

"In the beginning, I learnt a lot about what I should be doing with the kids, especially Sharon, she's my real worry, but now it's more about friendship. I go because I get to see people who know what it is like. It's nice. And that Tony, he's gorgeous. I'd give anything for a ride with him. Why can't we meet fellas like that, eh?" Tina broke into a loud laugh that made people look up from their food.

Hazel knew that she wasn't the quietest person on earth but Tina was really noisy.

"Yeah, why can't we?" she replied absentmindedly. She thought of Mark and how kind he was to Iris. It wasn't fair.

"Oh, cheer up, Hazel, and count your blessings. That's what I do every day now. I say, thank God my two girls are safe and healthy. I have a part-time job so if my ex doesn't pay up each month, I can feed them myself. I have a council house in my name that no man can throw me out of. Life is great!" She smiled broadly.

Hazel looked at Tina as if she'd gone mad. She certainly has low expectations, she thought to herself. But she also wondered if Tina was right. She was surviving as best she could and had pulled herself out of a terrible situation. Hazel wanted to do the same and was trying to but something kept pulling her back. Every time she tried to start afresh something happened to weaken her. Perhaps she didn't have the strength of Tina or Iris. Perhaps she never would.

"I wish I felt like that," she replied solemnly.

"You can. You just have to believe you can."

Hazel smiled at Tina. She sounded like a born-again Christian and was certainly a changed woman. She had been a tough girl at school and even though she was younger than Hazel, she had been afraid of her in school. She remembered the bruises Tina and her sisters used to come into school with. Their dad had been a violent man who beat them for the least thing. It had obviously affected Tina because she used to hit anyone who came within a few feet of her. Even though neither Iris nor Hazel had experienced violence in the home, they had been affected in a different way. They were as damaged as Tina but she had managed to face her past and move on. It inspired Hazel.

"Hey, a few of us are going to see a film on Sunday night, want to come?" Tina asked.

"Oh, I don't know," Hazel replied nervously. She didn't know who the other girls were and was afraid they might be some of the girls that had bullied her in school.

"They're nice, you don't know them," Tina said, reading Hazel's thoughts. "I had to lose contact with a few of – with most of my friends. When they started doing drugs, well, let's say they weren't the best of company to have around my kids."

Tina's honesty amazed Hazel. She had bared her soul in the coffee shop and Hazel hadn't told her one thing about herself.

"My son won't talk because . . . because I put him in a position where he felt he had to protect me," Hazel blurted out, surprising herself.

Tina did not blink an eye. She was used to hearing awful stories in the group.

"I know. I heard about Doyle. He'll get his. Bet you wish it was you and not your kid who did it?"

Tina knew about Doyle and his brother and knew that sooner or later either the suppliers or the locals would get him and she didn't care which.

Hazel nodded.

"You've made your mistakes," Tina said. "You can make things better for your lad because he has you and you love him. And remember, good things happen when you least expect them." It seemed an odd statement to make, given the conversation.

Hazel smiled at Tina. She really believed that it was that simple. She hoped she was right.

Chapter 38

When Iris woke up after her first night home, she went for a short walk and then opened the shop. She knew she shouldn't be working but it would be lonely in the flat all day and she reasoned that she might as well sit out front where she could see people passing by. Besides, she was keen to know if she had any regular customers left and, if not, she needed to think about how she was going to make a living. She picked up the ferry tickets that Hazel had dropped in the previous evening and scanned their departure times.

She had said nothing when Hazel said she had bought tickets for the boys. There was no point in fighting about it. Four more weeks, she thought to herself, and felt like a child counting down to Christmas but she reminded herself that Christmas could also be a disappointment for children and that this trip could turn out the same way. She had to focus on the fact that she was going to see her son graduate from school and that she shouldn't expect it to be a straightforward visit. She knew Kevin still had issues with her. It was to be expected and might always be that way. She hoped Mark hadn't talked him into inviting her. She was glad that Hazel would be there to make conversation and ease the awkwardness.

The bell went and Iris looked up from her tickets. Mrs Maguire stood stone-faced in the doorway.

"Back, are ya?" she said in her flat Dublin accent.

CAROL COFFEY

Iris was tempted to say 'No, I'm an apparition' and smiled at the thought.

"Yeah" she replied. "What can I do for you?"

She was glad to have some repairs to do. It would take her mind off her illness which, despite her best efforts, still worried her.

"Are you better?" Maguire asked flatly.

"Yes," Iris said softly.

"God is good," mumbled the old woman as her false teeth slipped in and out of her mouth.

Hazel sang to herself as she cleaned the house and tidied up the boys' room. She hadn't been in their room in weeks. She couldn't bring herself to go in, to smell their clothes, see their toys, so she had shut the door and had not gone inside during her many visits to check her post. She felt in an especially good mood.

At her last meeting with George, he had told her that Luke would be transferred that day to the Egans' foster home. A social worker she had not met before came into the room and introduced herself as the senior social worker. She said that when George had recommended that Luke have weekend visits home, she had liaised with Jack's social worker and they agreed that both boys could spend Saturday night with their mother initially and that, all going well, the time could eventually be increased.

Hazel felt a surge of energy and raced around the house making everything ready for them. She had phoned Iris who went quiet initially and she knew that her sister was overcome with the news, that she had missed the boys and would be looking forward to seeing them.

She put on a wash and sat down for a cup of tea and a breather. Her eye fell on the metal box that held the letters. She realised that she still had a few of the ones Grace had sent her mother to read and took one of these from the box.

Dear Liz
How are you? I haven't heard from you in ages and you have me worried. I've written to you about three times but have

had no reply. I called to your house when I was home and there was no answer.

My mother died. I was surprised that you weren't at the funeral. I thought you'd have heard about it from your mam. It was in her sleep so she didn't suffer. Lord rest her. I'm heartbroken though. It won't be the same knowing she's gone for good.

Mary Whelan thought you were home when I knocked next door. I left some things in for the girls. I hope they liked them. I am worried about how you are doing on your own. It can't be easy. Could you please phone me to let me know you are alright or even drop me a line? I won't be home again for a while.

Love
Grace

Hazel wondered if this was the last letter Grace had sent her mother and leafed through the others to check their dates. It was. She wondered why her mother hadn't answered, especially as her friend was grieving for her own mother and obviously needed someone to talk to. Perhaps her mother was also grief-stricken at the loss of her husband and couldn't write. That would make sense, she thought. Poor Mam. She suffered so much. Although she hated reading about the drinking, she knew her mother had found life tough and she didn't judge her for it. Iris was different though. She was bitter and she didn't want to understand why her mother drank so heavily.

Hazel thought about her planned visit to see Grace which she still hadn't told Iris about. She'd decided that she'd rise early and leave a note, asking Iris to watch the boys until she got back. It was only an hour on the train so she'd be back before lunchtime. She felt like a private investigator on a stakeout. She was sure that she would learn much more by talking face to face with Grace. A large part of her past would become clearer and who knows, it might even help her to become as happy as Tina Lawler.

Chapter 39

On Saturday morning, Hazel rose at seven o'clock which was unusual for her as she normally dragged herself out of bed. She couldn't sleep in, the excitement of having the boys overnight too much to return to sleep. She got up and made herself a coffee. She had agreed to bring the boys to Iris's for dinner so her sister could spend some time with them.

Luke had settled into the Egans' household well and was delighted to be reunited with his little brother. She planned on bringing them back home after dinner for a DVD and some treats and could imagine herself sitting on the sofa with them, Jack curled up into her like he loved to do and Luke sitting on the other side, happy to be home and chatting away.

She had started her training course, an introductory day, and she had enjoyed it. In the FÁS training centre, she had sat in a group of around twenty people and listened to the instructor giving them an induction. She was glad that there were so many people on the course and felt that she could hide among them. There were only three women there besides her but Hazel didn't care about that. She got on better with men anyway. The course instructor told them about what they would be doing each week and how they would be tested. She felt a surge of excitement. She loved tests. She usually did well and her results always gave her a boost for a few days. The instructor gave them a handout on what outdoor clothing they would need and where to buy it. It sounded expensive and she drifted off wondering where she'd get the money from and had to bring herself back, hoping that she hadn't missed anything important. Hazel remembered that even though she got good results at school, her concentration was always bad and she found herself day-dreaming on a daily basis.

At three thirty, Hazel left the centre and walked with a bounce in her step to the bus stop. Everything was working out. Soon she'd have her boys home and she hadn't even had to go to court like she had previously thought. The social workers could see that she was making every effort and that while she had some personal issues to address, she loved her sons. She knew that Luke would remain under the supervision of the juvenile liaison officer for some time but things could have come out a lot worse, for all of them. When she arrived at the Egans' house, both boys were still getting ready for their first night home. She went into the kitchen and saw Joe sitting at the table with Vinnie's two adopted children. He invited her to take a walk with him in the garden. She noticed that, while not classically good-looking, he had grown into an attractive man. He was no longer the tall scrawny teenager he had been but had filled out from years working as a bricklayer in London and San Francisco. He had not gone to college as Vinnie had but preferred to work with his hands. He had come home seven years ago. He began to feel lonely in the States and was looking for a more permanent lifestyle. He had not married – he told her that he had never met the right woman and that, due to his own upbringing, he'd rather stay single than marry or have children with the wrong partner.

"So, are you bitter then, about it all?" she asked.

"Bitter? No. Cautious maybe, but Vinnie and I were lucky. We often talk about it."

"So you don't mind?"

"Having been fostered? God, no. We were lucky. That's what I think. I did struggle with it when I left the home first. I spent a few years beating myself up about it. I was never like Vinnie. He always

207

saw the bright side of everything. It took me a long time to see things as he did. I think you have to arrive at a stage where you accept the past and don't let it destroy your future."

She tried to absorb his words. He sounded like Tina, full of hope for the future. If only their attitude was contagious.

"When . . . I mean . . . how long did it take you to accept your upbringing?" she asked.

"In London, I started to see a counsellor. Saw her for almost two years. I even made contact with my parents. I saved, did my time as a bricklayer and bought my own house. Life was looking up."

"How did you get on with your parents?"

"Well, it didn't go that well but it was, well, sort of cathartic for me. It gave me closure."

Hazel didn't know what *cathartic* meant but she memorised it and decided to look it up in Luke's dictionary later.

"What about you?" he asked directly. "How have things turned out for you?"

She took a deep breath, not knowing where to begin. She didn't mind telling Joe because he understood. It was other people she dreaded.

"Well, there's really not too much to tell. I live in my parents' house. Well, you know about my boys . . ." She reddened slightly. "I'm doing a horticultural course. I think my dad would have been pleased. He was a gardener. I . . . I'm trying to get my life on track."

"I'd love to have kids myself some day. When it happens, it will be the best part of my life."

Hazel laughed at his enthusiasm. "Be careful what you wish for!" she warned. "You don't know what trouble they can be."

He stared at her for a moment and she felt uneasy. She was only joking and hadn't meant to come across as crass.

"I'm kidding, they're great," she said. "It brings pressures of course but I'm trying my best. It's not easy doing it alone. It wasn't what I planned for myself. I made lots of mistakes but I am trying."

Joe nodded thoughtfully, digesting her words.

The patio door opened and Vinnie's wife May beckoned for

Hazel to come inside. Hazel left Joe in the garden and went into the house, noticing that May looked uncharacteristically serious.

"Sit down, Hazel. I just need to talk to you about Luke."

Hazel swallowed. "Has he done something wrong?"

"No, no, nothing like that. We started him back at his school on Thursday. I had my suspicions that he talks to Jack. They're sharing a room and a few nights I was sure I heard whispering from the room. I asked Jack and he denied it. You should have seen how upset he got when I asked. He looked really worried about it. I mentioned it to Jack's teacher and she said the boys were seen talking together in the yard during play-time. So, I don't know why Jack lied and what it is that Luke is telling him. I thought you might try broaching it later with the boys, separately if possible."

Hazel's mind raced for a moment. Luke was speaking. A rush of relief came over her. Surely he'd start talking to others soon? Yet May seemed worried about it.

"It's progress, isn't it?" she asked the concerned-looking woman.

"Yes, but . . . what worries me is that he might confide too much in Jack. He is only five and it's best if he doesn't know the details of that night. Luke needs to confide in an adult. You might try talking to him later and to Jack. You just need to find out what exactly Luke has told him."

Hazel agreed but left the home a little bit depressed. She had arrived there full of enthusiasm and with a renewed sense of motherhood and its responsibilities but she suddenly felt overwhelmed by the extent of her son's problems. What if she said the wrong thing and set his progress back? What if her questions upset him and she wasn't allowed to have them overnight again? She worried about taking the risk of losing what she had gained. Maybe she should let someone else sort out Luke's mental problems. But no, she reasoned, that was what she was there for. She was his mother. She decided that when an opportunity presented itself she would ask the boys about their little conversations, even if it meant upsetting her plans to reunite her family. The boys' welfare had to come first.

When she stood to leave the room, Jack came running in with no shoes on. He ran to her and threw himself at her. "I can't find my shoes!" he laughed.

Luke was standing in the doorway, eyeing her suspiciously. She moved towards him but he withdrew into the hallway and put his coat on, turning his back to her and facing out towards the glass-panelled door. He stood with his head bowed and hands dug into his pockets, waiting on her.

May touched her hand and mouthed words of encouragement.

When Iris finished her alterations that afternoon, she sat down on the bed for a rest. She was still exhausted and wondered when she'd feel right again. She had even started going for short walks which she loved but her energy levels didn't seem to increase and only encouraged her fears that cancer was still lurking in her body, waiting to resurface. She wondered if most cancer patients felt this way but she had no idea. She didn't know anyone else recovering from cancer and had kept to herself on the hospital wards. Earlier that morning she had taken the bus into town to have her hair done and had gone into Clery's to buy a new dress for the graduation. She hadn't bought anything new for herself in years. She had no reason to. It had taken her ages to find something that was suitable for the event. The dress's deep blue colour matched her eyes and didn't make her look as pale as the brighter colours did and hung in deep pleats to cover her thin body. She hoped Hazel was going to wear something appropriate and worried that her sister would turn up in a skimpy outfit and embarrass her. Kevin attended a private school and Iris could just imagine the snobs that some of the people might be. She took the photo of Kevin out of her drawer and smiled a sad smile at the youngster looking back at her. She wondered how her son really felt about her coming. He still hadn't phoned her but she knew he was a little shy, the only trait she passed on to him as he looked nothing like her.

Hazel would arrive in an hour with the boys and although she was really looking forward to it, she wasn't sure she had the energy for a long evening with them. She took out the pizza delivery menus and left them on the table for the boys to choose. She was too tired to cook and it'd be a nice treat for her nephews. She was relieved that when her sister called the previous day, she had not noticed that Iris had removed some of their mother's letters and that the pile was smaller than when Hazel had given them to her. She had torn the letters up. There were some things that Hazel did not need to know.

When the boys arrived, she stood at the door and hugged Jack for the longest time. Luke stood back and looked at his feet. Then she grabbed him and pulled him towards her, smothering him in kisses, but his arms hung loose by his sides and he did not complain loudly as he would normally do if she got too soppy with him. She stood back and looked at him. His little face seemed to have aged and there were dark lines under his eyes.

"Are you not sleeping, Luke?" she asked, forgetting that she would not receive an answer. He looked away and Iris thought she could see his chin tremble. It broke her heart. She stood and ushered them through the shop and into her tiny sitting room. The table was pulled out and set for dinner.

"Pizza? Cool, we're getting pizza! And Coke, can we order Coke, pleeaasse?" Jack begged as he jumped around the living room.

Iris glanced at Luke and thought she saw him smile at his little brother's antics but he caught her looking at him and his face turned to stone.

When the pizzas arrived, only Jack ate ravenously. Iris noticed how much more talkative she was now that Luke wasn't speaking and that Jack too had more than the usual amount to say. Hazel, on the other hand, said very little and answered questions with short responses, her eyes fixed on her older son as though at any moment he would disappear. After dinner, Iris offered the boys ice cream and flakes. Jack again jumped around wildly as if he'd never had anything like that before. Luke on the other hand simply nodded when she asked him if he wanted some. When she handed it to him, he left the table and ate his dessert on the sofa, away from the others. Iris beckoned for Hazel to join her in the kitchen, loudly stating that she needed help with the dishes. As they left the room, they saw Jack sitting down close to his brother and leaning against him. Luke did not pull away but stared at the evening news that had just begun on the television.

In the tiny kitchen Hazel leaned against the wall while Iris rinsed the dishes. She heard Hazel exhale loudly.

"I don't know what to do with him, Iris. Do you see the way he looks at me? It's like he blames me for what happened."

Iris turned the tap on louder to ensure the boys could not hear their conversation.

"Hazel, I don't think that's it. I think he looks . . . scared."

"Of what?"

"I don't know. He's been through an awful lot. I think we need to give him time."

Hazel opened her mouth to tell her sister that Luke had been seen talking to Jack in school and that May Egan had heard them whispering in their room but just then she heard Jack shout loudly from the sitting room.

"Mam, Pete's on the telly, look!"

Iris and Hazel both ran into the room and saw a photo of Pete on the Six O'clock News.

"Turn it up!" Hazel ordered.

Iris looked at Luke who had gone as white as a sheet. It angered her that her stupid sister didn't think about the effect seeing Doyle on telly would have on her traumatised son.

"*A suspected drug dealer has been reported missing by his family. Pete Doyle was last seen by his brother in the city centre three days ago. Doyle, who is known to the police and who was facing charges of possession of ecstasy for sale, was last seen wearing jeans and a blue jumper. He is described as . . .*"

Iris quickly turned the TV off and, sitting by Luke, took him in her arms. She could feel him shaking.

"It's okay, Luke. He's not coming here. Listen to me. If he wanted to come here or to your house he would have done it days ago. He's been out of hospital a while. He is not looking for you. I promise."

"Easy for you to say," Hazel retorted. "He didn't try to kill you!"

"Hazel!" Iris roared.

Hazel quietened and looked towards the ground like a sullen child.

"Your mam's only joking, aren't you, Hazel?"

"Yes. Course I am."

Luke sprang out of Iris's arms and grabbed his brother, almost knocking the little five-year-old over. He looked into Jack's eyes and then bent his head and appeared to whisper something in his brother's ear. Then he straightened up and began to rock back and forth while Jack nodded as if he understood what his brother's strange behaviour meant.

Hazel and Iris could see that Luke was shaking.

"What's wrong with him, Jack?" Hazel asked, the sound of fear audible in her voice. Jack loosened his brother's strangling grip and looked at his mother.

"He wants to go to May's. He doesn't want to go home."

Hazel almost crumpled, her dream of a lovely evening with her boys shattered.

"But I've got lots of lovely treats in and, Luke, your favourite cereal. Wait till you see the DVD I got. One of those wrestling ones you like. Luke, it'll be okay!" She moved towards him.

Luke tightened his grip on his brother but his eyes moved toward Iris. She didn't need him to speak to know that he was begging her to intervene.

"Hazel, I think you should take them back. There'll be another day. Come on, I'll ring for a taxi." She put her hand on Hazel's shoulder. She could see the bitter disappointment on her sister's face.

Vinnie Egan was surprised to hear his doorbell ring. It was almost ten and he was sitting watching a movie with Joe. May was upstairs trying to ease Lisa from one of her night terrors and all of the boys were sound asleep. He paused the DVD and opened the front door to see Hazel with her arm around Luke and a half-asleep Jack.

"He's shaking," she said as Vinnie opened the door wide to allow her to pass.

"What happened to him?" Vinnie asked. He was suddenly alarmed that his recommendation to the HSE that Hazel have the boys overnight was a wrong move and that she had done something to frighten the boy. He had even stated that he did not feel that Hazel needed a child-worker with her for the overnight stay as he had spent plenty of time with her over the past few weeks and did not think that she presented a danger to her children.

"Can I put him to bed, please?" Hazel asked.

She did not want to mention Pete Doyle in front of Luke. Vinnie reached out and led Luke in and up the stairs. Hazel staggered up the stairs behind them, Jack trailing behind her. As she looked down she could see Joe standing by the sitting-room door. He acknowledged her and moved back inside the room to give her privacy.

Vinnie sat Luke down on his bed and took his shoes off. Hazel wanted to scream at him to go away, to let her look after her own son, but just then she heard a gentle voice from the doorway. It was May Egan, carrying the little girl they were fostering.

"Vinnie, why don't you take Jack downstairs for some milk? Hazel can look after Luke."

Hazel shot the woman a look of gratitude and May smiled before she disappeared. Vinnie left the room silently, taking Jack by the hand. Hazel changed the trembling Luke into his pyjamas and managed to get him under the covers. Then she stood for a while looking at her son who was lying on his side, eyes wide open and staring out into space.

"Luke, won't you tell me what's wrong? Won't you talk to me?" she asked but he did not look at her and shifted his body to face the wall. She placed her hand gently on his back and she could feel him trembling still. "What is it, Luke? Please . . . I can't help you if you won't talk to me." She sat down on his bed and moved her hands up and down his back. She remembered that this used to calm him when he was a toddler and had got into one of his temper tantrums. He did not pull away from her but she could feel him tense up. What had she done to make him hate her so much? She couldn't understand why he was punishing her so. Hazel could feel someone watching her and turned her eyes to the doorway where Joe Egan now stood. He looked at her and she could see pity on his face.

"Why don't you come downstairs? You could check on him later."

Hazel stood and looked back at her son, waiting to see if he would resist her leaving him but he did not look up and kept his face to the wall. She could feel every ounce of energy leave her body and felt like collapsing into the bed beside her silent son. She felt that Joe Egan sensed this as he took her hand and led her down the stairs and into the kitchen where Jack was drinking hot milk and eating biscuits. Vinnie stood as soon as she entered and excused himself. Hazel briefly wondered if May had told him to give her a chance to talk to Jack also. She sat beside her younger son and smoothed his hair back.

"Did you have a nice time tonight?" she asked.

He nodded and continued to stuff May's home-made biscuits into his mouth.

"Jack?"

"Mmm."

"Does Luke talk to you?"

He nodded. He didn't want to be in trouble with Luke but he didn't want to lie.

She stood and took his nebuliser from her bag.

"What does he say?" she asked as gently as she could while she plugged it in. She didn't want to sound too keen.

Jack looked at her and then looked towards the door, checking to make sure that his brother wouldn't hear him.

"He only whispers, Mam. Not like real words."

"Why does he whisper?"

"'Cos he doesn't want to scream," Jack replied, pleased that he remembered what Luke had told him.

"Why?" Hazel asked. None of this made sense to her. She had no idea what was going through her son's head.

"Because, Mam," Jack replied matter of factly, "then you won't think he's brave." He smiled serenely at her and lifted the nebuliser mask over his face.

Hazel stifled a cry. So that was why he wouldn't speak! She bent forward, feeling an almost physical pain for her child. She hadn't realised just how much he was suffering.

When Jack was finished with the nebuliser, Hazel brought him up the stairs and put him into his pyjamas. She pulled back the covers on the bed at the far side of the room.

"Is this your bed? It's very nice," she said, trying to make the situation as normal as possible.

"I prefer my bed, Mam," he said. "This is just a holiday bed."

Hazel kissed him and moved to the other side of the room where Luke now appeared to be sleeping. She ran her hands over his dark curly hair and felt him stir. She knew he was pretending to be asleep.

"You need a haircut, mister," she said gently.

He did not stir.

"Luke? I know things are bad for you but you can talk to me. You can tell me anything."

Luke moved away from her, confirming that he was awake.

"You don't have to be brave, love. You're just a little boy and this is my fault, not yours, and I'm sorry." Hazel swallowed hard.

She could feel herself becoming upset but she had to be strong for Luke. She could hear small short sounds emanating from his throat and realised he was trying to stifle his tears.

"If you want to talk to me, Luke, you can. Anytime."

When he didn't answer, she sighed and went back downstairs and into the sitting room where she found Vinnie and Joe sitting quietly, May nowhere to be seen.

Vinnie stood and poured her a cup of coffee from a fresh pot someone had placed on the small table. She wrapped her fingers around the hot steaming cup and hugged it into her chest.

When she felt as though she would not cry, she told the brothers about Luke's reaction to Pete Doyle's reported disappearance. Both men remained quiet throughout her account of the evening. When she was finished, Vinnie reassured her that Luke would recover, that he'd seen lots of traumatised children over the years. She feigned interest in his story of an anonymous child who had come to him some years ago. The child, he said, had become mute from the shock of something he had seen. Vinnie proudly reported that after six short months of counselling, the child had completely recovered. Throughout the lengthy story, she could feel Joe's eyes on her. She glanced at him and decided that he had the kindest eyes she had ever seen and that, unlike his brother, he knew when to speak and when to be silent.

She finished her coffee and put the cup on the table. "I'd better be going home," she said.

Joe stood suddenly and offered to drive her. She accepted. She was too tired to go searching for a taxi and she didn't know if there was a bus route that would take her home.

She decided she would ring Iris when she got home to put her sister's mind at ease. She dreaded the thought of going home to the house alone, knowing that she had laid out fresh pyjamas on the boys' beds. She was thankful that she had no alcohol in the house as this would be one night when she could easily have opened a bottle of wine and drunk it all to ease her loneliness. It was going to be a long night.

Chapter 40

On Monday morning Iris answered the phone in her shop. It was almost eleven and she wondered who it could be.

Sunday had gone by slowly. Hazel had come over and had moped around, upset to be without the boys and yet simultaneously giddy about Joe Egan who she said had driven her home from the foster home and had been a perfect gentlemen. Now that Hazel was doing her course, Iris rarely had any phone calls during the day and missed having someone to talk to.

"Hello?"

"Iris, it's Mark."

She smiled to herself. Mark phoned her a couple of times a week and she loved hearing his voice, no matter how foolish this was.

"Hi!" she said excitedly.

"Iris, my dad had another stroke yesterday. He died a half hour ago," he said sadly.

"Oh, Mark! I'm so sorry!"

"I'm flying in tonight to make the arrangements."

"Can I do anything?" She was hoping he'd say no. She did not want to see Mark's brother and sister who she knew resented her for leaving their brother. Not that she blamed them. She just didn't want to have to face them.

"John and Karen are flying in tomorrow. I'll be calling in to check on Mam and Aunt Kate. But could you meet me later for dinner?"

"Isn't Miriam coming with you?"

"She'll fly over for the funeral with Kevin. He has exams at the moment," he said flatly, the sadness audible in his voice.

"Oh right," Iris replied, looking forward to seeing Mark but hoping that he didn't expect her to go to the funeral.

When Mark arrived at Iris's flat, she hugged him and expressed her sympathy. He looked as though he'd been crying and Iris loved him for that. He never forgot how much his parents sacrificed so that they could pay his way through medical school. He had made sure that their old age was comfortable and even moved them from their modest council house to a small cottage he'd bought when they were both unable to manage the stairs. Mark had booked himself into a nearby hotel. His mam's sister was staying with her tonight and the cottage only had two bedrooms. His father's wake would be held there from tomorrow.

They had dinner at the hotel and talked about Kevin. He had applied to study medicine in Trinity but it would be a while before he knew if he'd got a place. The thought of having her son in the same city as her filled Iris with hope that they might see more of each other and develop, on some small scale, a relationship. The conversation was subdued and Mark looked lost. Iris wanted to hold him, to comfort him. At ten Mark suggested he drive her home. He had hired a car and the drive would take his mind off his grief, if only for a while. As they drove towards the flat she wondered if she should ask him in and went over the question again and again in her head.

"You look well," he said, breaking the silence.

"Thanks. I still get tired and it worries me sometimes – but it's normal I expect?" she said in a questioning tone.

"It'll take you a while to regain your strength," he said flatly.

Iris noticed the spark was gone out of him and that he was miles away.

When he pulled up outside her shop, she kissed him on the cheek.

"If you need anything, please call me," she said, squeezing his arm. She didn't know if it was a good idea to talk about whether or not it was appropriate for her to go to the funeral. The fact that he didn't raise the subject worried her because it meant that he either expected her to go so didn't even see the need to raise it or didn't want her to go in case it upset his brother and sister. She wished she had the courage to ask him directly but he looked so upset that she decided she'd ask Hazel what to do, something that didn't happen very often.

Hazel sat outside the training centre, enjoying the bright weather. It was one o'clock and she had just finished eating lunch alone. She was getting on well with the men on the course but found the women distant and bitchy. She reasoned that they were probably jealous of her. All three were not the slightest bit good-looking and were probably envious of the attention she got from the male students. She thought of Joe and how much she had enjoyed the conversation they had when he dropped her home on Saturday. Even though she was upset about the boys, she had found him easy to talk to. She loved the way he listened to what she had to say, to her feelings, and noticed how he didn't jump in with comments like her sister did. She had even talked to him about her past because she felt that he understood how she felt because he, too, had been through it. She never thought she could be friends with a man before. Most men, she reasoned, were only after one thing but Joe didn't seem like that. He was polite and respectful and hadn't even asked to come in when they pulled up outside her house. They had sat in the car for ages and she told him all about Gerry Henan and about her boyfriends previous to him, many of whom were a lot older than her. She had even told him about Pete and all the trouble he had caused her.

Hazel loved the way he had shown a genuine interest in what she thought. No one had ever done that before.

He told her all about his counselling in London, about how painful it had been but how it had set him free from his past.

She had never met a man like Joe. He was sensitive and kind. She briefly wondered if he was gay. He wasn't married and never mentioned a girlfriend but he had told her that he wanted kids so she wasn't sure. Before he left he invited her and Iris to his house on the weekend. He said the boys were welcome and that Vincent and May would be there with the other kids anyway. Hazel accepted and found herself looking forward to the weekend, not only so she could see the boys but because she was becoming interested in Joe Egan. All she had to do now was talk Iris into leaving the comfort zone of her tiny shop for an afternoon, and that wasn't going to be easy.

Chapter 41

Iris sat at her sewing machine and stared out into the street. The weather had finally started to improve and she noticed people starting to dress in lighter clothing. The sky was clear and the sun shone in her shop window, reddening her cheeks. She had gone to Mr Carey's funeral a few days previously after Hazel insisted she should, reminding her of all that Mark had done for her recently, as if Iris needed reminding. She wondered what she was thinking these days, asking for advice from Hazel. When she'd arrived there alone, she was glad that it was such a large funeral. The Careys were well respected in Cabra and there seemed to be hundreds of people at the church which made it easy for her to hide among the crowd. But when the hearse brought the coffin to the old graveyard, the crowd thinned out and only close friends and family walked the rest of the journey behind the coffin. Mark and his brother John carried the coffin with Kevin and three other men that Iris did not know. She could see tears in Mark's eyes as he made the final journey with his beloved father. She found herself crying as she walked behind, trying to keep her distance and hoping that none of the Careys would recognise her.

When the crowd arrived at the graveside, Iris stood beside a small clump of old yew trees where a few local women were standing. Even though it was a nice day, a cold breeze blew through the graveyard. She joined in the rosary and glanced nervously around her occasionally to ensure no one had spotted her. She wanted to be able to tell Mark that she was here, that she cared. She could see Miriam standing beside Mark's mother. Mrs Carey looked so much older and so feeble that it brought tears to Iris's eyes. Mark's sister, Karen, stood beside her mother and held her own little girl's hand. His brother John had aged a lot. He was younger than Mark but his hair was greyer and she noticed that he had put on a lot of weight. He stood there, white-faced, with his wife and three children.

Iris looked at the group and pondered how a few short years could change your life, how she once belonged to this family but now found herself hiding behind a tree, hoping to escape their accusing eyes. She could hear the priest chanting the last blessing and watched as Mark and his brother threw soil on top of the coffin. Miriam hugged him as he wept. That should have been me comforting him, she thought sadly to herself. Iris could see the crowd move forward and shake hands with Mark and his siblings. She moved to go and walked around the trees out of view. As she looked back, she saw Mark move forward to hug his mother. Their eyes locked and she noticed a small appreciative smile move up his face, his sad eyes smiling weakly at her. He nodded. She gave him a teary smile and walked down the mucky path alone and away from people who had once loved her, away from people to whom she had once belonged.

Mark phoned her the following day and thanked her for coming. He put Kevin on and they had an awkward conversation about his exams and his applications for university. Mark did not ask her why she didn't speak to the family or attend the lunch that the priest announced from the altar. He told her that he was really looking forward to seeing her in London and ended the conversation with small talk about arrangements to collect them from the train station. Then he seemed to pause, waiting for her to respond. He seemed nervous and Iris wondered if he was worried that she might not go to the graduation, after her experience at the funeral. If so, he was close to the truth. Seeing Miriam and Mark's siblings at the funeral made her realise that the trip to London might not be such a good idea after all. She was worried about a confrontation. She wondered what Miriam thought of Mark inviting her and, if she hadn't promised Mark that she would go, she would have cancelled the whole thing. But she had promised him and so she assured him she would see him in London.

Somehow, she thought, being in company made her loneliness seem more real and made her question if she would ever really belong anywhere or to anyone.

She hoped that the invitation to Joe Egan's house on Sunday would not be the same and that she would enjoy going over old times with the brothers whom she had really liked.

Hazel sat in front of George Kane and informed him of Luke's reaction to Pete Doyle's disappearance. She had come to see him after classes, at his request.

She had spent a lot of time thinking about the news report and had decided that Pete wasn't really missing and the whole thing was probably a ploy to avoid jail time – that he was really living it up somewhere in Spain and his whole family were in on it, crying for the cameras about how something bad had happened to him. She had almost fallen for it herself and had actually felt sorry for Doyle at the time.

George questioned her closely about Luke's reaction and how she had dealt with his fear.

"Look, I've told him that he can talk to me. I've told him that Pete is not coming after him," she said sharply.

"He has no reason to believe you," George replied quickly.

Hazel could hear the tone in his voice, polite but direct. She didn't want him to go on but she knew he would anyway.

"You have lied to him so many times that he no longer trusts you. I know that's hard for you to hear but that's how it is, at least for now. Is there anyone else that he'd have confidence in?" George said all this matter of factly, as though he hadn't just insulted her.

Hazel bristled but tried to hide her annoyance. "Not really. He won't talk to my sister. I'm hoping to take the boys to London – if the social workers agree. We're planning on going to see my brother-in-law in a couple of weeks, ex-brother-in-law, that is. I could ask him?" It was worth a try. She was out of ideas anyway and felt like giving up on ever hearing her son speak again.

"Well, let me know how that goes. But there's something else," he raised his thick eyebrows at her. "I don't see much point in you bringing Luke here every week. In fact, I think it might be making him dig his heels in even more. I'll be doing workshops at the school next week and I'll see him there instead."

George felt that part of the problem was the fact that Hazel had begun to dread the sessions. He knew she was under stress and had to take time off from her course to come here but her frustration at Luke's lack of progress was probably hindering the boy's recovery. He knew that Luke was genuinely afraid of Pete Doyle and he decided to leave Hazel out of the sessions and see if this would help.

"You're not giving up on him, are you?" Hazel said, alarmed. She knew that she couldn't help her son and was now worried that George couldn't help him either.

"No," George replied quickly. "Not at all. It's just better for me to see him at school."

Hazel stood. "So I can still see you myself on Friday?" she asked, hopefully.

"Yes, if you're happy that it's helping."

"Yes, it's helping," she said.

She smiled weakly and left.

Now that she was doing the course, Hazel wasn't able to attend the parents' group and actually found that she missed talking to the other parents. She spoke on the phone to Tina who filled her in on what was happening with everyone. Hazel was genuinely interested in hearing how the others were getting on and especially loved hearing good news. She felt that if other people were making progress, then there was hope for her and her boys.

Chapter 42

Joe Egan's home was a modest three-bedroom house at the end of a quiet cul-de-sac in the south side of the city. Like Hazel's, it had a large back garden which Joe had spent years working on. When he finished cooking lunch, Joe walked around the garden with Hazel while Iris and Vinnie caught up in the kitchen.

From the garden, Hazel could hear Iris laughing heartily at one of Vinnie's stories about their foster mother "Aunty Joan", stories Vinnie's wife must have heard many, many times.

As they sat down to eat, Hazel expressed her amazement that Joe had cooked such a lovely meal by himself. On the table there was fancy chicken dish she had never seen before, a roast beef joint for the red-meat lovers, a Moroccan vegetarian dish for May and an assortment of colourful roast vegetables that she didn't even know the names of.

"That's sexist," he responded jokingly. Jack sniggered, thinking that Joe had said something dirty.

Later, Iris watched her sister's expression as Joe played with the kids in the garden. She knew her sister had designs on the gentle man but she worried that they would not be a good match. Joe had, after all, experienced the same neglectful childhood as she and Hazel had. She had hoped her sister would meet someone without baggage, someone who had had a normal upbringing, someone like

Mark. Yet Joe was different from Hazel's previous love interests. He didn't drink or smoke and seemed good with kids. Maybe his background didn't matter, she mused. Maybe he was the right one for her sister and she should put aside her reservations and encourage the couple.

"What a coincidence, eh?" Vincent said loudly, breaking into her thoughts. "Us meeting up like this after all these years!" He looked over at Hazel who had flushed with embarrassment.

She looked away. Vinnie didn't know when to keep his mouth shut. She didn't want any reminding of how they were reintroduced. It wasn't as if they had run into each other in the supermarket. Vinnie didn't seem to notice her discomfort and continued.

"Eh, Daddy Long Legs! I'm talking to you!" he said to Hazel who continued to ignore him.

With the exception of Hazel and May, they broke into fits of laughter, remembering the nicknames they had for each other. They had been like sisters and brothers once, like a family within a foster family. Hazel decided to join in. If you can't beat 'em join 'em, she thought.

"Donkey!" Hazel roared at him in revenge.

Vinnie had always had a strange laugh when he was younger which only improved after he had his tonsils out.

"Marty Feldman!" Joe shouted at Iris who squirmed.

She had hated her nickname which was given to her because she was "all eyes". The others had tried to make a nickname out of Iris, as in the iris of the eye, which they felt suited her due to her tiny face and huge blue eyes but failed to come up with something funny so instead teased her about her likeness to the bug-eyed actor.

"Can't you remember mine?" Joe asked Hazel. He'd noticed that she had gone quiet.

"Denis the Menace!" she laughed.

Aunty Joan had bought Joe a red-and-black striped shirt one year for Christmas which she made him wear for years, even when it was far too small for him. Everyone at school teased him about it.

"I hated that shirt" Joe said, shaking his head.

As their laughter died slowly, the group settled into a comfortable silence.

"It's been really nice having you here," Vinnie said suddenly.

Iris looked at him and could see that he was overcome with emotion. What lovely men these brothers are, she thought to herself.

When Joe insisted on dropping them home, Iris agreed to stay with her sister to avoid him making two stops. Hazel had the boys overnight and this time the evening seemed to have gone well. Even though Luke still hadn't spoken, he didn't seem as nervous. She wondered if it was because Vinnie and Joe were around. Perhaps he thought they weren't safe without a man to fight Pete Doyle if he arrived at the house but, in truth, she had no idea what was on her poor nephew's mind.

Iris wished she'd had a chance to get her sister alone to talk to her about not leading Joe on. She didn't want him hurt, didn't want to see either of them hurt. More than anything else, she didn't want the boys becoming attached to Joe knowing that sooner or later the relationship would sour.

As soon as the car pulled up, Jack invited Joe in. Joe laughed and looked at Hazel.

"Yeah, come in," she said, glancing briefly at her sister's worried expression. Iris put the boys to bed as quickly as she could so the couple didn't have too much time alone. She could hear them chatting in the kitchen, Hazel laughing easily at something he had said. She rarely saw her sister at such ease and decided that Joe's calm ways were having a good effect on her anxious sister. She tucked Jack in and kissed him goodnight.

"Did you have a good time, love?" she asked him.

"Yeah. I love Joe, Iris. So does Luke. He's the best daddy we've had yet."

Iris smiled at him but his words broke her heart. Joe wasn't even dating Hazel and the boys had already taken him into their hearts. Over the years the boys had had lots of daddies, none staying more than a few months. She decided that even if Hazel and Joe didn't go the distance, at least the boys would have had a good role model for a change.

She looked up at Luke in the top bunk and leant forward, kissing him lightly on his forehead. She tousled his hair which still hadn't been cut.

"I love you," she said and thought she saw him give her a small smile.

Iris raced downstairs and put the kettle on to make tea. Hazel and Joe appeared to have gone into the sitting room and she wondered if she should join them or if they wanted to be alone. She decided to go in with the tea and then to excuse herself if she was in the way.

"Thanks for today, Joe," she said as she placed the tray on the coffee table. "We really had a nice time, didn't we, Hazel?" She was aware it sounded as if she was treating Hazel like a child forgetting her manners.

"Yes," Hazel replied, wondering why Iris was reminding her when she had just thanked him only minutes before. She gave her sister an icy look.

Iris sat down and began to pour the tea. "So, Joe, what about you?" she asked. "Vinnie talked all night so you didn't get a chance to tell us about yourself."

"That's Vinnie!" he laughed good-naturedly. Well, there's nothing much to tell," he said softly. "I told Hazel everything I've been up to these past few years."

"Oh," Iris replied, unsure where she could go from here and thinking that she'd just have to be blunt. "So are you seeing anyone yourself? Any bells on the horizon?"

Hazel glared at Iris. She was well able to find out information herself and didn't need her sister to play Cupid for her.

"No, I had a few relationships that didn't work out but I haven't given up," he laughed. "I might get down the aisle yet."

"Fine lad like you! You'd be a catch," Iris said, looking at her sister.

Hazel's mouth dropped open. She was astonished at Iris. She wasn't usually this forward. She decided that she would squeeze the last bit of life out of her skinny sister when Joe left.

She rushed to change the subject, remarking on how well suited Vinny and May were, which was the first thing that came to mind.

"Well, I'm off to bed," Iris said as soon as she had drunk her tea, satisfied that she had at least cleared up the question of Joe's availability.

"I'll be up later," Hazel said sternly.

Iris knew that what she actually meant was "I'll get you later" but she didn't care.

Hazel turned to Joe. "Sorry about Iris," she said, flushing. "I don't know what's got into her. She's normally so reserved and then she tackles you like that! She's just concerned, you know . . . well, as I've already told you, I haven't been great at choosing boyfriends."

Joe chuckled. "Don't worry. I get that a lot," he said, glad that Iris had opened a door for him. Unlike his brother, he was shy at times and had been trying to think of a way to ask Hazel out.

"I bet you do. People can be nosy alright. Sorry."

"It's fine really. Iris is really nice."

It was Hazel's turn to giggle. "Ha! You need to spend more time with her!"

"Truth is, when I dated before I never felt that I'd found the right woman," he said, looking directly at Hazel. He tried to think of what he might say next. His heart was beating loudly. He had planned on asking her out today but was worried about how she would react. He knew she had a lot on her plate at the moment and the time mightn't be right to start seeing someone. If she said no, he would have to face her often when he ran into her at Vinnie's. It would be too uncomfortable. It was true that his previous relationships had ended in disaster but he felt that it was because his keenness to get married and have a family of his own had scared his girlfriends off. But he was different now. He wanted to find someone he really wanted to spend the rest of his life with and that didn't happen when you rushed things.

He stood abruptly, taking Hazel by surprise.

"Well, I'd better go. I'm glad you came over. I enjoyed it. They're lovely boys you have." He began to move towards the door.

Hazel followed him, bewildered. She couldn't believe that he wasn't going to try it on with her now that they were alone.

At the front door she leant forward and kissed him on the cheek, smiling to herself at how shy he was.

"I enjoyed it too. Thanks again," she said.

Before she climbed the stairs to throttle her sister, a thought occurred to her. If Joe was looking for a girlfriend, why hadn't he asked her? She knew she was good-looking and that they had a lot in common. This was a new experience for her. She stopped on the landing and looked into the mirror, turning from side to side and peering closely at her reflection. Even though Joe wasn't her usual type she couldn't help but feel irked that he hadn't tried it on with her.

As she passed Iris's room she was too deep in thought to stop to tell her sister off but she banged on the door.

"I'll get you tomorrow!" she called out.

She went to bed wondering what kind of woman her friend was looking for.

Chapter 43

Two weeks after Hazel had the boys for their first successful overnight stay, she arrived for her regular monthly meeting with the social workers at the local health centre. Vinnie had told her that most meetings occurred on a two-monthly basis and that she was lucky to have her case reviewed so frequently. But she didn't feel lucky. She felt victimised by the system and was barely able to keep her mouth shut in those early meetings when the boys were first taken into care.

Hazel had been allowed to take the boys on three further occasions for an overnight stay, one of those being a school night. She didn't realise how happy she would be walking her boys to school and ignored the looks from neighbours who had become used to seeing a foster mother drop the Fay boys off each morning. She knew that the HSE were testing her, waiting to see if she would measure up and she wasn't going to let herself down. She wasn't going to let her boys down. Jack had begun to ask her when he could come home and it hurt not to be able to give her son a definite answer.

Hazel sat on an uncomfortable chair and stared at the three women on the other side of the table, one of whom she was told was there to take notes. She wondered why it had to be this formal, why they couldn't give her the usual rant about how the boys would be staying where they were, that while they knew she was making good changes to her life they didn't feel she was ready to take full responsibility for her sons. She had been attending these meetings for months and wore the same formal outfit each time. A long navy skirt, navy court shoes and a simple white blouse. Fuddy-duddy clothes she called them but she knew that this is what these women wanted. They wanted her to look like someone's mammy, sensible and respectable.

The older woman leant forward and gave Hazel a rare smile. She began her usual recount of the issues that had led to the boys being taken into care while the woman at the end of the table took what seemed to Hazel like excessive notes. The social worker updated Hazel on psychologist George Kane's latest report on Luke's progress and that the child psychiatrist had also reviewed him.

When she finished, the other social worker reported on Jack's placement needs. As they neared the end of their lecture, Hazel dug her nails into her thighs. This was the moment she hated, the last line which told her that the case would be reviewed in another month and the boys would remain in HSE care until then.

But when the older woman smiled at her and said that it was obvious that her circumstances had changed and that the consensus was that the boys were ready to return home with HSE supervision, Hazel almost jumped off her seat and hugged the women.

Her boys were coming home! She couldn't believe it. It was over and they could get back to normal life, whatever that was going to be or whatever the HSE told her it was, because she wasn't going to mess up again. She was going to take every bit of advice they gave her, whether she liked it or not.

She waited until the boys were home for two days before telling them about their intended trip. She wanted to keep it as a surprise and didn't want to overwhelm Luke who seemed to move around the house in a daze, staring at everything as though he had never seen it before. His sleeping problems continued and the Indian psychiatrist whose name she could never remember had given her a prescription for a night-time sedative which she hated giving to

Luke. Each morning he could not wake up and she would have to physically lift his legs out of the bed and help dress him. She had begun to accept that her son would never be the same again, that this new Luke, the nervous, watchful, anxious boy had replaced her tough-as-nails son, her rock.

On the morning of their trip, Iris tried to ease her own anxiety as she double-checked the bag that she had packed weeks before. She rose early and took the bus to Hazel's house, following which the whole family would travel to the port by taxi together.

When she arrived at the house, she found that the atmosphere in the house was chaotic. Lucky I came early, she thought as Hazel opened the door hurriedly with wet hair dangling down her back, running back upstairs and slamming the bathroom door behind her.

Hazel complained loudly that she hadn't been able to get Jack to wake up while her older son ignored her and stared out of the sitting-room window.

Amazingly, Jack was ready and was sitting quietly on his gear-bag in the hallway, amused at his mother's frantic dash from room to room, looking for what he didn't know.

Iris followed Hazel upstairs and peeked into her overloaded case which was still open, trying to see if her sister had bought a new outfit for the graduation but apart from jeans and T-shirts, she couldn't see anything.

"You'll never get that closed!" she shouted in through the bathroom door but Hazel did not reply.

"I'll phone the taxi, okay?" Iris called.

"Fine!" was all Hazel replied though the door.

Iris raised her eyes to heaven as she walked down the stairs which made both boys smile.

When the taxi arrived, Iris's heart thumped as they loaded their luggage into the boot. She was glad that Hazel and the boys were going with her. She couldn't have faced this journey alone. If it went wrong, she would be alone in a city that was now foreign to her.

She was glad of Jack's constant questions.

"How long does the ferry take, Aunty Iris?"

"Over three hours."

"How long does the train take?"

"About four hours if we get the quick one."

"How long does the slow one take?"

The taxi ride should have taken no longer than twenty minutes but traffic was slow and Jack did not let up for the entire journey.

Hazel looked out of the passenger-seat window and watched people going to work in the May sunshine. She had lain awake for hours thinking of her visit to Grace. She had even made a list of questions, just in case she forgot anything. She wished Grace had known her father better because she would have liked to find out more about him, but at least Grace could fill her in on her mother, about what she was like when she was younger, but most of all she wanted to ask Grace what had happened that led to her mother drinking heavily. Even though the letters were informative, they only told her a small part of the story. Hazel stretched and could see the taxi driver glancing at her long legs. She felt fully awake now and turned back to the boys.

"Are you excited, boys?"

Jack nodded but Luke ignored her and focused his eyes out of the window.

Hazel turned around, looking once again at the early-morning walkers. She tried to look at their faces, normal everyday faces of people living everyday lives. Soon she would be one of them, when her course finished and she got a job as a gardener. She would be just like everyone else. She had taken two days off the course and would miss out on some of the lessons but she would catch up. She also knew that she would miss Joe whom she had seen a couple of times since the boys left the Egans' home. Each time he visited her home he made it clear that he had come to see the boys and she continued to wonder why he wasn't interested in her. She had done her best to show him that she was interested in him but it didn't seem to result in him asking her out. She had thought of inviting him to Luke's Communion but she wasn't sure if it would make her seem overly interested. Since their late-night chat in her kitchen he had not raised the subject of girlfriends again so she took it that she was definitely not his type.

By the time the ferry left the port, Jack had already fallen asleep from the excitement and missed the whole land-disappearing-from-view experience.

"He'll be disappointed," Iris warned Hazel as they sat looking out of the window in the cafeteria.

Luke stared out of the window, in a world of his own. It occurred to him that all of his problems were on that land and he felt his shoulders relax as the ocean grew and all he could hear was the sound of seagulls circling the ship. He wanted to go out on deck and take a better look. He stood up.

"Where do you think you're going?" his mother asked crossly.

"Leave him, Hazel" Iris scolded. "He's excited." She turned to Luke. "Do you want to go out on deck?" she asked him softly.

Luke nodded.

"Be careful then and don't talk to strangers," she said.

Hazel looked at her and raised her eyebrows.

"Don't talk to strangers!" Hazel echoed. "That's rich, Iris. I don't care who he talks to as long as he talks!"

Iris could hear the anger in her voice.

No wonder Luke gets annoyed so easily, she thought to herself. That's all he knows.

Iris stood and moved out of her seat to follow him.

"Just stand right outside where we can check on you, Luke," she said as Luke charged on ahead.

On deck Luke went to the railing and stared at the deep blue ocean. He thought what a wonderful sight it was.

Iris stood inside and watched him through the glass panel in the door. She wanted him to feel free, independent. She watched him as his eyes squinted against the bright sun glistening on the water. Then, with a sigh, she went back to her seat.

The sea was calm with only a gentle breeze blowing. Luke smelt the fresh sea air and it lifted his spirits. He wondered if he could get a job at sea when he grew up. He could get away from all of his problems, from his mother who he knew was planning to visit someone even though Iris told her not to, from Pete Doyle and even from the kids at school. But he would have to get Jack and

Aunty Iris jobs on the ship too because he would miss them too much. Luke wondered if there were jobs you could do if you didn't speak.

He looked up and saw a man standing beside him. He was smoking a cigarette while he looked into the water. He threw his cigarette in and Luke watched as seagulls dived, thinking it was food. He gave the man a dirty look. Luke was worried that the birds could be poisoned. He hated people being cruel to animals. The man looked at him and smiled slowly. He had dark curly hair, going grey at the sides and deep brown eyes.

"Ah, don't worry, lad, they won't eat it," he said.

No response.

"What, you don't talk to strangers?" Gerry Henan asked.

Luke nodded.

"Good boy," he said, smiling and revealing a row of stained teeth. "You never know who you're talking to."

Luke looked up at the man and studied him. His face was lined and deeply tanned. He wore a dark trousers and shirt with an emblem on the pocket. Luke was dying to ask him if he worked on the boat and whether or not they give jobs to people who don't speak. But then he realised that this was a silly question because, if he asked him, then he wouldn't have needed to ask the question because he'd no longer be afraid to use his voice.

"Ya like boats, son?" Gerry Henan asked.

The boy nodded.

"Well, they're alright for a while. It's an adventure – but you know what?"

Luke shook his head.

"It gets lonely out here. The ocean is like an island. Do ya understand?"

Luke nodded even though he didn't know what the man meant. How could the ocean be an island?

The man took a step forward and tossed Luke's hair.

"Good lad. Stay on land, that's my advice," he said, smiling.

Luke watched as the stranger walked to the other side of the ship and disappeared down a stairway.

Nice kid, Gerry Henan thought to himself as he returned to the bar area where he faced another long shift.

Luke arrived back to the others just as Iris was coming to look for him.

Jack was awake and had got over the disappointment at missing the departure because Hazel had promised him that seeing the land come into view was much better. He stood and looked out the window near their seats.

Hazel went off to buy tea and cakes for them all.

"Did you have fun?" Iris asked Luke as he sat down.

He smiled.

"Good," she replied.

Luke sat beside Iris, leaning into her. It was the first time he had actively looked for a cuddle since the episode with Pete Doyle.

"Aunty Iris?" Jack asked from the window. "Tell us a story about when you came to London all on your own."

Iris wet her lips and began the story of how she took this same boat journey to start a new life for herself when she was only eighteen years old. Jack returned to his seat and placed his elbows on the table, anxious to hear every detail of what was one of his favourite stories.

Chapter 44

When the long train journey from Holyhead was over and they finally arrived in London, Hazel and Iris made their way through the crowds with the boys who were by now exhausted.

It was almost seven o'clock and they had been travelling all day. The train had been delayed and they had sat on the platform at Holyhead for almost two hours until it eventually arrived and took them on the final part of their journey to London. Even Jack had quietened down and his questions were restricted to "How much longer?" which he repeated every ten minutes or so for the entire delay. Iris now wished that she had talked Hazel into facing her fear of flying. They would have been in London in an hour and would have settled into their accommodation hours ago. She was nervous and wanted to get the reunion over with as soon as she could.

"Mark! Mark! Over here!" Hazel shouted loudly which slightly embarrassed her sister.

Mark waved and smiled. Iris could feel her heart lurch. She could see Kevin squinting, looking for her.

Then father and son were striding towards them.

"You look great!" Mark said, beaming as he hugged her tightly.

Hazel coughed, pretending to be offended that he hadn't noticed her first.

"Hazel!" he said, smiling and hugged his ex sister-in-law.

Mark hugged both boys as Kevin stood shyly, looking at Iris.

Hazel shoved Iris forward, almost knocking her into Kevin.

She reached out her arms and hugged him. It felt strange and caused the awkward teenager to blush. She had not talked to him during the funeral and this was the first time she had seen him since she was in hospital.

"How are you?" she asked nervously.

"Fine, M . . . Iris," he replied. He was not sure what to call her. He wanted to say 'Mum' but he wasn't sure how she would feel about that.

Kevin had practised this meeting over and over in his head for the past few weeks but it was always awkward and no matter how many times he rehearsed it in his mind, he knew he would be embarrassed when it actually happened.

"You look better," he added politely.

Mark stood and watched the two.

Even though he was smiling, Hazel thought his eyes looked sad.

"I'm sorry about your dad, Mark," she said.

"Thanks, Hazel," he said quickly.

She could see he was still hurting.

"Right," Mark declared. "There's too many of us for my car so some of us will have to follow in a taxi."

"I want to go in your car!" Jack declared loudly.

Everybody laughed.

"I know, why doesn't Kevin come in a taxi with me and the boys and Iris can go in your car. Give you a chance to catch up?" Hazel suggested.

Iris looked at her sister and felt a rare surge of gratitude. Spending time alone with Mark was exactly what she wanted to do even though she knew she shouldn't feel this way.

Hazel noticed Kevin looking worried. He looked at his father.

"Okay," Mark replied, and added, "Kevin can tell you if the driver is taking you on the scenic route."

On the journey, Iris filled Mark in on the news about Pete Doyle and thanked him for the one hundredth time for paying for the convalescent home.

"I am going to pay you back," she reminded him.

"I know," he said, laughing.

The two broke into easy conversation and chatted as Mark pointed out restaurants where they used to eat and parks where they used to sit and read on weekends when they were dating. It had been the best time of Iris's life, her happiest. It was a time when she had felt secure and felt that her life was finally her own.

"I've organised dinner at a restaurant and afterwards I'll drop you off at the hotel. Is that okay?"

"Will Miriam be joining us?" Iris asked.

Mark took his eyes off the road and looked at her.

"Iris, I'm glad we got this chance to talk. About Miriam . . ."

Iris watched him tense. She suddenly became afraid that he was aware of her feelings for him and was going to let her down gently. She felt her face and neck heat up and hoped she wasn't blushing.

"It's just that . . . well, I need to tell you that . . ."

Iris couldn't let him finish. It was too embarrassing. She wanted to enjoy tomorrow and if he said anything like "Look Iris, I'm happily married but you know I care for you . . ." she'd never live it down and might not even be able to go to the graduation tomorrow. She had to stop him.

"Mark, I know. You don't have to say anything. I am only here for Kevin's graduation and I'm glad you were kind enough to invite me. That's all."

He took his eyes off the road again and searched her face.

"Oh," he said.

An uneasy silence fell between them and Iris was relieved when they pulled up outside the bistro. She noticed that he had chosen what had been their favourite restaurant and felt a slight stab as they walked in and saw Miriam and her daughter waving at them.

"Iris," she said warmly, "it's so nice to see you."

Iris shook Miriam's hand and returned the compliment but felt guilty. Miriam was so welcoming and would obviously have no idea that Iris spent her time coveting her husband. Miriam's daughter Anna was now a fully grown woman and showed off her engagement ring. Iris heard Anna call Mark 'Dad' which surprised her because she would have been already a young girl when Mark came into her life.

Iris felt rather embarrassed when Mark sat down beside her while Hazel sat next to Miriam at the other end of the table.

Iris felt like an intruder who had somehow found herself sitting at dinner in a stranger's house. She had thought things might be awkward but Miriam's friendliness had taken her by surprise. She realised that Miriam did not see her as any sort of a threat to her marriage and that any thoughts Iris might have had, consciously or unconsciously, about Mark were simply that – thoughts.

She could see Hazel looking at her, mouthing something at her. She thought Hazel was saying "Enjoy yourself", but she wasn't sure.

She could hear Hazel and Miriam laughing a lot. The restaurant was getting busy so she couldn't hear what they were saying. They seemed to be getting on well which surprised her. She couldn't think of anything that Miriam would have in common with her sister. Kevin seemed brighter and more relaxed. He spent half an hour trying to talk Mark into letting him have a beer but gave up and settled for a Coke. Kevin seemed to have a good relationship with Anna and the two ribbed each other like a sister and brother would. Mark initiated most of the conversation with Iris as she looked around the table and tried to see where she fitted into this group or if she fitted in at all.

"Do you remember the night we came here for your birthday?" he asked, smiling.

Iris nodded. "It was my first year in London and you proposed even though we weren't a wet day going out," she replied quietly. She was afraid that Miriam would hear her and noticed Anna leaning forward to listen, interested to hear how her stepfather proposed to his first wife.

As Mark told the story with relish, Iris noticed that Hazel and Miriam had settled into a quiet conversation. She looked at Kevin who was smiling at her. She flushed. She didn't want all this attention on her. As the story progressed to the part where Mark got on bended knee and a waiter tripped over him, everyone started to laugh and Iris realised that the whole group, even Miriam, was listening. Everyone clapped as Mark concluded his story which involved the waiter being covered in a plate of spaghetti which the restaurant made Mark pay for. He looked at Iris and grasped her hand. His face was slightly flushed even though he only had one glass of wine. Iris reddened as he leant towards her and kissed her on the cheek, saying how nice it was to recall the story in this restaurant with her beside him. Miriam leaned forward and looked directly at her. Iris couldn't place her expression but she looked wistful and perhaps a little amused. There was something so strange about the whole evening. She wondered what Mark was thinking, kissing her in front of his wife, even if it was on the cheek.

She excused herself and went to the bathroom where she stood looking at her reflection. She took a deep breath. It was hot in the restaurant and her face was flushed. She heard the door open. It was Hazel.

"You alright?"

"Yes. It all feels a bit strange, you know . . . seeing Miriam and all." She had thought she would deal better with seeing Mark with Miriam but it was very uncomfortable.

"Yes. It's strange all right," Hazel agreed. She glanced at Iris, wondering what to say. Miriam had told Hazel that Mark and she were divorced for years now and had been separated for some time before that. The divorce had been amicable and Mark and she had remained good friends. The information had taken Hazel by surprise. The attention Mark gave Iris during her illness now made sense. But she couldn't understand why Iris hadn't told her. On the other hand, Iris was always secretive and abnormally reserved so maybe her silence on this touchy subject wasn't so strange.

Iris washed her face and fixed her hair in the mirror.

Hazel put an arm around her. "Just take it day by day," was all Hazel could think of to say.

Iris nodded and reapplied some lipstick. She rarely wore make-up and always felt that it made her look a bit clownish.

"Thanks. You're right. It's just hard. I didn't know I still felt this way, you know?"

Hazel nodded and the two returned to the table where the waiter was now serving coffee.

Good, Iris thought. The meal is almost over.

Mark dropped them to their hotel and helped them carry the luggage to their room. Jack ran about investigating everything and gabbling to Luke who also seemed quite excited, judging from his flushed cheeks and bright eyes.

"Is this alright for you?" Mark asked Iris in particular after she had looked around.

"It's fine," she replied.

"Right, well, it's late, so I'll see you in the morning. About nine? The ceremony is at eleven but it's a good distance by car."

"Okay, nine is fine," she said. She noticed that Mark seemed a bit nervous. He looked as if there was something he wanted to say.

He moved towards the door and she followed him. At the door he paused and called goodbye to Hazel and the boys, who had disappeared into the bathroom. They chorused goodbye as Mark stepped outside.

"Goodnight," Iris said.

He seemed to hesitate but she smilingly closed the door on him.

"What are you two boys whispering about?" Hazel was asking crossly as Iris joined them in the bathroom. It annoyed her that Luke spoke to Jack but still had not uttered one word to her. "Have some manners!"

"Mam, Luke said Uncle Mark fancies Iris!" Jack giggled.

"See?" Hazel said loudly to Iris. "Told you he speaks when he wants to!"

Hazel and Iris quickly got the boys into bed and got into bed themselves. Within minutes Hazel and the boys were asleep.

It had been a long day and Iris's fears were realised. She loved Mark and it hurt. But she was going to have to deal with it.

Chapter 45

When Mark arrived to pick them up, Iris was already waiting in the foyer of the hotel with the boys. She was relieved when Hazel came down the stairs in a long black dress which complemented her fair skin and hair. Hazel smiled at Iris, knowing what her sister was thinking.

"What? You thought I'd be wearing a mini?" Hazel said mischievously.

Iris laughed. "Yes, I did."

The graduation ceremony was held outdoors at the large boys' college that Kevin attended. It was a beautiful May morning with a clear blue sky and bright sunshine.

As the guests sat on rows of wooden chairs, Iris looked on proudly as Kevin received four academic and sports prizes. Mark looked handsome in a dark blue suit and glanced at her occasionally as the ceremony progressed. Miriam had arrived separately with Anna and her fiancé, James, and was sitting two rows behind them. Iris thought it was strange that Mark had not kept seats for them but did not dwell on it too much. She wondered if Miriam felt that it was better if Iris sat with Mark as Kevin's biological mother, but she had no idea what the other woman was really thinking.

After the ceremony ended the group went for lunch in a nearby restaurant. Mark insisted on paying the bill which embarrassed Iris although Hazel didn't mind and sat beside Miriam, happy to have found a drinking partner as both women ordered expensive wine. Iris hoped Hazel wasn't going to get drunk and embarrass her. She noticed that Miriam seemed quieter today. Mark sat in deep conversation with James who was training to become a doctor.

Luke hadn't spoken the entire time but seemed to be enjoying himself, looking around the room and smiling at his big cousin. When Jack spilled a glass of Hazel's red wine on himself, she took him to the bathroom after she moaned loudly at him for wasting good wine.

Miriam leant forward. "Are you enjoying yourself, Iris?" she asked kindly.

"Yes, thanks," Iris replied politely.

She wondered at what point, if ever, she should thank Miriam for everything she did for her son. She tried to rehearse it in her mind but it seemed to her that there were no words to thank someone for something like that and that anything she would say would seem inadequate. Still, she knew she had to say something and decided to express her gratitude simply and with sincerity.

"Miriam, I want you to know that I appreciate all you did for Kevin. He's grown into a lovely young man."

Miriam smiled. "Thanks, Iris," she said earnestly. "But Mark had a hand in it. He's a great father. I – I know it must be hard being here. I can't imagine what it's like for you but it was good of you to come. It means a lot to Kevin even if he doesn't say so."

Iris looked at the end of the table where Kevin was laughing at something James was saying. She noticed Mark looking at her. There was a concerned look on his face. Perhaps he thought that she and Miriam would not get along? Iris smiled at him to allay his fears.

"Is it awkward for you, you know, me being the ex-wife and all?" Iris asked.

"Well, we're both the ex-wives now so no, I don't mind at all," Miriam replied.

"What?" Iris asked, thinking she had misheard Miriam in the crowded restaurant. Several other graduation parties had come in and the restaurant was very noisy.

"I said we're both ex-wives now," Miriam repeated louder, laughing. Then she noticed the stunned look on Iris's face.

"Ex-wives?" Iris repeated stupidly. "You . . ."

"You didn't know?" Miriam asked, amazed.

Iris shook her head. "When?" she asked.

"We've been separated now for five years. Divorced about three," she replied.

"Why?" Iris asked, her astonishment reducing her to monosyllabic questions.

Miriam rolled back her head and laughed. Her face was flushed and she appeared to be slightly drunk although Iris knew Miriam had only had about two glasses of wine.

"Why does any marriage end? We were different, that's all. We drifted apart."

"But you're both doctors, you were both single parents. I don't understand."

"It's not as simple as that, Iris."

Iris could hear her tone change. She sounded sad.

"I don't know why he didn't tell you. You'll have to ask him about that but we married for all the wrong reasons. Yes, we had a lot in common. We were both alone, both had kids. It suited. I'm not saying we didn't love each other, we did, but as the kids got older we realised that we just didn't have enough in common."

Iris stared at Miriam, trying to digest her words, and looked quickly towards Mark who was now staring at her. He blushed and lowered his head. Iris couldn't understand why he hadn't told her. What was he afraid of? Did he think she'd want him back and he'd have to let her down? A flush of embarrassment reddened her cheeks. She stood and left the table quickly, almost bumping into Hazel who had tried in vain to get the wine stain out of Jack's good shirt. She walked out into the air and leant on the small wall in front of the restaurant, taking deep breaths of the evening air into her lungs. She wondered if that was what he was worried about, that her letter to Kevin was really about him, about her wanting to be part of his life again. But that didn't make any sense. It didn't explain his kindness to her when she was ill, his visits to Ireland. Or did he bring Kevin to see her only because he thought she was dying? She didn't know. She had no idea what was going through his mind or, indeed, what was going through her own.

The door opened and she turned. It was Mark. She stared at him, trying to think of what question to ask first.

"Why didn't you tell me?"

"I tried. I just didn't know what to say or how you'd take it . . . and . . . a part of me didn't want to admit that I had another failed marriage. I mean . . . it doesn't normally happen twice, does it? I was afraid you'd think it was my fault."

"Why would . . . I wouldn't have thought that," she said quickly. Mark had been a great husband to her and she could see no reason why he'd be any different to Miriam.

Mark did not respond but stood staring at her, unsure what else to say.

"Look, I'm sorry. I know I should have said something but . . . can we go back inside and join the party?"

Iris bit her lip. She had no idea what was troubling her but something was weighing heavily on her mind and refused to let her in on the secret.

"Okay," she replied meekly. "But no more secrets, alright?" she added, even though she knew she had no right to say this to him, no right at all.

"In that case, before you go inside, I want you to know that Kevin's been accepted to Trinity to study medicine, providing his exam results are as expected. You'll have to act surprised when he makes his announcement later! And . . . I'm planning on returning to Dublin to look after my mother. I thought that if Kevin was accepted to Trinity, I might as well move over sooner rather than later. She needs a lot of help now that Dad is gone."

"So you're both coming to Dublin . . . to live?" she asked, amazed that they would all be living in the same city.

"Yes, there's nothing for me here now. Anna is fully grown and almost a married woman. So I thought, why not?"

Iris nodded. She could feel her heart quicken. A wave of excitement rushed over her and she felt her cheeks redden.

Mark moved forward and gave her his arm.

"Shall we?" he said, opening the door and leading her back into the restaurant.

As they took their seats, Mark and Iris were aware that everyone in the group was interested in where they'd been. Hazel gave Iris a knowing smile while Kevin looked worried.

When Kevin made his announcement that he was going to university in Dublin, everyone congratulated him and Mark ordered champagne. Jack moaned that he didn't get any. Iris could see Luke's expression. His eyes shone. He was delighted that his cousin would be living in Dublin, another role model for a child who needed more male company than he got.

When the group returned to Mark's house, Miriam and Anna left with James while Kevin made arrangements to go out with his friends.

"Well, boys, I think we are gooseberries here," Hazel replied. "So why don't we leave Aunty Iris here and go back to the hotel?"

"Hazel!" Iris said loudly, embarrassed.

"What's a gooseberry?" Jack asked.

"It means we are in the way," his mother informed him.

Iris protested but Hazel insisted on leaving.

When Hazel and the boys had left, Mark showed Iris around the house that he had moved into when he separated from Miriam. It was a modern house with expensive furniture. Iris wondered what Mark had thought of the hovel she lived in, that morning when he arrived unexpectedly on her doorstep. So much had changed since then.

He brought a bottle of wine into the garden and poured them both a glass.

"I don't really drink," Iris said nervously. She felt awkward being alone with him.

Mark picked up on her nervousness and put the both glasses onto the table.

"I know. Let's go for a drive," he said.

"Where?" Iris asked.

"You'll see."

It was a beautiful evening and the sun was still shining despite a forecast of rain. Mark drove the car down several streets that Iris was unfamiliar with. She did not know this part of the city but when he swung left onto Broad Street, she recognised the park that they used to sit in whenever they had the same day off. Their flat was facing the park. It was the flat they lived in when they married, the flat she had taken Kevin to from the hospital, the flat in which he had reached up to her the morning she left for good.

She darted her eyes to Mark who was looking for a parking space.

"Why did you bring me here?" she asked.

Mark thought she was just nervous and did not recognise the anger in her voice.

She had no idea what Mark had in mind. She could think of no reason to bring her here and wondered why he would do something so cruel.

He looked softly at her. She could see the look of pity on his face.

"Why?" she demanded. "Are you angry with me, Mark? Is that it?"

"No," he replied, a look of hurt on his face. "No, I'm not angry but, Iris, until you face the past, you cannot move with any confidence into the future."

Iris was amazed to think that less than two hours before they were having a nice, cordial conversation at the restaurant. She couldn't believe that he could do something like this.

"Take me home!" Iris demanded. She could not face it. She couldn't see that flat, those stairs, that long narrow road that she walked down on the morning that changed her life forever.

Mark moved towards her and tried to hold her. She pulled back.

"Please Mark, take me to the hotel."

She started crying and finally allowed him to hold her.

"Iris, this may be your only chance to do this. Please?"

Iris looked at him and felt every ounce of energy leave her body. Perhaps Mark deserved this? Perhaps this was some sort of penance for her actions. He was taking her here to where she had turned his life upside down.

Iris opened the car door and walked the few yards to where their flat had been. She looked up to find a high-rise block of apartments in its place.

"What? Where's the . . . was it here?" she asked, confused. She could see the narrow green gate into the park and knew the steps to her apartment used to be almost facing it.

"It's gone," Mark said quietly. "They tore them down a few years back."

"Then why? Why bring me here?"

"To show you that life moves on, that everything changes, that you have to forgive yourself for leaving. You have to move on."

"Because the building is gone? Do you think it's that simple, Mark? God, if only it was!" she said sarcastically. "I can't, Mark. I can't forgive myself. I know that at the time I felt I had no other choice but it will haunt me until the day I die." She was speaking more to herself than to Mark who remained silent and stood with his hands in his pockets, looking at her, watching her return to her most painful memory, her biggest regret.

"I forgive you," he said softly. "So does Kevin. Now all you need to do is forgive yourself."

Iris moved her eyes from the new building in front of her to Mark's face.

"I don't know if I can," she replied quietly. "Nothing turned out as I planned. I want you to know that. I loved my life. I loved you. The person I am is not who I wanted to be, you know. I didn't want to be like my mother or my father. I had a whole other plan and I don't know when that changed. I'll never understand what happened to me back then but I didn't have the strength to fight it. I gave in and ran away."

"Iris, you were ill. You needed help. You felt alone although you weren't alone. This time, don't shut me out. Let me help you."

"Why are you so kind to me, Mark?"

"Because I'm your friend and I always will be."

Iris started to cry. She felt a weight lift off her shoulders. A heavy dark cloud broke above her and poured out its contents through her tears.

"I don't deserve you, Mark Carey!" she sobbed.

Mark held her and they stood there in the street. Several passers-by looked at them but they were oblivious to their stares. They were two people suspended in time, two people looking to move forward by trying to put the past behind them.

"Now will you have that glass of wine?" Mark asked.

Iris laughed and wiped the tears from her eyes.

"Yes, I will."

"My place?" he asked mischievously as they walked arm in arm back to the car.

Chapter 46

Iris was awoken by the sound of Jack playing with an imaginary toy train in their hotel room.

"*Choo- choooooooo!*" he roared.

She raised her head and grimaced. "Jack, please be quiet."

She remembered that she'd had two large glasses of wine with Mark which was unusual for her and, despite her headache, she smiled at the memory of their evening together. They had sat in Mark's living room listening to music and talking quietly about their lives and the future. It had been a lovely evening with an old friend. There was a part of her that felt sad though. Mark was a special man and she wondered what her life would have been like if she'd stayed. She tried not to think about it and to be just glad that they had managed to put the past behind them and that they were friends.

Iris raised her head and looked over at Hazel's bed but, instead of seeing her sister fast asleep, she saw Luke sitting on her bed with a note in his hand.

"Where's your mam?"

He handed her the note.

Gone to Sussex to see Grace. Don't be annoyed. The boys were asleep so I didn't want to wake them. I'll be back by nightfall. Hazel.

"Oh no!" Iris said as she sat bolt upright.

"When did she leave?" she asked but the boy did not answer. "Oh please, Luke, you have to speak. It's important."

Luke lowered his head until all Iris saw were two guilty eyes looking back at her.

"You knew she was going to Sussex?" Iris asked.

A single nod confirmed this.

"Why didn't you tell me? I thought you and me had a deal. We agreed if your mam was doing anything that worried you, you were to tell me, didn't we?"

Luke nodded again. Iris could see tears forming in his eyes.

"He didn't tell because it was a secret," Jack said from the bedroom floor where he continued to play with his imaginary train.

"A secret?" Iris repeated crossly. "I told you boys not to have secrets, didn't I?" She started to pace the floor. Sussex was at least an hour by train and Mark had told her that it was about twenty minutes to walk from the hotel to the tube.

"She left when *Power Rangers* was on. I watched it!" Jack added, delighted that there was a TV in their room.

Iris looked at Luke. She knew Jack couldn't tell the time.

"What time was *Power Rangers* on, Luke?"

But he did not answer. He wanted to remind Iris that she kept secrets – secrets about Mark and Kevin – and he was glad that he had decided not to talk because otherwise he'd have told her so.

He was also wondering why Iris was so worried about his mam's trip. She was only visiting a friend of his grandmother who he had never met and what harm could that be?

"*What time, Luke?*" Iris shouted, frightening her nephew who was not used to her shouting.

"Nine o'clock," he said in a voice so quiet that she barely heard him.

She remembered what the counsellor said and tried not to look shocked that he had spoken, but she hugged him as tears flowed down his face.

"I'm sorry for shouting at you, Luke. I'm worried about your mam. There are things I prefer her not to know, things that might hurt her."

254

"Secrets?" he whispered.

"Yes, love. Secrets. And secrets are always bad," she said sadly.

Iris phoned Mark. She didn't have enough time to catch the train and needed a lift to Sussex.

When Mark arrived Iris had the boys dressed and waiting outside the hotel. She had no choice but to take them with her.

"Will it take long?" she asked.

"About an hour, maybe less. It's mostly motorway and there mightn't be much traffic on a weekend."

Iris looked at her watch. It was almost eleven. If Hazel had taken the ten o'clock train, she'd almost be there by now. She could feel herself start to sweat and part of her knew that no matter what she did now, today her sister would know the truth, a truth she had tried to shield her from for so many years. Iris began to fidget in her seat but relaxed when Mark placed his hand on her knee. She could feel his warmth through her jeans. She placed her hand over his and could hear Jack giggling in the back as she stared at the empty motorway before her.

Hazel sat comfortably in the armchair in Grace Mooney's house as Grace's daughter, Molly, made tea. She'd found the address easily enough and now that she was here, there was something so relaxing about the place that Hazel felt like she belonged here. Grace looked older than she had imagined her. Hazel realised that if her mother had lived, she would be roughly the same age as the grey-haired lady sitting in front of her.

As Grace reminisced, she told Hazel stories about her single days when she and Liz came to England in search of work, about how confident Liz had been then, chatting up the fellows she liked and turning down as many.

"You're the image of her," Grace said softly.

Hazel could see that the visit meant a lot to her.

"Yeah, people say that," Hazel replied. "Iris is different. She's short and she has dark hair. Don't know where Mam got her."

"Yes. Iris looked a lot like Eileen when she was a little girl," Grace said. "Do you remember your mam's sister?"

"Yes. Sure. She looked after us for a while after Mam died."

"It was the least she could do!" Grace spat. Hazel could hear the sharpness in her tone and wondered if it was because Eileen and her mam hadn't got along.

"Thanks for the letters. They made me realise how bad things were for my mam."

"You're welcome, love, but I often think no good comes from delving into things. Sometimes we are no better off from what we find out."

"I know but it is helping me. You see, I was bitter about Mam's drinking and how it affected Iris and me but now that I know how tough things were for her, being on her own and that, I think I understand."

Grace absorbed Hazel's words and sat there for such a long time that Hazel didn't think she was going to say anything more. She wondered if the elderly woman was a little senile. She could see Grace's mouth open and close as if she was speaking to herself or perhaps reliving old memories.

"You know," she said slowly, "it didn't have to be that way for your mam. I mean, when she met Jack we were working in the nursery here. Your mam had secretarial training – her mother saw to it that both she and Eileen had qualifications – so she got a job in the office as soon as the manager found out that she could type. We were picking mushrooms before that, ten hours a day."

"What do you think happened to her then?"

Grace dropped her chin down and thought about the question. It was a question she had asked herself many times over the years and for which she had never come up with a satisfactory answer. Her eyelids were drooping and heavy and she looked as if she was asleep.

"I don't know, love," she said in a raspy voice. "She could have had a good life but it seemed to me that every time your mam found happiness, she found a way to make herself unhappy. I'm not making sense, I know, but you would have needed to have been there. It was almost like she didn't want to be happy. If she wanted something, she got it, but as soon as she got it, she wanted something different. That's the best way I have of explaining it."

Hazel tried to absorb Grace's words. She hadn't expected Grace to say anything bad about her mother and it took her by surprise.

"Do you mean, she . . . she was to blame for what happened?"

"Oh no, love. I'm not saying that. It's just that she seemed to be always looking for something else, always thinking she'd be happier somewhere else or with someone else. Like I said, it's hard to explain a person in a few sentences. She was complicated. I still miss her."

Hazel looked at her and wondered what else she should ask. She could hardly take out her list. Grace looked more feeble than she had imagined she'd be and she was worried that she might not get another chance to find out about her mother's life. She was planning on catching the one o'clock train back to London. Iris had phoned her mobile twice already but she'd ignored it. She'd explain her reasons for coming here later when her sister had calmed down.

"Do you think she loved my father?" Hazel asked.

Grace raised her thin grey eyebrows in surprise and thought about her answer.

"Yes. In the beginning anyway. It's hard to know where it went wrong. I think her drinking got to him and he strayed but Liz said at the time that his roving eye made her drink. Truth is, it was probably both. She was lonely, that's for sure. She always felt alone, even with lots of people around. She told me that at a party once before either of us was married."

Hazel was amazed to hear that her mother shared this trait with her. She, too, had felt lonely her whole life and she had never met anyone that could take that feeling away.

Grace moved her lips back and forth. Hazel waited. Grace had something else to say.

"It's a pity that she's not here today with us. Maybe she'd laugh at all the foolishness of the past and wonder what she was fussing about?" Grace said sadly. "We used to have some funny times."

Hazel could see a far-off look in her eyes as she reminisced – probably remembering going to dances in London when they were young and out of the watchful eyes of their mothers.

Grace looked up and sighed heavily, bringing herself back to the present where she was an old woman who depended on her daughter for almost everything that she used to take for granted, a long way from dance halls and back-row kissing. She stretched and yawned. She still got up early every morning and normally took a nap at this time.

"I don't know if I've been much help, love, but I suppose your dad can fill you in on the rest."

"My dad?" Hazel said. "What do you mean?"

"Your dad – when you see him."

"See him? I don't understand," Hazel asked in confusion.

"I thought that's why you were here?" Grace asked, equally confused. "To see him."

"He died years ago, Grace," Hazel replied. She was surprised that Grace was confused about such a thing when only minutes before she seemed so coherent.

"Died? He's not dead, love. What made you think that? He lives here, in town, just out the road."

"Grace . . . he died, in an accident. You don't remember that?"

"No, love . . . he . . . well, I don't understand why you . . ." Grace was lost for words. She had no idea why Hazel thought her dad was dead and stared at the young woman whose face was slowly beginning to crumble in front of her.

"My mam . . . my mam told us . . ." Hazel tried to finish her sentence but her head was reeling. She could not take it in.

Her father was alive. He was alive and he was living in this town.

Her mother had lied to her.

"I thought you knew . . . I'm sorry," Grace said.

"Why . . . why would she say that?" Hazel asked herself aloud.

Grace stood up and took her walking stick from the seat beside her. Her feet were unsteady and she looked as if she would fall over.

"I don't know, love. I'm sorry, I didn't know that you . . . well . . . I just don't know . . ." Grace's mind was racing. She had no idea why her friend told her daughters that their dad was dead.

"Where? Where does he live?" Hazel asked. Her throat was dry and she could hear her voice crackle and halt with nervousness. Her head was spinning and she felt her legs weaken. Her mother, with whom she had tried to make her peace, the mother she tried so hard to understand, had lied to her and she felt cheated for a second time, deceived by the woman she was ready to forgive.

"It's only about fifteen minutes' walk."

"Good."

"Hazel . . . Hazel . . . he . . . he's married . . . Look, maybe this is a bad idea. I thought . . . I thought you had arranged to visit him, to put the past behind you. Maybe you should think about this, sleep on it?"

"No!" Hazel replied. "I'm going there right now. I deserve some answers."

"Will we phone first – tell him you're coming?" Grace asked nervously. Jack Fay and herself didn't exactly move in the same circles and since he had returned to the town she had rarely seen him but she didn't want to bring trouble on his doorstep. It wouldn't change anything. It couldn't undo the hurt that had been done.

"Where does he live? Just tell me which way to go."

Grace could hear the emotion in her voice and knew that the young woman was about to cry.

"It's an old house. It was his parents'. It has a white picket fence all around." Grace was feeling extremely uncomfortable and wished she could take it back, that simple sentence that was about to cause even more hurt. "Are you sure this is a good idea?" she asked Hazel again, gently trying to dissuade her.

"Yes. I'm going to get some answers from the one parent who can give them to me."

"Hazel," Grace said gently, "you may not like the answers you get."

"But they'll be answers just the same. Answers I need and that I deserve."

Grace nodded. Even if she didn't agree, she understood. She had written to Liz all those years ago, telling her that Jack was living in his parents' house with a woman only days after he arrived in England. Liz was hurt but at least she knew that he was not coming back, that he was gone for good.

"I'll get Molly to drive you," Grace offered kindly. She had started this and she might as well make it easier on the girl.

"No. I'll walk. I'd prefer to go by myself," Hazel said, moving towards the door.

Grace stopped Hazel and hugged her. "Parents are just people, love. They make mistakes that sometimes they cannot fix."

"These mistakes are too big, Grace. They left us, in one way or another. They left us and didn't care what happened to us."

"That's not true, love. They had problems, both of them, but you were loved. I know that. They were just not right for each other and you two girls suffered."

Hot tears began to fall down Hazel's face. She took her bag from the kitchen table.

"Thanks for seeing me" she said before turning quickly and walking out the door and marching towards her father's house.

Iris wrung her hands as the traffic conspired against them. They had got out of London quickly and had now joined the motorway that would lead into Sussex but an accident had created a tailback for about a mile and the traffic crawled by with each driver stopping for a look at the tangled wreckage. Iris bit her nails and tapped her foot on the floor.

"I'll just try Hazel's mobile again," she said but it rang out.

Hazel could not understand why her mother had sat them down and told them that their father was dead. Why didn't she just tell them the truth? She wondered how a parent could be so cruel. The bitterness that she felt for her mother before she read the letters returned and increased with each step that she took towards her father's house. She knew though that her father was equally to blame as he had obviously left them and had not even bothered to come back for his daughters when their mother had died. She could feel her heart thumping and her jaw muscles tense as she rehearsed what she would say to him, the fury she would unleash on him. But the fury turned to an overwhelming need to cry and she bent forward on the main street as though she was in physical pain. She started to sob uncontrollably and moved quickly into a small empty park off the town's main street.

"How could you?" she cried aloud to both her parents. "How could you do that to us?"

Hazel sat on a hard wooden bench and felt more alone than she had ever felt in her entire life. No one had wanted her, not her mother and not her father. She realised that her feelings of worthlessness were rooted in her parents' abandonment of her all those years ago. All the men who had used her, the sporadic employment, it was all down to them. It was their fault. Despite the mild spring weather, Hazel felt cold. She wrapped her arms around herself and stared out into space, thinking of what she would say to this man, this man whom she had idealised.

She rose and dried her eyes on her sleeve and wondered how she would ever recover from this, how she would ever feel valued, ever feel loved. Her parents had left a hole inside her that she had tried, but failed, to fill.

Hazel took a deep breath. She had nothing to lose now by confronting her father. Nothing he would say could hurt her any more than she had already been hurt.

Hazel rejoined the main street and walked slowly in the direction of her father's house. It was time for the truth, no matter how much it hurt.

Chapter 47

As Mark's car finally arrived in Balcombe, Sussex, Iris tried to remember the way to her father's house, a road she had travelled many years ago.

After Kevin was born she had begun to think about her father. She thought it was sad that he now had a grandson he would never know. She decided to find out where he was buried but, when there was no record of his death, she spent some of Mark's hard-earned money on a private investigator. She knew he had no relatives and a part of her fretted that he had ended up nameless in an unmarked grave. What she found out made her wish that she had spent the money on something frivolous or on some much-needed furniture for the flat. Her father was alive and living in Sussex. She still remembered the range of emotions she went through. Disbelief, upset, anger and finally bitterness which, despite the passing years, had not gone away. A few weeks after she learnt the truth, she rose early and took the train there, leaving Mark looking after Kevin in London. She made up an excuse about needing to go into the city for some new clothes.

When she arrived in Balcombe she asked discreetly where he lived and walked the mile journey out of town. It was not hard to find his house. She recognised the garden immediately. It was laid out almost identically to their own garden that he had designed when she and Hazel were small. The house and garden was picture-postcard perfect with a neat lawn and low picket fence. There didn't seem to be anyone home so she stood and looked into the garden for what seemed to her even now to have been the longest time. She remembered an almost surreal feeling overcoming her. She found it hard to believe that the man she had pined for, the man she thought had died, had been here all that time, living and breathing. She could not understand it. What did he think happened to his girls when he left them in the care of an alcoholic mother? Did he ever think of them? Worry about them?

Iris walked slowly the whole way back to town and waited for the next train. When she returned home, she burned the letter from the investigator and tried to put her father out of her mind. She decided never to tell Hazel as she knew that it would destroy her sister who romanticised their father. Her sister didn't need to know but she did need to hang onto the hope that at least one of her parents hadn't abandoned her, hadn't chosen to leave her but that an accident had cut his time with her short. Iris sometimes wondered if finding out about her father triggered her to abandon Kevin only months later but she knew there was more to it than that. Perhaps knowing he was alive all that time did not help but she had been anxious from the moment she became pregnant.

Now, even though her visit to Sussex was over sixteen years ago and her father could have died since then, Iris felt that he was still alive.

As Mark's car turned a sharp bend on the country road that led out of town, Iris saw her sister first, standing inside their father's garden, mesmerised by the similarity to her own, a garden Hazel had maintained in honour of a man she thought was dead. Iris got out of the car and asked Mark to keep the boys inside. She had explained everything to them and she watched as Luke struggled with yet another secret. She told the boys that there could be no more secrets. They were too costly, too dangerous and caused too much hurt. She could not describe the expression on her sister's pale face but thought Hazel looked as though she was sleepwalking.

"Hazel," she said softly as she wrapped her fingers tightly

around the picket fence. She did not want to go inside those gates. She could not face him. Hazel turned and looked right through Iris. "You knew?"

Iris nodded. She could hear the sadness in her sister's voice. Hazel's hair fell around her as she bent her head forward, looking at the plants and shrubs. A large hazel tree stood on one side of the garden, surrounded by daffodils and a thick mass of purple African violets. A rockery lined the other side and was adorned by deep blue-bearded irises and white crocuses. Hazel shook her head and turned back to where Iris stood. Tears were flowing down her face.

"Look at this garden, Iris. It's exactly like . . . ours."

Iris started to cry, her sister's pain obvious to her. "Come out, Hazel, come home with me."

"He's been here all this time. All this time when we needed him. He was planting trees and flowers for someone else."

Iris could not hold back her tears and let out a loud sob. "Hazel, I love you. You don't need him, not any more. Please come out. The boys are waiting for you." She dug her nails into the wooden fence and glanced around the pristine garden which seemed at odds with the devastation this man had left behind.

Hazel looked up and had started to speak when Iris saw him, standing there, an old man. He moved forward and Iris watched as he limped towards them. There was nothing familiar about him except his piercing blue eyes, but he knew them, he knew who they were. He walked slowly down the neat, winding path and stopped a few feet from where Hazel stood. He did not speak but looked at her, waiting.

Hazel stared at him, her eyes moving from his head to his feet. She did not know him. He was a stranger to her. Her mouth moved, trying to search for words, the right words.

"You built the same garden," she said, her tone incredulous.

Jack Fay maintained his gaze, his cold blue eyes watching the two women, his daughters, all grown up. They looked exactly as he imagined they would. He swallowed hard, revealing his unease. He never thought this day would come, never thought that the past he tried so hard to put behind him would resurface. It was over thirty years since he walked out on Liz and he knew even then that he was not coming back, that the marriage was over. He had fallen in love with Sarah and decided to make a life with her. He reasoned that he could not take the girls with him, he could not expect Sarah to take them on and he couldn't take them from Liz. They were all she had left. Over the years he knew that these were excuses he made to explain his behaviour. He had wanted to break away, to have a clean slate. To cut Liz and all the heartbreak she brought on him out of his life forever. He made it easy for himself, pretending it was in the girls' best interests, but he couldn't hide from his conscience, a conscience that spoke louder as he aged, and tortured him with guilt and regret. He told himself that he would contact them when they got older, when they were old enough to understand the situation he had been in, but the years passed quickly and somehow it became too late for explanations, too late for excuses. When his two sons were born, he thought of his girls even more and realised what they were missing out on, a loving mother, a secure home, and his guilt grew, nurtured by every Christmas, every birthday party and every school play he attended for his boys.

When Liz died, Eileen contacted him and pleaded with him to take the girls to live with him but instead of prising open the door that was still ajar, he placed his hand against it and slammed it shut. To this day, he still did not know why he did that. Perhaps it was fear of seeing the hurt in their eyes, of knowing exactly what kind of a man their dad was, a dad who had once been their hero. Eileen reluctantly stayed on to look after them, probably through guilt as she too owed a penance to Liz.

Hazel waited for an answer, something from his lips, but he did not speak. Iris could see the curtains move in the front room and wondered if his wife was watching the scene unfold before her and if she knew who they were, if he had ever told her that he'd abandoned another family for her.

Hazel struggled with her thoughts. There was so much she should ask and yet nothing that was worth asking because his presence here told her almost all that she needed to know.

"Why?" she said finally. "Why did you leave? Why did you not come back when our mother died?"

Iris watched him tense up and took pleasure in his discomfort.

"Please . . . please come inside," he begged, anxious not to have this reunion, this awful scene, aired outside.

"*No, I want to hear it from you here, in your beautiful garden!*" Hazel screamed, frightening the aging man.

"Your mother and me . . . it was never going to work. I tried, I just couldn't get through to her," he replied simply as if that was enough, as if that was a reason.

Iris thought that she had forgotten his voice. When she remembered things he said to her, it was always in her own voice, in her own head as if with his departure he took his sounds and smell with him and left behind only a memory of his face disappearing down a flight of stairs. Now his voice came rushing back to her like a flood, washing over her and returning her to the vulnerable little girl she had once been.

Heavy tears rolled down Hazel's face as she absorbed his words.

"I tried everything to make her happy but nothing was good enough. Then she started drinking. When your brother died, I gave up. I had nothing left to give her. I had started to hate her. I had no idea what else to do but leave."

"*What about us?* Did you think about leaving Iris and me with an alcoholic mother?" Hazel roared. In her anger she had reversed roles with her sister who stood almost catatonic at the gate. Hazel had nothing to lose. She had no memory of this man. Her only feeling was anger.

"I couldn't take you with me. It was different then. Kids stayed with their mother."

Hazel could see his eyes water and a recognisable expression on his face. Guilt.

"What about when she died? You knew that she had died. Grace Mooney told you."

"I was married then. It was complicated," he said in a low old-man voice.

"Well, life was complicated for us too!" Hazel screamed. "Did you know we went into care, that there was no one to look after us? Did you think of that when you were planting a new garden, making a new life?"

"I thought Eileen was looking after you," he said solemnly.

"Eileen? She didn't love us and neither did you. She died a few years after she came to look after us and we had no one. We thought we had no one but you were here . . . you bastard!"

Iris moved towards the gate, anxious to take her sister from here, but Hazel wasn't finished.

"Was it true, what my mother suspected? She thought you were seeing Eileen, her own sister! I read her letters. She also said you were having an affair with your boss's wife."

Jack Fay looked away from her and settled his eyes on a hedge of beech trees that he had planted as protection from the strong breeze that sometimes blew up from the ocean, the only difference to the garden he had planted all those years ago in Dublin.

"It's not true about Eileen," he replied, acknowledging the affair with his employer.

"You . . . you bastard!" she said angrily. "You cheated on her!"

He met her eyes and the anger glinting in them.

Jack Fay tried to ignore his daughter's rage. There were things she could never understand. He was lonely. He was always lonely until he met Sarah.

"I thought of you but time passes and sometimes it is too late to make amends."

Hazel was unmoved.

"When you leave, it is hard to go back. Everything changes," he said, looking at Iris as if he knew her past, as if he knew that they had something in common.

Iris swallowed. She was not the same as him, she was not. She glanced back at Mark who remained in the car with the boys as she had requested. She was not the same.

Finally, she spoke.

"You left us with someone who could not care for us and you knew that, you knew that very well. You need to know what happened to us after you left. You need to hear that she drank most of the money we had to live on. She left me to care for Hazel. She put us in danger on so many occasions that I spent many years trying to forget them. We depended on you. When Eileen died, we went into care. Yes, we were fed and clothed but we were not loved. We were never loved and you will have to face that fact until the day you die. I don't know what happened between you and our mother but I do know that when she wilted, you found yourself a new garden to grow and you left us to rot with her!"

Without thinking Iris opened the gate and walked over to the neat flower-bed and pulled every iris from its roots. He did not try to stop her.

"Don't you ever plant any more irises!" she barked. "You don't deserve any memory of us."

Hazel looked up at the mature hazel tree. She wished she had an axe and imagined herself swinging at it for hours, damaging the roots of the tree as he had damaged their roots, their beginning.

Iris took her sister by the hand and walked her to the gate where they both turned to look back at him.

"I called my son after you," Hazel said sadly. She knew that this would be the last time she would lay eyes on her father. "You should have come for us," she added as she closed the gate gently and walked towards the car where her two sons waited.

Iris turned back again and took a long look at the man whom she had cherished, watching them with old watery eyes as they walked away from him.

He remained there until their car disappeared from view.

In the car, Mark held Iris's hand as she cried in the front seat while Hazel broke down in the back.

Luke leant over and hugged her tightly. "Mam, you don't need a dad if you have people who love you," he said quietly as Hazel sobbed loudly at the beautiful sound of her son's voice.

Chapter 48

As Iris settled the boys into a seating area on the ferry, she glanced towards her sister who had hardly spoken since they drove away from their father's house the day before.

"You hungry?" she asked her.

She shook her head.

"Right, well, I'll get the boys something. Will you watch them?" She was worried about her sister and didn't want to leave the boys with her when she was like this.

Hazel pulled a face at her sister and turned away while Iris signalled for Luke to watch Jack while she was gone.

At the café, Iris joined a queue – the sea was choppy and people were swaying slightly while waiting on their orders. She brooded on the past few days and everything that had happened. She was still coming to terms with the fact that Mark was single. She still didn't know how she truly felt about that but knew that in some way it was easier when he was unobtainable. She tried to put these thoughts to the back of her mind and focus on more immediate problems such as Hazel's reaction to knowing their father was alive. She knew her sister was devastated but hoped she wasn't going to cave in and go back to her old ways.

She had found it hard saying goodbye to Mark and Kevin but hoped to see them soon. Mark said he'd be over during the summer and had asked her to help him look for a house in Dublin. He decided to buy a house nearer to the city centre that could double up as his practice and also so that he could see Kevin, who was going to stay on campus, as often as possible.

As Iris waited on her order, Luke took advantage of the situation and asked Hazel if he could go on deck with Jack.

"Yeah," Hazel replied absentmindedly, already used to her son now speaking and waving them away.

Luke guided Jack through the crowds of people and past a girl who was vomiting into a plastic bag.

"Oh, that's gross!" Jack said, holding his nose as he passed her.

As they opened the door to go on deck, they heard someone call "Hey!" behind them.

Startled, the boys looked around.

"If it isn't the little sailor!"

It was the man Luke had met last time.

He tossed Luke's hair and smiled at him. Luke grimaced. The man smelled of cigarette smoke which, like his Aunty Iris, he hated.

"Are ya going to talk to me this time?" Gerry Henan asked. "I'm not a stranger any more."

Luke nodded. "We're going out to look for seagulls."

"Is this your brother?"

"Yeah. He has asthma." He was unsure why he added that last piece of information.

"Well, the sea air is great for asthma."

"Really?" Luke asked. This was great news because if he did get a job on a boat and took Jack with him, they might not need to bring a nebuliser.

A silence fell between the three.

Jack looked up at Gerry Henan through small sharp eyes.

"I'm making my Communion in a few days," Luke said, hoping the man might give him some money.

"Are you? Well, we'll have to give you something for that" He rummaged through his pockets and handed Luke a two-euro coin. "There you go!"

Luke's eyes lit up.

"You shouldn't take money off strangers!" said Jack.

"It's alright, son. I won't hurt you or your brother," Gerry Henan said, rubbing his hand through Jack's mop of dark hair. He smiled at the boys. He didn't really like kids but these ones were cute. They reminded him of his son Gerard Junior when he was younger.

Jack stared up at the man and bit his lip. There was a smell of beer off him. It reminded him of Pete Doyle and made him nervous.

"Come on!" Jack said, pulling his brother towards the exit door. "Let's go."

When Iris returned and found the boys gone, she almost spilled the tea over Hazel who did not seem to have moved.

"Hazel, where are the boys?"

"Relax, Iris!" she snapped. "They've just gone outside."

"Alone! Have you lost your mind, Hazel?"

Hazel looked away from her sister and stared into space. Yes, she had lost her mind or at least felt it slipping away from her. She could not digest the fact that for all those years, the man she had adored, the man who she thought had been taken from her in a tragic accident had not wanted her. It was too hard to comprehend, too hard to accept and she could feel it eating away at her.

Iris turned away from her sister and looked quickly around the room. From the corner of her eye she spotted the boys coming in the door that led to the deck.

"Boys, come over here!" she barked. "I told you not to go outside without one of us with you!"

"Sorry, Aunty Iris," Luke whispered.

"A man gave Luke money," Jack offered.

"What? What man?" Iris asked, worried at what might have happened to her nephew on this crowded ship.

Luke gave his brother a dirty look. "He's nice – he said I'd make a good sailor," he said quietly.

"Were you . . . alone with him?" Iris asked gingerly, fearing the worst.

"Just me and Jack," Luke answered quietly.

He was sorry now that he had started talking again as it was definitely going to get him into trouble but when he saw his mam so upset about her dad not wanting her he had to talk. He had to protect her because that was his job, that and looking after his brother.

"I didn't like him," Jack said.

"Why?" Iris asked, her eyebrows raised, waiting to hear some awful story about a dirty old man interfering with her nephews.

"I don't know," Jack answered glumly. He didn't want to mention Pete Doyle, not when his brother was finally talking again.

Iris looked at the two boys, unsure if there was anything else she should ask them. "Okay, but if either of you leave my sight again for the rest of the journey, I'll be very, very cross!" she said in her best cranky-aunt voice while Hazel continued to stare out the window towards home.

When the ferry finally arrived into Dublin port, the weather had turned dark and dismal and the heavy rain darkened Hazel's foul mood, matching the bleak day. As they walked down the crowded gangway, Iris held tightly onto Luke while Hazel carried Jack who had started to wheeze from the change in the weather. People were pushing each other trying to get to the few available taxis and the noise of children crying and people shouting was getting to Hazel who yearned for quiet so that she could be alone with her thoughts, with her troubled mind.

On the crowded gangway, Gerry Henan was only twenty feet behind her as he made his way through the crowd. His shift was over and he faced four days off which he dreaded. Gerry had come to hate this job but somehow he hated his long stints off even more. He was living in cheap digs now and found that he spent his time off either sitting alone in his damp hovel or sitting in the pub, still alone despite the crowd of rowdy port workers. Summer was coming and he dreaded the long bright evenings as families out walking passed by the window of his basement flat. He would sometimes spend hours watching all sorts of legs pass by his window – children's legs, men's legs, old people's legs, all with someplace to go – and it made him feel even more alone. Not that he ever thought he didn't deserve the situation he was in. He knew it was his fault and he had chosen freedom over family, but that the freedom had imprisoned him into a life of loneliness and isolation. He glanced up at the thundery sky which promised more rain.

Just ahead of him, Jack was still in Hazel's arms.

"That was the best holiday, Mam," he said breathlessly.

Hazel could not help but smile despite her mood. It was the only holiday the child had ever been on.

"Good," she said, kissing him on the cheek, unaware that Gerry Henan had passed by her as he headed for home, alone.

When they reached Hazel's house, Iris set about unpacking the boys' things straight away and made them some dinner while Hazel sat alone in the living room. By eight, Iris had bathed the boys and tucked them into bed. She needed to talk to her sister before she fell into a depression.

She went into the sitting room where Hazel sat staring at the telly which wasn't even switched on.

"I might stay the night, Hazel."

"Okay," she replied, glad of it. Even though she didn't feel much like talking, she didn't want to be alone.

Iris sighed, not knowing where to begin.

"Hazel, I know this is hard for you but nothing you or I did made him leave and there is nothing we can do about it. It's in the past."

Hazel looked up at her sister. "I know that . . . it's just that . . . I . . . I can't get over it, Iris . . . can't believe he did that to me."

Iris could see her sister's bottom lip quiver.

"We'll never understand it, Hazel. It's a waste of time to even try. I know. I tried to understand why I left and have never worked it out. I don't know if I ever will. Hazel, I am angry with him too but . . . I did the same thing, didn't I? Abandoned a family who needed me? I don't think I'm in the best position to hold onto my anger towards him. I have tried to forget about it. You need to do that too."

"But you left because you didn't think you'd be a good mother, you left because you thought Kevin was better off without you. This is different. He wanted to start a new life and he threw us away as if we were nothing."

Iris went and sat beside her sister on the sofa.

"Look, I know you're hurt. I was too when I found out. I didn't tell you because I wanted to protect you."

Hazel nodded, fighting back the tears.

"I know. I'm not angry with you," she replied. "How long have you known?"

Iris told her the story of how she went looking for her father's grave but found that he was not only alive but married with two almost grown-up sons.

"It must have been hard to keep it to yourself. I realise you did it for me. I just . . . I would have liked to have known sooner. I'd be over it by now."

"You'll get over it. Look at the changes you have made. You cut down on the drinking, did that parenting course and now your gardening course. Joe seems nice . . . he's a good friend, right? Don't let it get you down, don't throw all your achievements away because of our father. He's not worth it Hazel."

Hazel shifted on the sofa. She was entitled to her bitterness, even for a while. She knew her sister was right but she was hurt and she was finding it hard to regain the positive attitude she'd had these past few weeks.

"I just don't understand it, Iris. Why they had to be the way they were . . . why we had to have them as parents. It's like we never stood a chance, you know?"

"Maybe that was true then but we came through it, didn't we? Look at Vinnie and Joe. God, their parents left them alone all night while they drank. Things could have been worse. You have to put it behind you, otherwise it'll eat you up."

Hazel stated blankly back at her sister. "Put it behind me?" She didn't think she'd ever be able to do that, not in this lifetime anyway.

Chapter 49

Hazel lay on the sofa as the boys watched television before bedtime.

After her trip to London she had not returned to her course. Somehow she couldn't find the energy to rouse herself. Her muscles felt like lead as she dragged herself around the house in her dressing-gown. She had spent every waking moment thinking about her father and had even tried to put herself in his shoes to see if she could see things from his point of view but nothing worked. No matter how she tried to look at it she could not forgive him for abandoning them. Iris had phoned her every day and tried to persuade her to go back to the course, but she couldn't focus on that. She needed to work things out in her head first.

The doorbell rang and Jack jumped up to answer it.

"*Wait!*" Hazel screamed.

Ever since the incident with Pete Doyle, she was nervous answering the door when she wasn't expecting anyone. She walked to the door and listened. She could see a tall person on the other side. She took a deep breath.

"Who is it?" she asked sharply.

"It's Joe!" a meek voice replied to her unwelcoming tone.

Hazel opened the door and looked at her skinny friend.

"Oh, come in," she said, embarrassed to have been caught in her night clothes and without a scrap of make-up on.

The boys were delighted to see him and started talking excitedly at the same time, telling him about their trip. She was impressed that Joe did not react with shock when Luke spoke but answered him calmly as if the child had never been mute.

"I was talking to Iris. Actually, she phoned Vinnie for my number," he said, coming clean. "She told me you hadn't been back at your course."

Hazel felt bad. She had meant to phone Joe but she didn't know what to say to him and felt that if she had a couple of days to think, she'd be fine.

"Oh, I had a lot on. I was going to call you," she said but Joe was studying her, watching her facial expressions and obviously knew she was lying.

"What's happened?" he said.

"Mam found her dad and he wasn't nice!" Jack said loudly, delighted to have news.

"Jack!" Hazel cried.

"Is that true?" Joe asked, amazed. No wonder she looks so down, he thought to himself.

Hazel nodded. "I'll tell you about it when I get my head around everything," she said quickly.

"Will you come to my Communion on Saturday Joe?" Luke asked.

Joe laughed and looked at Hazel who threw Luke one of her "I'll kill you later" looks.

Luke noticed her expression and decided to make himself scarce. "It's our bedtime," he announced quickly. "Come on, Jack."

"But I want to stay here!" Jack cried.

"Come *on*, Jack!" Luke grabbed Jack's arm and hauled him from the room.

Joe watched them leave the room and shook his head.

"You have them well trained," he said. "I can't believe they just go to bed like that."

"Well, they're not always like that," she said half-smiling.

Poor boys. The first nice man that comes along and they are looking for a daddy, she thought, realising that she had a lot in common with her boys. They were all looking for someone to love them unconditionally.

"Do you want a cup of tea?" she asked.

"Well, if I'm not interrupting."

"You're not. After the boys go to bed I usually sit here alone and moan to myself about life," she said, smiling.

"Yeah, it gets lonely at night," he replied sympathetically as he followed her to the kitchen and stood in the doorway while she put the tea things and some biscuits on a tray and waited for the kettle to boil. "I feel the same way. In the day, it's grand. There are people to talk to and that, but when I get home, well, I dread it really. I never got used to living on my own. I spend a lot more time at Vinnie's than I ought to. Don't know how May doesn't get fed up with me."

Hazel looked at him. She had never met a man who talked so openly about his feelings. "Yeah. I know what you mean. Sometimes I keep the kids up just to have someone to talk to."

The kettle clicked off and she made a pot of tea, then carried the tray into the sitting room.

They sat and talked for a long time. She told Joe all about her father and heard herself tell him things that she didn't even know she was feeling. She realised that this was a sort of therapy, having someone you trusted to talk to. Joe listened to the whole story with a sympathetic ear. He told her about the day he met with his parents. When he found out where they were living, he wrote to them twice and left several phone messages but never received a reply. Vinnie, who was older than him and remembered more about their parents, had warned him against it but he was glad he did it. He knocked at their door one day and was shocked when a younger boy answered. A boy of about fifteen, their son, a brother he didn't even know he had. It sickened him that they were allowed to go on having more children after what they had done. They brought him in and unleashed years of pent-up anger on him. He couldn't believe that they were actually annoyed that he told a teacher in school about their drinking, a revelation that resulted in both Vinnie and him being taken into temporary care and eventual permanent fostering. He didn't even remember doing that so he assumed he must have only been in primary school.

"What did you do about your brother?" Hazel asked. She knew her father had two grown-up sons and had briefly wondered what they were like.

"I phoned social services. Even though the house looked clean and he looked alright, I wanted to be sure. It was too late for a relationship but I owed it to him to make sure he wasn't in any danger."

"What happened?"

"They said they investigated and that he was fine, that he was being well cared for. You know, I admit that this made me angry. I know it's awful to say but I resented him. I mean, why couldn't they have done that for Vinnie and me years earlier? It made me feel less important. Also, I wanted to hurt them, I wanted social services to take him, to teach them a lesson. I was in a mess back then. As time went on and I got my life on track, I accepted it. Accept what you cannot change, as they say. Like I said, it freed me but it takes time." He paused and their eyes met and held the gaze. "Give yourself that time, Hazel, but don't give up on yourself in the meantime."

She nodded. She knew Joe was right.

"How do you feel about Iris knowing all this time and not telling you?" he asked.

"I know I should feel angry with her and I suppose deep down I am, but she's the only person who put my feelings first. She knew I'd be devastated. I've held onto his memory for so long . . . well . . . I feel that I've nothing to hang onto now. Except for the boys and Iris, I am really on my own in this life."

"You have me. You can talk to me anytime, you know that."

"Thanks, Joe. Yes, I know that but you know what I mean. Knowing that I had a parent out there all that time who could have been helping me, well . . . like you say, it'll take time."

"You know, you should tell him how you feel. I mean all of it, the whole story about how his leaving affected you. Why don't you write it all down. You know, send him a letter?"

"A letter?" Hazel repeated incredulously.

"Yeah. Iris might write it with you. Sounds to me you both feel the same way."

"I don't know. Iris coped better, she's stronger and she . . . she has her own reasons for not being as angry as me. It's a long story . . ."

"Well, think about it." He stood up. "Well, it's late. I'd better go. Will you go back to the course tomorrow?"

"Yes," she said.

They walked to the door.

"Joe?"

"Yeah?"

"Thanks for coming around. Can't think of anyone else except Iris who'd care if I went back to the course or not."

"You're welcome," he replied.

Even in the darkened hallway Hazel noticed him blushing.

There was an awkwardness about the moment, neither knowing what to do next. If it was Pete, he'd grab her and kiss her roughly before leaving but she could see Joe was a gentleman. Hazel leant forward and kissed him gently on the cheek. She could hear giggling and footsteps running on the landing.

"*Get into bed!*" she roared.

Joe laughed. "Leave them, they're only kids!"

Hazel slanted her eyes at him. "I can see that they have you wrapped around their little fingers!" she said in a mock-annoyed tone.

"So you'll definitely go back tomorrow?" he asked.

"Definitely," she replied.

Hazel closed the door and glanced up the stairs but the two boys had run for cover and were back in their bedroom. She sat in the sitting room and smiled to herself. Joe was definitely not her normal type. She had always preferred rougher types and definitely preferred older men but what if all this time her type was all wrong for her? What if Joe was Mr Right?

Chapter 50

Hazel had been thinking a lot about Joe since he arrived at her door a few nights previously. She liked him and felt happy when she thought of him. She had returned to the course the day after she promised him and it was going well. After her trip to London, she thought that she'd never want to see another plant or flower again and that she'd want nothing to do with anything that reminded her of her father. But when she returned to the course, she realised that she liked growing things so much that she couldn't let her father ruin that for her. Whether she liked it or not, gardening and a love of the outdoors was in her blood.

The same day, Iris put the finishing touches to a wedding dress and watched the bride-to-be swirl around her shop, smiling to herself.

Iris always had mixed feelings about making wedding dresses. There was certainly plenty of money in it and a part of her loved the look on the bride's face as she stepped into her wedding gown, looking forward to a new chapter in her life as a married woman. But sometimes she found herself feeling a little sorry for the bride. She didn't really believe the "till death do us part" bit any more.

As the bride went into Iris's living room to change, the bell went. She looked up.

"Mark!" she said aloud, revealing how pleased she was to see him.

He gave her a peck on the cheek as he gently squeezed her arm.

"Thought I'd surprise you" he said, smiling. "I got a call from the estate agents. There's a house they think will suit my needs. It's on Merrion Square. It seems to have everything I'm looking for so I thought I'd check it out before it sold. I was hoping you'd come with me?"

"Well, sure, if you think it'd help. When can you see it?"

"They should be finished painting it today so I have an appointment to see it tomorrow at nine. Does that suit you?"

"Yeah, I'm closed tomorrow anyway for Luke's Communion. Oh, will you come to that? It's at three o clock."

"Yeah, I'd love to. Hazel invited me but I didn't think I'd be able to make it so my timing is great!" He paused. "Are you doing anything tonight?"

"Hmm, let's see . . ." Iris replied sarcastically. "After shopping for the Communion with Hazel, I have a ball at eight, a ballet at ten . . . there's something else . . . just can't think of it."

They laughed together.

"Well, you'll need to eat somewhere along the line. Fancy having dinner with me?" His deep brown eyes became serious and locked with hers.

Iris felt a shiver run through her. He could still do that to her, even after all these years.

"Yeah, that'd be nice," she replied softly.

"Okay, see you later then," he replied, smiling broadly.

As Mark left, Iris's bride came back into the shop.

"Oh Elaine, sorry, I forgot you were in there! Were you alright getting the dress off by yourself?"

"I was grand. I didn't want to come out. I could hear that you were being chatted up!" she laughed.

"Chatted up! No . . . definitely not . . . that's my . . . well . . . he's an old friend." Iris hesitated. She didn't want to tell her bridal customers that she was a divorced woman. It might not look so good. "I definitely wasn't being chatted up."

"Well, that's not how it sounded to me! It sounded like he was asking you out!"

Iris laughed. The younger generation, they do have romantic notions, she thought to herself, already wondering what she'd wear that night.

Chapter 51

Luke shifted uncomfortably in his smart, navy, Communion suit. The crisp new tie felt like a noose around his neck. Hazel and Iris thought he looked so cute in his new shiny black shoes and white shirt, his red rosette pinned neatly to his lapel. He had even had his dark curly hair cut tight for the occasion. According to his teacher, he looked like an angel.

"Stop pulling at that tie!" Hazel hissed as they left the church.

Jack was also dressed in new clothes and wore brown trousers, a cream shirt and brown leather shoes that squeaked when he walked and were much tighter than his runners.

"Luke, will you share your money with me?" Jack asked with wide eyes. He could not believe that lots of people would give his brother money today and it wasn't even his birthday. He couldn't wait for his own Communion even though it was three long years away.

"Jack! For God's sake, you're making a show of me. It's not about money, it's about the sacrament!" Hazel muttered through clenched teeth, even though she didn't really go for all that lark herself.

Jack looked down at his new shoes. He hated when his mam was annoyed with him, especially since it was a happy day and they were having a party afterwards.

"Sorry," he whispered.

"It's okay," she replied, sorry that she had been annoyed with him.

She wanted this day to be special. She still remembered how disappointed she was on her own Communion day and had vowed that her sons would have happy memories of theirs. It was on occasions like this that Hazel really felt aware of her single-mother status. Even though there were a few other women there alone, most children were flanked by couples – mammies and daddies taking photos. Joe was coming to the house later for the party and while she knew she could have asked him to come to the church also, she didn't want to become dependent on him. She still remembered what the social worker said to her, that she had to be strong on her own before she entered another relationship and she was trying to stick to this even though she was lonely and, on days like today, she felt she stuck out like a sore thumb.

"Mam, can I get my photo taken with you and Mark?" Luke asked, looking over at the other boys having photos taken.

"Course," she said, understanding why he was asking.

Iris understood too and a lump rose in her throat as she saw Luke smile broadly at the camera, proud as punch.

When they arrived at the house, Mrs Whelan came with two apple tarts. Joe arrived with a home-made lasagne. Hazel couldn't believe it – she had just about managed to make two trays of ham and cheese sandwiches. Joe was almost too good to be true.

Everyone cheered as Luke blew out the candles on his cake. He'd made over €100 and hoped his mother hadn't noticed him counting it.

"What, no wine?" Iris whispered to her sister.

"No, Iris, no wine," was the quick retort.

She hadn't bought any because Joe did not drink and she didn't want him to think she was an alcoholic, drinking at a child's Communion party.

Iris laughed. "So you do like him then?" she teased.

"Stop it!" Hazel replied. "He's listening!"

Iris walked away, smiling to herself, and sat beside Gerard who she could see felt a bit out of place. He had been talking to Joe earlier about football but Joe was now following Hazel around like a puppy, even dishing up the food and doing the washing up.

"It's great to finally meet you, Gerard. Luke never stops talking about you."

"Really?" he asked, smiling.

Iris nodded.

"I can't believe I have two brothers" he replied. "I always wanted a brother. I know they're a lot younger but they're great kids."

Iris could see what Hazel meant. Gerry Junior was a very mature young man.

"And you don't mind, you know . . . about Hazel?"

"No, my mam said he was always carrying on . . . em, sorry, I didn't mean any offence to Hazel."

"It's okay," Iris replied. "Do you ever want to see him?"

Gerard took a deep breath and let it out slowly. "I used to. But, it's too late now. Even if we did meet up, it's not like he'd ever be like a father. I don't see any point really."

Iris thought he sounded a little sad and that, even though he had come to terms with his father's abandonment, he still felt the loss. She thought back to Luke getting his photo taken with Mark in front of his pals and, now, talking to Gerard, she realised that must be how Kevin felt now as a young adult. That it was too late. She looked around the room at the group, at Hazel, Joe, Gerard, Luke and Jack, and even Mark. So many damaged souls. She could see Mark looking over at her. He seemed to be enjoying himself. They'd had a lovely meal the night before and had talked into the early hours like old times. Mostly they talked about his divorce from Miriam and how he felt about it. He told her that he found life pretty lonely now. Kevin was practically reared and he had never really got into dating. He found it too contrived and preferred to meet someone out of the blue, when he was least expecting it. When he left to go back to his hotel, Iris wished she had an extra room. She felt completely comfortable with him and would have liked him to stay.

He had picked her up early that morning and they'd gone to see the house he was thinking of buying. It was an old, three-storey Georgian house. The ground floor was actually a basement and had a separate entrance. It had been used as an office so was prefect for Mark's needs. The living areas of the house were split across the two upper levels and the large spacious rooms had high ornate ceilings and old wooden panelling. It seemed too big for Mark on his own as Kevin would be staying on campus from October but she told him that she loved it and laughed heartily when he said, "That's fine, then I'll buy it." Iris wasn't sure if he was joking. When they left the house, it was still only a little after ten so they went to Bewleys and had a quick breakfast before going to Hazel's house to help organise the food for the Communion. Mark had her in stitches with stories about the things kids said when they came into his practice and how much he was looking forward to hearing the same kinds of things from Irish kids when he set up in the autumn.

By eight thirty, the boys were tired and cranky and Hazel got them to bed. Mrs Whelan had left about an hour earlier and Gerard excused himself after playing computer games with Joe and the boys for most of the evening. Just before ten, Mark suggested he drive Iris home and she was only too happy to leave Joe and Hazel alone.

As they pulled up outside her shop, Iris asked him if he'd like to come in for a coffee.

"I thought you'd never ask," he replied.

Joe Egan sat beside Hazel on the sofa as they watched a late-night movie. Hazel could not believe that he didn't try it on and gazed at him as he sat upright beside her on the sofa. She moved close and placed her head on his shoulder, thinking he needed some encouragement, but while he placed his arm around her, he did not move towards her.

When the credits rolled up, Joe stretched and yawned.

"Well, it's been a long day" he said slowly. "I'd better head home."

Hazel couldn't believe that he wasn't going to try to get her into bed, especially as he wouldn't have to try very hard.

286

"Em, why don't you stay a while longer? Sure there's no rush," she said quickly.

"Ah, I'll head off," Joe replied, ignoring her hint. "I was training today and I've a match in the morning. I coach junior league. Maybe the boys would like to join?"

"Em . . . yeah, I'll ask them," Hazel replied, annoyed that his focus was back on the boys when she had other ideas on her mind.

Hazel saw him to the door and stood for a moment. She thanked him for coming. When she realised that he wasn't going to kiss her, she put her arms around his neck and pulled him close to her, kissing him on the lips. He did not pull back even though she could see that he was surprised.

"Night," he said, smiling.

"Night," Hazel answered, closing the door behind him.

Not for the first time she wondered what the hell was wrong with Joe Egan.

Chapter 52

Iris made Mark one of her hot-chocolate specialties and sat beside him on her worn couch.

"Luke looked smart in his suit," he said. "He seems to be over the worst."

"Yeah," she replied. "He still goes quiet at times but I suppose it'll take time."

"How's Hazel? She didn't mention your father today so I didn't raise it."

"She's still upset. She doesn't blame me for not telling her but she's so angry. She says she'll never get over the shock."

Mark nodded. He looked around the room and noticed a small piece of tinsel still stuck to the ceiling.

"Do you leave that up all year around?" he joked, trying to lighten the mood.

"I couldn't reach it," she laughed.

Mark remembered back to the January morning that he stood waiting outside the shop for her. She still had her little Christmas tree up. Seeing her walking up to him, her small face red from exertion, he realised that he still loved her. He wondered when, if ever, it would be a good time to tell her. He didn't want to ruin the friendship that they had but he needed to know if she could ever feel the same way about him again.

"It's been a strange few months since I came here to your shop. When I saw you coming towards me . . . you looked lovely with your red Rudolph nose."

Iris opened her eyes wide and reddened slightly. She was taken aback and felt a thrill of excitement rise within her.

"I'm glad that we've become good friends, Iris. It means a lot to me and it's important for Kevin, but I wonder if you could ever see me as more than a friend, if you'd ever want more than that again?"

Iris swallowed. She couldn't believe her ears. "You still want that, after all that happened?"

"I still love you, Iris. I knew that the morning I saw you coming towards me outside that shop. I never stopped loving you really."

"Mark, I – I don't know what to say. You could have any woman you wanted . . ."

"I want you," he said quietly, pulling her to him and kissing her softly.

She embraced him as they kissed more passionately now, more fervently.

She missed this, this tenderness, the warmth of another person's touch. Memories of her youth returned, memories of the passion they had once shared. Her body yearned for this, for his familiar touch.

She stood and Mark looked at her, worried that he had moved too fast and frightened her. She grasped his hand and pulled him up, looking into his deep brown eyes. Neither of them spoke as she led him to her bedroom, closing the door behind them.

When Iris awoke the following morning, she found herself looking straight into Mark's open eyes as he smiled at her.

"Morning," he said sleepily, his large body crushing her in her single bed.

Iris reddened. She had no clothes on and wondered how she was going to get out of bed without him seeing her naked. She was older now and knew she didn't look the same as she did during their marriage. Her heart thumped at the situation she found herself in and she wondered how she could have been so stupid, how she allowed herself to be swept up by the moment and ignore the consequences. It was not normally her style and was something she scolded her sister for on so many occasions. She blushed again, wondering if she'd gone mad.

She remembered him touching her breast. She had flinched and blocked him with her arm. He'd moved it gently away and kissed her scar. Her eyes had filled with tears and she'd hoped in the darkness that he could not see them. It had been a beautiful moment but now, in the morning light, she wondered what on earth had possessed her. She knew that Mark was lonely and vulnerable and there was no way that she was going to hurt him or Kevin again.

Mark picked up on her discomfort. He rose first, and went to her bathroom to shower.

Iris jumped from the bed and pulled some clothes on. When she heard the water running in the shower, she ran to the phone.

"Hazel?"

"Iris? It's only half eight. What's wrong?" she sister replied, annoyed that her Sunday morning lie-in had been disturbed.

"I slept with Mark last night. It just happened," she said nervously, waiting for her sister's response.

"So?" Hazel replied, annoyed that this is what she was awoken for.

"So?" Iris asked annoyed. "So . . . so . . ." Iris couldn't think of a reason why she should not have slept with Mark.

"God, Iris, live a little, will you? Anyway, was he any good?"

"Hazel!" Iris said angrily. "Not everything is a joke."

"Iris . . . I'm going back to sleep. Just enjoy the day, will you?"

Hazel was dreaming of Joe. He was a Manchester United player in her dream and scored three goals in front of a sell-out crowd. At the end of the game he asked her to marry him over the PA system. The camera moved to her and she was shouting "Yes, yes!" when the phone rang.

Bloody Iris again, Hazel thought, closing her eyes and trying to replay the scene.

Less than five minutes later, the doorbell rang.

"Christ!" she screamed, jumping out of bed and hoping it was not someone selling anything because they were about to get a piece of her mind.

She pulled on her dressing-gown and thumped down the stairs noisily. She opened the door to find Mrs Whelan standing white-faced on the doorstep.

"What's wrong?" Hazel asked. It was unusual for her neighbour to call in without an invite.

Mrs Whelan handed her the newspaper.

"Body of Drug Dealer Found in Wicklow Mountains," the headline said.

Hazel looked up at her neighbour, her mouth dropped open.

"It's Pete Doyle," Mrs Whelan said anxiously. She was unsure how Hazel would take it but she wanted to make sure she knew before she took the boys to Mass. Pete was a local man and the priest might mention the death during prayers.

Mrs Whelan watched as Hazel's face crumpled and she started to sob on the doorstep. She came inside and led Hazel to a seat in the kitchen.

"I didn't want him to die," Hazel sobbed. She hated Pete for what he did to the boys and for the way he treated her but, at the same time, she didn't want this to happen to him. The paper said that because he had been dead for several weeks, he had to be identified by dental records and that he had been badly beaten before taking a single gunshot to the head.

"He didn't deserve that death!" she cried. "No one deserves that!"

Mary Whelan hushed her but did not reply. She knew from her daughter that Pete and his brother had been selling drugs for some time and she did not feel sorry for him. When she moved to this area, the worst the teenagers could do was drink too much cider in the field but now drugs were destroying the lives of families, local families who were struggling even before heroin and ecstasy wreaked havoc on their lives.

"What will I tell Luke?" Hazel asked, worrying that Pete's death might induce her son to muteness again.

"Tell him the truth. You don't have to show him the article. I know kids in school might tell him how he died but you can't do anything about that. For now, just say that Pete's body was found and try leave to it at that. It'll be enough for him to take in."

Hazel took another tissue and wiped her eyes. She could hear the boys getting up. "Thanks for telling me, Mrs Whelan. You're a good friend." She was thinking how wrong her mother had been to shun the friendship Mrs Whelan had offered.

"You're welcome, love. I'll be next door if you need me." Mrs Whelan picked up the newspaper and let herself out quietly.

When the boys came down, Hazel gave them breakfast and when she put Jack's nebuliser on him, she took Luke into the sitting room. He already knew that something was wrong. He had noticed his mam's swollen eyes and hoped Iris wasn't sick again.

When she told him, he just stared back at her. She wanted to plead with him not to let Pete's death affect him. She couldn't bear for him to stop talking again. She could see his forehead crease as he digested the news.

"I'll say a prayer for him, Mam," he said, taking her completely by surprise.

"You'll pray for him?" she repeated, amazed.

"He'll need lots of prayers to get into heaven, Mam, and I don't want him haunting me," he replied seriously.

Hazel almost laughed except it wasn't really funny. Her son really thought this was possible.

"Okay. We'll light candles after Mass and that'll help as well," she said.

"Mam, he'll also have to be sorry. At Communion class the priest said that you can't get forgiveness unless you're really sorry."

Hazel pulled him close to her and hugged her son tightly, kissing his head and rocking him. She thought of her father and wondered just how sorry he was for his actions. She would probably never know.

"I'd say he's very sorry, Luke. Very, very sorry."

Chapter 53

On Monday afternoon Iris set about her repairs, occasionally glancing out the window at passers-by, as the boys played in the back waiting on their mother to collect them. Hazel had phoned her the previous evening and told her about Pete Doyle. She had spoken to Luke but he seemed fine about it which really surprised her. She wondered if it would hit him later and decided she'd keep a close eye on her nephew.

As she pinned a dress together, she closed her eyes and felt the warm sunshine through her shop window. Summer seemed to have come early.

She had taken Hazel's advice the previous day and focused on enjoying the day with Mark who had a Sunday evening flight back to London. They had spent the entire day together, walking around St Stephen's Green and lunching on fish and chips. Mark held her hand which made Iris glance around nervously. She hoped none of her customers were in the park. She'd hate having to explain who Mark was and the gossip that would surely follow. She had enjoyed the day and it had given her a lift but she had an uneasy feeling that she could not shake off. On one hand she felt happy at what had happened between them and she was thrilled that he was still interested in her. But she knew that the real Iris was worried about him wanting her, worried that she could not give him the love and commitment he seemed to be looking for. She did not want to hurt him again.

Before he left, he pulled her close and kissed her passionately. He told her that he had missed having her in his life and that he'd ring her about the house they had looked at together. She wondered if he was planning on asking her to move in with him and, if so, how would she react to such a commitment. Iris plugged in her sewing machine and pressed the foot pedal to the floor as she thought about just that.

Chapter 54

On Saturday night, Mark phoned Iris to tell her that the offer he made on the house had been accepted and that he'd be moving in over the next couple of months. She congratulated him and told him she was just on her way out to baby-sit for Hazel as Joe had finally picked up the courage to ask her sister out.

When Iris arrived at her sister's house, Hazel was dressed in the same black that she had worn to Kevin's graduation. Her long fair hair was tied up at the sides and fell around her shoulders in neat curls.

"You look lovely," Iris said genuinely, admiring her sister's statuesque figure.

"Wish me luck, sis," said Hazel.

"I do."

The sisters smiled at each other and, in that moment, they caught a glimpse of what their relationship could be in the future.

Iris returned to her flat the following morning after listening to her sister rave about the night out with Joe and how she felt things were moving in the right direction. She had barely got inside the door when she heard the phone ringing. She lifted the receiver, expecting to hear Mark or Hazel's voice on the other end.

"Hello?"

"Iris?"

"Yes."

"It's Dad."

The colour drained from her face. She had not expected to hear from her father ever again.

"What do you want?" she said slowly.

"I want to talk to you, to explain everything."

Iris could hear his voice shaking, a mixture of old age and nervousness.

"I think we already know your side," she spat. "You never came to see us. You never checked to see if we were all right."

"When your mother died, Eileen wrote to me about you. I – I can't explain why I didn't come. She said your mother told you I was dead and somehow I didn't want to open it all up again. I admit I was wrong and that I took the easy way out."

Iris wanted to slam the phone down but couldn't. She felt hypnotised by his voice.

"It's Hazel you need to talk to," she replied. "I knew you were alive years ago."

She could hear him breathing heavily as though this revelation shocked him.

At last he spoke. "I got your number from directory enquiries. They didn't have any Hazel Fays listed and I didn't know her husband's name."

Iris thought he sounded upset. "She's not married," she said. She remembered that Hazel had to change her number and made it ex-directory after a spate of crank calls that she was sure were from an old boyfriend.

"Iris . . . I'm not expecting you girls to forgive me but I just want you to know why I left. Your mother was impossible to live with. I couldn't keep up with her. She was always angry."

"With good reason! You weren't exactly a good husband," Iris retorted.

"I swear, in the beginning, we had a good marriage," he protested. "Later, when she started drinking, well, I was lonely. Can you understand that?"

"What I can't understand is why you left *us*. We were innocent victims in your battle with each other. You could have visited us, you could have provided for us."

"I sent cheques every couple of months for about a year but she sent them back, every last one of them, unopened."

"But why did you not come and see us? How could you just cut us from your life?" Iris asked sharply. She could feel herself becoming angry. She did not want to have this conversation.

The line went silent and she could hear his heavy laboured breathing.

"It was too hard to see her, that's why I didn't visit. I felt bad for leaving Liz but I was drowning. If I'd stayed with her she would have destroyed me. Back then, when a marriage broke down, men did not take their kids. They always stayed with the mother. By the time she died, I was married with kids. It was too late but I thought about you every day. I want you to know that. Every single day. I never heard that Eileen died, that's the truth. When she stopped writing I thought it was because she was annoyed with me. She . . . she didn't want to . . . look after you girls. She resented leaving her life in London. Years passed and you slipped away from me."

Iris did not want to hear any more. Heavy tears fell down her face. She dug her nails into her thigh. She did not want him to hear the hurt in her voice.

"Well, I don't accept that you couldn't have come. No matter how hard it was for you, we were your children." She cringed, aware of the irony in her words. "You ruined our lives by leaving. We never got over losing you."

"Iris," he said softly, "I am trying to explain. That's all. I know I hurt you. I know it is different for mothers. Women are always stronger."

Iris took the receiver away from her ear as though it had burned her.

"I . . . I have to go," she said, slamming the phone down.

When the phone rang again a half hour later, Iris let it ring. Her heart had not stopped thumping since she had slammed down the phone on her father and she did not want to hear whatever else it was he had to say. When it kept ringing she worried that it was Hazel and walked slowly over to the phone, lifting it to her ear in slow measured movements.

"Hello?"

"Iris?"

"Yes."

"I hoped you'd be in."

"Kevin?"

"Yeah. Sorry, should have said who it was! I'm coming to Dublin to organise a few things for the coming year in a couple of weeks and Dad said you might like to catch up."

"I'd love to but . . . is it your dad's idea or yours?" She didn't want her son to think he had to see her. Even though it was a few months now since they had reunited, they still had not developed any sort of relationship. She knew she had to give him time but she accepted that they might always be strangers to each other.

"He suggested it but I'd like to. Maybe you could show me around? Every time I came over the see Nan and Granddad, we never did any sightseeing."

"Well then, yes, I'd really like that," Iris replied, astonished that within the space of half an hour she had spoken to both the father who had abandoned her and the son she had abandoned. She knew there had to be a message in this but did not want to think about it any further. She wasn't ready.

"Great. Em . . . could I stay with you? I thought it would give us time to get to know one another."

"Yes . . ." she said slowly, aware that Kevin had never actually seen her flat. "But I warn you, it's quite modest." She felt slightly embarrassed. "It's pretty much a fold-out sofa-bed."

"I don't mind," he said quietly.

Iris could hear his shyness returning. "I'll meet you at the airport – let me know the flight details. I'm really looking forward to it, Kevin. Bye."

Iris put the phone down and replayed both conversations in her head. She looked at the clock. It was almost eight and Hazel would phone as soon as she put the boys to bed. She'd tell her everything then.

She made herself a cup of tea and settled down to watch the soaps but she couldn't concentrate. A thought was niggling at her. She thought back to when she sent Kevin a letter explaining her actions. She was not looking for forgiveness, nor did she expect it. She simply wanted him to understand why she had left. She wondered if her father was doing the same, trying to explain his actions.

Iris lifted the phone, unable to wait any longer for her sister to ring.

"Hazel. It's me. D-Dad phoned." Iris now understood something else. She understood why Kevin did not call her 'Mam'. You had to earn the right to be called that.

Hazel listened as Iris recounted the conversation, leaving the part about Kevin's call till last, hoping that her sister would see the connection, the irony.

"Iris, I've been so upset these past few weeks knowing that all that time he was alive. I am only now beginning to put it behind me. Nothing he said tonight makes that any different. Don't forget, he could have contacted us at any time. He could have written a letter to us, phoned us."

Iris knew Hazel was right but there was a part of her that knew she had no right to enjoy Kevin's company if she would not forgive her father. And she wanted that right. She wanted to form a bond with her son.

Iris took a photo of her son out. She felt a mixture of excitement and nervousness at the thought of spending a few days alone with him. They barely knew each other.

Chapter 55

Two weeks after she and Joe stated dating, Hazel was thinking of making other changes in her life. Ever since her visit to Sussex, she felt differently about the house. It didn't hold the same meaning for her. The security she once felt there now seemed childish. Although she knew that she had a lot more growing up to do, she felt it was time to stand on her own two feet.

One afternoon as Joe drove her home she noticed a new development of houses near the training centre. The billboard in front of them said: "*Looking for a fresh start?*" Hazel felt that there was a message in it. It was as if the advertisement was talking directly to her. She asked Joe to stop and took a look around. The houses had an average-sized back garden, smaller than her own, and a small front lawn. They were semi-detached and had three spacious bedrooms and a playroom where the kids could watch their own television and leave her in peace. With the recession in full swing, the houses were very reasonably priced and if she sold her house which was larger and in a slightly better area, she should come out even.

She was amazed when her sister agreed that it was a good idea, that it would be good for the boys to start in a new area where no one knew what had happened with Pete Doyle. Iris teased her, telling her that she thought she'd be buying the new house with Joe and she surprised her sister by saying that it was too soon for that, that she was taking her time with this relationship.

When Iris met Kevin, they embraced awkwardly and made their way to the taxi rank. By the time they settled into her flat, they had already talked about his course and Mark's new practice in Dublin. Iris felt that there was nothing else to say and filled the next few hours asking him about his life, about school and friends and anything else she could think of. The atmosphere was awkward and she felt like she was interviewing her son. She noticed his discomfort as he answered questions in short sentences and shifted uneasily on her sofa. He looked huge and awkward in her tiny sitting room. It was as if his presence made her flat and her predictable life untidy. She looked around the room as an uncomfortable silence fell between them.

"It's not what you're used to," she joked uneasily.

"It's fine," he answered. "Do you like it here?"

"I got used to it."

Kevin nodded.

Iris felt the weight of the strange atmosphere in the room. The tension was wearing on her and she felt that the air needed to be cleared.

"You must find it strange, being here alone with me."

"A little," he replied, blushing, "but Dad thinks it's important."

"And you, what do you think?"

He thought about his answer. He did not look at her but kept his eyes on the ground. "It feels a bit strange. Dad said it'll take time for us to get to know each other."

"But . . . how do you feel about me . . . about my leaving?" she asked nervously.

"I felt a bit angry," he admitted. "I know you were sick but I . . . well, I missed having you."

Iris gulped and straightened her spine in defence. "And . . .?"

She needed him to have his say. If they were ever to become friends, he needed to tell her exactly how he felt.

"I . . . hated you for what you did to Dad," he said, blushing and lowering his head.

"Kevin, can we start over? I'm not asking to be your mother. I know it's too late for that. I'm asking for a second chance though, to be your friend."

He nodded through watery eyes.

They hugged and Iris raised her hand to his face and wiped a tear from his cheek, embarrassing him.

By the time Mark arrived seven days later Kevin and Iris had almost walked every street of Dublin's city centre, visiting all the ancient churches and medieval ruins that were littered throughout the city. She took him to the Botanic Gardens and showed him the tree she and Hazel had carved their names into as children. She showed him her school and told him about her life – about her parents and her grandmother and how their problems had cascaded through the generations and affected her and Hazel and now Luke, Jack and himself and how she hoped that they would be strong enough to stop the cycle of damage for their children and grandchildren.

Iris joined Mark and Kevin for their first meal in their new home. The entire house had been newly painted in bright creams and warm autumn colours which were complemented by the expensive wooden floors that ran throughout the two upper floors. Mark had arranged for a small amount of his furniture to be sent over and had purchased only the bare necessities, asking Iris to help him pick out new stuff. As the three sat together at a makeshift table, Mark opened a bottle of wine and toasted their new life, their new beginning.

When the evening came to a close, Iris rose to leave. She kissed Kevin and Mark saw her to the door.

"You could stay, you know."

"I know but I have an early start at the shop tomorrow."

"I mean . . . you could move in, on whatever terms."

Iris looked up at him.

"I – I don't . . . know . . ."

"Don't answer yet. Think about it," he said as he held her close and kissed her softly.

Iris opened the door to her waiting taxi.

"Night," she said.

As the taxi pulled away she could see Mark and Kevin returning to the sitting room. Even in the bright summer evening, the room looked cosy and inviting. A new life at her fingertips, if she wanted it.

When she arrived back at her flat, she opened the door and sighed. She could hear her voice echo around the empty flat as she talked to the cat who stared back at her, meowing periodically. She hung her coat on the door and sat on the sofa. She had a lot of thinking to do.

Chapter 56

Hazel was delighted when her house sold only three weeks after she put it on the market. She had made enough to cover the stamp duty and could move as soon as the contracts were signed on the new house which was almost ready for her to move into. She enrolled the boys in a new school for the following September and was surprised at how excited they were. Her relationship with Joe was blossoming. Everything was looking up. Even her sister seemed happy. She went to Mark's regularly and even though she was thinking of moving in, she was determined to keep her little shop going.

That evening when her sister came to help her pack up, Hazel picked up the box of their mother's letters and smirked over at her sister.

"You hid some of them, didn't you?"

"Just the ones about him being alive," Iris admitted sheepishly.

Iris glanced over at Hazel, amazed at how much she had matured these past few months.

"Well, I think that's everything. That's as much as we can pack away until moving day." Hazel taped up the last box and brushed the dust from her jeans.

The sisters glanced around the empty room that looked shabby now with all the photos and ornaments gone. There was a dent in the plaster where a large scenic painting had hung and you could see the layers of different wallpapers that had been hung over the years, some of which were there from the previous owner's time. The sun had faded the deep red carpet underneath the window and the once-white skirting boards, now void of furniture to hide them, were yellow and chipped. They could picture their mother on the old sofa, calling them to make her a cup of tea or shouting for them to keep the noise down. Iris could visualise her father, dirty and tired after a hard day's gardening, asking her about her lessons and listening intently as she practised her tin whistle. They had so many memories here, good and bad. They looked at each other and both felt the same wave of emotion as they burst into tears and hugged each other. They were saying goodbye to their past, to their lost childhoods and looking forward to a new beginning.

"Do you think we'll ever have contact from him? I mean, could you see yourself ever wanting it?" Iris asked.

Hazel shrugged as though she didn't care but was betrayed by the tears in her eyes.

"I don't know. I've tried but I don't think I'll ever get over the shock of knowing he was out there all that time. It's like a part of me is tied to what happened and I can't get free of it, do you know what I mean?"

Iris nodded. "But when I think of Kevin and the second chance I got, I feel I have no right to that chance if I won't give it to others."

"You mean you want to see him?"

"No, not that. I just want him to know I've moved on and that even though he hurt us, I want a future. I want to put it behind me."

"So what are you saying?"

"I want to forgive him," she said simply.

Hazel looked at her sister and frowned. "Me too," she whispered, surprising her sister. "Joe said I should write to him. I tried one evening to put how I felt on paper but it was so full of anger. I knew there were other feelings but I couldn't get past that resentment. Almost thirty-five years of hurt can't fit onto a tiny piece of paper."

"Then why don't we make it simple? Think about what it is that *we* want?" Iris said, taking a copybook from Luke's schoolbag.

The two sisters sat on the floor and talked about what they wanted to say. After an hour they had put their feelings on paper and signed their names.

It read:

> *Jack,*
> *We want you to know that we have moved on with our lives and are looking forward to a very different future. We forgive you. Forgive yourself.*
> *Iris & Hazel*

The two women sat together in silence, absorbing the release this pardon gave them and looking at the past while imagining the future. They held hands and cried tears of relief and sadness, anger, disappointment and acceptance. They sat there surrendering their emotions in the empty room that was once their home while a new life beckoned.

The front door opened and noise filled the air as the boys returned with Joe.

"What are you crying for?" Jack asked while Luke stared at them with large, concerned eyes.

Joe looked at the women and moved the boys from the room.

"They are saying goodbye, boys."

"To a room?" Jack asked, with a confused expression on his face.

"Yes, Jack. To a room."

Chapter 57

On a Saturday morning in late July, Mark, Kevin and Iris went for a walk in St Stephen's Green after a nice breakfast on Grafton Street. Kevin walked ahead, embarrassed that anyone, more notably any girls, would see him walking with his parents. He had been to a few "information" evenings at the college which were really excuses for drinking and he knew that a few of the other students lived around here. Mark took Iris's hand in his as they walked in the bright sunshine. She had begun to stay over on the weekends and, while she was enjoying the company, she felt depressed each Sunday evening when she returned to her flat alone. She no longer wished to live like this and knew that she no longer had to. She had people who loved her, people with whom she should have been sharing her life all along. She had lost so many years but it was not too late. Her feelings for Mark were deepening and Kevin had made a special effort to get to know her, to trust her.

Even though it was still early, the park was busy with lots of tourists and families enjoying the sunshine.

"Remember when we were going to call Kevin 'Stephen'?" he asked.

"Yes, you loved this park. God, you were going to tell everyone he was conceived in here!" she laughed, embarrassed at the thought.

"Have you given any thought to my offer?" Mark asked.

"Sorry, what was your offer again?" she teased.

"About moving in!" Mark pretended to be hurt.

Iris could see he was nervous.

"Yes," she said.

"Yes?"

"Yes," she reiterated.

Mark beamed. "We could make it all above board, you know."

Iris raised her eyebrows. "What do you mean?"

"We could get married. We don't want to give our son a bad example!"

Iris's turned sharply and looked into his eyes, expecting him to laugh and say he was joking.

"Mark, I . . . well, let's take it one step at a time, okay?"

"Okay," he replied, pleased that at least things were moving in the right direction. "You won't regret it," he said, lifting her clean off her feet.

Iris screamed. Kevin blushed and walked even faster ahead of them.

"Put me down, we're like pair of teenagers!" she squealed.

"Well, let's catch up to our 'might be' best man and embarrass him even further, eh?"

"Yes, let's do that."

Chapter 58

On the last day of the school term, Hazel dropped the boys off to school and returned to the house to finish the packing with her sister. The removal truck was coming at eleven and they had some last-minute packing to do.

"Hey, we almost forgot the garden tools!" Hazel said.

The two opened the old wooden shed and passed the items out one by one.

They quietened as they looked through the tools that had been their father's. Forks and spades that he had dug this very garden with. Pruning sheers and old torn gardening gloves that he had tended the shrubs with.

An old wheelbarrow squeaked as Hazel pushed it out to the front for loading.

"Should you bother bringing that?" Iris asked. "It looks like it's seen better days."

Hazel lowered her head. "Yeah, but I'd like to keep it," she answered putting the barrow down and brushing her hair from her face.

Iris gave her sister an understanding smile.

"I can't believe I'll be sleeping somewhere else tonight," Hazel said nervously. "How long did it take you to get used to Mark's?" she asked, knowing that her sister spent most of her nights there now.

"It is surprisingly fine. It's . . . it's . . ." Iris struggled to find the right words. "It's home because the people I love are there."

Hazel nodded. "Yes. Yes, you're right. I'll be fine."

"Right, that's everything," Iris said as the removal men put the last box into the truck.

As they walked out the door, Hazel beckoned for Iris to pull it closed with her and together they slammed the old wooden door shut for the last time. The sisters laughed as their odd behaviour caused the removal men to smirk at each other.

As the truck pulled away, Iris and Hazel walked together down Mobhi Road. They planned on catching a taxi to meet the truck at the new house.

Hazel stopped suddenly, looking at her watch.

"I think there's one more thing we have to do."

Iris and Hazel linked arms as they walked into the large ancient cemetery, buying a small bunch of roses, their mother's favourite, on the way in. They held hands as they stood at their mother's grave and told her what they now knew about her life and that they understood there were things they would never know or understand. They told her that they were letting her go, they were forgiving her and they were moving on, that they were looking for peace and that her two little girls hoped that she had finally found hers.

As they walked arm in arm in the summer sunshine, Iris and Hazel allowed their tears to flow, a final cleansing so that they could start afresh.

"Well?" Iris asked, drying her eyes. "What about you and Joe?"

Hazel smiled broadly as she did each time Joe was mentioned.

"We're taking it slowly, day by day. And Mark?"

"Same. One step at a time," Iris replied as they walked arm in arm into the future.

If you enjoyed
Winter Flowers by Carol Coffey,
why not try
The Penance Room also published by Poolbeg?
Here's a sneak preview of Chapter One

The Penance Room

CAROL COFFEY

POOLBEG

Chapter 1

"Mum!" I scream as I jump from my bed and stare into the darkness. Sweat drips from my face and, as my breathing eases, I realise that I have dreamt the same dream once again and have woken as usual just in time to feel the vibrations of the 3 a.m. freight train to Sydney as it passes by the back of our house. I can never understand how its passing doesn't wake any of the residents in my mother's nursing home where I live. I am the only one who is woken by its passing and left to roam the hallways unable to return to sleep.

I slip quietly from my room past the nurses' station where Aishling is sitting writing her notes. She doesn't notice me and I am relieved about that. She doesn't like me creeping around at night but I can never sleep after that dream and feel a need to be near my mother. I walk downstairs. When I reach the hall I can see a sliver of light coming from under the door of the bathroom beneath the stairs and I wonder if my father is also awake. I move towards the front of the house where the vibrations of the trains are not so disturbing and where my parents' room is. I pass a large ward on my right whose residents are referred to as "the babies": nine men and women who can no longer do anything for themselves and who lie in bed all day, looking at the ceiling or with eyes closed so tight you'd think they were afraid to open them. I pass the kitchen, the dining room and the large bay-windowed lounge room where the residents while away their days, and then I turn the handle of my parents' room across the hall. I look down at my mutilated foot from which I still feel pain, a punishment for my stupidity. It happened almost five years ago when I was eight years old. I was playing with my friends on the train line, something my parents didn't want me to do because of my hearing.

I can see the accident like a film reel whose middle is caught in the projector and you can only watch the first part of the movie over and over. I am throwing stones into the small waterhole on the opposite side of the track at the back of our house. It is almost lunch-time and I decide to walk along the tracks behind my friends. They don't want to play and I plead with them to spend more time outdoors. I try to entice them by trick-acting on the tracks but they ignore me and walk down the line towards their homes. My memory goes fuzzy then, and there are things about that day that I cannot remember or perhaps that I don't want to remember. Foolish things. But I do remember the rumble of a distant train, the vibrations running up my feet and moving through me like a bolt of electricity. I remember my friends' mouths opening and closing quickly. Simon, who used to be my best friend, is jumping wildly and waving his arms. I realise that he is trying to warn me and turn around just in time to see the train bearing down on me. I know the timetables by heart and think that it is earlier than normal, which I guess is a strange thing to think about when a train is coming at you. Everything seems to move in slow motion and it is like I am describing something that happened to someone else in another lifetime. Frame one: I try to run but my lace is caught. Frame two: I fall and try to get my shoe off as the rumble of the train increases. Then the reel snaps and my next memory is being carried by my mother towards the house. I want to close my eyes but her mouth says, "Stay awake, Christopher, stay with me," as I drift into a deep sleep. When I wake up I am in a different place. A tight bandage is tied around what is left of my foot. I can see my mother crying at the bottom of the bed. She looks faded and misty in the strange light. My father's big shoulders are drooped forward as though I have taken the very life out of him. I have never seen his face, usually scorched by the hot Australian sun, so ghostly pale. I can tell that all his hopes for me, his only child, are gone.

I don't think I have recovered from the shame and regret I felt that day and although I try, I worry that I can never make it up to them.

I limp closer to my mother's bed where she is sleeping soundly. My father is missing so I know it is him in the bathroom. She looks as though she is smiling and her long dark hair falls over the white pillow. She is beautiful and I have often seen my father say this. I think she senses me since she touches the locket around her neck in which she has a photo of me when I was younger. She half-opens her eyes. "Christopher?" she asks but I slink back into the darkness and leave the room. My mother doesn't get enough sleep and has to get up twice during the night to help Aishling turn some of the patients to prevent bedsores.

I am fully awake now and feel that it would be useless to return to bed. I decide to wander around the nursing home, which is a habit I have developed since my accident. The home used to be a boarding house for workers when the mine was busy in the 1940s. It is the last house on Menindee Road and lies at the bottom of a small hill that sweeps up steeply on either side of it – which is where the name "Broken Hill" comes from. There is rolling countryside to the right and the town is a short distance to the left.

I climb the stairs. There are five rooms on each side of the narrow upstairs corridor. Aishling's room and mine face each other at the back of the house and are divided by the narrow stairwell that leads to the lower floor. She is the only nurse who lives in and has worked for my mother almost since she arrived in Australia about fifteen years ago. Not everyone here needs nursing care. Some of the people are boarders but have no family to help them, so they live here on the upper floor.

Wilfred Richter sleeps in the room next to mine. He is from Germany and is in his fifties, younger than most of the residents. One of the nurses said he was a Nazi during the Second World War but I don't know if this is true. He knows I love history and used to tell me all about his life in Germany when he was a boy. But he doesn't talk much any more.

I pass his room and the bathroom and stand for a moment outside Jimmy Young's room. His door is slightly ajar and I can see him curled up in his bed. He is one of the few residents who was born in Australia and came to live here after he had a stroke and could no longer run his farm. His speech is hard to understand and the left side of his body doesn't work very well. I look at him as he sleeps and like how still he is. When he wakes, he bangs things around his room, looking for attention. I understand how he feels. It is hard when people ignore you because they cannot understand what you want. I have a voice but I don't use it, unless I am afraid or get a fright like when the train wakens me. When I was little and still had some hearing, I didn't like the sound my voice made. My words didn't sound like other people's. The staff ignore me like they do Jimmy but, unlike him, I don't bang things and I try to stay out of everyone's way.

Martin Kelly is next. He has a disease in his lungs which makes him cough up black phlegm and a clot on his brain that gives him headaches. My mother says that one or other of these conditions will kill him some day.

When I get to his room, I notice that Aishling is standing in his open doorway. He is out of his bed and flailing his thin arms around the room.

"Help! Help me! Someone, please!"

He looks straight at me and then turns to Aishling. He says something to her and I watch as the side of his mouth moves backward and forward. He has forgotten that I am deaf and I can only lip-read if he faces me. I wonder if he is dying. I see death a lot around here. I am used to it. My mother says death is simply another part of life and is nothing to be afraid of. I think she is right. I move around him to make sure I can follow his words.

"Can you see her? Can you?" he asks.

"Martin, there is no one here, now go to sleep. You're waking everyone up," Aishling tells him crossly.

"It's my wife. She's come for me. She's right behind you. The boy can see her." He looks at me. "Can't you?" he asks and I hang my head.

Aishling blesses herself quickly and takes a deep breath. "There is no one here. Your wife died fifteen years ago, Martin," she scolds him. "And if she were here, she'd probably be haunting you, you old scoundrel!" Locals in the town have told her that Martin was known to beat his wife throughout their marriage. "I'll leave your light on, all right?" She's feeling slightly sorry for the old man who is tormented day and night by imaginary attackers.

I follow Aishling out and watch while she returns to her small desk outside my room. I look out the window at the other end of the hallway which faces the front of the house. It is a beautiful night and a full moon shines directly on to our sign: "*Broken Hill Nursing Home and Day Care – Vacancies. Proprietors Emma & Andy Monroe.*" I look at the large gum tree, which is shining in the moonlight, and remember swinging from its branches when I was younger. I can see our cat, Paws, licking his lips and meowing on the fence although I cannot remember what this sounds like.

I walk along the other side of the hallway. Mr and Mrs Klein's room is first. They are the only married couple here and at the moment they are the people I am most interested in. Neither of them can remember our names any more or the fact that they were once prisoners in a concentration camp. Neither do they remember that their son Jacob died at the camp, which my mother says is a blessing. Despite being in his eighties, Aron is still a tall, broad man. His face is deeply lined and his eyes are a sad deep brown and always look far away, even if he is staring straight at you. Iren is a tiny woman who sits shrivelled up in a chair all day. She calls his name most of the time even though he is right beside her and rarely leaves her side. He pats her hand and hushes her when she cries and she settles if only for a while. I walk over to their bed and watch as he sleeps with his arms wrapped tightly around her tiny shoulders. My mother says he has cancer in his lungs and that she will soon have to move them downstairs. He coughs loudly and shifts. I am afraid that he will wake and I leave their room quickly.

I pass by Mina Jensen's room on my tiptoes. She never seems to sleep and if she hears me she will start shouting that the Japs are coming and Aishling will know that I have been creeping around. Mina was a prisoner of war in Indonesia during the Second World War. She boards here as she was afraid to live on her own when her husband died. She walks with a frame and has two long scars on her hips. She is not as confused as some of the other residents but sometimes it seems like she doesn't remember that the war is over. She hides food underneath her clothes and is afraid of Li, our cook, who is Chinese not Japanese but Mina doesn't seem to know the difference. Each night, when the staff help her to her bedroom, they take away the food that she has hidden in her clothes. She begs for it to be returned to her and my mother has to calm her down. She doesn't believe that there will be more food tomorrow and the day after that and my mother says it might have been better if she had died back then because her mind is still a prisoner and only her body is free. I worry that when she dies her soul will be trapped in the war and she will spend eternity searching for food. I am like that, an unusual child. I worry about things that most other kids probably don't even know about.

Next to Mina is Father Francis Hayes. He was a Catholic priest and is from the same part of Ireland as Aishling. He is senile now and often forgets how to speak English but my mother says that, long before he became confused, his mind broke and his Church sent him here. He often cries for no reason and sometimes Aishling is woken from her day-time sleep to comfort him in Gaelic. She hushes him and he smiles and calls her 'A stór' – which Aishling says means 'my darling'. My father, who is from the Hebrides in Scotland, can speak this language even though some of the words from his island are different. I see him speaking with Aishling sometimes and watch as their mouths move in a strange fast way. My mother doesn't like to see them speak together but I don't know why. Perhaps it is because like me, she doesn't know what they are saying and she feels left out of this part of my father's life.

Two sisters, Penelope and Victoria Miller, live in the room before Aishling's. Their father was a lieutenant in the British army and they spent their childhood in army camps all over the world. Despite being born in and eventually settling in Australia, they speak with upper-class English accents and the nurses sometimes mock them if they think my mother will not hear. The spinsters dress almost identically and live their lives by a strict routine. If a meal is late, or they cannot find a belonging, they become so distressed that my mother has to send them on top-secret government work around the nursing home which quietens them for a while.

I wander slowly back to my room and stare out my window at the tracks that are visible even in the darkness. The train has long since passed and I feel a sense of relief even though I know that I will relive it all again tomorrow night. All day long trains pass here carrying goods and passengers to and from Sydney but, for some reason, only the 3 a.m. train frightens me. Perhaps that is because in three short hours the house will come alive with the movement of staff and residents and in the vibrations of life, or what is left of it, I will not notice the trains coming and going. As I ease myself back into my bed, I gaze around the room. As every other room is occupied by residents, the staff sometimes have to use my room for storage. Large boxes of medical supplies line the wall on the right making large, unusual shapes in the darkness. I lie down and turn on my side. As I enjoy the cool breeze from my open window, I stare at the ceiling and pray that I may drift off again into what will hopefully be a peaceful sleep.

·◆·

If you enjoyed this chapter from
The Penance Room by Carol Coffey
why not order the full book online
@ www.poolbeg.com

·◆·

ALSO BY POOLBEG.COM

The Butterfly State

CAROL COFFEY

Tess Byrne has a secret. Alone and forgotten in an institution for troubled children for the past ten years, Tess has kept the secret with her. But now, at the age of twenty-one, she is coming home.

Waiting for her at home on the farm in Árd Glen, County Wicklow, are sister Kate and brothers Seán and Ben. But why are Kate and Seán dreading Tess's return? What lies behind Seán's hostility towards his young sister? And just what is the secret that threatens to destroy the Byrne family?

Can Tess finally live the normal life she craves with the people she loves, or will their tragic family history tear them all apart forever?

ISBN 978-1-84223-397-9

POOLBEG WISHES TO

THANK YOU

for buying a Poolbeg book.

If you enjoyed this why not
visit our website:

www.poolbeg.com

and get another book delivered straight
to your home or to a friend's home!

All books despatched within 24 hours.

POOLBEG

WHY NOT JOIN OUR MAILING LIST
@ www.poolbeg.com and get some
fantastic offers on Poolbeg books